For Lionel C.—Film maker

CLAIRE RAYNER

POSTSCRIPTS

Michael Joseph
LONDON

MICHAEL JOSEPH LTD

Published by the Penguin Group
27 Wrights Lane, London W8 5TZ, England
Viking Penguin Inc., 375 Hudson Street, New York, New York 10014, USA
Penguin Books Australia Ltd, Ringwood, Australia
Penguin Books Canada Ltd, 2801 John Street, Markham, Ontario, Canada L3R 1B4
Penguin Books (NZ) Ltd, 182–190 Wairau Road, Auckland 10, New Zealand

Penguin Books Ltd, Registered Offices: Harmondsworth, Middlesex, England

First published 1991

Typeset in Linotron 202 11 on 13pt Sabon by Wilmaset, Birkenhead, Wirral
Printed in England by
Clays Ltd, St Ives plc

Library of Congress Catalog Card Number: 90-63779

A CIP catalogue record for this book is available
from the British Library

ISBN 0 7181 3457 5

POSTSCRIPTS

Also by Claire Rayner
A STARCH OF APRONS
THE MEDDLERS
MADDIE
CLINICAL JUDGEMENTS

One

London was not at all as Abner Wiseman had expected it would
be. That annoyed him; not because of the difference between
reality and expectation but because it made him aware of the fact
that he had any expectations at all. He had been so careful not to
let himself be influenced in any way: to forget all those cosy
Ealing comedies and the gritted-teeth war films that he always, in
a kind of shamefaced fashion, enjoyed so much; above all, to
ignore all his father had ever said about Europeans and European cities. He was coming to London with an open mind, he
had told himself, a mind unpolluted by any hint of prejudice. Yet
here he was, standing on the South Bank in the pearl-grey
twilight of a damp February evening, staring at the National
Film Theatre and finding it unexpected. It was infuriating.

The girl beside him seemed to have the air of divination.

'It *is* a little dwarfed, isn't it? The Festival Hall and the
National are so very overpowering, don't you think? And, of
course, the bridge does sit on it rather, doesn't it?' And she
peered up at the spans of Waterloo Bridge immediately overhead
as though remonstrating with them.

'Mmm?' He was startled again. To hear someone really
speaking to him in those strangled British tones and saying
'Don't you think?' and 'rather' in that diffident way; it shouldn't
be like that. Reality was supposed to be different from the
movies.

The girl led the way now, pushing past the littered tables
where people sat in the dampness hunched over coffee cups in a
way that amazed him (to sit outdoors in *this* weather? They must
be crazy), and opened the doors and ushered him inside.

'They built this place well after the others, of course. Or at
least, I think so. I'm not sure whether the National Theatre was

already there when they — well, it doesn't matter. As Spencer Tracy said, "There ain't much, but what there is is choice." '
And she threw a glance at him, sideways, so see how he responded to her attempt at a Spencer Tracy sort of accent. Kindly, he pretended she hadn't, and smiled at her.

'I'm sure it's a great place,' he said. 'And it was very good of you to invite me. I'm looking forward to it all.'

'Don't expect too much, though, will you?' she said anxiously. 'I mean, the place is — well, the audiences we get aren't *huge* you see. Just the ones who understand the medium and love it.'

He managed a grin again. 'I guess that means you haven't had much of a show at the booking office for me.'

She went a rich crimson, and he watched with interest as it flooded up from her neck and then slowly subsided.

'Oh, it's impossible to say. I mean, lots of people just drop in, and it does rather depend on what's on the box, you see. Sometimes they have films on television that are almost as good as anything we have here. And they can rent videos too, can't they? It all depends on people's interests, of course.'

'It really doesn't matter,' he said and patted her shoulder. 'I couldn't give a damn — ' and he almost added, as Clark Gable said, but stopped himself. That wouldn't be kind. 'You paid the air ticket, lady, you fetched me here and I appreciate that. I don't break my heart because they don't come battering down the doors. Anyway, they never do at home. I'm just another film maker, is all. I still don't know why you asked me in the first place.'

'Oh, we wanted you,' the girl said earnestly. 'Truly we did. I mean, we've had a lot of interest lately in the drama-documentary form, and you did a wonderful job on *Uptown Downtown*. I'm sure a lot of members will be interested — I mean, the sort who are interested in . . . ' Her voice trailed away as another girl came hurrying across the lobby towards them.

'I say, Amanda!' she called in a high treble, and at once Abner was gripped again by that *frisson* of surprise. People called Amanda. People saying, 'I say', in that breathless way. Jesus! '

'I say, is this Abner Wiseman? Yes? Oh, I'm so glad I caught you. I've got someone from *Look and Listen* here. She tried to get you at your hotel, and you'd already gone. The thing of it is, she's in a bit of a rush, can't stay for the screening and the question time after. Wondered if you'd mind awfully giving her a few moments now? Do you mind, Abner, may I call you Abner? It does *so* help to have something in *Look and Listen*. It's one of our most important magazines and we're running the film for the rest of the week of course and – '

'Sure,' he said. 'Glad to. Anything you say,' and followed her down a long corridor into a small cluttered office, leaving Amanda hovering outside.

'Good evening, Mr Wiseman.' The woman in the room looked up, nodded, and made a half-hearted attempt to get to her feet. Abner leaned towards her and shook her hand vigorously, and she looked a little startled; and he thought, goddamnit, now I'm behaving like a stereotyped Yank in one of those British movies. It gets worse and worse.

It was all getting too much, he told himself, as he allowed the fussy girl who had brought him in to provide him with coffee and generally mother-hen him; it was all too much. A bit of jet lag, maybe? And he took a deep breath to check on how tired he was. But that told him nothing. He just knew he felt as tight as a freshly boiled frankfurter trying to burst out of its skin. His nerves seemed to stretch over the surface of his body in a net that twanged and resonated, and he took another deep breath, this time to calm himself. Crazy, all of it. To be like this just because he had come to London? It wouldn't be the first time he'd spoken at one of those art theatre-type places. New York was crawling with them, and he'd spoken at more college movie clubs than he could remember; they even had one in Newark, and last time he'd been home to see the folks he'd spoken there, and that hadn't worried him, even though there'd been an audience standing at the back, the place was so full.

'It's good of you to give me this time, Mr Wiseman.' The woman sitting on the other side of the desk dragged him back into the present. He'd been on the verge of sliding into that damned morass of memory again. Just thinking the word 'Newark' had brought it up in front of his eyes, blotting out the walls covered in movie posters and stills, the desk piled with paper and the battered filing cabinets. 'I find it so much better to get a one-to-one conversation if I can at these events. So difficult to really get any questions dealt with in depth don't you agree, when you're in a crowd?'

'It won't be that much of a crowd,' he said and practised his smile again. He'd done a lot of smiling since he'd got here. He felt it was necessary, faced with people who, on the whole, did not use their faces to express much at all. She looked back at him seriously and then bent her head to her notebook and scribbled.

'Why should that be?'

He shrugged. 'Hell, I don't know. I'm just telling you what Miss – um – what the girl from the office said. She picked me up at the hotel and brought me here and she said – '

'Yes?' the woman said, not looking up, clearly quite uninterested in how he had reached the chair facing her. It was enough he was here; and something in her manner chilled him, made him feel the way he had when he had gone through his oral examinations in graduate school.

'Tell me, Mr Wiseman, why have you chosen to come here to London now, when in the past you've always refused? I remember when you got your Cannes award for *Uptown Downtown* the NFT invited you for a lecture, but you wouldn't come, and I understand that the distributors wanted you to do a tour and told you they could make a lot more of your film if you'd agree to come and sponsor it, but you wouldn't. But now, for a showing all these years later, here you are.'

She lifted her head now and looked at him and he stared back, at the long face with its unhealthy pallid skin, dark eyes behind round deliberately unfashionable glasses and the lank dust-coloured hair that framed it all. Her expression was politely enquiring but there was no real spark of humanity in there, he told himself, and felt anger begin to tighten in his belly.

'It wasn't convenient at the time,' he said, and gave her a winning smile. It was important, he felt obscurely, not to let her know she had got under his skin, though why it was important he had no idea. Who was she after all? Just a goddamned journalist.

She lifted her brows. 'Ah. Not convenient.' And again she bent her head and scribbled in her notebook as though he'd said something of great significance. 'It wasn't that you didn't think it worth your while to come to Britain with your film?'

'Oh no! Of course not!' He knew where he was now. This was wounded chauvinism; he'd heard New York scribblers put British directors and writers through the same hassle and now he felt more comfortable. He wouldn't have to explain to this wall of unfriendliness about his father and the real reason he hadn't come here before. 'It was truly a personal thing – family – you understand?'

She lifted her brows again, and to his fury he heard the words come tumbling out of him and cursed yet again his own volubility. As if it mattered what this woman thought, as if he had to apologise. He had nothing to apologise for, but here he was, going on and on, the words rolling out of him, and he sat and listened to himself talking, knowing himself to be a fool and unable to stop it.

'Listen, my father – I got a father, you know? And the old man got very worried about some things. Like Europe. He got very screwed up if I talked of coming to Europe. Since he was an old man, and it mattered to him – I didn't come. It's as simple as that, no more. An old man has a notion; so I'm a young one, but what good does it do to me to ignore his notions? He was entitled, God knows – '

'Yet you've come now.' The woman had her head a little to one side now, like a bird, watching him through those damned round glasses.

'I've come now because he died,' he said and tried to smile again. 'I thought, this time I can come.'

'Oh.' It wasn't a question, just a non-committal sound, and he shook his head at her, irritated again.

'Now it's convenient. So tell me, do you want to talk about me or about the film?'

'Oh, about both,' she said and looked down at her notebook. 'I was just interested to know about why you were here. I thought perhaps that now the British film industry is less – anguished, shall we say, than it was, you might be planning to make your next film here.'

Relief flooded over him and beneath it, anger at himself. He did it over and over again; getting defensive when there was nothing to be defensive about. The woman hadn't been getting at him at all, hadn't been anti-American either. He could see that now. Her questions were perfectly reasonable, and he'd given her all that guff about his father. Goddamnit – and he sighed once more and produced his practised smile.

'Well, not precisely. Let me say I have ideas for a film that could involve Britain – in a way.'

'Can you explain that a little more?' She stared at him owlishly.

'Well, at this stage it isn't – there isn't a lot to explain. Let me just say that I'm doing some – um – research for a new movie.'

'Is that all?' Still she looked owlish, and quite without any real interest. 'I'd heard that finance might be of interest to you here.'

He stared. 'Who told you that?'

She waved one hand vaguely. 'Oh, here and there. People talk, you know. In this business. You know how it is.'

'I don't see how anyone could talk about me and my plans,' he said and now he let his irritation show. 'I mean, goddamnit, I hardly know what they are myself yet.'

How the hell did this woman know that he was trawling for backers here? Did she know, too, that at home he wasn't regarded as worth a bent dime? That he'd tried all the usual ways and got nowhere? *Great stuff you make, Abner*, they'd all said, or something like it. *Great stuff. For the art houses, you know. Not commercial, hey? And right now we're looking for returns on our dollars. Not a good time, Abner. Come back in a year or two.*

So he'd talked to one or two people and they'd told him there was money in Europe, if he went looking for it, and then Hyman had died and – but he didn't want to think about his father and so he didn't. Instead he glared at the woman opposite him.

'I'm still at the preliminary stages,' he said stiffly.

She nodded. 'So I heard right. Will it be the same sort of film as *Uptown Downtown*?'

'You mean will it be about drugs and kids on the streets? No.' He was tired of it, sick and tired of it. He'd made half a dozen films, on a hell of a lot of different themes, but the only one they ever remembered was *U.D.* Not that he had anything against it; it had won him his Oscar, albeit in a largely disregarded documentary category, though it wasn't really a documentary at all – but there it was; that was how the Academy had categorised it. And it wasn't a bad film. In fact, it had been a damned good one and he wasn't ashamed to admit it. But then *Yesterday's Babies* had been good too, and that had been about something quite different; and what about *Wall of Silence*? Yet all these goddamned people ever asked about was *U.D.* Well, he'd change all that. Wait until they saw what he'd do with this one. It was going to be –

'What then?'

'At this stage I'd rather not say – ' he began but she shook her head at him.

'Oh, you should, really you should, Mr Wiseman.' For the first time she smiled, an odd little wriggle of the lips that vanished almost as soon as it appeared. 'If you're looking for backing it could do a lot for you to have something about it in *Look and Listen*. We're quite a powerful magazine, you know.'

'Everyone says that,' he said and stared at her. He was sick and tired of puffed-up scribblers labelling themselves and their two-bit rags as the be-all and end-all.

'And everyone's right,' she said, almost heartily. '*Look and Listen* is the best. So you might as well tell me. It'll be a useful thing for you to do.'

He was amused then; the thickness of some skins! And his amusement made him relax. After all, where was the harm? And she had a point at that. Maybe someone in the business would read about him and what he was looking for, and come out of the woodwork looking for him instead of leaving him to make all the running.

'Well, why not? OK, I'm planning a film to be called *Postscripts*. It'll be a feature film again, but like *U.D.* – I'm sorry, *Uptown Downtown* – based on real people in a real situation. The fewest actors I can get away with, real people living their own lives is what I want – '

'What sort of lives?'

'I beg your pardon?'

'American lives like *U.D.*? Or Brazilian lives like *Yesterday's Babies*? Or even prisoners' lives like *Wall of Silence*?'

The last of his hostility faded in a wash of gratitude. Someone who remembered his very first film; it was as though she'd kissed him. 'You liked *Wall of Silence*?'

'It was fascinating,' she said primly, and he laughed aloud.

'Wow, that was some put-down,' he said and made a rueful face. 'I should know better than to ask.'

'Well, it was a first film. There'd be something wrong if it was your best, wouldn't there?' She still wasn't smiling, but it was clear to him now that this woman wasn't at all unpleasant. Her seeming hostility was no more than shyness taken to a painful degree, and he wondered briefly how come someone as in-turned as this lady clearly was should be a journalist. And he shook himself a little. How come anyone like him should be a movie-maker? We all do what we fall into doing. These things happen to us; we don't ordain them. And he grinned at the pomposity of his own thought and nodded at her.

'Well, I suppose so.'

'So, what sort of lives?'

'Pardon me?' He had been thinking his own thoughts again and blinked at her, a little confused.

'The new film. What sort of lives will it be about? These people living their own real lives in real situations. What sort of – '

'Oh yes. Well, now, this is a difficult thing to explain. But I'll try. The Holocaust – '

Her face seemed to stiffen. 'Oh, I see. You're making a fiftieth anniversary film?'

'I don't follow you,' he said, genuinely puzzled, because she had seemed to show a flash of contempt. 'Fiftieth – ?'

'Anniversary of the War,' she said. 'We've had a considerable flurry of memoirs, books, TV, films – 1989, you see – ' She lifted her eyes to his, and they glinted behind the round glasses. 'Of course, for you it's a different anniversary, isn't it? It started in 1939 for us. Rather later for you.'

Anger lifted in him again. 'No,' he said and his voice was very level. 'Rather earlier. In 1936 for me. That was when my parents were picked up by the Gestapo and put into a labour camp for the first time. And I didn't have anniversaries in mind when I planned this movie.'

There was a little silence and then she said, 'I'm sorry. I didn't mean to be offensive.'

'No?' he said. 'I'm glad to hear it.'

'So, a film about the Holocaust?'

He didn't see why he should explain any further. The woman had been very offensive, in that snotty way only Brits could be, and he remembered all the Manhattan dinner parties he'd sat through, listening to Broadway people bad-mouthing these people and how he'd argued on the Brits' behalf, saying that they were good at the business of plays, they really were – no good pretending they weren't; and wished he hadn't. But that was stupid, childish even, and he looked at the woman and said flatly, 'No.'

'Not about the Holocaust? But you said – '

'*After* the Holocaust. About what happened when they came out and got married and had kids. About living happily ever after. Do I look the sort of movie-maker who's into exploitation? You've seen my other work? Where do you get off thinking I'd make a film that used and abused the people who'd – '

'Look, I'm sorry, Mr Wiseman, if I seem to offend you. I really don't intend it. I'm just trying to get the – I mean, you mentioned the Holocaust, I didn't.'

He calmed down at that. 'Well, OK. But try letting me explain, hey, instead of jumping in on me? The film's about – I'm interested in the left-over life they had. I'm concerned about the children, and the grandchildren too. What has it been like to grow up in the shadow of that? Not something in the history books, not something in scratchy old film clips, but people you know, people who are part of you, and you look at them and you think – he was there, he went through that. And here am I, and it's not like that for me. Why isn't it? That's the film I want to make.'

She was scribbling hard, and he sat and watched her for quite a while, angry with himself yet again for letting so much out. If he'd known it would be like this, he'd have said no, made her wait to ask her questions with everyone else after the screening; and then his belly tightened into ice with sudden fear. He had to go on to that stage, to sit there and have questions thrown at him and answer them. Would they be like those she'd asked here in this cluttered smelly little office? Would the people in the theatre be as cold and confusing as she had been? He wanted to get to his feet and run out and leave them to show his film without him; and he had tightened his thigh muscles almost ready to get to his feet when the office door opened, and the girl Amanda poked her head round it.

'I really think we ought to – I mean it's almost five to – please, would you mind, Miss – ah – and the photographer's here and wants some shots and I thought on stage, perhaps? There's a really nice audience here already, a good little crowd, really very good in fact, and we should be moving . . . '

He let her cluck him out of the office and on down a corridor lined with more stills and posters, leaving the woman with the glasses and the expressionless face behind. He was glad to be rid of her. She'd probably write something godawful in her lousy magazine and that would be the end of it. The whole damned trip would turn out to be a waste of time, and he'd have to go home and start over. A new idea, a new plan, something that'd bring the backers in from the West Coast. What did he need with these lousy Britishers and their choked voices and their arrogance? God knows what they'd be like after this showing; well, he'd show *them*. And he pulled his shoulders back as the girl Amanda, with one last despairing word flung back at him over her shoulder, opened the door to the side of the stage and pulled him in. He'd show them and then he'd go home and forget all about it.

Two

'No,' Abner said. 'It wasn't bad at all.' He smiled then. 'In fact, I kind of enjoyed it.'

'Oh, I'm so glad!' The girl Amanda was now flushed and excited, as relaxed and happy as he was that it was all over. She stood beside him in the lobby watching the last of the audience drift away and then grinned up at him so widely that he could see the fillings in her teeth at the back. 'I told you it'd be all right, didn't I? A big audience, after all – '

'Hardly big,' he said. 'How many does the place hold? A hundred and sixty, or so? If that. For a national film theatre it isn't what you'd call – '

'Oh, that wasn't the main theatre we used! That one's much bigger! We used the more – well – intimate one for you.'

'The one that makes ninety-three people look like a crowd?' He laughed at the look on her face. 'Sure I counted. I sat there while that guy talked and I counted. What else could I do?'

'Well, it's pretty good for a Monday night in winter, believe me,' the girl said. 'I've known nights here where we've barely filled half a dozen rows. They liked you, they really did. And it's not as though you weren't a specialist type, is it? You are – not like the Losey season we've got in the big theatre – that really pulls them in. But then they're different sorts of films, aren't they?'

'They're feature movies. So are mine,' he said, enjoying seeing her squirm. Why didn't she just shrug him off? He hadn't been forced to come, he'd only agreed because he had his own reasons for being here and getting a free air ticket had charm; she didn't owe him any apologies.

'I was told documentaries,' she said, and looked at him doubtfully. 'That's what they said when – '

'Oh, it's OK,' he said, bored suddenly. 'Believe me, it's all OK. I'm just – take no notice. He was good, the guy in the chair. Talked a lot to start with but shut up after that.'

'He's very good,' Amanda said stiffly. 'He's one of our best-known film critics.'

'Then I'm sure he was great,' Abner said solemnly. 'Listen, do I go now? Or is there something else you want me to do?'

'Well, you said you didn't want to have dinner but – '

'I have a date,' he said hurriedly. 'At the hotel. I'm sorry.' The mere idea of sitting down to dinner with his chairman, a man who had droned on in as dull a fashion as Abner could ever remember hearing from anyone, had given him the horrors – thank God, the guy had gone! – and it would be better to sit at the hotel on his own than sit and listen to more of this girl's gush. She meant well, and what worse could you say? 'Maybe a cab?'

'I'll arrange it,' she said and went away a little huffily, and he thought – I've done it again. Said the wrong thing in the wrong way. I keep getting it wrong. It's like being in a foreign country, the way I give – and get – the wrong messages all the time; and then was amused at himself. Of course, he was in a foreign country. It just seemed strange to think that way about England, where people spoke his own language – or an approximation of it – and where he had lived a large part of his secret inner life for so very long.

Because he had always been particularly fascinated by British movies, and now he drifted across to a section of wall where a display was mounted about a forthcoming attraction, a week of Ealing comedies, and remembered how very important two of those films had been to him once. When he had first discovered about Hyman and Frieda, after that evening when he'd stood there in the kitchen and made them tell him and had at last understood about the arguments that had been the constant backdrop to his growing-up years, he'd gone slamming out of the apartment in a sick fury – sick at himself as much as at them – and gone to the little movie-house, six blocks down from the workshop where his father spent all the hours God sent, and seen *The Ladykillers* and *The Lavender Hill Mob*, part of their regular Alec Guinness *hommage* and felt better, much better. Watching those comfortable people in their comfortable Fifties world had made it possible for him to forgive his parents for their duplicity. For that evening at any rate.

Had this evening gone well enough? He made himself think about it; anything rather than let himself walk the treacherous path of long ago memory. He'd been doubtful at first, when they had introduced him briefly from the stage and then led him to a seat in the auditorium so that he could watch the film with the rest of them. He'd seen it too often, that was the trouble, and could see its flaws all too clearly. But this time wasn't so bad; he hadn't sat through the whole of it for over a year, come to think of it, and it offered him a freshness he'd quite forgotten. In fact, listening to those kids he'd railroaded into his movie all those years ago and made into startled once-only actors (kids who were now grown men and women – if they were alive at all, of course, which was doubtful for some of them), he'd become as enmeshed in their story as he had been when he'd made the movie as a fresh-faced twenty-five year old barely out of film school. Nine years ago; Christ, but time was dribbling away. He'd be forty next week at this rate. Not to be thought about. Think instead about the evening that lay just behind him. They'd shown him on to the stage after the film ended and fussed over him a bit, and then the dull voice of the chairman had introduced him with a few sharp comments about the 'less mature' aspects of the work mixed in with the careful praise; and then the questions had come, and he'd been first startled and then gratified.

When he'd spoken to movie clubs before at home there had always been one or two people who had a genuine understanding of the film-maker's dilemmas and asked intelligent questions, but most of the queries were dull and predictable, coming from dull and predictable people with their perceptions warped by the liberal sprinkling of stardust in which they lived, movie stardust. At home people were in love with movies in a much less critical way; they were dazzled and delighted and not ashamed to admit it in their questions. But these people were different: knowledgeable, equally in love with the film as a medium but much more analytical about it, and he settled down to respond to their queries and comments with all the skill he could. It had been good. Like when the guy who had accused him of being a bleeding-heart liberal – because he had allowed the pusher in the

Bronx to talk about himself in person, and explain why he was in the trade – had accepted his argument that the pusher was as much a victim of the system that allowed drug abuse to flourish in New York as any dead kid on a slab in Bellevue. It had got a bit uncomfortable there for a while after that, though, when they started asking questions about his next film, and he had been very grateful that the woman from *Look and Listen* wasn't there; he didn't want to talk about *Postscripts* too much. It could damage the whole project, dammit; and he had regretted bitterly at that moment telling her anything about it at all. It had been a dumb thing to do, the fault of his jet lag. He yawned jawcrackingly then turned as the girl Amanda came back and told him she had a cab waiting for him at the front of the building, on Upper Ground.

'Upper Ground?'

'That's the street. If you'll follow me.' And she led him out again, along narrow corridors adorned with more movie posters and stills, until at last they came out into the darkness of the street; and he was startled again to find it quite so dark. He'd forgotten how long he'd been in this building. It seemed a long time since he'd left the plane this morning and been driven into the middle of London, gawping at everything like the greenest of tourists. Damnit, it *was* a long time.

'Goodnight,' he said. 'You've been very kind. I truly have appreciated it, Amanda.'

'If there's anything else you need while you're here, do let me know,' she said, holding the cab door open and not looking at him. 'You can get me here any time. Well, most of the time.'

'Oh, I'll be fine,' he said. 'Just fine,' and got into the cab.

'You'll be going back home now, then?' she said. 'Or staying a bit to do some sightseeing?'

'Sightseeing, sure. But more than that. I might stay to work a little.' He grinned at her, placatory now. He'd not been as friendly as he might and she'd tried, after all, tried very hard to take care of him. 'It's not for everyone to know, but I do have some work of my own to deal with while I'm here.'

'Then I'm glad you were able to get to us,' she said with a moment of spite. 'It was convenient for you that we brought you over.'

'It was,' he said. 'And I do appreciate it. Well, so long then.'

'Goodbye,' she said, and closed the cab door on him firmly and he sat back against the leather padding and sighed as the cab driver leaned back and called over his shoulder, 'Where to, squire?'

'Squire,' Abner said, amused. Ealing again.

The cab driver twisted round more in his seat and winked at him. 'She said you was a Yank, and I like to give value for money. All-purpose label. Beats guv', doesn't it? Where to?'

He laughed. 'The West Park. In Leinster Terrace.'

'Blimey, they got themselves on the itineraries, 'ave they? Comin' up in the world. Not exactly the 'ilton, is it?' He let in the clutch a little noisily and turned the cab neatly in a full circle and headed westwards. 'Lookin' after you all right, are they?'

'It's fine,' Abner said. 'Just fine.' And sat and stared out at the passing scene as the cab wheeled left and went up on to the bridge. It was still misty, and the river shone on each side as though he were seeing it through a mesh over a lens; and he shook his head as the simile came to him. He wasn't in a movie-house now, for God's sake! This was real life. That really was the Houses of Parliament away on his left and that really was the dome of St Paul's shimmering on his right. He was here in London. He was thirty-four years old and for the first time in his entire life he was in Europe. Where, if the world hadn't gone mad sixty-odd years ago, he should have been born.

Piecing together the story of who he was and why he was where he was had – it had seemed to him, walking home from the Alec Guinness movies the night he had found out – taken all his life. When does a child know his world is different from that of other children? You grow up thinking everyone in the world, every-where, eats corned beef for dinner on Sundays, always has chicken on Friday nights and gets to eat an ice-cream on walks in the park once in a while – a very few whiles – and you think that's normal. And then you find out, slowly, that it isn't. That in other houses they eat food you never even heard of, and that some kids get ice-cream every day. That in other houses parents talk to each other and laugh, and sometimes bawl and shout, but don't spend long swathes of the days in total silence. That other people's parents speak as you do yourself, American, not foreign with a thick sound at the back of the throat that makes you think they want to cough. Some people have parents who talk that way, and some have parents who talk different ways, but most have American speaking parents. That this is a very strange thing to discover when you're six years old and never knew it before.

At first it hadn't mattered. There was school and there were other kids and sometimes other adults from the Shoah Club his parents went to, though they never took him there. Once or twice in a year – and no more than that – there would be strangers in the apartment, sitting in the living room at the big round table with the red plush cover and drinking tea out of glasses like his parents did. They didn't talk to him a lot either. They talked about him, of course – all the adults did that – but mostly he was sent away, out to play, sent to be anywhere but with them, when visitors came. And that didn't happen in other people's houses, he learned painfully. Other people stayed around and didn't get sent out of the room all the time. It didn't happen to other people. Only to him.

I'm seventeen, he'd thought that evening as he had walked the long blocks back to the apartment, his head still half dazzled by the joy of the movies he had seen, his ears full of those creamy English voices. I'm seventeen and I've only just found out where I come from. They robbed me, all those years they robbed me. When they talked at school of the Holocaust I sat there and listened as other people talked of it; I sat there and felt sick and angry and a million miles away. I listened to Joey Stein crying when he talked about it, and heard Amy Greener saying what happened to her grandma and it was like listening to the teacher talk about the Civil War. Important and never to be forgotten, but nothing to do with me, none of my business.

Only, of course, it was. It always had been, and he hadn't known. They should have told me. To leave me to find out the way I did, to have to sit and hear that drooling old man going on and on about it, telling me what happened to them both, and not have *them* tell me. To have him speak of the babies they had had that had died, to have him explain how precious a child Abner was to his parents, and never have heard it from them? It was an obscenity, that was what it was.

As he had walked past the A & P supermarket, past Kresge's and Woolworths' five-and-dime, he had seen that old man in his

memory silhouetted against everything he looked at, heard his
thin voice grating in his ear above the rattle of the traffic.

'They never told you? Hyman and Frieda, always a funny pair
those two, always like that to us, but to you you'd think they'd
be different? Three babies they lost – my old woman, she knew,
worked at the hospital so she knew, and she said it was three –
and then you and you'd think they'd tell you – ' And he'd
hawked and swallowed convulsively and then sniffed thickly and
Abner, seventeen-year-old Abner, had almost thrown up.

But the old man hadn't noticed, had just sat there hunched
over his coffee and doughnut at the tall counter, talking and
talking. And because there were no other customers there, just
half an hour before closing time at the coffee shop, Abner had
had to stand and listen to him, had to stand there in his short
white coat and stupid round white hat that barely stayed in place
on his over-exuberant curly hair, had to hear how he'd been
cheated of his childhood. Had to hear it from a stranger.

Because he had been cheated – robbed, spoiled, left with huge
blanks in his self-knowledge, because they had never told him
anything of what had happened to them. *Weren't their lives part
of his heritage?* he'd asked himself with a vast and painful
passion as the old man went on and on about Hyman and Frieda
in their labour camp. *Hadn't he a right to share their pain, help
them to assuage it?* To be seventeen and aching to change the
world and then discover from a stranger, who happens to walk
into the coffee shop where you're earning a few dollars at night
for your college funds, that your own parents had suffered so.
What could be worse?

And the anger had boiled and steamed in him, almost enough
to overwhelm the other feeling, the guilt, cold sick guilt to have
lived so soft, so easy, if so lonely and remote from his parents,
when they had suffered so. To find them both so very unlovable
when they had gone through such hell simply so that he could
exist – seventeen-year-old Abner had needed so much to weep
and had been so unable to do so. *They had been wrong, wrong,
wrong. Wicked even, to treat him so.*

So he had mouthed to himself, walking the city blocks back to
the apartment he had lived in all his life and had thought the be-
all and end-all of his parents' existence. He would make them tell
him, make them explain, all of it – not just the bald admission

he'd heard earlier this evening – and he had gone into the apartment and slammed the door loudly behind him, to show that he meant business, and walked heavily into the living room to face them both, screwing up his anger tightly in case it ran out of him and left him speechless.

Only to find Hyman, his father, alone. She had gone out without him: Frieda, who never went anywhere except sometimes to their club where the other Polish people went, and certainly never without Hyman, who sat and twisted her hands silently, staring dead-eyed at the wall, when Hyman was only five minutes later than he usually was coming back from work, Frieda out, *alone*?

But so it was, and Hyman had told him she had gone specially so that she wouldn't have to talk to her son.

'She can't, Abner,' the old man had said, sitting there in the armchair under the lamp with the scarf thrown over it so that it didn't tire his eyes. He worried a lot about his eyes, Hyman. 'She wants me to talk to you.'

'She wants you to – ' Abner had stopped and then realised he was still in his heavy overcoat and had taken it off and, daringly, dropped it on the sofa. She always looked at him if he did things like that, looked with those heavy dead eyes that filled him with so much guilt, and so he had always put it away in the closet, for her passionate need for perfect order was stronger than he was. But he had left it there that night in a gesture of defiance as pointless as it was pitiful, and turned to look at the old man and had opened his mouth to speak, then stopped and stared and thought – he's not so old, after all.

That had been the second great shock of the evening, and in some ways it made his world reel under his heels even more than the first had.

'How old are you, Pa?' he'd said abruptly, and his father had looked up at him from beneath his grey brows and said, 'How old? Who remembers? I suppose, forty-eight. As if I could forget. November 30th I'll be forty-eight.'

'I never knew when your birthday was,' Abner had said and gone round the table to sit in the shadow so that he could stare at his father without being stared at in return. Not that the old man would. 'You never said.'

But he wasn't old, that was the trouble. The thin straggle of grey hair and the eyebrows were a lie. So were the lines running from nose to mouth to throat in deep ravines, and scoring his forehead to split his face into segments. The tired sagging skin, the wattles of the neck, all of them were too soon. It should have been another twenty years before they appeared. And he said sharply, 'And Ma? How old is she? And does she have a birthday? Or is that a dirty secret, too?'

Hyman had winced a little at the word dirty, but had said only, 'Frieda is older than I am. Not that it matters to her or to me. But she's older. She has a birthday. April. April 9th. She was fifty-two last April.'

'Why do you behave so old, goddammit?' the boy Abner had burst out, aware of the youth and spring in his own bones and hating the lack of them in the only two people he had to call his own. If they were so old so young, what hope was there for him? 'Christ, there are people twenty, thirty years more than you who don't look so crabby – '

'It's not something you choose, Abner,' Hyman had said. 'It's something that happens to you. It won't happen to you, though. To me and your mother it happened. It won't happen to you. Not here in Newark.'

At once he had felt the guilt come down on him, like a great cold blanket. He could hardly breathe for it, and he pushed it away, twisted it in his mind and forced it to become anger.

'How could you lie to me for so long? I'm your *son*. How could you lie to me that way?'

Hyman had lifted his brows at him, half comically. 'Who lied? To say nothing is now to tell lies? Oy, have we got problems if that's the way of it.'

'You know what I mean!' Abner had roared. 'You know what the fuck I mean – ' and then had reddened as Hyman had winced.

'You know what I mean,' he had said more quietly. 'I asked you, the times I asked you! "Why no relations, Pa?" I'd say, six, seven years old I was and I'd ask you. And you? You'd look at me and you'd say nothing! Neither of you ever said a goddamned word.' That at least was a safe adjective, and he revelled in it, needing to swear, unable to find other words to show the depth of his pain. 'You sat there like some dumb sonofabitch and said nothing when I asked you.'

Hyman had gone suddenly white and leaned forwards into the light, his eyes very bright. 'Never say that to me, you hear me? My mother was – she died in that place, you hear me? Never use such words to me again.'

That had been the relief. At last he had wept, great big seventeen-year-old Abner, all six foot two of him, had sat in the shadow of his father's lamp and knuckled his eyes and felt his nose running as he wept, and the old man had got to his feet and come and stood behind him and set his hands on his shoulders and held him until the tears stopped. And then he had sat down and told him, answered all the questions, every one of them. And Abner had listened and asked questions and listened again, and afterwards, as soon as he could, had made his arrangements to go to City University in New York. Not too far away, but far enough. He had never lived in the apartment ever again.

There were messages for him at the hotel, and the very young girl on the desk gave them to him with a goggle-eyed pride in being part of so important a transaction, and he smiled at her and took the faxes away to his room. It wasn't much of a hotel, the West Park. He'd been sent a list of recommended places by the NFT when they'd invited him over, making it clear that they could only provide the air fare (and he had a shrewd notion that they'd made some sort of special arrangement over that with the airline) and could not pay any more of his expenses, and he'd assured them that that wasn't a problem. But, of course, it was. There was never enough money, and that didn't apply only to making movies. It applied to living, too, and he had looked at his bank book and called Irving Sasha, who'd been at school with him in Newark and now had his own travel agency there, and got him to advise him. So now here he sat in a dull little place, full of dusty plastic plants and smelling of tired over-cooked food and elderly beer, and was grateful it was so cheap. Comparatively cheap, that was; he had looked at the prices of other London hotels and been horrified. If things worked out the way he hoped, he'd have to do something about finding an apartment maybe, just for the time he was here. Hotel life was out of the question. Even though it did double as a sort of office for him; and he looked down at the piece of paper in his hands, grateful that the place had at least its own fax machine.

And then the tiredness that had been crawling ever closer to the centre of him receded a little. There was one closely written sheet and he looked down at it and thought — she did do it then. Frieda had done it.

He always tried not to think about his mother. Hyman had been hard enough but at least he was dead. Abner had been able to draw a line under him and live with what there was. But she, so very much alive still — and he dodged away from the implications of that thought in his head — she was a different matter. Yet she had asked him if she could help and when he'd said shortly that all he needed was to talk to people who had shared the same experiences she and Hyman had had, she had shrugged and, as always, said nothing. Yet here it was in his hand; a list of names. And he stared at it and he thought — I'll have to go back to see these people. Isn't it like her, to send me this after I've gone to London? Too late to use it; always she gives me information when it's too late.

But this time she hadn't. He peered again at the fax and saw the addresses and his face smoothed out in amazement. He felt it happen. There were several names here and matching addresses, and all of them were in London.

Three

He slept dreamlessly for over ten hours, crawling out of the depths to blink at the thin morning sunshine spilling in through the dusty window and to gawp at the clock on the side table. Gone ten? Christ, what had happened to him? And he rolled over in the rather lumpy bed and dragged himself out, aware that he'd be sleeping yet if it hadn't been for the insistence of his bladder. God, he'd been tired! For the first time he understood what people meant when they yammered on about jet lag; he'd always thought those people who talked about it were only bragging about how widely travelled they were; now he knew it was a real problem.

But by the time he'd shaved and bathed – no shower in this hotel's bathroom – and eaten a vast English breakfast, which was a great deal better than the quality of the hotel might have led him to hope, he felt better, and went back to his room to sit on the crumpled bed and look at the list of names and addresses Frieda had sent him.

No phone numbers; well, that shouldn't be a major problem, and he pulled the phone towards him. Half an hour later he was realising just how very much abroad he was. Dealing with British phone operators was no ball game; they were slow and unhelpful, and the systems they used were not at all what he was used to. But at length he had numbers for five of the people on Frieda's list. The other two would need letters, he decided. Add to those five the seven names and numbers he had brought with him from New York and Los Angeles on his own account, of academics in the field, and film people, and he had a long morning ahead of him.

He started with Frieda's numbers, feeling an obscure need to get them out of the way, and drew a blank with the first two. A

Mr Joseph Hempel was dead. The daughter who answered his call seemed uninterested in the fact that someone with an American accent was calling; she said merely that her father had died six months ago and what did he want? And when Abner tried to explain that he was doing research for a film she had said flatly, 'Well, you're too late,' and had hung up. And he had sat with the phone in his hand as it buzzed dumbly at him and thought – what would I have done if someone had called me to speak to my father about a movie, had had an English accent, and explained as I had explained? Would I have just hung up in that brusque fashion, showed no further interest? I might have done, he thought then, as he cradled the phone and drew a line through Joseph Hempel's name on his list. I might have done.

The second blank came at the home of Mrs Marie Morgearn. A tremulous voice answered, an old man, Abner thought, and his heart sank as he struggled to explain what he wanted to someone who was clearly very deaf – for he kept asking for words to be repeated – and equally clearly agitated. At dealing with the phone call? Perhaps. Some old people, he knew, didn't like the instrument. But when he shouted that he wanted to speak to Mrs Morgearn, the old voice shook even more and said, 'Hospital. She's gone to hospital.'

'I'm sorry to hear that,' Abner said, trying to sound sympathetic while shouting at full blast. 'Will she be home soon, do you think?'

'Kept wandering, you see,' the frail voice said fretfully. 'Wandering. And wouldn't eat – and the laundry – I can't do laundry, can I? Not at my time of life. So I got the meals-on-wheels and the home-help comes in and Marie's in hospital and I go when I can, once a week they try to take me, but she don't know me, so what does it matter? And she wanders, you see . . . '

He drew a second line on his list. One dead, one demented. A great way to start. Already it was approaching noon and he'd have to make the calls he'd promised he would before lunch; how long was lunch in London? Did it start early or late? He'd try one more of Frieda's list and then abandon it for a while.

This time he struck oil. Hilda Fraister answered the phone herself and seemed not at all surprised to hear from an American.

'Who sent you? Frieda Wiseman? Nah, this one I didn't know. Where from? Newark? Ah, well now, you should ha' said! Newark, I know. Got *mechutanim* there – my son's wife, you understand, her people. He married a girl from New Jersey, and punkt! It turns out her father came from the *haim*. My town in Poland, you understand.'

His pulse actually quickened. This sounded hopeful. She was a vigorous woman – he could tell that by the bounce in her voice – with only a trace of an un-English accent, and talking to her should be easy. 'I'm doing some research, Mrs Fraister,' he said. 'For a film.'

'On the telly?' Her voice grew bouncier still. 'Get away!'

'For the cinema, but maybe it could be on TV.' Goddamned TV. The way it always made eyes light up made him sick. 'I hope you can help me.'

'Me help you? So tell me how!'

'The film's to be about what happened after the camps. In Europe. In America, too. What happened to people who were in the camps, and to their children and grandchildren.'

There was a silence, and then she said with a sharp note in her voice, 'Children? Grandchildren? What can they know about the camps? Who wants them to know?'

'That's my point.' He became eager. 'I want people to – to understand how long the shadow is. They know there was a Holocaust, they know the camps happened. They know there were people who came out, started to live again. But how was it not just for them but for the children they had? It had to affect them – '

'Listen, the children they had – they're fine. I know, believe me. They're fine.' She was truculent now and Abner felt the familiar frustration welling up in him. He could hear remote notes of Frieda's stubborn silence in this woman, for all her volubility.

'You don't want to go sniffing around the children,' she said then, hectoring now, a matron embattled. 'Enough's enough already. We got to get on with the future, you understand? I got seven grandchildren, lovely kids – why should their heads be *verdrainischt* with such stuff? For me, its over – '

'But I needn't talk to your children or grandchildren, Mrs Fraister,' he said, mendaciously. Let me get to you, lady, just let me get to you. Later, who knows what will happen? 'It's you I'd be interested in. You were in the camps?'

There was a long silence and then he said almost despairingly, 'You must have suffered.'

'Suffered?' she said sharply as though she'd been stung. 'Stupid word. Doesn't mean anything. I was there. Say that and you've said enough.'

'How long were you there?' Let me get what I can. Later maybe she'll relax, tell me more. Who knows? 'A long time?'

'All my life,' her voice had changed. No bounce now, but still strong. 'That was what it felt like, I never remembered a time before – listen mister, I know you know Hetty and Jack, but – '

He was startled. 'Hetty and Jack?'

'My daughter-in-law's people. Isn't that who sent you?' Her voice had sharpened even more. 'You said that was why you called. Hetty and Jack in Newark, they gave you my name and number – '

'Not exactly,' he said and then had to tell her, hating having to do it. 'It was my mother who did. She was – she belongs to the same club they do. I asked her to find me people who could help me and she sent me this list. You're on it.'

'Your mother – your mother's in the same club? Then she's from the camps, too.' Not a question, that. A statement.

He took a deep breath. It was like stripping them naked in public, talking this way. All those years when they refused to talk about it, and now he was using them to open his own doors. Hateful. But he'd have to get used to it. It wasn't going to get any easier if he put it off. 'Treblinka,' he said.

'Ah!' A soft sound, not a sigh, but the breath of recognition. Whatever it sprang from, it made her voluble again. 'Your own mother, hmm? So she told you all about it, hey? You've shared it with her – '

'No.' He couldn't let that ride. 'No, she – they preferred not to speak of it.'

'They?'

'My father – '

'Ch-ch-ch.' Another soft sound, almost a croon this time. 'Two in one family. Well, maybe it helps. My husband, he could never deal with it, you know? Didn't understand. Even though I was so young. I mean, I got out, I was only five. I don't remember a time before. Only a little time at the end of it all.'

Disappointment thickened in him. 'You were five when the war ended?'

'That's it. Five I was. A baby! But I remember – '

'Do you?' He let himself become hopeful again. 'How much?' He could almost see her shrugging at the end of the phone.

'This and that – listen, I can't talk for ever, you know. I got a part-time job, got to go out to it. Call me again, maybe?'

'Perhaps you'd let me give you lunch? If you could spare the time?'

'Lunch? Out to lunch? Me?' She laughed. 'Nah, you come to my place. When my husband's here.' He grinned at that. She must be over fifty, and still being coy about meeting a man she didn't know. 'These days, who knows what sort of villains there are? You could be anyone. You can come when my husband's here. Maybe my son as well. That bother you?'

'Not at all,' he said. 'I thought you didn't want me to talk to your children?'

'Yeah, well, we'll see. If you want to talk to me, you have to come to see me when there's family here. I don't go out to no lunches. Where are you?'

He gave her the name and number of the hotel. 'I'll phone you,' she said. 'I'll talk to my husband and my son and maybe I'll phone you – ' and hung up.

He sat and stared at the dead phone for a long time before starting again. Would they all be like this, defensive, that rather queasy amalgam of come-on and stand-off? Should he forget the whole project right now, go home, look for some other subject?

'Ch-ch-ch,' he said under his breath, using Mrs Fraister's sound, but making it harder, like a teacher reprimanding a child, but reprimanding himself. 'Ch-ch-ch!'

And very deliberately he folded the fax from Frieda and pulled out of his briefcase a slim folder. He'd make his own calls. The others needed more time than he could give them right now. And maybe it would be better to go calling on them instead of phoning first. It was too easy for them on the phone. To go to see them would be to give himself some advantage.

Researching a movie was like planning a battle, that was the trouble. You had to fight the very people you needed to be your allies eventually. But that was the nature of the business, so what else could he do? Postpone it, that was what – or at least postpone the hard part of it. Dealing with academics must surely be easier.

But first he made a half-dozen crisp and businesslike calls to secretaries in distant offices. He had the names of people who could be approached about making a package deal for a movie, names culled from the film people in LA he had used in the past. It would be good to have a scatter of appointments that were sure; better than having to go cold-calling on strangers like Mrs Fraister. Not that she felt like a stranger now; English accent or not, she had been too much like those adults who had come visiting when he'd been a child in Newark. Then they'd sent him out of the room; well, Mrs Fraister wasn't going to send him out of any room. He was on his own now, an adult like them. No more silence or secrets for Abner.

With the appointments made he relaxed and looked at his watch. Almost one-fifteen; had he been talking that long? Most people would be out to lunch now. He'd had trouble with the last two calls he'd made for that reason. Time to go to the next list then; not film people, not possible subjects, but solid background research people. The academics. They, surely, didn't waste time on long lunches. And he looked at the last of his contact sheets and pondered. None of them in London, that was a drag. How far away were these places? Liverpool? He had a notion that was way up in the North, Beatles country; and there was a query against the name anyway. Joe Lipsher who'd given him that one had been dubious.

'Might be anywhere now. I talked to him back in 'sixty-three, when I was making *Evil Eyes*,' he'd told Abner on the phone from his Hollywood poolside, making Abner very aware of the state of the street outside his Manhattan apartment block where the wind chill factor nearly cut off the legs of passers-by. 'But you could try. He was a good guy – a Middle East specialist, very up on Israeli politics, you know?' And then had gone on to talk interminably about his own new film, a space fantasy extravaganza, which had made Abner want to grind his teeth with fury, because he'd placed the call and it was costing him. But what can you do? Climbing painfully on to the film bandwagon always cost you — money as well as effort.

There were two more he'd got from the history professor at his own university, one in Hull — another doubtful starting point, according to Joe; he'd have to check that one on the map — and the other Oxford; and he let his finger stay on that one. Here he knew where he was. One of his older friends at college had gone off to Oxford to get a degree there after he'd finished in New York and he'd written long gossipy letters about it. The nineteen-year-old Abner had been deeply jealous of the life Wallace had led there; accounts of rowing and partying and general whooping-it-up, and damn all about work. He'd spent time poring over maps of England to see where the place was and read a lot about it, especially novels. And when Channel Thirteen had run *Brideshead Revisited* he'd been glued to the screen. He'd definitely start with Oxford.

'Geoffrey Hinchelsea,' he read. 'Professor of History. 309 Bainton Road, Oxford.' And he picked up the phone again and dialled the number his own professor had given him.

It rang for a long time, and he was ready to hang up in despair, when there was a click and a rather gruff voice said, 'Yes?'

'Eh? Oh — good afternoon,' he said carefully. No more risks were to be taken. He'd gone in much too hard on Mrs Fraister. Time to be careful. 'My name is Wiseman, Abner Wiseman. Professor Jansen of City University in New York suggested that Professor Hinchelsea could give me some assistance with a project that — '

'What sort of project?' The voice was still gruff and very abrupt but, he now realised, a female one. Full of bad temper, he thought and bit his tongue to stop himself snapping back.

'It's to do with the effect of the German concentration camps on survivors,' he said even more carefully. Tell this woman — clearly the dragon the professor kept at his gate — that he was engaged on a movie and he'd get no further. He'd come across these bitter old battle-axes before. If they could stop people getting to their employers they always did. He'd have to be very skilful, very delicate with this one.

'I could write to ask for an appointment,' he said, not exactly threatening but making it clear he wouldn't be easily put off. 'It really is important to me to have some access to the material the Professor – '

'Not much point in that,' the voice said sharply. 'Waste of time. When do you want to come?'

He was taken aback. He'd expected more stonewalling than this. 'Well,' he hesitated. 'What would suit you?'

There was a short silence and then she said, wearily. 'It really makes no difference. Just give me a day and a time, and you can see the material you want.'

He lifted his eyebrows. Just like that? Was she that much in control of her employer?

'Tomorrow?'

'Tomorrow then. What time?'

'Ah – it depends on trains,' he said, startled at the promptness of her acceptance. 'I'm staying at a hotel in Leinster Gardens in Bayswater, and – '

'Paddington's round the corner,' she said. 'There are trains every hour or so as far as I know. I don't come up all that often. Morning or afternoon?'

'Ah – morning?'

'Right. I'll see you then. Three-oh-nine Bainton Road. Just off the Banbury Road, halfway to the big roundabout. Goodbye.' And the phone clicked and left him once again holding on to a dead buzzing line.

He hung up, irritated. Was this a pattern of life in this country? Did everyone slam the phone down on everyone else? It had all stopped being at all like cosy film comedies.

Suddenly he'd had enough. He needed air and a lot of it. Abner shrugged on his overcoat and packed away his briefcase, and went out, passing a sour-looking chambermaid in the hallway outside who had been waiting to come into his room to fix it; and that reminded him. He'd have to think hard about where and how he was to live if he was staying any length of time. And if he was staying at all.

But right now, he decided as he came out into the street and stood in the thin February sunshine staring round, right now, I'm a tourist. Tower of London, Buckingham Palace, the whole foot-slogging schmear. And he turned on his heel and began to walk towards the main Bayswater Road at the far end of the street, aiming for trees he could see in Hyde Park just beyond. This was London, and he was here and it was time to enjoy it. Whatever happened in the future.

Four

The train journey to Oxford pleased him enormously. He liked Paddington Station, big, shabby and cavernous and not remotely like the sort of train stations he was used to; and found the train equally delightful, looking strange and interestingly foreign as it did; and above all, the passing scenery captivated him. First the decrepit housing and factories and shop backs they passed, all of which was familiar in its spirit if not in its detail. Every city has tattered edges to its skirts, he thought, as the buildings slid by the windows, and he could look down into battered yards and piles of rusting cars and assorted junk, and then grinned at his own flight of fancy. You'd think he was writing a fancy novel rather than setting out to make a gritty honest movie. But then the buildings and the suburban stations stopped passing and they were in countryside, soft for all its winter harshness, and remarkably green. It made him marvel a little; he'd heard that Ireland was the green place, but southern England was emerald enough for anyone, though there were plenty of yellows and buffs and browns as well to set off the starkness of the skeletal trees that lined the railway. He liked the houses they passed, too: small, stocky and infinitely cosy looking, with tidy back yards and swings for children, and here and there a paddling pool; and he tried to imagine what it might be like to be a child living in such redbrick neatness, playing on that swing and in that minute pool, riding in those little cars that trundled on the wrong side of the roads which snaked past the train windows, and felt a sudden tightness in his throat.

He mustn't do it, he must not; to think about children was to push him back too close to memory. Not permitted at all.

At Oxford station he lingered for a while, standing by the bookstall and pretending to check out the magazines and papers there while he gazed round covertly. It had a dusty dishevelled look; people hurried by with their heads down as though ashamed to be seen or else loitered sulkily, and he thought, why is it that places of travel are always so very melancholy? The pleasure he had been feeling ever since the day started began to drain away, and he turned over one of the magazines, staring down at it sightlessly. He did want to make this movie, he really did; he wanted to make it for himself, for all the other people like himself and, he could not deny, for Hyman. The old man had lied to him, cheated him, had robbed him of his youth and heritage, but still he owed it to him even though he wouldn't have wanted it. No matter what, the movie had to be made. Yet here he was, on his way to collect useful background research and filled suddenly with uncertainty and a sort of – what? And he prodded at and turned over and over the mood in his mind, finally identifying it. Distaste. He felt dirty, as though he were pushing himself into intimate places where he had no right to be. So his parents had kept silent about what happened to them? So that woman Hilda Fraister didn't want to talk to him, had left a message at the hotel while he was out that she'd rather he didn't visit her, thank you? So what? Hadn't they the right to be quiet? To hold back their memories just as he did? Had he any right to go turning over the stones under which they had crept to comfort themselves?

But he couldn't allow that thought to take root. It had become almost an obsession with him, his anger with his parents. The first memories he had were of lonely emptiness, of being different, of being unloved. They had erected barriers between themselves and him, and he would never forgive them for that, he told himself, standing in the dusty melancholy of Oxford station. Never.

This really was crazy behaviour, he thought then. It had to stop; and he put down the magazine and turned on his heel, ignoring the disapproving stare at his failure to buy from the woman behind the counter, and followed the signs for taxis. He had a map of the town and could have walked, he suspected, but he wanted to get there now, before he changed his mind again.

The cab rattled him over a bridge – they called that river the Isis, didn't they? Or was it the Thames? He knew both were around here somewhere – and then through commonplace streets, travelling northwards as far as he could tell. And he made a grimace at himself in the dimness of the rattling old taxi. In this country they didn't seem to bother much with defining the compass points. And after all, why should they? It made sense in a town like Manhattan on its grid, but here where streets twisted and turned so absurdly it made no sense at all.

But then he was in a long, very straight road, which definitely ran north; he was aware of the morning sun moving up to its zenith from his right, and he stared out of the window at the heavy dull houses and wondered what sort of home this Professor Hinchelsea might have. As big as some of these bold brick places with dripping gardens overgrown with dingy bushes? Or would it be somewhere smaller and neater with the sort of charm the houses he had passed on the train had offered? A big place, he decided as the taxi trundled on. Big and handsome with the smell of expensive cigars about it, and perhaps good brandy. Wallace had written a lot about the high life these dons enjoyed. An odd word, he'd thought, 'dons', but maybe apt enough after all; maybe it was a sort of mafia they ran here. He'd heard that places like this, where everyone fed on everyone else, were like that.

The house at which the taxi eventually stopped after turning sharply left surprised him so much that he checked it with the driver, who stared at him in bucolic patience and said, 'You said Bainton Road, didn't you? Well, this is three hundred and nine. See? On the gatepost?'

And he looked at the battered letters, the three dangling awkwardly sideways on a single screw, and paid the man and then stood and stared as the vehicle went chugging away back to the Banbury Road.

It was a narrow street and the houses that lined it were equally mean and small. Attached to each other in a long row, with occasional breaks between the blocks and with garbage cans sitting drunkenly beside some of the battered front gates, each house had a minute garden and scrubby hedge in front of it. They looked dusty and tired, as though they'd been there for a very long time. Staring at them he felt a wave of tiredness of his own. Two days since his arrival; plenty of time to get over the effects of his journey, but now he felt the weariness and thought – I should have had something to eat first. It's been a long time since breakfast. Maybe the Professor will offer me some lunch of some sort? It may not be the kind of house I thought it would be, but maybe the hospitality will be there, all the same.

The path was made of old red bricks set on edge, and there was a row of rather battered tiles also set on edge to separate it from the patch of lank grass that lay in the very middle of the very small front yard. Clearly the hedge had drained away what nutriment there was in the soil, leaving it dispirited and dingy, and he thought suddenly of the row of plants on his window sill in his Manhattan apartment, and how carefully he fed and tended them. There was a stab of homesickness sharp as a needle, and he rang the doorbell firmly to push it away.

He heard it ring inside, muffled and forlorn as though it was as tired as the hedge and the grass behind him and he stood there listening, needing the sight of a cheerful human face, an open door, a warm welcome – and he tugged at his tie in the manner of a man steadying his spirits, and squared his shoulders a little, preparing to set his practised smile on his face.

By the time the door opened the smile had long faded. It seemed that whoever was inside was in no hurry to respond and he glanced at his watch irritably and then lifted his hand to ring again. It was eleven-thirty, for Christ's sake; no one could say this was too early and the woman, whoever she was, had said, 'morning'.

But the door opened silently even as he reached again for the bell push and he pulled his hand back sharply, as acutely embarrassed as though he'd been caught trying to steal something. Abner quickly pushed his smile back into place, albeit a little lopsidedly.

The door had opened only a little and he could just see someone peering out, but it was hard to see who or even what it was. Man, woman? Could be a goddammed dog for all he could see. Though it would have to be a tall one.

The silly thought helped and he relaxed a little. 'Ah, good morning. I'm Abner Wiseman? I called yesterday, made an appointment to see Professor Hinchelsea. I was told this morning would be fine, so can I see him please?' And he widened the grin, deliberately ingratiating.

Grudgingly the door opened more widely and he could see the person behind it. Definitely a person. A tall thin figure, with a pale face that was a blur in the dimness of the house behind until the figure stepped forward and he could see better. A girl, about – and then he stopped. Definitely a girl and not a woman, yet there was no way he could judge her age. She could be as young as twenty or as old as ten years more; or even older than that. Usually he was a shrewd judge of such matters; movie directors had to be. But this girl with her taut pale face and cloud of frizzy dark hair was one of the inscrutable ones. She had a pair of large round glasses behind which wide dark eyes were very watchful, and as he stared at her she pushed them from her nose up to the top of her head, where they sat incongruously looking like car headlights. That was the way the beach girls – tall, tanned and luscious California beach girls – wore their shades. To see the same mode on this rather gawky and very unluscious creature was decidedly odd.

She was wearing shapeless dusty black trousers over old sneakers and over that a white T-shirt and long black cardigan, obviously a man's for it was far too large and had the sleeves rolled up in bunches over thin arms and bony hands. She saw him glance at her hands, which he could see were red with roughness, and shoved them deep into the pockets of the old cardigan.

'You'll have a job doing that,' she said shortly. 'Come in,' and stepped back, holding the door wide.

'I beg your pardon?' He moved forwards into the house, and she closed the door behind him. There was a smell of age; old paper, old books, old food, *age*. It was an unappetising sort of smell and it made his voice sharpen. 'I understood from whoever it was I spoke with on the phone that I had an appointment.'

'You have. It was me. I spoke to you. I told you to come.'

She led the way through the hall, in which he could just make out pieces of large heavy furniture to a door on the right and pushed that open, to lead him in.

'So I can see Professor Hinchelsea?'

She sounded suddenly irritable. 'Oh, for heaven's sake! He's dead!'

He stopped short on the threshold of the room. 'But I was told I could come – '

'You said you wanted to see material. I told you it was a waste of time, but you said you wanted to come, so – ' She thrust out one hand in an awkward little gesture. 'So help yourself.'

He stared at the room into which she was pointing and saw the piles of boxes and the heaps of papers on the tables that were scattered around. There were a couple of chairs and no more furniture at all, though one bar of an elderly electric fire burned in the grate under a mantelshelf on which even more papers were piled.

'There are three more rooms with more than this. I've started the best I can. This room is late nineteenth century and early twentieth century Germany. It goes up to 1945. The latest stuff I haven't started on yet. The dining-room next door is mostly Italy and France and you'll find the other European stuff upstairs – ' She waved her hand vaguely towards the ceiling and he looked at her and thought – she's exhausted. There were faint violet smudges on her temples and the skin beneath her eyes looked stretched and dull. 'I can't help you with any sort of catalogue, I'm afraid. I've got all I can do just to sort it into rough categories right now. He wasn't the tidiest of men . . . ' Her voice trailed away, and she looked at him and he saw the hint of panic in her expression and said impulsively, 'Hell, I'm sorry! If I'd have known I'd never have made any sort of nuisance of myself – '

She shrugged. 'You're no nuisance. The stuff's here. People came to use it when he was alive and he wanted it used now. So use it.'

She moved to the door. 'If you tell me what your subject is I can maybe start you in the right place. You don't have to, of course. I know how it is with you people working on theses. Though why any of you should think I'd do any harm if I knew is beyond me – I'm not likely to try to cut in.'

'I'm not working on a thesis,' Abner said after a moment. 'It – it's a movie.'

She stopped in the doorway and stared back over her shoulder at him. 'A *what*?'

'A movie. A film.' Here it comes, he thought and braced himself. 'A documentary in a sense, but not entirely. Real people most of the time, but I'll need to use some actors, tell a story, so it'll be a feature. About – it's about what happened after the war. The second war.' He looked down at the packing chest in front of him. The chalked information on the side was clear: '1914–1918'.

'The people who were in the labour camps. I want to make a film about them. Not the ones who died. The ones who survived. And their families – '

She was leaning against the door jamb, staring at him, her arms folded over her chest. He was suddenly aware that thin as she was, she was heavy breasted; he could see the swell above the taut muscles of her arms and an odd *frisson* slid across the small of his back. Not desire, no way desire. Just recognition.

'Christ almighty,' she said with great deliberation. 'Christ all-bloody-mighty! Is that what I'm working myself stupid for? All those weeks of digging into this stuff, sorting it, dragging it around, piling it, choking on it, and all to make some cheapjack film? Christ almighty!'

He was stiff with fury. 'Cheapjack is not what I am about, Miss – Miss whoever you are. Who is the – the executor? I'll deal with him.'

She stared at him and then laughed, a high sound that had no humour in it at all. Just tired anger. 'Who's the executor? I'm the executor. I'm the cleaner and the porter and the fireman who burns the rubbish and the garbage collector who humps the bags and the boxes. I'm the only one you can talk to. And if I don't choose to talk to you, you can go to hell. Now get out! Because I don't choose to talk to you. I've got enough to do without wasting time on a *film*.' And she almost spat the word.

He stared at her and then very deliberately unbuttoned his jacket and sat down on one of the chairs. 'I'm not going anywhere. There must be someone else who can give me permission. A relation, maybe, a – '

'Me,' she said again. 'He was my father. So now what are you going to do?'

He looked back at her, nonplussed, and then couldn't help it. He began to laugh, genuine amused laughter, and she watched him, quite unresponding, until at last he stopped and took a handkerchief from his pocket and blew his nose.

'Hell, this is funny – you have to admit it, it is funny! I come schlepping all the way here from London – all the way from New York, for God's sake – and what do I get? Some stonewalling piece who thinks "movie" is a dirty word! I come to the world expert on modern European history and what do I get? A sourpuss who's too tired to give a damn about anyone or anything but herself. You have to laugh!'

'I'm not laughing,' she said, still leaning against the door jamb. 'Are you going?'

'No,' he said, and grinned at her. 'Now, what are you going to do?'

She shrugged. 'Not a thing. I've no time to waste on stupidity. Do what you like.' And she walked out of the room and closed the door behind her. He heard her footsteps go slapping away across bare floor boards, and a door slam somewhere.

He waited a while to see if she'd come back and then shrugged in his turn, took off his jacket and set it over the back of the chair. He'd come this far so he might as well see what there was to see. And he began to prowl among the packing chests, peering at the labels on their sides, seeking what he could find.

He struck lucky quickly. The fourth chest he looked at proclaimed, 'Rise and Fall of National Socialism, 1919 – 45' and he sat down on the floor beside it, heaved it effortfully on to its side – it was very large – and began to pull out the contents.

There were great piles of them, mostly tied with string, yellow dusty paper interspersed with bound notebooks, and there were also envelopes filled with faded newspaper cuttings, and he pulled a notebook and a pen from his jacket pocket and set to work.

Within fifteen minutes he was totally absorbed. Much of what he was reading about he knew of, since he'd read it in other historians' books, but this was different. This was first source material: private letters from individuals who had been involved in the Germany of the period; letters from people who had been directly affected by the Nuremberg Laws of 1935; records of people who had been in the camps, many of them in Dachau; and that, for the first time, made him feel sick as he read it. His father had spoken to him of Dachau – that had been where he had been sent in 1936, a Pole though he had been. He had been studying in Germany and that had been enough. He mustn't think of Hyman now, he mustn't; and he reached down into the chest and pulled out more paper and more still.

It was a long time before he remembered how hungry he was.

·

His belly grumbled loudly and he stretched his back and glanced at his watch and was amazed. Gone two, and he was still here.

He lifted his head and listened. There was no other sound from anywhere in the house and after a moment he got to his feet and started to brush off the dust that covered him. The floor was dusty, the papers were dusty and his mouth and throat, he suddenly realised, were dustier than any of them. He needed something to eat and drink; and he pushed his notebook into his pocket and then shrugged on his jacket. He'd have to get something and then come back and go on; there had to be material here somewhere that he could use.

He stopped suddenly then and stared blankly at the window. If he left now, she'd never let him come back. Did he have to stay here starving to get what he wanted? Nonsense! Of course, she must let him come back. He thought for a while. Then, moving firmly and with no attempt at being quiet, he went out of the room and along the dark hallway, deeper into the house.

He knocked on each of the three doors he found and was greeted with silence; so, boldly, he opened them one after the other, and found her in the last, a surprisingly large kitchen at the very back of the house. And for the first time felt he was in a home rather than in a dilapidated and half-abandoned ware-house.

It had a red-tiled floor, which reflected flames from an old-fashioned fireplace that was set in a gleaming black range of the sort he had seen in carefully and very self-consciously restored Connecticut farm houses inhabited by over-moneyed Manhattanites on their weekend and summer vacations. There was a brightly coloured rug on the floor in front of the fire, and on that a large rocking chair in which the girl was sitting, curled up, a pile of books on her lap. She looked up at him and her glasses, low on her nose, reflected the light from the window on the far side of the big room and made them glint blankly. He thought — Little Orphan Annie. For she did look for a moment so very like the cartoon character of his childhood.

He risked it. 'You look very sad sitting there. Are you?'

'Not particularly,' she said and bent her head again. And now her glasses stopped glinting.

'Look, I'm sorry if I — well, I'm sorry. Please, can we start again? I know I'm researching for a film and not for a thesis, but believe me, films can be serious too. They're not all schlock.'

'Schlock?'

'Rubbish. Garbage. Call it what you like. Some of them have quality. I have quality.'

'If you say so.'

'I do.'

'Well, so, you have quality. But that doesn't mean I have to help you – '

'Of course it doesn't,' he said swiftly. 'There's no obligation ever to anyone, is there?'

'Oh yes, there is,' she said surprisingly. 'For academics, for historians. I have to let them get at that stuff. Geoffrey told me that. It's not mine. It wasn't his. It's for anyone who needs it. It's history.'

'That doesn't include me?' And he lifted his brows at her.

She looked back at him consideringly. 'I've been thinking about that. I suppose it does. I'm sorry if I was rude. It's been a bad week.'

He moved further into the room. 'That's OK. No problem. Forget it. Does that mean I can come back and do some more on that stuff?'

'If you like.'

He looked at her consideringly. 'When did your father die?' There was no need to show this girl any sort of special concern over her bereavement, he thought. She'd be offended if I tried it. Be crisp. Be matter of fact. Be very, very British.

'Two weeks ago,' she said after a moment.

'And there's no one to help you? You've no other relations?'

'If it's any of your business, no. None at all. What's it to do with you?'

'Not a damn thing,' he said cheerfully. 'Just a bit of human feeling. Fellow feeling. I know what it's like when fathers die.'

' "All that lives must die",' she quoted, ' "passing through nature to eternity. Why seems it so particular with thee?" Is that what you're saying?'

He was sitting in the chair on the other side of the fireplace facing her now. The warmth of the flames was agreeable on his legs and face. 'No. I'm no Hamlet. I just said I'd been there. Know what it's like. My father died a couple of months ago.'

'Really,' she said chillingly and bent her head again. 'I've told you that you can come back to do more work if you want to. What else do you want? Are you going now?'

'I'm hungry,' he said. 'And thirsty. I need something to eat. Can I come back afterwards?'

'I've told you. You can come when you like. If I'm not here, you can have the key. Though I usually am.'

He got to his feet and went to the door. 'I hoped you'd offer me some lunch if you — well, how about me offering you? It's the least I can do, after making such a pest of myself.'

She sat and looked at him, her eyes blank behind her glasses. 'What on earth makes you think I'd come and eat lunch with you?'

'Maybe you're hungry,' he said. 'And maybe you've got a car. It's a hell of a way back into the town and I passed no coffee shops on the way here. If you come with me, you act as my guide and you get lunch in exchange. Is it a deal?'

And to his amazement she suddenly laughed and said, 'Why not? Why bloody not?' And got to her feet.

Five

———— ⌇⌇⌇⌇ ————

She was, he decided, the most bewildering person with whom he had ever had to deal. She shifted from one attitude to another so swiftly it was seamless. She did not, for example, make any effort to make herself street smart to go out. She just uncoiled herself from the chair, and set the room straight, poking the fire, refuelling it and closing the damper to keep it in, knuckling the cushion on her chair into tidiness and setting the books she had been working on neatly on a shelf. She did not give herself one glance in the mirror over the fireplace, but walked out through the door he held for her without a backward glance.

In the street outside – and he noticed she merely slammed the door shut and made no effort to lock it – she led him to a battered old Volkswagen that was parked on the far side. Its outside was grimy, clearly not having been washed for weeks, if ever, but inside it was neat to the point of fastidiousness, and faintly scented with lavender from a bunch of the dried flowers that were lying tucked into the open glove compartment. The car was unlocked too, and he said curiously as she manoeuvred it round to take them towards the town centre, 'You must have very honest neighbours.'

'Why?'

'You didn't lock your front door. The car was open too. Doesn't anyone around here ever help themselves to other people's property? You're very fortunate.'

'Oh, I dare say they do,' she said, uninterested. 'If they want to they're welcome. It doesn't really matter.'

'Doesn't matter? I wish I could be so easy! I couldn't afford it.' He was nettled by her coolness, and she grinned, without turning her head to look at him.

'Neither can I,' she said. 'The difference is I couldn't care less.'

He stared at her profile for a while as she pushed the little car through the traffic with casual skill, and then said, 'Are you always like this?'

'Like what?'

'A bunch of thistles. About as approachable as a – well – '

'A bunch of thistles,' she said. 'That's about right. Keep off. That's the message.'

'Why?'

'Why not? Is there any reason I should be sweetness and light to every idiot who comes along and fancies a chat?'

'Thank you,' he said stiffly. 'I'm sorry I bothered you. I can't see why you agreed to come out to lunch, feeling that way about me – '

'Who said I felt that way about you?' she said calmly and pushed the car expertly between a pair of buses and a massive van. 'Don't be so conceited. I said any idiot who comes along. You're not any idiot.'

'Oh, I see. What am I then?'

'Someone who offered me lunch. And I'm hungry. And broke. I don't get out to eat often. So, here I am. I wasn't being prickly. If I were you'd know it. I just don't talk to people at all unless I want to.'

Now she turned her head and threw a glance at him, and her eyes were wide and amused. Her glasses she had again pushed up to the top of her head and she looked softer as a consequence.

'Look, let's get something straight, shall we? I'm not one of your giggly girls who like to go around fluttering their lashes at every man they see. I can't be bothered with that. But if someone seems interesting, then a conversation might be agreeable. You seem tolerably interesting.'

'How the hell can you know that?' he said and refused to let any pleasure in her sudden loquacity show, though he was feeling it. 'You've hardly given me the chance to say much – '

'Because you sat tight and got what you'd come for instead of scuttling off in a panic. That's what most of them do.' The sneer in her voice was very clear. 'There've been three of 'em this week alone. Coming bleating about wanting to look at Geoff's stuff, and what they really want is to talk to me – God knows why. And when I'm rude to them, they scuttle. You didn't scuttle.'

I can't think why they did, he thought, again staring at her profile, which was agreeably clean and sharp against the light of the far window. This girl's interesting, very interesting. Well, more fool they.

'Who were they, these three?'

'Oh, people who'd worked with Geoff. Postgraduate students. Boring little twits – as if I'd waste time on them.'

'You talk a lot about wasting time,' he said. 'What are you saving it for?'

She threw him a startled glance and then let her eyes slide away. 'Look, there's a pub where they do pretty good bar lunches. We should be just in time. Or you can go to a fancy restaurant if you'd rather and can afford it. You're paying. I can't.'

He laughed then at the baldness of it. 'Yes, I'm paying. And I'm on a tight budget, so the pub it is.'

'Go on in and find a place to sit then, and make sure they've got some food left. I'll park and find you.' And she leaned across and opened the door for him, and he smelled a hint of soap and clean hair and liked it.

'I'll come with you – ' he began but she pushed him irritably so that he had to unfasten his seat belt and move over.

'Don't waste time. That lorry behind's shoving – go on. I'll be there in a minute or two.'

He watched the car disappear into a side street and then turned and went into the pub; an extraordinary woman, and an extraordinary day, he thought. Quite extraordinary.

The pub was quiet, its dark brown interior smelling of tobacco and wood smoke, beer and vaguely savoury things, and he was glad there were only two or three groups of people there. He glanced at his watch; almost two-thirty.

The girl behind the bar looked sourly at him when he asked about food and said, 'All the hot's off. Been gone this past half-hour or more. There's a bit of salad left, and you could have a ploughman's. Bit late to be serving lunches, by rights, but – '

'Ploughman's?' he said.

'Bread and cheese and pickles,' she said, clearly scornful of his American ignorance, and rubbed a glass in a bored fashion and put it away. 'Best we can do. Wouldn't recommend the salad. It's mostly been picked over – ' And she jerked her head at a covered counter beside the bar.

She was right. A few sad lettuce leaves and curling onion and cucumber rings seemed to be about the limit of its offerings and he sighed and said, 'Two ploughman's lunches, then, and – ' He stopped. What would she drink? What can I give her? he thought then, a little savagely. I'm paying, after all. 'A couple of beers.'

'What sort?'

'Eh? Oh, the best you do, I guess.' And she looked less belligerent and reached for a couple of glasses.

'Halves?' And she seemed to assume that was what he wanted so he said nothing and watched her as she pulled the beer handles and the dark stuff filled the glasses and topped itself with a high creamy collar. He'd never get to like this stuff, he thought gloomily. Warm and sweet, probably.

It wasn't. By the time Miss Hinchelsea appeared at the pub door he was settled at a table beside the log fire with the beer and two respectably full plates of crusty bread, good stilton and celery, together with the biggest pickled onions he'd ever seen; and had sipped his beer. It wasn't that warm, and had a mellow bitterness he found he liked. It was all a bit like Miss Hinchelsea herself, contradictory, never quite what he'd expected.

He watched her come towards him through the long room and noticed how well she moved. Long legs and haunches that moved smoothly beneath that hideous old cardigan; he could see her better now for she had her fists thrust into the pockets of the trousers in a way that tightened them over her thighs. And again he felt that *frisson* of interest.

She sat down beside him without a word, reached for the plate and began to eat. He watched her; she was indeed hungry, and ate with a sort of controlled fierceness that he found touching. Abner opened his mouth to speak to her, but she caught his eye and looked at him challengingly, and he found his gaze falter, so reached for his own food and began to eat.

It really was very good indeed; whether it was his hunger or the warmth of the fire in the dark room or the company of the girl beside him he didn't know, but it seemed to him that all his tastes were sharpened. The bread was crusty and nutty in his mouth; the cheese sharp and yet creamy and the onions wonderfully tart. The beer slid down his throat cheerfully and later, when the girl at the bar brought them coffee and a couple of pieces of apple pie plentifully laced with cloves and cinnamon, that too tasted remarkably good. He gobbled it all with relish, as did his companion and then they sat, one each side of a long settle and stared at the flames.

'Thanks,' she said after a long silence. 'I needed that.'

'Me too,' he murmured, a little sleepily. 'You don't always notice when you get hungry – '

'I do,' she said after another little pause. 'I *needed* that.'

'You're not that broke, are you?' he said then and turned his head, all trace of sleepiness gone. 'Is that really the only reason why you said you'd come with me?'

She made a little grimace. 'Not entirely. I said I'd come because I was hungry, yes. But also because you're not a twit. However hungry I got, I wouldn't spend time with a fool. As for being broke, well, let's just say I often don't eat, mainly because I'm too lazy to bother most of the time.'

'Too lazy to bother with what?'

'Shopping. Eating. It seems such a chore. So I just go on till I just have to get something and then I go out. It's cheaper that way too. I'm not completely on my uppers but I have to be careful. He left bugger all.'

'Your father?'

'Who else?'

There was another little silence and then he said carefully, 'You were dependent on him? I mean, you don't have a job.'

'I did have. But it died,' she said, and then lifted her brows at him. 'I looked after Geoffrey. He was a full-time job. I tried to help with the work as well, of course. The papers – but he was too much for me. Kept it all locked away, wouldn't let me disturb anything. Kept all his filing systems in his head, damn him. So now it's driving me mad, sorting it all out.' She shrugged. 'Well, it won't be so bad. When I get straight and the house is sold, and I find a room or something somewhere, that'll help.'

'Then you'll eat more often?'

'Oh, I doubt it. Shopping and cooking – it'll still be a problem. God, what a bore! But at least I'll be able to get out and find something without having to worry about how much it costs.'

'Was it like this for your father too? I thought he was a professor of the University – '

'Oh, he was, and there was some money from that. And he had an annuity. But that all died with him. Like my job. So, there's very little. But I can manage.' And then suddenly she turned and flared at him, 'Don't you dare feel sorry for me!'

'Like hell!' he said. 'I'd as soon feel sorry for a rattlesnake!'

'Good! Glad you could hear the warning.' She settled back in her seat, pulling her legs up so that she had her heels tucked beneath her and her arms circled her knees. 'Keep listening for it.'

Another silence as the pub slid into emptiness around them with the last people leaving. And he stretched and yawned. 'Don't they close soon? I've heard about your crazy drinking laws.'

'They've changed them. This is one of the places open all day now.'

'Good,' he said. 'Another beer?'

She nodded and the same bored barmaid served them. They sat and drank, both staring at the fire and not speaking. Until he stirred himself and said, 'May I know your name?'

She slid her eyes sideways. 'Hinchelsea.'

'Oh, for Christ's sake! Do you have to be so – '

'Miriam,' she said. 'Miriam Sipporah. As biblical as yours.'

'I beg your pardon?'

'Abner. Do you have another name too?'

He felt his face redden. 'What if I have?'

'What is it?'

'I'd rather not – '

'Too bad.' She smiled, and it lifted her whole face so much that it cheered him, and he found himself speaking before he realised he was doing it.

'Shlomo,' he said. 'I ask you! Shlomo. When the kids at school found out, they called me shlemiel. What else?'

'What's wrong with that?'

'Shlemiel? It means idiot. Fool.' He stopped then and looked at her sharply. 'I only just realised. How come you've got a Hebrew name?'

She looked at him levelly. 'My mother was Jewish,' she said.

He was so surprised that he said nothing, just stared, and she burst into laughter. It was the first time he had heard her laugh and it was a pleasant sound; throaty and filled with genuine amusement. 'Don't tell me I don't look it,' she said. 'I couldn't bear that.'

'But you do,' he said. 'I should have — it just never occurred to me. That here, in Oxford — and a father who's a professor — it didn't seem likely.' He looked at the cloud of frizzy hair and the wide dark eyes again and nodded. 'You do look it.'

'I do?' And there was a note of amused jeering in her voice now. 'What sort of Jewish do I look? The red headed blue eyed kind you find all over Israel and all over the world come to that? Or black like the Ethiopian Jews? Or Chinese like the Shanghai Jews? Or — '

He threw up both hands in mock surrender. 'All right, all *right*! I'm a racist pig who thinks in clichés — '

'Something like that,' she said and again smiled at him. It was a real smile, wide and friendly and he could have warmed his hands at it.

'This is better,' he said, off his guard. 'It's good to be so comfortable together.'

It was as though he'd pulled a shutter down over her. The warmth and the laughter vanished and she sat up, setting her feet firmly on the ground.

'I have to get back,' she said abruptly. 'Have you paid? I've got the car round the corner in Pusey Street by St Cross. They'll clamp it if I leave it much longer. You want to come back to do some more work? Or come another day? I could drop you at the station.'

He stared at her, bewildered again. 'Can't you — I mean, do you have to rush back? I want to do some more work, of course I do. And if you worked with your father on this stuff, I'd like to have some guidance from you. But right now, I thought — we seemed to be — I mean, how about showing me the town? I've never been to Oxford before. I had a friend who was here, used to write me about it, but I've never actually seen it. Show me the colleges.'

She stared at him. 'The dreaming spires bit? I suppose so.' Another sudden change. She looked approachable again, but the moment of real intimacy that had seemed to grow between them a little while ago had quite vanished. She was polite, no more; and then turned and led the way out of the pub.

'We'd better check the car's still safely parked,' she said. 'And then I'll walk you around a little. It's hopeless any other way.' And she went swiftly along the pavement, her hands in her trouser pockets again, and the old black cardigan swinging behind her. He noticed now that she had a neat round behind and that pleased him. Neat behinds were good to look at, and he might as well get what pleasure he could from her company. Certainly talking to her was an occupation fraught with disappointment. So he watched the muscles move in their rhythmic way and enjoyed it all the way up to Pusey Street.

The car sat demurely tucked between two much larger ones and since none of the vehicles had been clamped or ticketed and there were plenty of them, she nodded briskly.

'We'll gamble. Should be all right till a little later. They get tough around the rush hour. So, you want a tour. Right. This is St Cross College. That one over there's Regent's Park College. Come on, you can look into the quads as we go by, and I'll take you into one or two. Oriel, maybe, and Balliol.'

She took him round the city at a rate that left him breathless, and made even his long legs ache, weaving her way in among the strolling passers-by as deftly as she had manoeuvred her little car, throwing information back at him over her shoulder.

'That's the Ashmolean – not a bad museum, though for myself I rather like the University one. That's St John's College over there, and the other one's Trinity. If you go down there, Broad Street, you'll come to the Bodleian – old Bodley – and the Radcliffe Camera's on the other side of that. We'll work our way round in a minute – '

Her energy seemed unflagging, and she did not shorten her step at all, however breathless he got. He wasn't used to this much exercise, though clearly she was; most of his time at work was spent hunched over a desk or a camera or an editing set-up. There had been a time when he had considered taking up jogging like everyone else in Manhattan and then had discarded it as mere fashion. Now, as he panted after those swift legs, he wasn't so sure. It was shaming to be left sweating and red-faced in this manner.

But as time went on he got his second wind and it got easier, and he could actually stop and stare at some of the things she showed him; great old stone buildings of such solidity they made him feel fragile, and he tried to encompass the dates she gave him for some of them; this place had been largely unchanged, it seemed, for hundreds of years. Some of these buildings could almost have grown out of the ground, they were so much a part of the landscape, and he worked to control his sense of awe. He wouldn't for the world display to this odd girl his American naïvety in terms of the antiquity of buildings. It was too easy to be overwhelmed by such minor matters, he told himself, and just nodded and asked the most intelligent questions he could, as she rattled on with her guided tour, for all the world like a city employee.

It was getting dark by the time she had taken him all round the centre of town and at last she stopped on the pavement in the middle of the hurrying home-going shoppers, and said flatly, 'Well, that's it. Today's gallop through the dreaming spires.'

'Nothing dreamy about that. I'm aching all over.' He grinned at her, inviting her to laugh, hoping his admission of frailty would soften her. It didn't.

'Shall I take you to the station? It's not much of a walk. Down there, along to the right and then first left. Once you're over the bridge turn left again and then right. You'll see the station there.'

'Well, yes. Thank you. I'll walk. I can come back again?'

'I told you. The stuff's there if you need it.'

'Even for just a movie?'

'It's history,' she said and turned away. 'Geoff said everyone who needed access was to have it. You need it, you have it. What I think doesn't come into it.'

'I'll phone then, and make a time,' he said and then had to call after her, for she was already walking away from him. 'Miriam! I'll call you!'

She didn't turn round. She just lifted one hand above her head in an absent sort of way, wriggled her fingers, and walked on, and he watched her go and felt oddly bleak. It had been an effortful afternoon, and his calf muscles and heels were aching dully. They'd be screaming blue murder at him tomorrow. But he'd enjoyed it. He'd enjoyed her too. Coming back would be worth while for more than one reason.

Six

'Listen,' the fat man said. 'You've picked a good time and a bad time.' He leaned back in his chair and grinned expansively at Abner, clearly pleased at his gnomic utterance, wanting to be asked what he meant. Irritated by his self importance, Abner refused to ask and just sat and looked at him, waiting.

He was very aware of the room around him; it was over-furnished to the point of being embarrassing, with heavy leather sofas and armchairs set on deep Chinese rugs, a vast glass coffee table piled with movie magazines and trade papers from every country in the world that published them. The walls were covered with self-consciously modern paintings as well as the ubiquitous movie posters that everyone displayed in offices involved in the industry – only these had been expensively framed. There were a couple of framed gold and platinum records, too, and very large photographs of grinning performers with great sprawling signatures on them. 'To the Divine Monty' he could read clearly right over on the other side of the room, scrawled beneath a simpering face so rich in dimples and curls that their owner could have been a lascivious Shirley Temple, except that he was clearly male. 'The Bestest Agent a guy could have – with gratitude – Jonty Charteris.' One of last year's big names, Abner remembered hazily. A singer of banal sentimental ballads that middle-aged women all over the world had adored. He must have made a lot of money out of that one, he thought sourly and stared back at the fat man who was still watching him expectantly.

After a moment the man sighed and leaned forwards to tap his cigarette ash into the Cadillac hub cap he used as an ashtray. 'I'll tell you, Wiseman, there's money around. Oh, yes, there's money around.'

Again he leaned back and stared owlishly at Abner. 'For some films you just hold out your hands and it comes running in. That's the good news.'

Still Abner said nothing.

'The bad news is, the ones that want to spend the money are mostly Arabs. And something tells me that they won't be so eager to go paying out to make a movie like this one you want to make, you know what I mean? Bad title too,' he said then with a fine judicious air. *Postscripts*? What sort of a title is that for a film? Sounds like – like a . . . ' he sawed the air with one hand, looking for a simile and ended lamely, 'It don't sound like a film.'

'Why not? I saw a poster coming in for a movie called *K9*. What sort of a title is that?'

'A money-making title, my boy, that's what that is! Anyway, it's a joke, see – *K9* – it means a dog. It's a buddy movie, only one of the buddies is an alsatian. Great for an agent, that is! Making stars of bloody mutts. But it's making money, believe me. So who cares *what* they call it?'

'Precisely. My *Postscripts* then, is just as good a title – '

'If it'll make money.' The fat man seized on that. 'But where's the guarantee? No stars, no glamour, and such a subject! Movies about such subjects – do they make money? People want a bit of uplift now, entertainment, Spielberg stuff – '

'Spielberg makes Spielberg movies,' Abner said, as colourlessly as he could, though anger simmered inside him. 'I make mine.'

'Sure you do, sure you do!' The other was expansive, warm, sympathetic. 'Of course you do! I'm just saying, find a better subject, a good title, a star or two and there's backing for the asking. But this subject, this title – no Arab's going to give a damn.'

'Are you saying the only available investors in this country are Arabs?' Abner said. 'I understood from Joe Kass in LA that you knew the business on this side better than anyone. That you didn't just agent performers but directors as well and were involved in packaging. That was why I came to see you. I thought you'd know all the sources of funding and – '

'Of course I do! I was just telling you where there's easy monies to be found! Sometimes you have to do it the hard way, but why be stubborn if by changing a bit here and there you can have an easy time of it?'

'I'd rather make my own movie, Mr Nagel.' Abner said. 'If you're saying you're not interested in handling that, then – ' He made a move to get to his feet and the other waved him down again.

'So what's your rush? I was just going through the options for you. What sort of a businessman would I be if I didn't look at all the options and spell 'em out, hey? And call me Monty, for God's sake. Everyone does. All through the industry, you just say Monty and everyone knows who you mean. So, you've set your mind on this subject, this title. Hmm.' And he pursed his lips and sat staring down at the sheet of paper he had picked up from his rosewood desk, looking for all the world like an elderly and evilly disposed baby. 'You've got a good track record, I'll grant you, but in the wrong places, if you know what I mean – '

Abner stared at him and thought – he's a great deal smarter than he looks or sounds. He's not going to let go of a possible earner, even if he's not sure yet I can make him a couple more of these godawful leather sofas; and he let his shoulders relax. He was used to men like this agent. LA and New York were littered with his carbon copies.

'I know,' he said wearily. 'Of course I know! Art houses, public service television, who's interested? In the States, no one wants to put money in my sort of stuff. That's why I'm here. To hell with using people who are now in the States for research for the movie. I'll use people here in Europe. Why not? It doesn't matter where the survivors ended up, does it? Their stories'll be much the same – So that's why I'm here. I thought I'd do better. You've got a long tradition of art house movies. You've got the BBC, you've got your Channel Four, you've got – '

'And much good they do any of us,' Monty said gloomily. 'Awards, sure. Long fancy reviews in the *Guardian* and *Look and Listen*, big deal. But money? Fourpence and if you're lucky another tuppence abroad. But real money, you need to be *popular* for that – and let's face it, Wiseman, you're not what you could call popular. Classy, yes. But money-maker, no.'

'I'm as interested in money as most people,' Abner said. 'But let's get one thing clear, Mr Nagel – Monty. I don't want to make money more than I want to make my own movies. A living I'm interested in, sure. But I can't eat more than I eat now, and who needs more than one car or — '

'I've heard that sort of talk before,' Monty said, more gloomily than ever.

'Well, I mean it,' Abner said. 'I want to make a reasonable living from my work but I'm not into putting the cash before the credit. If I only cared about that, I'd make porn, for Christ's sake!'

Monty shook his head with great seriousness. 'You wouldn't. You'd be surprised how little there is in that. Sure, the videos sell and there's a black market for the really ugly stuff, but it don't make what I call money. For that you need your Crocodile Dundees, your Batmans, your Dick Tracys — '

Abner waved that away with some impatience. 'I want it clear. If you want to represent me here, fine. But on my terms. I'm not going to make the sort of big money some of your other people do — ' And he swept a slightly scornful glance round the framed photographs. 'But if you get me the backing I need, help me set up a package with a bit of backing, there'll be enough to be worth your efforts. *Yesterday's Babies* and *Wall of Silence* kept me going for a long time, all through till I got *U.D. — Uptown Downtown* — on the floor. I had no complaints and you won't either — '

'But you're not exactly flush now, are you?' Monty said shrewdly. 'You ain't in no suite at Claridges! And you said to me you're going to be wanting some work while you're here, to keep you going.'

Abner reddened. 'So, I'm not one of your savers. When I earn I spend. Right now, I'm not earning, so there isn't much slack I can take up. But there it is. That isn't what I'm in the business for — and if you are, I'd better go now and stop wasting time for both of us.'

'So high minded,' Monty sighed. 'Well, I could get me a bit of class, at that. I'd like to sit there at the Oscars, watch you walk up and get another. And maybe a BAFTA. Wouldn't be bad, that. Though I still wish it was a different subject. This one — ' He gave a sudden shiver and now he didn't look at all like a baby. There was a bleakness about his eyes and mouth and Abner looked at him sharply. He was learning to recognise that look.

'You got some personal reason for not liking it?'

Monty shook his head, sliding his eyes up to look at Abner and then flicking his gaze away to the window. 'Me? This is business I'm talking here – '

'But you don't like the subject for personal reasons,' Abner said, pushing at him, actually leaning forwards in his chair to get closer to the fat little man on the other side of his ornate desk. Monty Nagel reacted by leaning back, pushing his chair back a little so that he could put his feet in their chocolate pumps on the blotter in front of him, so restoring the space between them.

'Who does like it?' he said. 'You're a Jew, you should understand these things.'

'So, I'm a Jew. What's that got to do with it? I could have been a Gypsy. Or gay. Or whatever. A lot of people went into those camps, not only Jews.'

'Mostly it was Jews,' Monty said flatly. 'And in this business that means there'll be people who won't want to be involved with this film of yours. Look what happened in the States over *Playing for Time* – an uproar. People didn't like it.'

'They didn't like Vanessa Redgrave cast as Fania Fenelon. The woman's anti-Zionist so the fuss was political. But the picture was great. It got great notices and – '

' – and made no money and upset a lot of people. There's a lot who won't ever watch this sort of stuff. They see it's going to be about the Holocaust, and they say, who needs such misery? It's over, already – they switch off, they don't buy no tickets.'

'Not all of them,' Abner said. 'This one they'll watch. They'll have to – ' And he stared at the fat man who stared back at him and then rubbed his face a little awkwardly.

'Well, yes,' he said. 'All right, I've agreed, haven't I? I'll consider taking you on, find you a bit of work, see if I can put you in touch with some people who might help. But don't expect me to like it – '

'Because you've got some connection with it all,' Abner said, coming back like a terrier to the thought that had come with the man's uneasiness. 'Your own family, perhaps?'

Monty shrugged. 'Perhaps. Hasn't everyone? Listen, let me give you some people you can talk to about money. Tell them I sent you – you've got a notebook? Good.' And he reached for his intercom button and shouted, 'Tania? Put up the B seventeen lists will you? I got the wrong disc in here.'

There was a little fussing as the secretary came in and set a
floppy disc into the gleaming computer that sat on its own table
alongside the rosewood desk, and then Monty sat there, flicking
at his keyboard and staring at the screen. Abner hitched his chair
closer and leaned forwards so that he could read it too. It was
easy to see the screen and he watched as Monty stared at
columns of names with letter and number clues alongside. This
was clearly, he told himself as yet another key was hit and a
different list appeared, one hell of a well-run organisation. With
contact lists like these, surely Nagel was worth being with?
Abner hadn't warmed to the man on a personal level, which was
a pity in an agent, but the important thing was to find someone
who could deliver. So what if he couldn't be a bosom buddy?
That he'd have to find someone else. And he refused to think at
all about Oxford, even though his legs and feet still carried the
ghost of an ache from yesterday's walking.

'Try Simmy. Yeah. Simmy'll be good news – here, can you see?
This one.' He pointed at the screen with a stubby finger and
leaned back to light another cigarette as Abner wrote in his
notebook. Simmy Gentle, with an address in Wardour Street.
Where else? Everyone in movies seemed to be in this knot of
streets around him. Monty's office was in the area, too, tucked
into an unprepossessing building in D'Arblay Street that belied
its internal opulence; no doubt this man, Gentle, would be in the
same sort of accommodation.

'And try that one bottom of the list, see? Jo Rossily. Good
news, Jo – well worth a visit.' Abner scribbled again, and then
Monty returned to the keyboard and again punched it. More and
more names flashed up, and he sat and studied them as Abner
stared over his shoulder. At length he said, 'Yeah, this might be
worth a minute or two of your time. He's a real wide boy, you
know? But all the same.'

'Alexander Venables,' wrote Abner, and this time the address
was very different. 'The City? Isn't that the financial district?'
And he looked at Monty with his brows up. 'Not a movie man,
then?'

'You're fast, aren't you?' Monty grinned and seemed suddenly
a nicer guy to Abner. 'Not here five minutes and already you
understand about addresses, hey? You're right. He's a banker –
well, kind of banker. Got access to cash that's mostly Arab, but

he might have a few bob from other sources. In fact, I know he does. A smart fella. And he's got an interest in – ' He stopped then. 'Well, let him tell you himself. If he wants to.'

'Tell me what?' Abner was alert at once. There were messages here if he could understand them.

'I told you, ask him yourself.' Monty's voice had sharpened but then he relaxed and it seemed to Abner he had made a conscious effort to do it. Odd. 'Now there's just one other possibility here – Barney Milner. You'll like Barney. Good fun, and there ain't anyone he doesn't know and who don't know him. You can't even begin to think films in this town without him. Here you are – '

'Another banker?' Abner asked, writing hard. 'Where's this place? Not round here. It's a different zip code altogether.'

'Out in the suburbs. Way over the river. He's the gear man. Cameras, lighting, equipment, the lot. And he's a studio owner, too. One of the best. Not the cheapest but good. And he dabbles in funding now and again. "To keep his gear out of the warehouse," he says, but it's more than that. He's crazy about the business, he is. Crazy. He'd work for nothing, if he had to, I swear, as long as it was films.'

'I like him already,' Abner said. 'My sort of guy. Great, Monty. I'll get on to all of them.' He finished scribbling, and snapped the notebook shut with its rubber band. 'Tell me, who's Matthew Mayer?'

Monty gaped at him. 'How the hell do you know about him? Don't tell me he's got to the States as well?'

Abner jerked his head at the computer screen. 'He keeps coming up there. I saw most of the names you've got there only once, but that one keeps turning up after other people's names. Like he was in partnership with them or something of that sort.'

'Oh,' Monty looked oddly wooden. 'Something of the sort. Nothing that'd help you there though. Now, you've got four names there, right? That'll do for openers. If you can't crack something with one of those, I'll be surprised. Mind you, it could mean I'm right and there isn't going to be any backing for you. But I'll be glad to be wrong – let me know how you get on. Maybe I'll make a bob or two out of you yet. What do you say?'

Abner said, 'No contract then?'

'Not yet,' Monty said and stood up. He was surprisingly tall,

Abner thought. Sitting there he'd seemed to be a stocky sort of man, but he had long legs under his heavy body that gave him a slightly unbalanced look. 'You take that stuff as a present from me, OK? You seem a decent sort of a chap – wouldn't cheat me. If you make it start to work with one or two of those, begin to get somewhere, come back, we'll talk again. But I don't make contracts till I know the sort of people I'm dealing with. Only been wrong twice. That singer, the French one, calls himself Rousseau, you know the one I mean?'

'I ought to,' Abner said dryly. 'Biggest thing since Presley as far as I can tell. Can't escape him anywhere.'

'Came to me as a raw kid from Dagenham, about as French as my arsehole, and nothing to look at. But he had a bit of a spark and I thought, maybe, maybe. Sent him for a start off to one of the best voice people we got, and a stylist, and told him to come back and let me have another look at him and I'd talk contracts. And what does the little bugger do? Takes himself off to the Charter lot, signs on with them and makes 'em a bleedin' fortune. May his bollocks fall off. But me, I still take risks. You won't go and do nothing so crooked, will you? You look an honest enough man.'

Abner grinned. 'That's not what makes you so easy on me,' he said. 'You just don't reckon I'm a money maker, that's what it is.'

Monty laughed. 'Well, I don't think I'm sending the next *Gone With the Wind* out of the door, that's for sure. But like I said, it's time I got a bit of class around the place. You get fed up with the Rousseaus, believe me. Good luck.'

He held out a hand and Abner shook it and turned to go. The outer office, which was about half as opulent as Monty's own room but still highly over-decorated, was quiet, but one man was sitting waiting, and Abner looked at him casually but then more sharply, because he was puzzled. He looked harmless enough, a small man, rather wizened, as though he'd shrunk since he'd first bought the suit he was wearing, and with a dull flat face that bore little expression. Yet at the sight of him Monty at his side had stiffened, and in the big bronze mirror that had been faked to look antique and which covered the wall facing Monty's office door, Abner had seen the reflection of the fat man's face. Monty had looked at the man sitting in the corner armchair and had been alarmed; had first frowned and then very slightly, but definitely, had glanced sideways at Abner and then shaken his head and made a warning *moue* with his rather full lips. It had been an unmistakable reaction and Abner was intrigued by it. It was none of his business, but his was an eye that missed nothing and a mind that stored memories of all it saw. And he needed a lot of information about the way the film industry worked in this town and who was involved in it. There was no reason that he could think of that one man, whom he had met for the first time this morning, albeit after bringing him a very warm letter of introduction from an important Hollywood contact, should be alarmed because another total stranger appeared while he was with Abner. Yet alarmed he had been.

'Oh, Mr Nagel,' the girl behind the desk said brightly. 'Here's Mr Heller to see you and − '

'I've got eyes in my head!' Nagel growled, and the girl flushed and subsided, clearly put out, and bent her head over a pile of papers. Monty slapped Abner amiably on the back then, and said loudly, 'Well, then, Abner, I'll be seeing you. It's been a good meeting. Keep up the good work.'

'I will,' Abner said, carefully ignoring the man in the armchair, and nodding affably at the secretary at her desk as though the little scene with her boss hadn't happened. 'You'll be hearing from me.' And went out into the shabbiness of the outer stairwell and down to the street.

It had been, he decided, a productive morning so far. To have a list of four more contacts with a firm introduction from a powerful agent was a beginning, and having that agent probably willing to take him on was even more than a beginning. Now, what next?

He stood in D'Arblay Street and looked round at the mid-morning hubbub, which was considerable, and pondered. Start at once by going to some of these people Monty had suggested? Or just continue with his own list of possibles? Monty had been the best of them − Kass had been right with his assurance that this was the guy to see − but all the same, the rest might add up to something. He had appointments with three or so of them, but not till the next day; Monty Nagel had been the only one available this morning. But then Abner brightened. He had his list from Newark, the fax that Frieda had sent, and he reached into his document case and pulled it out.

Four names there and all of them attached to addresses. All in London or nearby. And he peered at it and made up his mind. To hell with phone calls. It was worth taking a chance and just going to see if any of these people were right for his movie. Maybe by the end of the day he'd have more than an agent, and a list of possible money people; he'd also have some people to use as material for the movie.

And that, he thought illogically, should show Miss Miriam Hinchelsea a thing or two, if nothing did.

Seven

That London was big he knew, but he hadn't understood quite how big, until now. The girl in the coffee shop where he had stopped to collect his thoughts, as well as to rest his aching legs, had advised the tube, and he'd liked the thought of that. The first time he'd used the subway in New York, after arriving at City University, he'd felt like a real New Yorker; there was something so very domestic about being rattled along underneath the city cheek by jowl with people who pretended you weren't there at all, so jealously did they guard their own space; and though such a journey now wouldn't make him into a Londoner, it would at least mean he wasn't just another tourist. The town seemed to be crawling with them; he'd heard every sort of American accent — from the flat of the mid-west to the fluting of California via New York's nasal jabber — and had shrunk a little from the stereotypical behaviour of some of their owners. What was it about Americans abroad that made them so very embarrassing? But it wouldn't be like that in the tube. There he could sit and watch the stations run by the window and watch his fellow passengers ignore him and feel comfortable.

But it was such a distance and took so long that when at last he emerged from Burnt Oak station, where the coffee shop girl had assured him he needed to go, he felt uneasy. To have come so far on impulse without calling first had been crazy. The guy probably wouldn't be there. At work, possibly. Though perhaps not, he thought then. He could be old, too old to be anything but retired. He reviewed the club in Newark, trying to squint back down the years at the people there. He hadn't gone there often, but often enough to have been aware of the sort of people who belonged and to his young eyes then they had been really old. Perhaps in their fifties, even sixties, he told himself now as he

looked round at the street in which he found himself in Burnt
Oak – another sixteen years or so and that'll be me – and he was
caught with a sudden sense of desolation as he contemplated the
shortness of his life. So little time lived, and so little left to live.
And then, irritated at his own melancholy, Abner reached into
his document case for the list of addresses and the book he'd
bought in a newspaper shop after he left Monty Nagel's office. It
was going to be his bible, he thought now, as he leafed through
the index looking for the address. A London street map – how do
they manage ever to get round without one in this town of
snaking roads and tiny streets?

He found the street he needed easily; Silkstream Close seemed
fairly near by, and he started to walk, turning right to pass cosy
local shops, along pavements full of mothers with bawling
children in buggies and old men wrapped in overcoats walking
with careful steps from post office to tobacconist and from
supermarket to corner pub. Was one of them his quarry? he
wondered and looked at the men who passed, trying to see which
one of them looked Jewish; and then felt anger at himself,
remembering Miriam Hinchelsea's jeering response when the
question of her Jewishness had come up. Who could say what
was a specifically Jewish look, anyway? Yet here he was thinking
in the same bigoted fashion. He should be ashamed.

But still he looked; peering at old faces pinched with the cold
over tightly wrapped mufflers, or beneath carefully arranged
hats, looking for – what? – Hooked noses? Dark eyes? Ringlets?
Or was it something less obvious and nothing to do with such
simplicities? Perhaps he was looking for an expression of
suffering, or of nobility. He turned sharply to cross the road, as
though to leave behind him the foolishness of his thinking,
looking for the side road that would lead him to Cyril Etting's
house, and made himself think about him.

On the other side of the road, two women were standing
gossiping, and beside them a bored child in a scarlet duffle coat
pushed a toy car along a garden wall, making engine noises with
his mouth. Abner looked at him, and memory stirred. Almost
panicking, so important was it to keep it dammed back, he
hurried on, forcing himself to think about the man he was about
to see.

How old *would* he be? His own father, Hyman, had been

sixty-four when he had died; not old really, but old enough. He had been just eleven when he'd been taken with his family to Dachau, and as the thought formed itself in his head, memory could no longer be controlled. Suddenly Abner was no longer walking along a London suburban street, with its fringe of little houses and gardens on a chilly February morning in 1989; he was sitting in the living room of his parents' home in Newark in 1973, in the glow of the lamp with the cloth thrown over it, listening to his father's low voice coming from the shadows behind the pool of light and telling him how it had been. He had felt the chill of fear, icy in his belly, when he'd heard his father's story that first time and now he felt that coldness again as the memory did not just come back into his mind, but flooded his whole being, as though it was an actual experience he was recalling for himself. He couldn't stop it. He was no longer Abner but Hyman, the son of Yossel and Bryna, eleven years old and asleep in his bed, and now it was 1936.

He'd been lying awake a long time that night because it had been so strange a day. His parents had sat up long after he'd gone to bed in the little cupboard-like space, which was all the room they could find for him in that poky Berlin flat, talking in frightened and hushed voices; and he remembered how at school the other children had refused to talk to him, had left him and Issy Rabin alone in the corner of the playground surrounded by emptiness, the only Jewish boys there. But he had at last fallen asleep and then, almost as soon it seemed as his eyes had closed, the noise had started; bangings and men shouting, the high wailing notes of his mother's voice, and his baby sister crying in the way she did, with huge gulps and then roars; and he had tumbled out of his bed as his father had arrived at the door and told him sharply to dress. He had looked so strange to young Hyman, his smooth hair not smooth at all but rumpled, so that his bald patch showed, and that had startled Hyman more than anything else, for his father had never ever looked like that before. He had always combed his hair in the morning before anyone had a chance to see him leave his room. But not this time. Hyman had dressed and picked up his little wooden car, the one he liked best even though he was really too old for it now, but for some reason he'd picked it up and put it in his pocket. And they had gone out of the flat, all of them, Momma and Poppa and the baby Minka and Hyman, eleven years old and very puzzled and only a little bit frightened. Then.

As suddenly as the memory had come to him, it went; Abner was himself again. He was standing quite still in the middle of the pavement of Silkstream Road, in north London, his face cold with sweat and his eyes unfocused, aware of someone standing in front of him and peering up at him, and he blinked and looked, and the small woman with the shopping trolley stared back with birdlike intensity and said in a thin high voice, 'Are you all right, young man?'

He looked at her stupidly. 'Pardon me?'

She seemed to brighten. 'You're an American! Visiting someone, are you? Can I help you if you're lost?' Her curiosity hung around her as thick as a cloud, and he looked at her eager face, hating her for intruding into the pain of his memory, and grateful to her for dispelling it, all at the same time.

He blinked yet again and said carefully, 'Ah – no, thank you. I'm not lost. I have my map.' And he lifted the book in his hand.

She looked at it and said, 'Oh, I just thought – well, good morning then.' And went, leaving him looking down at the book and pretending to check his route, shaken, embarrassed and with an oddly desolate feeling taking the space that the fear had occupied.

For he had been very frightened. It had been as though he had been walking along this rather dull little street with his father, hearing him speak of his experiences for the first time and reliving them. And the recollection of the fear that had engendered created even more fear in him. He felt panic rise for a moment and lifted his head and said aloud, 'Hey, fella, watch it!' That had been the way he'd learned to stop the feelings coming all those years ago at City, in his second year when he'd been so knocked out by the flu he'd caught from Wallace. Panic attacks, the doctor had told him, free-floating anxiety caused by the flu, and she had made him learn relaxation techniques to control them, but the only one that had worked had been that silly spoken phrase: 'Hey, fella, watch it!' And he said it again now and took a deep breath. At last the feeling began to ebb away, and he could start walking again. But his legs felt jellied and his head felt light. He wished he hadn't come.

But he had and was nearly there; and he had to deal with it, had to make his move. To turn and go now would be the end of it all. No *Postscripts* would ever be made, and that failure would mean there would be no peace for him. Ever. Not to be thought of.

The house was on the corner of a side street, looking sideways across the road to a pretty little park, which was dank and grey now and sodden with tired wintry trees, but which would bloom soon. Even on this February afternoon there was a faint blush of green on some of the trees, and he felt a little better as he looked at them, and then pushed open the creaking gate and walked up the path. Not brick-made this time, like the path of the Hinchelsea house in Oxford, but paved with worn grey stones. The garden through which it ran was neat and well cared for, with clean empty flowerbeds in which a few green spikes showed, promising daffodils soon.

The house had a watchful look, he thought, and then was annoyed with himself for being fanciful. How can a house be watchful, goddammit? And he reached forwards and pressed hard on the bell.

The door opened so promptly that he realised the old man had been standing behind it waiting for him. He must have seen him coming up the path from behind the curtains that shrouded the stained glass window set into the front door, and he thought with a twitch of amusement – I was right, the house *was* being watchful.

'Mr Etting?' he said with great care, and smiled. Not too eager, not too ingratiating, just a smile. The old man stood and stared at him; a bulky figure in a dust-coloured cardigan that drooped in front almost to his knees, bulging in shapeless grey trousers. The cardigan reminded him for a fleeting moment of Miriam Hinchelsea, and again he was amused at himself and began to feel a little better.

'Who wants him?' the old man said. His voice was scratchy and thin as though it wasn't accustomed to being used.

'My name is Wiseman, Abner Wiseman. I'm a researcher on a movie – a film. I was given your name as a possible – um – advisor and helper by the Shoah Club – you know, the Survivor's Centre – in Newark, New Jersey. In America. I'm not filming yet, you understand. Just looking for some guidance.'

The door began, very slowly, to close. The old man standing

there with one hand on it was pushing it inexorably forward and
Abner had to hold on hard to his impulse to put out a foot and
prevent him; that would be no way to reassure a possibly
alarmed old man – for indeed, he looked very old – that there
was no risk.

'Someone has to tell the story, the way it really was,' he said
desperately. 'It's all I want to do. Tell it the way – ' He
swallowed, seeing the need looming in front of him, hating to
have to do it, knowing it was inevitable, knowing he would be
lying. 'The way my father would have wanted it told. He told me
what happened to him, and now he's dead. I have to tell it for
him. That's all I'm trying to do.'

Oh, God, he thought. Hyman would have hated a film, Frieda
will hate it too even though in her own way she's helping me. But
I've got to make it, and if that means lies, then lies there will be.

The bulky old man stared at him dully, but the door stopped
moving and Abner stood there waiting, feeling the cold air on his
face, still chilled from the sweat that had filmed it when he had
stood there in the street lost in the panic of memory. And at last
the old man grunted and opened the door wider.

'So come in,' he said, and his voice sounded a little less thin,
and he turned ponderously and shuffled slowly along a narrow
hallway. After a moment Abner followed him in and closed the
front door behind him.

The hallway was dim and smelled powerfully of a thick
chemical; and he knew it immediately and at once felt at home;
the scent of naphtha, thick and clinging and daring any moth
anywhere in the world to come near. Every step on this heavy old
carpet under his feet sent up a new wave of it. It was a comforting
smell, and he relaxed into it. He was on safe ground.

'So, a film? Haven't there been enough yet?' The old man
settled himself into a deep armchair beside an electric fire, in
which one bar was burning at a meagre half level, and pulled a
rug over his knees. The room was cold and dank, and Abner
thought – does he choose it like this? Or is it money that's the
problem? It was hard to tell. The room was heavily furnished
with a style he knew to be forty years old, square and
uncompromising, but there was a lot of it. The shelf over the fire
and those on the walls were full of books and assorted orna-
ments, all piled in an agreeable jumble, and the carpet was as

thick in here as in the hall. But there was no sense of comfort for all the display of possessions. Abner looked at the old man and then, uninvited, sat down in the chair facing him. 'There haven't been any films about the – about afterwards,' he said. 'That's what interests me. Not what happened there. We know, God help us. It's been told and we all know.'

'Know? You think you know?' The thin voice was a little stronger now, growing comfortable with being used. 'What can you know, a boy like you? Were you there? What can you know unless you were there?'

'No, I wasn't there. But there have been a lot of films. So many. And books. And television programmes – '

'And you think that makes people know?' the old man said. 'Much they know. You had to be there, believe me you did.'

There was a little silence, and then Abner said carefully, 'Well, yes, I'm sure you're right. But this time I want to make a different sort of film. About what came after – it's called *Postscripts*.'

'*Postscripts*? How come *Postscripts*?'

'At the end of a letter, after you've said it all, or think you have, and there's a bit more to speak of, that's a postscript. And my film comes after all that the other people have said. It's what came after – so that's what I'm calling my movie. About the people who came out of the camps, about their children, and their grandchildren.'

There was a long silence as the old man stared at him and then grinned slowly. It was an unlovely grimace displaying dirty teeth like a broken old fence but there was real amusement in it, and Abner found himself smiling back.

'Now I see what's what! You're thinking about yourself, hey? Not about the people in the camps at all.'

'No! Not at all – I mean – ' Abner stopped, and the old man still sat there grinning at him and after a long moment Abner lifted his shoulders slightly. 'Well, OK. A bit, maybe. Who can say why anyone does what they do? All I know is this is the one I want to make. It's more. It's one I've *got* to make. Can you see what I mean? It's not about me. It's not even about my parents. It's about all of them. Everybody, then and now.'

'What happened to your father?' the old man said.

'I'd really rather not talk about – ' And the old man gave a crack of laughter.

'*You'd* rather not? You come here asking me to tell you all about what happened to me, and you don't want to talk about what happened to your family? Why should I, tell me that? Just tell me, why should I?'

Why does it matter so much? Abner thought, staring at the face, bluish in the cold and blurred with fat but with those bright peering eyes set in it like raisins in a cake. I hated Hyman and Frieda for not telling, but aren't I as bad as they were, wanting to hold back? Why should I be so queasy? What right have I? And he opened his mouth, and let it come out, any way it wanted to.

'My father was Polish, and his family went to Berlin in the middle Thirties. His father was a goldsmith and there was good work to be had there. But there was some sort of trouble with his employer and the family were picked up in 'thirty-six and sent to Dachau. They got out of there – they were Poles, and someone somehow pulled strings. I don't know. He never told me that. And they went back to Poland, to Cracow. My father left school, apprenticed as a goldsmith to his father, and then in 'forty-two they were warned they were going to be picked up – the whole family. So they tried to get away, to Bialystok, but they caught them and put them in Treblinka – '

'Treblinka,' the old man said, and his eyes were as sharp as ever. 'Cracow Jews in Treblinka?'

'They'd tried to get to Bialystok. Almost did. So they were close to Treblinka. My father said his father had a brother there, a rich man. They thought he could help.'

'Some help,' the old man said, a little sardonic now.

'I don't know. Anyway they were taken and never got the chance. They were all in Treblinka, but my father – '

Abner stopped. He could hear Hyman's voice again, telling it all to him that evening in the apartment in Newark – that low regular voice, not particularly expressive – could hear the detachment in it and shook a little. And the old man sitting opposite him stirred in his chair.

'He got away, hey?'

'Not then,' Abner said. 'Not for a long time. Not till 'forty-five. He lived there three years. His parents, his sister – they didn't make it – '

'Three years? He did well,' the old man said with a fine

judicious air. 'Me, I managed two years and thought I'd done good.'

'In Treblinka?'

'Where else? We lived in Warsaw. Where else would they send us?'

'Two years,' Abner said. Then with great care, 'And when you got out?'

'Out of Treblinka, or out of trouble?'

'Both.' Abner ached to get out his notebook. Would he remember all this? Surely he must; how could he not? It was possible, but he had to risk it. This man would be upset by notebooks. Wouldn't he?

'Out of Treblinka was first. They took us to Brok, on the river. Such a journey to Brok. In lorries and buses and vans – '

'Another camp?'

'Where else could they take us? We were stinking, lousy, starved – just let us out on the street, just like that? It wouldn't have worked. The Russians, they took us to another place. And then, after a long time, there were more places, and then more. Displaced persons we were, from everywhere, people where they shouldn't have been. Those were the terrible times.'

'Not as terrible as Treblinka, surely?' Abner said.

The old man seemed to think about that. 'I don't know,' he said then. 'In Treblinka, there was a war. We knew where we were, even why, crazy it was, but we knew why. But afterwards, in peace time – they called it peace time. What sort of peace was it for us? Still starving, nowhere to go, Poles still hating us – ' He stopped then. 'You know, they went on killing us after the Russians arrived, after the liberation? Just because we were Jews, the Poles went on killing us. Not all of them killed us, but enough. It happened to plenty – at Parczew, at Novy Tara. Jews there were trying to get back to their home towns, and punkt, shot by some anti-Semite Polish officer, or the Polish Home Army or some such. The Germans had gone but they'd left their poison behind. Not that there wasn't enough of it in Poland anyway. They hated us. It was in their blood, in their guts. For all I know, it still is. Who can say? Poison like that, it doesn't go so easy, hey? It doesn't go so easy.'

'No,' Abner said. 'It doesn't.' And the room slid into silence as the old man and the young one thought about poison.

The old man stirred first. 'Listen, we're going to talk, I got to have something to moisten the mouth. It gets dry – some diabetes I got, and it gets dry. The doctor says, get thin, the diabetes should go. But what do I care? After so long starving he thinks I'm going to get thin? What's left but eating, hmm?' And he laughed.

Abner looked up and said, 'Can I get you something?'

'Sure you can,' the old man said. 'Sure you can. There's a Chinese restaurant up by the station, right? Go fetch, and me, I'll make tea.'

'I'll go now.' Abner was on his feet. 'Is there anything you specially want? Or don't want?'

'Everything,' he said, and his eyes glinted with happy greed. 'Prawns, pork, the lot. Believe me, after those years, *kashrus* is the last thing I care about – what about you?'

'My family never cared about eating kosher.' He was embarrassed, suddenly. It should matter, he felt obscurely, it really should. But he couldn't pretend. Not to this old man. It would be an obscene thing to do.

'So, I'll make the tea. Don't be long.' And he shuffled out to the hall, and opened the front door, almost pushing Abner out in his eagerness. 'And don't be mean! I got an appetite, you know?'

'I know,' Abner said and set off to walk briskly back the way he'd come. It wasn't until he was sitting in the stuffy Chinese restaurant waiting for his order, amid the tinkling of the Chinese music and the rattle of the bead curtains over the door, that he saw how exquisitely funny it was; to be buying sweet and sour pork for a survivor of the Holocaust had to be the most black of jokes. And he began to laugh.

Eight

───※───

Cyril Etting, wrote Abner at the top of the sheet, and added the address and the phone number. And then stopped and stared helplessly out of the window of his room at the hotel.

He tried again. Perhaps if he concentrated on getting the bald facts down that would unlock it? The flood of words the old man had produced over the little foil containers full of greasy food, the information that had come out so casually from a mouth filled with barbecued spare ribs and piles of noodles, had been so horrific, had painted a picture so vivid, that Abner hadn't listened so much as watched the images unroll in front of his eyes; and now he couldn't find the words to précis it as he would have to to make any use of the material for the film. So he wrote: *Age: seventy-one. Country of origin: Poland (Warsaw). Camp: Treblinka. Special factors: member of Warsaw Ghetto resistance committee for three months till rounded up in purge, following assassination of German sergeant. Occupation pre-war: medical student. Lost relations: five sisters, three brothers, parents, grandparents, two uncles, ?one aunt (no death record ever found).*

Again he stopped. To try to get on to the page the sense of outrage that had filled him as he had listened to the old man talking so calmly of the misery and humiliation he had known was beyond him. It would have to continue to be simple facts. Were there any more he could dredge out of that long afternoon? He had sat and listened as the gravy from the chicken chow mein had congealed on his plate and tried to be as dispassionate a listener as the old man was a talker. He had somehow succeeded, but now he felt the exhaustion of the effort it had been. The only answer was to go on being dispassionate; and he bent his head and again started to write.

And now it came more easily. *Camp occupation: orderly in krankenhaus (hospital). Assisted at surgery (probably cause of survival; deft at the work, also to an extent befriended by senior surgeon).*

What was it the old man had said then? Abner stared again out of the window at the darkness and heard the old voice thin in his ears.

'Listen, do you think I didn't know what was happening? Those operations he did – it's better you don't know. It was better I didn't think about them. But at least they had an anaesthetic before it was done. They died comfortable, which was more than a lot of them did. The ones I had to work with, they had a decent anaesthetic and didn't know what was happening. If there'd been any percentage for me in doing any different than what I did, I'd have done it. There wasn't, so I didn't. What would you have done?'

Oh, God, Abner thought. What would I have done? And having no answer bent to look at his page again.

Post war; displaced persons' camp in occupied West Germany, then quota'd for UK emigration, 1948. Six months in resettlement hostel, Hackney, London. Two years in hospital in Epsom, Surrey UK with TB (tuberculosis). Married ward orderly from hospital 1951. Worked as hospital porter, Edgware, London, from 1952 until retired at age sixty-five, 1973. Wife died 1974. No children (probable reason, Etting's sterility following radiation in camp experiments 1943). House bought with legacy from wife's parents, 1959. Current source of income: old age pension plus social service welfare support (free meals delivered, home help). Present health: poor; considerable arthritis, mild diabetes and severe chest problems (emphysema).

He wrote the last word carefully, copying it from the scrap of paper Cyril Etting had given him. He didn't know what it was, but he would find out. And he stopped writing and leaned back in his chair to read all that he had set down.

How would it fit into his film? Would any of it? The long empty quiet years afterwards when Etting had pushed wheelchairs and garbage cans around a battered British hospital? The childless marriage – to whom? 'What was she like?' Cyril had echoed his question. 'Who can say? She was a wife. My wife.

Who's to know what that means except a husband? A good girl who knew nothing of Jews and misery. A good girl – '

It won't fit, any of it, Abner thought. I used the afternoon and none of it is any use. He tried to drum up some indignation at the waste of time, but he couldn't. Of course, it hadn't been wasted; even if he didn't use Etting as a participant in the film when eventually he got the money to start work on it properly, he had painted in the emotion, the background of it all in a way that Abner needed. He had some of it already, of course. His own father.

He stood up then and began to pack away the file he had started. The notes on Mrs Fraister – those *were* a waste of time, but he wanted to record every conversation he had – he set carefully after Etting's in the ring binder. Be orderly, alphabetical, keep it all correct and neat and then you won't lose anything. But he knew he was hiding from the confusion in his mind with such foolish detail and was once again angry with himself.

He bathed, put on a clean shirt and then reached for the jeans and windcheater in which he felt most comfortable. He'd put on a suit that morning, feeling that he ought to look businesslike and sensible but now he needed to be comfortable so badly that he ached with it. He had to get his head clear of the shadows of the afternoon and didn't know how to do it; as he turned away from the bedside table, strapping on the watch he'd left there while he bathed, he stopped and stared at the phone. After a long pause, Abner picked it up and dialled the number in Oxford. Why not? She had said to come back. So he would. But he would make an appointment.

She was cool on the phone, sounding as though she could barely remember who he was, and he said sharply, 'You told me I should call, arrange to come back some time. Have you forgotten?'

'Of course not. I told you, come when you like.'

'I thought I should make an appointment. Not just walk in on you – '

'Why not? I'm always here – or if not, you can wait, I suppose. I'm never gone long.'

'You must be out sometimes.'

'I told you, never for very long. Half an hour or so. If that's too long to wait, of course – '

'It seems unnecessary when I could make an arrangement,' he said.

She sounded exasperated. 'And that means I have to sit around and expect you, and you might not even bother to turn up. I don't do that. It's boring. Come when you like. I'm here, or if I'm not I soon will be. Take your chance like everyone else – ' And she hung up, leaving him holding the dead ear piece and feeling absurdly elated. She had been offhand to the point of being insulting and yet she hadn't been unfriendly, he knew that; behind the edged exasperation of her tone there had been a liveliness that had not been there the first time he had spoken to her. He'd get through the appointments of the next couple of days because he'd made them, and he had to be businesslike, but then he'd go down to Oxford. And that thought made him feel positive again and he reached for the light to switch off before going in search of supper.

The phone trilled and he was startled; who had this number for him?

'Mr Wiseman? Would I be speaking to Mr Abner Wiseman?' The voice was low and agreeable, the accent very precise, and he thought – Conrad Veidt. Those velvety careful tones were pure Veidt. Any moment the door would open and Claude Rains would walk in to the strains of 'As Time Goes By', with Bogart lisping, 'Of all the bars in the world . . . ' Fool, he thought and made himself concentrate.

'Yes?' he said. 'Who wants him?'

'Ah!' It was a soft sound, almost a sigh. 'I'm glad to have found you. My name is Garten, Eugene Garten. How do you do?'

'Er – glad to meet you,' Abner said rather absurdly as though the man was standing there, holding out a hand to be shaken.

'I thought it might be useful to talk, Mr Wiseman,' the velvet voice said.

'Er – well, that's very kind. But I – who are you? I don't think I know you – '

'No, of course you don't.' The voice laughed in a friendly sort of way. 'How could you? I understand you're doing some research into survivors of the German labour camps?'

Abner said guardedly, 'Who told you this? Are you a friend of Cyril Etting?'

'Who?' The voice sounded genuinely puzzled.

Abner sharpened. 'Obviously not. Who then?'

'Victor Heller,' the voice said. 'He said you were doing research for the purpose of a film, and that I should get in touch with you since I could be of some use, having been myself involved in those dreadful times.'

'Well, that's very helpful of you – who did you say?'

'An old friend of mine. It really doesn't matter.'

Abner had managed to tuck the phone between his ear and his shoulder so that his hands were free to scrabble in his document case for the list of contacts Frieda had sent him. Maybe the name Garten had said was on that? It certainly wasn't on the list of his own contacts; he'd have been sure to remember if it were.

'But it would help to know,' he said, a little abstractedly now, because he was looking down Frieda's list. There was no Heller there. And he lifted his eyes from the paper and squinted at the wall, concentrating on the caller. 'Just for my records.' And he knew that sounded fatuous and didn't care.

'Heller.' Garten seemed reluctant to say it now, but he repeated it all the same. 'Victor Heller. But it doesn't matter. The film world, you know what it's like, is a very small one. Everyone knows everyone else, and I dare say the word's gone round and people are talking. I'm in the business myself in a small way, you understand. I deal mostly with distributors. As a publicist.'

Now Abner understood. The hangers-on, the people who bustled about self importantly long after the real work was over, when the packages had been tied up and the film had been shot and edited and post production was almost complete so that they were about to hit the distributors. The people who then scuttled around talking and boasting and carrying on as if the film was their very own. Abner had hated the publicist on his first film who had oversold it so hard that he had made it seem tawdry in Abner's own eyes. In the event the flurry of newspaper and TV excitement had done no harm; the film had found its own recognition and acceptance and hadn't needed the hyperbole of the publicist, who thereafter regarded the film as a failure because it hadn't been a blockbuster – Oh yes, Abner thought, publicists I understand about.

'I shan't need a publicist, Mr Garten,' he said frostily. 'Not for a long time, if at all. I'm still very much at the research stage.'

'I realise that,' Garten said easily. 'I'm not touting for work, Mr Wiseman, rest assured. I'm simply offering my services as an object of research. I was in Birkenau, you understand. Not as long as some, thank God. A mere six months. I was fortunate. But I understand how it was for so many people and would be glad to offer any help I can in your interesting project.'

'How do you know it's interesting?' Abner was as alert as he had ever been. This bastard was a rip-off operator. That was the real threat – not unwanted publicity, but robbery. The film was a good idea and some bastard was trying to poach on his ground. 'What the hell do you know about it?'

'Oh, please, Mr Wiseman!' The voice was as soft as cream. 'There's no need to worry! I'm not trying to steal any of your ideas! It's simply as I said. I was told that you're interested in talking to people who have suffered in the camps, and as one who feels strongly that there should be no forgetting, that it is not possible to speak too often of the horrors of those days and those people, I wished to be of assistance. However, I quite understand your anxiety and if you prefer not to speak to me . . . '

He stopped invitingly and Abner stood there trying to think clearly. It was bad enough that the man had seen through so swiftly to his fears; was he now going to compound the problem by sending him off in a temper when he actually had something to offer? To hang up on him would be very satisfying, but if his suspicions were right and someone was trying to put a spoiler on his plans then it would be much more sensible to hold on to this guy, find out more about him and who set him on. And anyway, never forget that he could be useful.

'Well, OK,' he said now, carefully acting the part of an aggrieved man who was being won round. 'If I have your assurance there's nothing at all – you know how it is in this business. So many sharks around, you get yourself eaten before you put your feet in the water, unless you take great care.'

'I'm no shark, Mr Wiseman. Just an old man with a story to tell. May I suggest you join me at my club for a drink?'

'Club?' Abner lifted his chin in hope. Was there another Shoah Club here in London? 'What sort of club?'

'Ah, I'm afraid not one of your first-water types. Not Whites or Boodles! But decent enough for all that. We call ourselves the Philanderers, though most of us are much too old to do more than just reminisce over the days when we had the energy to do so. It's in Soho, you know. It will amuse you, I'm sure. In Romilly Street, on the corner of Vinegar Yard. Any cab driver will know it. In half an hour perhaps?'

Abner hung up the phone and stood staring at it sightlessly. This was all so silly and cloak and dagger; to get calls from total strangers and to accept invitations to drink in cheap clubs in Soho; first visit to London though this was for him, he knew about the area, that it was a dubious neighbourhood.

And then, suddenly, he knew what to do and seized his key and went down the stairs two at a time to talk to the man in the bar; a thin and pallid creature of indeterminate age who clearly knew all there was to know about life in London. Abner had sat over a late night drink the evening before listening to him talk to the other people there, and knew him to be useful. He'd tell him what he needed to know.

'The Philanderers?' the man said. 'Can't say I ever 'eard of it. Where is it, did you say? Romilly Street? – Oh, I know. It's 'armless, mate. Just another drinkin' joint. Not even any girls there. No one'll rip you off there. It's the strip joints you got to watch out for, Mr Wiseman. They'll take your wallet, your credit cards and sell your balls for soup before they let go of you, so watch it. If you want a girl I can do you better than any of those scrubbers.'

Abner declined the offer gracefully and swallowed the drink he'd ordered, out of good manners, as fast as he could. If he was going to meet Garten he might as well be on time.

He was comforted when the cab driver simply grunted and showed no special reaction when he gave him his instructions, and settled back into the leathery seat to think his way to Soho. Already his research seemed to be paying off; if outsiders were trying to horn in on it there had to be something there worth horning in on. So he'd got that side of it right, for a start. What about the money side? Nagel hadn't been all that forthcoming for all his largesse with names and phone numbers, and Abner thought again of the computer screen and its close packed lines of information and frowned in the dimness. All right, Nagel had given him four possible sources of financial help, and he'd thought that good, but what of all the other names he'd had listed there? Four seemed meagre compared with that; and he tried to recall some of the other names he had read. In his boyhood he'd had one of those memories for which other people at school paid him handsomely in hamburgers and bubble gum; he could stare at a sheet of writing for half a minute and then close his eyes and read it off as though it were still in front of him. He tried it now, shutting his eyes against the passing neon lights of Oxford Street along which the cab was now pushing itself and tried to read Nagel's computer screen again.

Matthew Mayer. He opened his eyes and stared at the passing scenery. That was the only name he could remember, and it wasn't strange that he did, after all. It had been repeated often enough and he had actually commented on that fact to Nagel. That was why he now remembered it, he told himself a little mournfully. I didn't read it off in the way I used to. I've lost that photographic memory of the old days, dammit.

Matthew Mayer, he thought again. Partner to so many different people, second in command to so many different companies. Odd, that. And then as the cab at last wheeled and began to thread through the side streets of Soho he nodded at himself in some satisfaction. He'd try that one on the man Garten. If he was really in the business as he said he was, wouldn't he know the sort of people who might have money to spare for a useful film like *Postscripts*? Wouldn't he know who Mayer was, and whether it mightn't be worth talking to him? After all, he might be only second name in any particular company, but he was up there. Couldn't he have some muscle? And mightn't he respond to an approach with appreciation? Second stringers, he told himself, often get left out. He might find it flattering to be asked. I'll have to find out more about him.

The cab stopped beside a narrow door with a row of battered brass plates outside it and he got out and paid, looking over his shoulder a little uncertainly. But there it was, 'The Philanderers', and he said to the cabby as he dug for change, 'Do you know this club?'

The cabby looked, uninterested, at the plate and then made a face. 'Can't say I do. But they're ten a penny round these parts. Keep one 'and on your wallet and the other on your private parts, mate. They'll skin you of the one and give you something very nasty in the other if you don't watch it.' And nodded affably and drove away.

The girl at the entrance to the club hardly looked at him as he gave Garten's name, just jerking her head in the direction of the end of the corridor; he walked along, barely able to see where he was going, and turned a corner to find himself in a small square room with a few lumpy old armchairs spread about and a bar at the far side, lit with alternate blue and red bulbs in a distinctly queasy fashion. Abner hated dives like this, and he peered around at the chairs, hoping now that the man he had come to see was not here so that he could legitimately turn and go. He'd tried, after all; no one could ask more of a man . . .

'You must be Abner Wiseman. May I be so bold as to call you Abner?' The man who had come quietly to his side was very small and round, little more than five feet two or three, Abner estimated as he bent his own head — fully a foot above him — to see, and with jowls like Alfred Hitchcock. The voice might be seductive and sophisticated; the man himself most certainly was not, for even in this light Abner could see that his clothes were unkempt and his shoes unpolished. Not at all an appetising figure.

'Come and sit down and try this claret. Not a good one, I'm afraid, not even remotely good, but it's wine and it's red, and you can't ask for more at these prices. I am not a wealthy man, Abner, but what hospitality I have is yours.'

Already repelled by the smoothness of the man, which sat oddly on his unpleasant appearance, Abner followed him. Half an hour, no more, he promised himself. Absolutely no more.

'Well now, Abner,' Garten smiled at him as he leaned back in his armchair after pouring a glass of wine for his guest with some ceremony. 'What can I tell you?'

'I don't know,' Abner said. 'You tell me what you want to tell me. You called me, after all.'

'Indeed I did. Well, now, I gather the film you're making is not about the terrible tragedy of the Holocaust itself, evil as that was, but the after effects. What happened to the people who came after. The children, the grandchildren . . . '

'You've been well informed. Who is this Heller man you say put you on to me? I don't know his name from – '

'Well, I dare say you don't,' Garten said soothingly. 'It's possible he got it from someone else, after all.'

'Who?' Abner demanded. The wine glinted in his glass invitingly but he was damned if he was going to drink it. He wouldn't be beholden to this creepy guy for anything.

Garten shrugged and drank deeply, and then refilled his glass. 'Who can say? Who have you seen?'

'Why should I tell you that?'

'My dear chap, so suspicious! Well, there it is. Understandable, I suppose. Well, let me see. Who does Heller deal with most? We'll try a few names on you. Benson, the distributor, no? Or Sampson, his colleague and – not that one either? Jimmy Brandon, Joe Mandelson, Lee Capetelli, Monty Nagel – ah! Is that the one? Well, now, Victor sees a good deal of old Monty! Did he know of your project? Perhaps he was the one who told Victor, wanting to be of some assistance to you.'

Heller, Abner thought, and suddenly the picture was there in front of him. The shabby little man in a too voluminous suit sitting in the corner of Monty Nagel's office and Monty snapping at the secretary who said, *Here's Mr Heller to see you* . . .

An odd memory of an odd moment and now it infuriated him.

'If he did he talks too much,' Abner said wrathfully. 'It's my project, dammit! I'm not even contracted to the guy yet, if I ever am. Where does he get off telling the goddamned world and its wife what my projects are and – '

'Now, Abner, Abner, calm down!' The voice added a satin quality to its underlying velvet. 'I know Monty Nagel too and a better man never breathed. He means no harm, I do assure you. He was just trying to help you, of that I'm certain. It's all I want to do, too. A man doing research needs to use every opportunity that comes his way. Why are you so paranoid on this matter?'

'Paranoid?' Abner said and then stopped. God, was that what

it was? Was he being like Frieda, looking for threat at every turn, convinced that there was ill will directed at him from everywhere? And he took a deep breath to calm himself and then without thinking, reached out and took up the wine glass and drank.

'There,' said Garten with satisfaction. 'That is better, isn't it? Now we can talk comfortably.'

And he did.

Nine

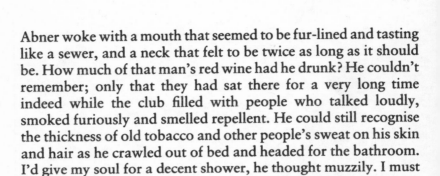

Abner woke with a mouth that seemed to be fur-lined and tasting like a sewer, and a neck that felt to be twice as long as it should be. How much of that man's red wine had he drunk? He couldn't remember; only that they had sat there for a very long time indeed while the club filled with people who talked loudly, smoked furiously and smelled repellent. He could still recognise the thickness of old tobacco and other people's sweat on his skin and hair as he crawled out of bed and headed for the bathroom. I'd give my soul for a decent shower, he thought muzzily. I must get a place of my own if I'm staying in this stinking town.

He made himself eat breakfast, remembering that half his trouble last night had been lack of food, and then sat crouched over his ringfile again. Note making, that was the answer, and he smoothed a new page and wrote at the top of it 'Eugene Garten'. And then stopped.

After all, how much had the man told him? Precious little. He'd burbled on about the camps, talking of the horrors of it, the wickedness of it, the evil of the Germans; but what had he actually said that was new? He had spoken little of his own experiences, and when Abner had tried to get facts about his time in Birkenau out of him he had been evasive. The level in the wine bottle had dropped and then seemed to rise again, and Abner tried now to remember how many bottles there had been. Three, at least – and he rubbed his face with one hand, feeling the slight numbness of his lips. He had never had a head for alcohol and that stuff must have been particularly poisonous. He really did feel lousy.

So, what did he know about Garten? That he was living in a flat in Edgware – not far from Cyril Etting, in fact, though Abner had managed not to mention where he had spent his afternoon –

and had his own business as a film publicist. Not a very successful one, Abner thought, for he lacked the glossy look of the breed. This man operated round the fringes of whatever he did, that was obvious.

So why had he come after Abner? That was the puzzle and Abner stared at his blank sheet and tried to order his thoughts. It had to be to tout for future work, surely. It was as he had thought; Garten had picked up from someone in this most gossipy of all businesses the fact that Abner was working on a project, and was trying to worm his way in on the ground floor. It was no more than that, and Abner closed the ringbinder and reached for another cup of coffee. He'd forget him; he had more important things to do now, like raising cash. And that would be a much bigger problem than some little runt of a man scurrying round trying to pick up a few crumbs to keep himself going. And for just one moment Abner felt a tinge of pity for Garten. But only for a moment.

The day ahead was a busy one. He had appointments with three of the people about whom Nagel had told him and he took the tube from Paddington to Oxford Circus, getting another *frisson* of pleasure from his increasing understanding of the system, and set off to walk up Oxford Street towards the first call. Simmy Gentle in Wardour Street.

Oxford Street was humming with people and reeked almost as badly as that club last night had done, but of fried onions from the cheap hamburger stands on the street corners – they called those things hamburgers? Abner thought, peering disgustedly as he passed. Christ! – and traffic fumes and human bodies; but there was the bite of winter air and a certain amount of wind between the buildings that sharpened him and made him feel better. He needed the walk and lengthened his stride, carefully checking the names on the side streets he passed, watching for Wardour Street.

Gentle's address was almost the far end of it, and Abner stepped it out, weaving his way along the crowded pavements, comforted by the familiar logos on the buildings he passed; Paramount and Fox and MGM; but even more so by the unfamiliar names. There were a great many independent film-makers here, and they all seemed to be making a living. They had buildings in what was clearly a costly part of the town and their display windows were filled with shrieking posters of their latest offerings. There'd be room for him and money to be found. There had to be.

Simmy Gentle's office was on the third floor of the small building Abner found just beyond a street market filled with gaudy fruit and vegetable stalls and shouting people. He climbed the stairs – why didn't somebody tell these people about elevators? – grateful to be feeling so much better than he had. The coffee and toast had done the trick, thank God. Never cheap wine again, he swore as he pushed on the door marked 'SIMON GENTLE ENTERPRISES. RECEPTION. PLEASE WALK IN'. From now on, Coke is my limit.

The girl behind the desk in the small office was pert and pretty and full of energy. She leapt to her feet as he came in, fussed over him with offers of coffee and told him Mr Gentle had just stepped out for a moment but would be back, and had said he was sorry, Mr Wiseman was to wait please. Would he like to see *Screen International*? Not this week's, she was afraid, on account of it always came late, but still not too old.

Gentle was actually half an hour late for the appointment, by which time all Abner's good humour had vanished. Sure he was coming cap in hand to this guy, but for Christ's sake, did he have to be so goddammed ill mannered? He wasn't asking for favours, he was offering the man the chance to invest in what was a real film, one that mattered, that could give him some credit higher than the stuff he'd already been involved with. Abner stared round again at the posters that adorned the walls, feeling the sneer rise in him. Cheap shlock thrillers, every one of them. Rubbish.

Gentle came in in a rush of apologies, a tall thin man with a harassed look, and some of Abner's anger evaporated as he fussed and chattered at him.

'Got caught up in a damned meeting – you know how these people are. Especially money people! They never think anyone else's time but their own matters, have you noticed?'

Abner laughed aloud at that. 'I'd noticed,' he said with heavy irony and looked at his watch with some point. 'I'd noticed.'

Gentle chattered on, oblivious. 'I said I had someone waiting for me, but would he let me go? Would he hell! But what can I do? He's – well, never mind all that. Just have some coffee, hmm? Did my little Tiffany look after you? A good girl, Tiffany. I don't know where I'd be without her, eh Tiff? Coffee, girl, chop chop!'

At last they were settled in his inner office, a small and cluttered room with a desk piled so high with papers that Abner couldn't see the man's hands in front of him, but then he cleared a space by shifting whole piles on to the floor and looked at Abner with a wide grin.

'Well, now, my old friend Nagel sent you, hmm? A good man, Monty. One of the best agents in the business. And tell me, who sent you to him?'

They talked personalities for a while, Abner mentioning his New York and LA contacts and sharing mildly salacious gossip about the private lives of some of the biggest names in the industry. It wasn't time-wasting, but a way of ensuring that he was for real. Knowing and talking about the right people and having the right information about them was a vital qualification everywhere in this business, and Gentle listened and laughed and chipped in with occasional tittle-tattle of his own, to establish his own credentials, and then they both relaxed. Now they could talk real business.

'Have you got some paper, a few pages we can use?' Gentle said. 'Monty is right. There's money around but they like to see something before they put their cash on the mahogany, you know what they are.'

'Sure.' Abner reached into his document case and pulled it out, the neatly bound but slender script of three pages. More than that no film man would ever read; how many of the bastards were able to read at all? Abner would ask himself, and knew the answer, and so had pared down his prose till it shone with meaning. The most elegant and important of the pages he'd sweated over longest, his budget forecast and cash breakdown, and he watched Gentle's face as he leafed through the pages, trying to look as calm as though it didn't matter.

'I'm not looking for too much hard cash up front,' he said then, unable to stay silent any longer. 'It's a promise of underwriting I need. I don't start with the sort of script most people expect, you see. It makes itself as I work. I write with the camera as much as anything else. It depends on who I find, what sort of people they are, how the project develops. Sometimes there have to be actors as well as the people it all really happened to, but even then it's an improvisation job. We work together, we talk of the story, what we're trying to do, and then it kind of just happens – so there's no need at this stage for big money, only underwriting for the research stage. But with me that's just about the most important – like a script, you see, but it's cheaper. No high flying writers to take too much of the cream.'

Gentle nodded, not looking up. 'I know your stuff. I saw *Uptown Downtown*. Bit arty for me. I like my blood thick, Winner style, you know?'

'I don't make that sort of film,' Abner said stiffly, anger starting to rise again. 'Death Wishes aren't up my alley and never will be – '

'If they were, I wouldn't be looking at this stuff,' Gentle said and looked up and grinned again. He had the dreadfully even teeth of the over orthodonted, almost Californian in their ferocious perfection. 'I've got a team already making that sort of stuff, and it's doing very nicely, thank you. But I'm looking for something a bit different, as Monty knows. I've been thinking romance. I reckon romance is on the way back in a big way. Big women's weepies, you know? Crawford, Davis, Stanwyck stuff – but this is interesting. It's certainly different. Maybe I could get some of the available Arab cash, if you tone down the Jewish angle a bit.'

Abner stared. 'Tone down the – how the hell am I supposed to do that? This is a post Holocaust movie, for Christ's sake!'

'Gypsies, queers,' Gentle waved a hand vaguely. 'Just an idea. But it's not written in stone. If you don't want to, you don't want to! It makes it harder to get the money this way, but not impossible. I could talk to my partner – '

'Partner?'

Gentle waved his hand again even more vaguely. 'He's a sleeping partner, you understand. I do all the real work. But when it comes to big projects we have to talk. That was why I was late this morning. We've got a big horror movie on the floor. Believe me, anything you can do with Stephen King, we can do here. We've got blood merchants so revolting you could throw up. So listen, can you leave this with me?' He waved the script package in the air.

'For a few days,' Abner said. 'But I need to know soon. I'm

offering this around. You know how it is. Can't wait too long
to – '

'You don't have to tell me,' Gentle said heartily and stood up.
'Haven't I been in this business since I was fifteen? Worked at
Elstree I did, when films really were films.'

'Ever work at Ealing?' Abner was suddenly eager.

'God, no! Not my style at all. I was on the big adventure stuff.
Stewart Granger, James Mason – the really good old days. Just a
boy at the time, you understand, but it was good.' He shook his
head in heavy reminiscence. 'Like they say, they don't make 'em
like that any more, more's the pity. OK, Wiseman, give me a few
days. I'll be able to do a Goldwyn then, hey? Give you a definite
maybe. But I'll do my best, I give you my word. If my partner
shows interest it'll help. He's the financial genius. Me, I put the
packages together. Given any thought to lighting or camera man
yet?'

'Too premature,' Abner said. 'Where's the use of looking at
availabilities till I've got a deal?'

'Sensible fella.' Gentle led him across the room with one arm
set in familiar fashion over Abner's shoulders. 'It's just the way I
think. Always trying to get people in bed together, and there's an
excellent fella I know I'm putting about a bit. Still, as you say,
let's get the first things first, hmm? Call me Friday.'

Out again in the street Abner turned left and started walking as
though he'd lived in the neighbourhood all his life and knew
exactly where to go. It pleased him to do that, made him feel
more capable and successful, and he walked fast, keeping in his
mind's eye the page he'd studied in his London street map,
making his way to Lexington Street. Maybe that photographic
memory hadn't quite vanished after all; he could see the map
closely superimposed on the rushing passers-by and the hooting
fuming traffic at a virtual standstill in the roadway. It was a
comforting thing to be able to do.

Jo Rossily, he thought. What sort of a guy would this one be?
The film people he'd met so far here had been an odd mixture of
the same sort that he knew in New York and on the Coast, and
what he regarded as stereotypically British; though how much of
that was due to their accents he couldn't be sure. As soon as
someone opened their mouth and that extraordinary sound

came out, he was back in a movie house, watching *Passport to Pimlico* or *The Ladykillers*. The characters in those hadn't been stereotypes, of course; and yet somehow they had. Like these people here —

Again he had to drag his thinking back to the here and now. It was crazy the way being in this town affected him; at home when he worked he had his nose down hard on the scent and thought of nothing but the job he was doing. Here his mind wandered, looped around itself, came back to the beginning and then went wildly careering off again. It couldn't all be due to just being abroad. Or could it? And there he went again, off the point.

He found the small building in Lexington Street he was hunting for; a narrow door had the inevitable row of plates beside it. 'R & M DISTRIBUTION' read the third one, and unlike the other plates, was well polished, with stains of the stuff they had used to give it its deep gloss whitening the brickwork around it, and he thought — a small company, run by someone who cares for nothing else but his work. And climbed the inevitable three flights of stairs inside after the entryphone buzzed in response to his ring.

'Mr Rossily?' he said to the girl at the desk marked ENQUIRIES. 'I think he's expecting me.'

'If you're Mr Wiseman,' the girl said tartly, '*Ms* Rossily is waiting for you now. You're almost half an hour late — '

'My last appointment ran late,' Abner said, and tried to look comfortable. Why be surprised that Jo Rossily should be a female? 'He was half an hour late and — '

'You could have phoned us,' the girl said and pressed a button on her phone. 'Jo, your eleven-thirty appointment has just shown. It's almost twelve. You have an early lunch, remember.' And she listened and then nodded dismissively at Abner as a door behind him opened.

'Mr Wiseman? Come in. Coffee?'

'No, thank you, Miss Rossily,' he said, and looked swiftly at the girl behind the enquiry desk with an attempt at humour. 'I wouldn't dare after being late and all. Your — er — receptionist here might put poison in it — '

'Ms Rossily makes her own coffee,' the girl said scornfully, and began to rattle at her word processor, and Abner followed the other woman into her office.

She was tall and square, with shoulders made even squarer by her black suit. Power dressing, he thought, vaguely remembering silly articles in magazines, but then, as she reached her desk and turned and looked at him, changed his mind. She wasn't trying to put on any show or to intimidate him. She was just a woman who was in charge of this setting and knew it. She needed no padding for her ego, whatever fashion put on her shoulders. And older than I am, too, he found himself thinking. As long as she doesn't try to put me down the way some of those bitches at home do.

'I gather Monty Nagel is our contact point,' she said and reached out a hand. It didn't match the square shouldered suit jacket, for the nails were short and rather broken and the skin reddened. 'You have a script to show me?'

He reached into his document case. 'Not really a script,' he said, and launched again into an explanation of his working methods and how scripts for his films grew organically rather than being deliberately writer-created, and she sat and leafed through it, listening and showing no sign of any reaction.

'I see,' she said at length and put the script down on the desk. 'And what do you want of me?'

'You're a distribution agent — ' he said, half questioningly, but she didn't respond, just looking at him, and he went on, 'And I'm trying to get the whole thing set up as best I can to get the money men going.'

'What money men?'

'I beg your pardon?'

'Who have you got already?'

He thought very briefly. To try to fool this lady would be crazy. Her clear eyed view of reality showed in every line of her face, and in the uncompromising stare she was fixing on him. None of the usual crap you had to use to bring people on board would work here.

'As yet, not a one,' he said as cheerfully as he could. 'It's one of the reasons I'm here. To set up cash, and — '

'No joy in the States? You've got a good track record. I know your stuff.'

' "Public service television" is what they say to me there,' he said with a hint of bitterness. 'Art-house movies. But they're all after big bucks. Anyone who isn't Spielberg or Lucas gets nowhere.'

'Not entirely true,' she said, still with that direct stare. 'Other people are making movies as well as them. I distribute here for quite a few.'

'I'm tough to work with,' he said then, after a long moment. 'I don't let money people get involved in production. They're separate functions from where I stand, so they don't get any input except their dollars. They don't like it.'

The shoulders seemed to soften a little as she relaxed and for the first time smiled. She wasn't that old after all, he thought. Tense, tired perhaps; there were shadows under the dark eyes and smudges of violet on her temples that looked even darker because her hair was a dusty fair colour that seemed to highlight her pale face. But not that old. His own age perhaps, if that.

'That's better,' she said. 'I can't be doing with the sort of people who play Aesop's ass carriers.'

'I beg your pardon?'

'One of the fables,' she said and picked up his script again and began to leaf through it. 'A man and his son taking an ass along the road try to please everyone they meet – sometimes they lead the ass, sometimes they ride it, sometimes they carry it. And they never get it right.' She looked up at him then. 'I prefer people who know what they want and make sure they get it.'

'Then we could do business,' he said. 'I hope,' and grinned.

She didn't smile back, but sat and stared at him consideringly. And then said, 'I think I might be able to get Channel Four in on this. I have a good relationship with them and it's their sort of project. They may even consider some financial involvement. Don't get excited,' she said then and he reddened a little. He hadn't realised that the little surge of hope she had lifted in him had been so obvious.

'I know better than to hold my breath, ever,' he said. 'In this business, you can die trying.'

'I'll see what I can do. What sort of percentage for me if I do?'

'I haven't got my agency sorted out yet,' he said. 'Nagel may be the one – '

'I can deal with him,' she said. 'He's straight and a good man. I'll call him.'

'You won't be the only one.' Abner needed to recover his sense of his own value. 'Everyone I've seen is showing interest. It's clearly a project people are going to want to be part of.'

'I'm sure,' she said and held out her hand and got to her feet in one smooth movement. 'I'll be in touch then. Leave your address and phone number with Maggy.'

'She'll take it, I hope,' Abner said, trying again to be a little lighter in the hand. 'She sure didn't take to the idea of making coffee.'

Jo Rossily shook her head. 'You'll have to understand something if you work with me, Mr Wiseman. We don't run any sort of hierarchy here. Maggy has her job to do and I have mine. Personal things we do for ourselves. We're not into servants, you understand? Any of us. We're all women in this office, and we all have equal value, even if our jobs are different.'

'I see,' he said. 'OK, I apologise. Maggy isn't into making coffee for the head honcho, right? I saw that movie too – is she the "M" of the company then?'

'I'm sorry?'

'You're "R and M Productions". The "R" I imagine is for you, Jo Rossily. Is the "M" for – '

'Oh!' she shook her head, and again that brief smile lifted her face. 'No, that's my financial partner. He doesn't work here. His name is Mayer. Good afternoon, Mr Wiseman. I'm running late so you'll have to forgive me . . . '

It wasn't until he was sitting over a sandwich in Chubby's Bar in Poland Street that he realised what she had said. Mayer. Could it be that all-over-the-place guy Matthew Mayer, again? If it was, it was time for him to meet the man face to face. Indeed he was getting very interesting.

Ten

'Quite a place,' Abner said approvingly and chased the last of his steak and kidney pie around his plate. 'That was incredible. How did you find it?'

'I didn't have it,' she said and leaned back in her chair. 'The menu said it was made with Guinness. Disgusting stuff. But you seemed to enjoy it.'

'I didn't mean the pie, though that was — well, anyway. No, I meant, how did you find this restaurant? You said you don't get out that much — '

'It's in the *Good Food Guide*,' she said, almost scornfully. 'And we used to come here, Geoffrey and I, when we could. You get value for your money.'

'That's important to you' — he watched her as the waiter, a lissom young man in a long apron, somewhat given to extravagant gestures, cleared their table and put a menu down in front of them — 'value for money?'

'It is to most people in Oxford.' She sounded even more scornful and bent her head over the menu. 'This is an academic city, remember. There are some people here with more money than judgement who go in for scampi in baskets and bottles of wine that cost enough to keep a family for a week, but by and large people here have more sense. That's why places like Browns do so well — I'll have the cheese. Stilton — ' and she pushed the menu away from her. 'And coffee at the same time.'

'Class never goes away here, does it?' he said and then nodded at the waiter. 'Cheese for two. And coffee.'

'Class? You mean it's snobbery to care about value for money? Well, Well.'

'No. To make judgements about people according to what they eat. What's wrong with scampi in a basket, whatever that may be?'

She stared at him for a long moment and then laughed, and he looked at her approvingly. The laughter lifted her face and banished her customary scowl and completed what was in many ways a transformation. When he'd arrived at the house she'd been wearing the same rusty black cardigan and baggy trousers, but when he'd said firmly – after spending several hours over the packing cases that held the *Rise and Fall of National Socialism* – that he wanted a proper dinner and she needed one too, she had nodded without argument and gone away for fifteen minutes, to reappear ready to go out and looking quite different. Still wearing black, but this time a dress that fitted her body well and displayed long legs in dark tights that made her startlingly elegant. She had pulled her hair back from her face and pinned it into a soft knot on the top of her head to reveal a long neck that looked very vulnerable. She had even powdered her face and applied lipstick, and he had looked at her almost shyly when she came down the dusty stairs.

'You're right, of course,' she said then. 'It shouldn't matter when people do unutterably naff things, but there it is – one notices.'

'Naff?' he cocked his head at her, and again she laughed and lifted both hands in a gesture of helplessness.

'I couldn't explain that this side of Armageddon. Live here a little while and you'll understand.'

'You're a difficult lot, you Britons. Like to be awkward. Just for the sake of it sometimes.'

'It beats being as eager as a puppy to tell people everything there is to tell within five minutes of meeting,' she retorted. 'And all that hand shaking and back slapping.' She gave a small shudder. 'It's too much.'

He said nothing, just sitting and looking at her and suddenly she went rather pink.

'That was snobbery too. And of a very nasty kind. I'm sorry.'

He still said nothing, just lifting his brows a little and not taking his gaze from her face.

'I don't know what right I have to be so. I suppose I learned it after we came to live here. God knows I've no cause to regard myself as anything special. Please accept my apology.'

'It's not necessary,' he said and considered leaning forwards to set his hand on hers and then dismissed the notion. That would be a mad thing to do with this young lady. 'You're right, in a lot of ways. There are some Americans who make one hell of an object of themselves just the way you say. "Hi there, Joe, whad'yaknow, you in Kiwanas or Elks? Put it there, pal." It makes me shudder too.'

She smiled and bent her head to the cheese, which had now arrived, and there was a long companionable silence as they demolished their platefuls. Then, when there was just coffee and the remains of the bottle of claret he had ordered, he said carefully, 'You said you learned to be fussy about the way people behave after you got here. Here to Britain or here to Oxford? I mean, you sound totally British but there's something – I don't know exactly. You could have been born some place else.'

She was silent still and then looked at him and lifted her brows. 'You're a perceptive person, Mr Wiseman.'

'I am? I'm glad to hear it. In what way?'

'I'm English in that I was born here. In London, actually, not here in Oxford, though I suppose the place has had quite an effect on me. We came to live here when I was around ten. My – my father was English, of course.'

There was an unwillingness in her; he could feel it as though it were a palpable thing, but there was a conflict there too. She seemed to be trying to hold back while something else within her was pushing words out.

'My mother wasn't, though,' she said then and bent her head so that her face was shadowed over her coffee cup. 'Perhaps I get my foreignness from her.'

'Wasn't English? I know you said she was Jewish, but I thought – she could still have been English.'

'Could have been, but she wasn't.'

He said nothing, leaving it to the inner conflict, whatever it was, to serve his purposes. It did.

'She was Polish,' she said then, abruptly. 'Her name was Basia Novak. Born in Bialystok, her father a doctor, her mother a schoolteacher, originally.'

He took the risk, looking at her bent head, feeling her need to talk and her shrinking from it at the same time, pitying her because he knew how she felt. Hadn't he felt the same? Hadn't Hyman? 'What happened to them?'

She made a faint movement of her shoulders. 'The same that happened to hordes of others. Six million others.'

It was as though ice had been trickled into his collar at the back of his neck to snake its way down his back, and he took a sharp little breath. 'Then you know, too.'

Now she looked at him. 'Know what?'

'How it feels. What's it like to be a – ' He managed to produce a small grimace, trying to make it a smile. 'Call it a postscript.'

She frowned, puzzled, and then her face cleared. 'Oh, your film. Your *movie*.'

'Yes, my film.'

Again there was silence and the waiter came and refilled their coffee cups and emptied the wine bottle into their glasses and they still sat silently until Abner said carefully, 'I'm not asking you to tell me, but there are things that – ' And stopped, not sure how to go on.

'Things you'd like to know,' she said harshly and managed to grin at him. It wasn't a friendly look though, as it had been last time. Her face merely twisted, for her eyes had no glint of pleasure in them. 'For your *film*.'

'No,' he said. 'For me. I'm still trying to understand how I feel. My parents were in the camps, but they didn't tell me until I was grown. Seventeen. I'm still trying to handle it.'

'You're lucky,' she said, still with that harsh sound in her voice. 'You had some good years, then. Seventeen? That was luxury.'

He blinked, startled. It hadn't been the reaction he'd expected. 'Luxury?'

'Of course it was! You spent seventeen years not knowing about it all. Not being reminded all the time, not feeling wicked because you were young and alive and – Christ, you don't know what luxury is if you don't realise that!'

'You knew from the start then? When you were a child?'

'There wasn't a time I didn't know. The whole bloody story over and over again, she told me. Other kids got Cinderella.

Not me. I got David and Sonia and the rest of them in gas ovens. Great stuff to go to bed with. Sleep well, kiddies.'

The ice moved across his back again. 'She told you – your mother?'

'Who else? She knew it best.' She shook her head then. 'My father tried to tell it sometimes. A better way. But there was no better way.'

'Will you tell me?'

'Tell you?' She lifted her head and stared at him. 'Why the bloody hell should I?'

'Because it's history,' he said carefully. 'Because your father told you that the material you have at the house was to be made available to people who need it. An obligation, you said. For historians and academics. And perhaps for a serious film-maker. Isn't speaking of your own experience in the same category?'

There was another silence, and then, moving sharply, she picked up her wine glass and drank the claret as though it were water, fast and without stopping to taste it. She put her glass back on the table with a sharp little gesture and said in an even tone, 'Right. David Novak, born in Bialystok, very middle-class and so forth, trains to be a doctor in Berlin, returns to Poland, sets up a good practice. Makes money, marries girl from equally middle-class sort of family, very full of itself, I suspect. Sonia. She's got a degree from a French university, very cultured, all that stuff. They have six children, and Basia is the oldest girl, with two older brothers, and one sister and two brothers younger. Good school, ballet classes and so forth all lined up. Got that clear in your head?'

'Yes,' he said, almost dazed with the speed at which she was talking. He ached for a notebook, or better still a cassette recorder, and prayed somewhere deep inside his head that his memory would be as effective for spoken words as it was for written ones. Would he be able to close his eyes and hear all this again? Oh, God, please, please let me hear it all, hold it all.

She had started again and he scrambled to fix his attention on her.

' . . . in a camp in Germany, I don't know why. Anyway, there they were, David sent to the men's side of course, Sonia and the children together elsewhere. David, it seems is valuable.

Doctor, you see. So he gets to eat sometimes and lives. Not the others, Sonia and Laszlo, and Frederic and Ben and Jacob, they die in the first year. Typhoid or some such – ' She shrugged as though it didn't matter. 'They were fortunate, clearly. At least it was what you could call a normal death. Basia and her sister Malka recovered. Amazing, wasn't it?'

'Amazing.'

'That's what Barbara said it was. Amazing.'

'Barbara?' he said, floundering now.

She shook her head irritably, as though he should have known. 'Basia. My mother. Afterwards she changed it to Barbara. It was easier for people to cope with. Basia and Malka didn't die of typhoid. Amazing. But later on, Malka died, probably of TB. Basia wasn't sure, but she said she used to cough blood. In the laundry – '

'The laundry – she worked in the laundry?'

'Very clean they were in Sobibor, Barbara said. Always scrubbing and cleaning. The inmates, you understand. Not the guards.' Miriam's eyes were wide and staring at him, but he knew she wasn't looking at him. 'They made them scrub and clean and wash and iron on the big machines and then scrub and clean again. On cabbage soup if they were lucky. What they could steal if they weren't.'

He pushed her coffee cup closer to her, as though to compensate for her mother's hunger; an absurd gesture.

'That was why she wouldn't ever clean again, she said. Even when Geoffrey was just teaching a bit and writing his books and they had no money to pay for help, even then she'd never clean anything. It had to be tidy, but clean didn't matter. She said it never mattered.'

'How – when did she get out of Sobibor?'

She blinked and then focused her eyes so that she was looking at him at last and managed a sort of smile. 'Get out of Sobibor? Oh, there's a story for you! A story and three quarters.'

'Tell me,' he said.

'I'm thirsty.' She drank some coffee and made a face, for it was lukewarm, and he waved at the waiter, who fetched more. And she drank and thought for a while and then said sharply, 'Are you going to use what I tell you? In your film?'

'I don't know' he said. 'How can I know till I hear it all? You don't want me to?'

'I don't give a shit,' she said and he actually leaned back at the venom that was suddenly in her voice. 'Why shouldn't you if you want to? It's not as though she didn't tell the whole bloody world. Anyone who'd listen. It was no secret. Not even from me.'

'Should it have been?' he said softly and she looked at him with her eyes as blank and opaque as pebbles. There was so much anger there that he felt he could strike sparks off them.

'Of course it should! I was a child, a small child. Wasn't it enough it had happened to her? Did she have to make it happen to me, too? Tell it to me so that I lay in bed, night after night, thinking of her, crying for her, *being* her, going through it the way she did? Only having the worse hell of getting up every morning knowing it hadn't been happening to me badly enough to make me feel better? For her there was at least the knowledge that she had paid for everything. For me there was never that. I had the suffering and the pain and the hatred and I never paid for it at all. I got up to eat cornflakes for breakfast and to watch Andy Pandy on the television and to be given chocolate on my birthday, while she told me how it was on her birthdays, working in that goddamned laundry. You ask if it should have been a secret from me?'

He shook his head. 'Mine never told me,' he said. 'I found out by accident. It made me – I was very angry.'

'Because you found out by accident? Or because they never told you?'

'Both, I suppose,' he said after a while. 'Both. They had no right to hide it from me.'

'She had no right to show it to me,' Miriam said roughly. 'She destroyed my childhood as hers had been. You, at least, had your good years undamaged.'

'Did I?' he said. 'How can you be so goddammed sure? What do you think I remember when I think of being a kid? Good things, happy things? Like hell I do. I never knew a time when I didn't feel alone and lonely. I remember – the first memory I have – waking in the night ill. Feverish, I think. And crying, calling for someone to hold me, make me safe and comfortable. And she came and looked at me and told me not to shout so loud, it was only a cold, and he watched from the door and said nothing. And they went away and left me alone. In the dark. For seventeen years it was like that. Alone and in the dark. All I remember is anger and distance. They were always so far away, both of them, it was like I walked round the outside of them. They had their Shoah Club and their friends, the people they talked to, the ones they saw every weekend and every Monday night, but me, all I had was TV and the kids from school – '

'And you slept at night without nightmares,' she said flatly and stared at him, daring him to argue with her.

He couldn't. 'Yes. No nightmares.'

'It wasn't so bad for you then,' she said and bent her head. 'No scores being kept here, but take it from me, it wasn't so bad for you.'

'No scores,' he echoed and then took a deep breath. 'How did she meet your father? How did she get to come to England?'

'Oh, that's the one-and-three-quarter story,' she said and leaned back in her chair. 'That really will entrance you. It entranced her. She told it so often to so many people and every time she did she lit up like a – listen to this, my friend. Just listen to this. And then tell me you can make a film that'll match it?'

'I'm listening,' he said as equably as he could, chilled by the rage in her voice. 'Is it all true?'

She flicked her eyes upwards and glanced sharply at him and then away. 'Why do you ask that?'

'You didn't seem to believe it, whatever it is. You sound' – he shrugged – 'contemptuous.'

'It's true, all right. My father told me the same story, but in a different tone of voice. You know what I mean? A story told one way means one thing. Told another . . . ' She shook her head. 'It's all a matter of the person doing the telling.'

'Tell me your way,' he invited. 'Let me judge for myself.'

'Not here.' She looked round then at the noisy restaurant and its potted palms and hanging plants. 'Not here. I couldn't bear it.'

'I'll take you home,' he said, and lifted his hand to call for the check. 'We can talk there.'

She hesitated, and looked at him, and he thought – oh, Christ, I've frightened her. She's going to go off into one of

those crazy moods of hers and I'll never hear all this. I have to
hear it, I have to. It's the most important information I've
collected yet. I need it so badly I can taste it. And I want to be
with her even more than I want to know.

It was that realisation that startled him the most.

Eleven

'It'll be cold in here for a while,' she said, as she pushed open the door to the room at the back of the house. 'I'll light the fire.' It was indeed very cold, with a deadness that came from air that had not been disturbed for some time, and it made him uneasy. It was as though a corpse was in there somewhere, and he looked round almost warily.

A cluttered room, an old man's room, full of the detritus of years of book-centred work. In every available space books were piled. The walls were lined with packed shelves, and he could see that they were stacked two deep; behind the smaller paperbacks at the front, taller hardcovers loomed. The floor was covered with faded carpet, though little of it could be seen between the books that were piled on the floor, too. Pathways had been left between them to reach the fireside, where she now crouched setting matches to the crumpled paper and rough sticks in the grate. The only surface that was not book-heaped was a rumpled old sofa covered in faded red velvet that faced the fireplace on the other side of an almost bald goatskin rug.

She sat back on her heels and looked at the result of her efforts. The flames lurked low in the heavy grate for a while, as though they too were dispirited by the place in which they found themselves, but then slowly strengthened and lifted, and the scent of newly burning wood moved across the deadness of the room as the sticks caught and began to crackle with an incongruous cheerfulness.

'That should help,' she said and stayed there crouched in front of the fire, staring at the flames as they climbed up the sticks and began to eat the logs set above them. The smell of the wood and the warmth made him relax and seemed to have the same effect on her, for she said suddenly, 'I'd like another drink, I think.

There's some sherry in that corner – ' and jerked her head a little, and obediently he went foraging. He found the decanter and the glasses perched a little precariously on the inevitable pile of books on a low table, poured the drinks and brought the glasses back to the fireplace.

She was sitting on a corner of the sofa now, her legs tucked up beneath her, still staring at the fire, which was settling nicely, and reached up one hand for a glass without shifting her gaze from the flames.

'This is familiar,' he said. 'Comfortable,' and sat down at the other end of the sofa. 'I had a friend with a place in Connecticut – where else? – and they'd ask me up at Thanksgiving. We'd sit by a fire like this on a winter night – ' And as he spoke he was seized with a sudden pang of homesickness that left him shaken by its intensity. What the hell was he doing sitting three thousand miles from home in this dank house in Oxford, with this graceless girl, who was about as enticing as a bad tempered cat that couldn't be trusted not to spit if you attempted to stroke it?

'Yes,' she said, almost dreamily. 'It was always comfortable and good in here.' She sipped at her glass and then said, 'When I laid that fire, Geoffrey was still alive. Odd, isn't it?'

'Odd?'

She shrugged. 'If you don't know what I mean, then there's no point in explaining.'

'If you mean the transience of experience – ' he began and now she did look at him.

'My word, aren't we serious!' she said mockingly. 'Transience of experience – there's some fancy language for you!'

He flushed. 'I'm sorry,' he said stiffly. 'I just wanted to – well, it doesn't matter.'

She said nothing and they sat in silence for a while and then she stirred and said, 'How are you getting back to London tonight? I'm not sure what time the last train goes.'

'I can stay over,' he said. 'I imagine there are hotels in the city that'll manage one night.'

'Extravagant, aren't you? Or just rich – '

'Neither,' he said sharply. 'Just practical. I worked it out earlier that I'd have to stay over. It's no big deal. I'm not going to the Hilton or wherever. Anywhere cheap'll do for me.'

'Well, hadn't you better be sorting it all out? For all you know the town may be full and no hotel rooms available.'

'Are you telling me to go? I thought you were going to tell me what happened to – '

'The moment's passed,' she said swiftly and uncoiled herself from the sofa and went across the room to refill her glass. There was a recklessness about her movements now that sent a couple of books tumbling to the floor.

'Why?'

'Because – oh, just *because*.' She was still standing by the sherry decanter, looking at him over the rim of her glass, watchful and alert, and he tried a smile.

'Not for me it hasn't. You said you'd tell me.'

'So I've changed my mind.'

'Why?'

'Oh, for Christ's sake, why nag me? The moment's past, I tell you.'

'Why are you so frightened?' He was genuinely curious. 'What harm can I do you that you stand there looking like that? I haven't bitten you yet, and I'm not likely to start now. For Christ's sake, lady, cool it! Come and sit down and stop behaving like some sort of movie queen.'

He thought he'd gone too far for a moment but then her shoulders, which had tightened as he spoke, seemed to sag a little and she made a small grimace and came back to the sofa to sit in her corner again.

'Damn you,' she said, but there was no animus in her tone. 'Damn you. You're a bloody nuisance, you know that?'

'Sure,' he said equably, and went and refilled his own glass. The stuff was warm on his tongue but had an agreeable nuttiness about it and added to the claret he'd had at dinner was making him feel a little glittery. Watch it, a corner of his mind murmured. Remember what happened the other night, with Garten.

'I've been talking to some odd people,' he said then, as he came back and sat down in his own corner. 'You're the least of it.'

'How odd? Crazy odd or just English and, therefore, odd to you? To a lot of people in this country you're about as odd as Dick's hatband – and no, don't look at me that way. I'm not going to explain.'

He grinned. 'So don't. I'll tell you how odd – all mixed up.' And he launched into an account of the man Garten, dressing it up a little to make the encounter sound even more interesting than it had been; she listened and then laughed, and he thought, I'm getting closer again. And then said carefully, 'Then, of course, there was Cyril Etting. He wasn't odd. He was plain heart-breaking.'

He knew he was taking a chance, edging her back to the subject he wanted to talk about. They shouldn't have left the restaurant, he was thinking. I should have got it out of her there and then, while the mood was on her. Now I have to recreate it all over again, goddamn it.

'Oh?' She sounded genuinely interested, relaxed and quite without the tension that had filled her so short a time before. The most unpredictable person I've ever met, he thought. Weird.

He told her of Cyril Etting and the deep loneliness of his life, painting as vivid a picture as he could of the old man sitting in his cold house, and then sharing Chinese food with him, and she sat and stared at him, showing no reaction. The gleam of interest that had been there seemed to have faded, leaving just a blank listening gaze.

'I have others to see,' he said then. 'A man who lives in – where is it? Streatham. In south London – '

'It's pronounced Stret'am,' she said. 'Not Street-ham.'

'Oh!' He was taken aback. 'I'm sorry.'

'No need. I don't give a damn but some people do. They'll just laugh. As if it mattered.'

'I dare say it does to some.' Then he said daringly, 'Like eating scampi from a basket?'

Now she did laugh and relaxed even more and he thought, now. Now, while I've got her.

'Tell me, Miriam,' he said. 'Tell me the story and three quarters. You said you would.'

'The story and three quarters,' she echoed, and then sighed and set her glass down on the floor at her feet. 'If that's the only way I can get you out of here – all right. But don't interrupt me. Don't ask silly questions – '

'I'll try not to. What'll happen if I do? Will it all turn into dead leaves?'

She managed a crooked little smile. 'This isn't fairy gold, believe me. It's – oh, hell. Just listen.'

'Yes,' he said softly and put down his glass and folded his arms, and looked at her. 'Yes, I'll listen.'

'All right. Where did I get to? Ah, yes. What happened afterwards? Well, the war was over, right? And the Russians came. People in the camps had an idea they were coming – the word got round, God knows how, and they were ready. And when they opened the camps people just came out. Pouring out, some of them. Others were too frightened to pass the gates and just stayed there. Nowhere to go and no strength to get there. But David, he had to get out to find his family. He didn't know who had lived and who had died. He'd done well enough in the camp hospital, even had reasonable food. He was pretty fit, considering. But he had to find the family. So he went to the women's section and started asking and found out. His wife, five of the children, all dead. Only Basia living. Where's Basia? Gone – '

She stopped and he opened his mouth to speak and then, catching her glance, closed it again. And she nodded in satisfaction.

'Well done you. So, there's only Basia left. But he doesn't know where she is because she got out as soon as the Russians arrived. Swept away somewhere, he doesn't know where. But he reckons he can find her. He just has to go to the various places the people from the camps go to – displaced persons' camps. So he starts. The first camp, near Treblinka, it's like a madhouse, Basia said. An absolute madhouse. Hundreds and hundreds of people all milling round and doctors and nurses from the Russian forces and from the other allies, too, eventually, and the Red Cross and God knows who. She was in one of them, but they'd moved her on by the time David got there. And she didn't know where he was, didn't think he was alive even. Why should she? Her mother and the other children were all dead. How could she know her father wasn't dead too? She didn't think to ask, she said. So, she goes off to a camp for children that's been set up in Northern Italy. No, I don't know why so far away. They were all over Europe, these camps. They had to get people sorted out as best they could and wherever they found a place they could use for displaced persons, I suppose they used it no matter

where the persons were displaced from. And so there she is in a
camp near Cuneo in Italy and her father wants to find her.'

Again she stopped, and then went on with a sort of jeer in her
voice. 'And as though it wasn't ridiculous enough to try to find
one child in all the mess that was in Europe in 'forty-five, he
decides he's got to find her in time to get her ready to be
batmitzvah! The boys are all dead so none of them will ever be
barmitzvah, he says, and he has to have one child of the law.
What else did so many Jews die for? One of his children has to go
through the experience of being called to the law, and if it has to
be a girl, well, there it is. They were part of the reform
synagogues anyway in the days when there had been such
synagogues in Poland and Germany. So he gets it hard in his
head that's what he wants, a batmitzvah daughter. And Barbara
was born in 1933, so he hasn't much time, has he? Not if she's to
be batmitzvah when she's thirteen, the proper age. Mad, isn't it?
To put a time limit on such a search. Barbara said he was mad,
but she was so proud of his madness.'

'It's understandable,' he ventured, but she ignored him.

'He walked, that stupid bastard, he *walked*. Sometimes he got
rides, sometimes he managed to get money to buy a train ticket,
but mostly he walked. She wasn't in any of the camps near
Treblinka. No one knew where she was but they told him other
places children were sent to. So there he goes, walking around
the madhouse that's Europe, and looking. And every camp he
gets to they say very brightly, "Sorry, no child called Basia
Novak here, sorry, try there, try somewhere else, try anywhere,
only go away." '

She reached for her glass and drained it and then dropped it on
the floor, making no effort to set it straight, not caring what
happened to it, and it lay on its side, its open mouth gaping up at
her.

'After he got to Warsaw – which he did because after the
Treblinka overspill camps, he was sent to the Auschwitz ones –
they had God knows how many children there. Surprising,
really, how many survived, of the kids. You'd think they'd die
fastest, wouldn't you, in camps and times like those they knew?
But they lived. Tough they were, like Barbara. Anyway he got
there. Took weeks, months, maybe. No Basia there, so they tell
him to try in Hungary and he gets himself to Budapest. Still a

crazy man. No camps with children at all near Budapest, it turns out. Just old people. So he goes north again to Vienna and the same thing happened. There are children there, but not his Basia. So, Strasbourg, and then south again to Basle, and then Evian, God knows why Evian – no camps there – and then eventually Cuneo – '

'Italy,' Abner said and she nodded, seeming not to notice that he had disobeyed her.

'Italy. It's been a year and a half he's been looking. It's the end of 'forty-seven by now. He's late for the batmitzvah bit. He knows it, but he thinks, well, girls can still be batmitzvahed till they're sixteen. I've still got time. But he'd made up his mind that if she wasn't in this camp near Cuneo he'd give in. Well, he'd have to. There was nothing else he could do, nowhere else to try. Not after the places he'd been to. So many of them. He had a few bob in his pocket by this time. He'd had to work to earn some money in Basle and he'd actually stolen some there – from the baker he'd worked for.' She laughed then. 'The perfect David, stealing! Barbara used to get embarrassed about that, would you believe it? She'd slide over that part of the story every time, but she always said it all the same. It was as though she had to, because that was how David had told her, but she was ashamed of what he'd done. Anyway, in Cuneo – well, about thirty kilometres away – there was this camp full of kids. And David found the Commandant's office, sort of wooden hut it was, full of buzzing flies and stinking with garlic and rotten food and old shoes, enough to make you want to retch, David said, and so many people it was like a hell hole. And the Commandant's a fat screaming Italian who cries a lot when he gets angry and he does that a good deal because he just can't do all the work he has to do. David asks him, have you got Basia Novak here? and the Commandant waves his hands around and says no he hasn't. And David – oh, you should have heard Basia tell this bit. Quite a performance it was! – David sits down on the only bench there is, under an open window, and starts to weep. It's the end of the road, his last child is dead, must be, even though he'd been told in Treblinka by one of the women that she'd been all right, had got away. It's the way it is. Basia's dead. And he weeps. A girl outside the window, sitting on the ground with a rag doll, looks over the window sill and says brightly and in perfect Polish, "Are you looking for Basia Novak? I heard you say – well, she's in my hut." And she takes David, who is now crying like a tap, to this long street of tin huts and into one of them and there's Basia, sitting on a bunk with a piece of paper she's drawing on and she looks up and says, "Oh, hello, Daddy." So now you have it. That's the way Basia told it to me, when she was Barbara. Now you know.'

She leaned back into the corner of the sofa, tucking her legs up even more tightly as though she could become small enough to disappear into the scuffed velvet and stared at the fire, where the logs were now glowing in a heap of crimson ash.

There was a long silence and then he leaned over and set more logs from the pile in the fender into the grate. He had to do something useful, and that was the only thing he could think of. He dusted off his hands carefully, and then said with equal care, 'Indeed a story and three quarters. It's more like twice that much. What happened then?'

'Heavens, for a film man, you don't add up!' she said and flicked a glance at him and then back at the fire which was already greedily licking the new wood. 'I give you the perfect happy ending, and you want to know what happened then?'

'Happy endings aren't true,' he said. 'I need real endings, if there ever are any. So what did happen next?'

She shrugged. 'They got themselves into a quota for the UK, came to London. David got a job in a mental home and Barbara went to school. Did very well – '

'Was she batmitzvah?'

'Hmm? Oh. No. She wouldn't learn Hebrew. Refused to learn even the little bit the Reform synagogues in England wanted. So she never was. But she learned good English and got herself into University only a year older than the rest of her set. Which seeing she'd had no education at all till she got to London, not to call education, wasn't bad going.'

'Not bad,' Abner said, trying not to sound as though he was being ironic. 'And then what?'

'Got a degree. A first class degree in English. Joseph Conrad, sucks. It's Barbara Novak who's the one, they said. Going to be a great novelist in the English language. Ha!' And she tried to laugh. It didn't come out that way, though; just a flat, 'Ha!'

'Did she write?'

'Of course not! She met my father and married him, didn't she? Just after David died. I was born a year or so later and then – ' She shrugged. 'That was it. Never wrote a damned word.'

He stirred in his seat. He'd been almost afraid to move till now. 'A pity.'

'Wasn't it just.'

'And after that?'

'I told you. She married my father and – '

'No,' he said gently. 'What happened to Barbara? Where is she now?'

Again a silence, and she said roughly, 'She's dead.'

He caught his breath. 'I'm sorry.'

She ignored that, and he tried again. 'She couldn't have been very old when she died – born in 1933 you said? She'd only be – ' he calculated fast – 'fifty-seven or so now.'

'She was thirty-nine when she died,' Miriam said in a faint voice. 'Thirty-nine.'

He was silent for a long time and said awkwardly, 'I'm sorry. It was like that for so many. Their health had been ruined in the camps and – '

She looked at him contemptuously. 'Sorry again? Who the hell are you to be sorry? You know nothing about it.'

'I was trying just to – well, there it is. It must have been hard for your father after she died – '

'Geoffrey?' She made a little grimace, turning the corner of her lips downwards and lifting her brows in a casual sort of couldn't-care-less fashion. 'I don't suppose so. He never said. He just went back to where he'd been. It didn't seem to matter to him that much. After all, they'd only been together ten years or so.'

'It's a sizeable period in a young man's life,' he said, chilled by the note in her voice.

'Not for him, it wasn't. He was sixty-six when she died. Ten years to him – what was that?'

'Sixty-six?' He sat bolt upright at that. 'He was *sixty-six*?' Then how old were you when it happened? When your mother died?'

'Ten,' she said.

'And ever since then there was just you and your father? Is that why you never had a job, no friends of your own? Because you were looking after him, an old man?'

'Who else could there be? He had no other relations alive. He'd been the youngest of a family from Scotland. And both his older brothers had died before I was born. I know of no other relation. And of course there were none from my mother's family, were there? Or haven't you been listening to what I've told you. So here I am, a poor ickle orphan. Boo hoo, isn't it sad?'

'It could be,' he said, 'if you didn't work so hard to make sure everyone you meet is turned off you – '

'How do you know how I am with everyone I meet?' she cried fiercely. 'How the hell do you know anything at all about me? You made me tell you all this crap and now you – '

It was extraordinary. One moment she was talking to him, even shouting at him, her eyes snapping with fury, and the next she had dissolved into helplessness and was sitting with both arms held tightly round her thin body and weeping great ugly tears, her face twisted into a mask of misery. And all he could do was sit and stare at her in amazement.

Twelve

But not for long. It seemed to be an eternity before he moved, but it was a matter of moments. He slid along the sofa and took her shoulders in both hands and pulled her hard, so that she could not resist him and had to sit with her head pressed against his chest. She was still holding herself tightly, her arms making a barrier between them, but she was so thin that he knew he would have no difficulty encompassing her, and now he did just that, relinquishing her shoulders so that he could put both arms round her and hold on tight. And she sat there with her head pushed hard against him and wept bitterly.

It stopped almost as fast as it had started. Miriam took a deep shuddering breath and raised her head, and then pulled back. At once he let go, and she lifted her hands and wiped her face with the open palms in a childlike gesture that was infinitely touching and made him want to reach out for her again, but he controlled the desire and sat with his own hands clenched in his lap, watching her.

'Oh, Christ,' she said huskily. 'Oh, Christ. Why do I do it?' There was no apology in her voice, nor even regret; just a sort of puzzlement. 'Why the hell do I do it?'

'You're entitled to cry,' he said.

'I'm not entitled to keep on digging it out,' she said and leaned back in the corner of the sofa again. 'That's what I can't understand. Why I keep on doing it. It always makes me feel so foul.'

'You want to blame me? I asked you to tell me.'

'No,' she said drearily. 'It's nothing to do with you. I mean, yes, you asked me, but what difference does that make? It's just saying what's in my head all the time, anyway. I can't get rid of it.

It keeps on and on, marching through my mind like a – oh, I don't know. I just can't get *rid* of it all.'

'Was it like this before? When your father – '

'Of course it was. But at least when Geoffrey was here I had something to do. Looking after an old man – and he was a stubborn one – it gave me an occupation of sorts. He had to be fed and kept clean. At least that made me tired. Hard work.' She stared at the fire. 'Eighty-three. I won't live that long. It's dreadful to live that long.'

'Was he very difficult?'

She shrugged. 'How can I know? I never looked after anyone but him. Maybe he was no worse than anyone else of his age. Better even. He knew who he was and where he was and he went on working till the day before he died. But he was so far away, so very far away.'

'My mother's like that,' he said abruptly.

'Old?'

'Not particularly. Sixty-eight, as far as I can work it out. She never even told me when her birthday was when I was a child.' He grinned a little crookedly. 'I sort of had the idea that only children had birthdays. But I didn't mean because of her age. She was always the way you said your father was. A million miles away from me. I could never get near her.'

'She's still alive?'

'Oh, yes. She's still alive. It was my father who died.'

'Was he that way too? Remote?'

He tried to remember, tried to see Hyman in his mind's eye and then sheered away from the effort. Whenever he thought of Hyman now it was the same; a blankness where the face should be. 'I'm not sure. I mean, he was like Frieda in some ways, secretive and quiet but not so far away. No, I think he'd have talked to me sooner and more, if she'd let him.'

'She cared about you,' Miriam said flatly. 'That's why she didn't tell you what happened to her. That's why she kept away. If Barbara had been the same I wouldn't have this bloody business now, would I?'

'Cared about me? Like hell she did,' he said harshly and to his amazement felt a sudden tightening in his throat. It had been a long time since he had shed tears, but he remembered the sensation vividly and was amazed it should happen now. This girl Miriam is an extraordinary influence, he thought. She wept and now I want to weep.

'Think about it,' she said and leaned forwards, and again threw a log on the fire, which leapt excitedly to greet it. 'Just think about it and you'll see what I mean. You'll never get a hotel to take you now, will you? What are you going to do?'

'I beg your pardon?' He was startled and looked at his watch and then up at her. 'Christ! It's gone two.'

'I know,' she said. 'You'd better sleep here. The fire'll last a while yet and there's a blanket around somewhere. I'll see what I can find.' She got to her feet and stood staring down at him. 'Unless you want to do something different.'

'I — no,' he said and shook his head as much to clear it as emphasise the word. 'I'd be grateful. You're right. No hotel'd take me at this time of night and — '

'I'll fetch the blanket,' she said and went, leaving him sitting listening to her footsteps on the stairs and then above his head as the old house echoed around him. He felt deeply tired and a little sick; the food at the restaurant had been good, but there was a metallic taste in his mouth now that soured its memory and he yearned for his toothbrush; and then she appeared at the door with a heavy blanket over her arm and a small package in her hand.

'I found this,' she said and gave it to him; a new toothbrush, still in its wrapping, with a tube of toothpaste set alongside it. 'You'll need it. I'm going to bed. Goodnight.' And she put the blanket down on the sofa, nodded at him and went, and again he stood and listened to her footsteps and marvelled. Really the most extraordinarily abrupt girl he'd ever come across.

Abner wandered then, looking for a lavatory — which he found tucked away in a sort of outhouse beside the back door at the end of the corridor that led to the kitchen — and somewhere to wash, settling eventually for the kitchen sink for want of anywhere else. The hot tap yielded only lukewarm water, but there was a piece of soap there and a roll of paper towels, so he managed well enough; then he went back to the living room to pile the fire even higher with logs and to strip down to his underpants, before wrapping himself in the blanket and making himself as comfortable as he could on the old sofa. Around him the house creaked a little, and now he could hear the wind outside, humming irritably to itself in the trees; he lay there, very wide awake, wanting to sleep and feeling he never would, because he had been so stirred by the whole evening and, he had to admit, by Miriam herself, as a woman. For a while he was very aware of this sexual hunger as he lay there under the rough blanket and considered the possibility of going upstairs to find her and try to make love to her — and then actually laughed aloud. It was a ludicrous notion; and slowly the need subsided and he could be comfortable again.

At last Abner slept. And dreamed, waking from time to time with a start as the fire hissed in the grate and then settled with a little rattle, only to sink into the same dream. Frieda was trying to find him, just as though he were the girl Barbara whom Miriam had told him about. He seemed to himself to be running away from her as hard as he could, dodging behind walls to escape her, climbing up a great tree at one point while she stood beneath it and wrung her hands and wept with loud sobs; and he woke again and thought drowsily, that'll show you, that'll make you know what it's like. He drifted off again, and this time Frieda was sitting in a corner of a room, alone, and rocking herself with her arms held around her in a tight grip; and though it was Frieda she had Miriam's face, and he went towards her because she was Miriam and held his arms out, and she came and let him hug her and pet her and he looked down at her and it was Frieda's face this time, and he pulled away; but she held on — and again he woke with a start, and the thought was there as sharp as a piece of broken glass. She did love me, she did. She just didn't know how to. That was why. She did, but she didn't know how. And then he slept once more, but at last the dreams, if they came, buried themselves somewhere out of reach, and when he woke next it was almost light, and he was cold, for the fire was no more than a heap of grey ash.

He got up and stretched stiffly and then, very aware of his bladder, went padding along the dark corridor outside towards the lavatory, not bothering to dress first, and stood there shivering, his feet curling on the ice cold tiles of the floor, yawning. He came out into the corridor to find her standing just inside the kitchen door and switching on the light. She was wearing the black trousers again but this time she had set over it a vast yellow sweater, and she looked warm and alert, even inviting, and he gaped at her, feeling his face redden.

'Hell,' he said. 'I didn't think you'd be around yet.'

She flicked a glance at his bareness, and he had to control an instinctive urge to set his hands over his genitals, even though he still had his pants on. To do so would be so ridiculous, like some sort of male version of the Boticelli 'Venus', and he began to edge his way back towards the living room to escape her, holding his arms awkwardly at his side.

'I'll get dressed,' he mumbled, and she nodded and said casually, as though there were bare men in her house every day of her life, 'I'll put the kettle on. I dare say you'll want to shave.'

'No razor,' he muttered as he reached the safety of the living room door and dived in, and she called, 'I've brought one of Geoffrey's down. Can you manage a cut-throat?'

'I'll try,' he called back as he began to climb into his clothes as fast as he could, though why he needed to rush he could never have explained. It was obvious she wouldn't come to him. 'Or I could go around with designer stubble. It wouldn't be the first time.'

'Hideous,' she shouted, now well into the kitchen, and her voice seemed to him to be more cheerful. 'I've seen 'em on television. They look dirty.' He buttoned his shirt and vowed he'd manage with a cut-throat somehow, and went back along the corridor, his tie thrown over one shoulder and his jacket, hooked on to a forefinger, over the other.

'Do you know how to use this damned thing?' he said and stared at the razor, a wicked looking object, yet with a certain charm; the curves of the glinting steel were handsome. 'Or better still, do you know how to cope when I start bleeding to death?'

'If a man of eighty-three could use it, so can you,' she said. 'There's some shaving soap, too. You can go up to the bathroom if you like but the light's better here, and it's easier to give you hot water. If you don't mind me being here. I'll make you some toast.'

It was an oddly companionable ten minutes. He soaped his face thoroughly, watching her covertly in the little mirror that was set over the sink as she moved around the kitchen cutting bread, finding marmalade in a cupboard, putting out cups and saucers, and she seemed to him to be glowing. It wasn't just the yellow sweater, either, he decided; she really did look better than she had at any time since he'd met her.

Gingerly he set to work with the razor, and she saw him and laughed and came over to him.

'Not like that, idiot,' she said, and her voice was relaxed and friendly. 'Like this.' And she leaned over his shoulder and rearranged the razor in his hand, and again he smelled clean hair and soap as he had on the day when he'd first met her; and this time it had the added dimension of being familiar; and the same stir of sexual hunger lifted in him and he was grateful he had more clothes on now than just a pair of underpants.

'You see?' she said. 'Now hold it flat to your face – no, not like that! You'll cut your throat. Like this – that's it. You see? It's not that difficult.' And she watched him as, carefully, he slid the blade through the film of pallid soap. 'You'll make an Englishman yet.'

'You reckon that's a good thing to be?'

'The sort Geoffrey was, yes,' she said and turned away to crouch down so that she could look at the toast beneath the old-fashioned cooker's grill. It was beginning to smell good and he felt a sudden lifting of his spirits. She had lit the fire in the old grate, too, and the overhead light in its red shade glowed richly. The whole feeling of the room was of stuffy cosiness and security, and he began to whistle softly between his teeth, the way he only did when he felt really good.

'Then I'll see what I can do to emulate Geoffrey, if you'll teach me,' he said and went on to finish shaving and then to dry his face, as she took a battered dark blue tin pot to the kettle, now singing at the back of the cooker, and filled the small room with the rich scent of freshly made coffee.

'I've got better things to do,' she said. But her tone was still amiable, bantering even. 'D'you eat butter? I've got some. I can't stand that margarine stuff.'

He reached into his jacket pocket to find a comb. 'Then you do care a bit about food? So far you've given me the impression that you're rather above it in some ways – '

'Then you took the wrong impression,' she said. 'Breakfast's ready!'

'May I comb my hair in here? In my mother's house combing hair in the kitchen was the crime of the century.'

She lifted her shoulders. 'I don't give a damn,' she said and poured coffee. Swiftly he fixed his hair and then came to sit down opposite her.

'If you want more toast there's bread in the crock over there.' She indicated a squat grey piece of pottery with a lift of her chin. 'And the grill lights with a match. Help yourself.' And then swiftly spread butter and marmalade on her own toast and pulled a book from the dresser beside her, propped it up against the coffee pot and started to read and eat at the same time.

It could have been an insult, but it didn't feel like that. Instead it made him feel that she regarded him as safe and good to be with, as comfortable as a pair of familiar old shoes, and he liked being cast in that role. Abner sat and crunched his way through his own toast, making another two slices — because he was hungrier than he would have thought possible — and drinking scalding hot coffee. He leaned over to replace the coffee pot with the marmalade jar when he wanted more, so that he didn't disturb her reading and thought absurdly, we could be married, we're so easy together, and then was amused at himself. Marriage had never been on the list of things he intended to do. There had been women, of course there had. He was as normal as the next man and far from attracted to asceticism, but a permanent sharing-a-kitchen sort of relationship had never seemed to him something he could handle or wanted. Yet here he sat, staring at a girl across a table as she read a book and ignored him, a girl with a scrubbed face and no attempt made to look good, with hair tied back, he now noticed, in a rubber band, and dressed rather like a New York bag lady. An uptown bag lady, perhaps, but still a bag lady.

'I must go,' he said and got to his feet.

'Mmm?' She looked up at him a little blankly.

'Time to go,' he said. 'I've trespassed long enough on your hospitality.'

She stared at him with unfocused eyes for a moment and then they sharpened, and she looked at his directly and laughed. 'My God, but you can sound pompous!'

He frowned, nonplussed. 'I'm sorry.'

'No need to apologise. I suppose it's me, really. I'm not used to being with people much. Listen — thanks for dinner last night.'

She got to her feet and stood there a little awkwardly as he shrugged on his jacket. 'It was very kind of you.'

'It was my pleasure,' he said stiffly, and knotted his tie with a savage little jerk of his wrist. 'I'm sorry I outstayed my welcome, is all.'

'You didn't,' she said, and stood back to allow him to reach the kitchen door. 'In fact – ' she seemed to hesitate and then went on with a little rush – 'in fact, you've been very good for me. I'm really grateful. I slept better last night than I have for – oh, ages. Maybe talking about things isn't such a bad idea at that. Someone said to me when Geoffrey died I should go to some sort of do-gooding counsellor and I said the very idea made me puke, but last night – ' She shrugged, looking now as gawky and shy as a schoolgirl. 'Well, you helped, you know? I'm sorry I cried.'

He was completely disarmed now. 'I'm not,' he said and smiled and held out one hand. 'I'm really not. It was a compliment that you were willing to talk to me. I truly appreciate it. Will you talk some more?'

She looked at him consideringly for a long moment. 'For my good or for your film?'

He didn't hesitate. 'Both.'

She nodded. 'Fair enough. Then yes. Not that there's a great deal more to tell you, really. I know little about how it was in the camps that I haven't told you, but I dare say you know most of that. It's hardly a secret any more. Geoffrey had a room full of books and papers on that upstairs. I'll show you next time you come.'

'It's afterwards, though, that interests me.'

'Yes, I know. I understand that. Well, it quite interests me. As you may have noticed. So, as I said, fair enough.' She held out one hand, holding it stiffly as a child does when doing as she is told. 'We have an arrangement. Goodbye.'

'Er – goodbye,' he said, taken aback yet again by the abrupt dismissal and turned to go. She made no effort to follow him. Abner left the kitchen door open behind him, and went along the dim and chilly corridor to the front door. Still she made no move, just standing there watching him, and he pulled on the door, which hadn't been locked and opened it.

Outside the morning air was damp and cold and slid across his face with an agreeable shock, and he stepped out on to the cracked door step and then looked back, his hand on the door knob, ready to close it behind him. She was still standing there, watching him, and seemed to have no intention of moving at all, but then just as he pulled the door closed behind him she lifted one hand and smiled.

All the long way to the station as he walked with long fast strides he saw that vision of her, framed in the soft red light of the kitchen, and it was a pleasant one. It wasn't till he was buying his ticket and had to speak that he realised he had been whistling through his teeth in his happy fashion ever since he'd left the house.

Thirteen

The next week was, for Abner, the most productive time he could ever remember spending, apart from when he had actually had a film out on location. He returned from Oxford filled with a vigour that made him realise just how under-stretched he had been, operating on only half of his cylinders since his arrival in London, and determined to get back into fast, hard action at once.

He started by finding himself somewhere to live, for it suddenly seemed intolerable to stay at the Bayswater hotel one more day. The cost of apartments in London horrified him, but a long morning spent chasing from one letting agent to another eventually paid off. He found someone with what was called a studio flat that she was desperate to let on a short lease and finally bargained hard to cut the costs and took it, biting back anxiety as he wrote the cheque for three months' rent in advance. It swallowed almost half of his entire living budget, but he felt it was worth it. The worst that could happen was that he'd live on baked beans and fried onions again, the way he'd had to when he was making *Yesterday's Babies*, and he'd survived that. He could again. And the apartment was perfect: one large room, with a sofa that became a bed at night, in a small block overlooking a canal near Camden Town, north of the centre of the city, was all he needed. The kitchen, so-called, was ludicrous – little more than a cupboard with a minute sink, an electric ring and a sandwich toaster set over the smallest refrigerator he had ever seen – but who needed more for baked beans and fried onions? – but the bathroom pleased him. No bath, but a real shower stall as well as a basin and the lavatory, and that was more than enough. The furniture was sparse but sound enough, with its major component being a very large pine table set in front of the big window. Somewhere to work, spread his papers and put a typewriter. What more could a man want?

The chance to make his film; that was the more this man wanted, he told himself as he unpacked his few clothes and prowled around his new domain. I've got this sorted out; now get the job going. Both strands would have to be pursued side by side still; he wasn't free yet to concentrate, as he longed to do, on the research and the preliminary work on the film. The money was still the major problem, so he went back to embark again on his haunting of useful people in the industry, hurrying from office to office around Wardour Street, hustling with all the energy he had. Monty Nagel was out of town, he was told, for another week, so he couldn't be sure that he had an agent, but he decided to assume he had. It was the best way to operate, after all; he needed a name to flash about, as well as a reason for flashing it, and it was clear that Nagel was a power of some sort in the industry here. People knew him and nodded sagely when his name was mentioned and seemed more co-operative. If Abner told enough people that he was a client of this man, that would in a sense make it so. Nagel would find it harder to repudiate him than he knew. And Abner grinned to himself as he thought that and marched into Alexander Venables' office in a little yard off Lombard Street, near Mansion House. This was the last of the contacts Nagel had given him and Abner was determined to make full use of him.

Venables turned out to be far from the elegant Englishman his name suggested. He was short, amazingly fat, though with a small and rather sweet face like that of a knowing cherub, and had as thick a European accent as Abner had heard outside the worst sort of US television comedy show.

'Vell, vell!' He beamed at Abner as he settled him in a deep armchair and pushed cigar boxes, glasses of wine and coffee cups at him all at the same time. 'So you're a friend of Monty, hey? Ach, such a good fella, zat Monty, a real *mensch*, the best in the voild!'

Abner looked at him sharply, convinced the man was putting him on; no one could be that from-the-*haimish* surely?; but Venables beamed back at him, his raisin-black eyes gleaming in his pastry face, looking as innocent of guile as any man could; and Abner, in spite of himself, smiled.

'I guess he is,' he said. 'Everyone says he's a good agent, that's for sure.'

'Like I said, the best in the voild, no one knows how good. Me, I know, on account of I'm a *mensch* too, you understand? Me and Monty, like this ve are!' And he actually crossed his first and second fingers at Abner.

Abner smiled even more broadly. 'I'm sure. So, are you enough like that to put some money into a project for one of Monty's clients?'

'He's your agent?' The raisin eyes gleamed more brightly still, and Abner heard the warning in the back of his head.

'Near enough,' he said cautiously. 'We've signed nothing, but he's the guy for me, and my movie's going to make good money for him. Once we get going. He's the man.'

Venables nodded in satisfaction and padded round his desk to insert himself with some care into the vast chair that stood there. He rested his pudgy hands on the desk – he couldn't get close enough, because of his belly, to put more than hands there – and said with great benevolence, 'So you haven't got going yet?'

'I'm clear in my head what I want to do,' Abner said and reached into his document case for yet another set of pages. He'd had a half-dozen more made at a ridiculous price at a local fast-print set up in Parkway, in Camden Town near his apartment, and he was going through them at a hell of a rate. He'd need another half dozen soon. Jesus, but he needed money for so much, and the awareness of that sharpened him; he leaned forwards and switched on all the charm he had. He'd done it before, persuaded people by sheer strength of personality to back him, and by Christ, he could do it again. He had to.

'I want to make the best film that's ever been made about the hell it was that people went through in Europe in the Thirties, the Forties. But I want to tell it through other eyes – their children's, their grandchildren's.'

He was launched, very well launched, and he sat there, his shoulders up and his face flushed – he could feel the heat radiating from him – and bathed the man in words and images and ideas and hopes. He painted pictures of the picture he would make that were so vivid they made his own pulses accelerate and increased the heat in him. His back felt wet from sweat and still he talked, and the little fat man sat and watched him almost unblinkingly as he went on and on.

'So, all right,' Venables said, as at last Abner paused for breath. 'All right. It's development money you need, hey? Development for development, I can maybe manage, you understand. Not the big stuff – none of your twenty-five thousands, your thirty thousands. This you get from somewhere else. But me, I could take a small percentage, a *bissel* of a *bissel*, you understand? To get you off the floor. On account of right now are you on the floor or are you on the floor? Chee!' And he pursed his lips into a damp pink round as he made the sound again. 'Chee!' And Abner remembered with a vivid mental picture the Hollywood kitsch he'd loved so much before he'd learned the greater value of Ealing comedies, and saw the fat man who had bounced his way through so many of them. Cuddles something. That was it, Cuddles Zakall. This man Venables was doing an impression of Cuddles Zakall and doing it rather well and he grinned widely and said, 'So, OK, Mr Venables. Would I lie to you? I'm on the floor. A nice floor, with carpets, and all that, but still the floor.'

'For Monty's sake, I'll do it. Not a lot, you understand, not a lot!' He was writing a cheque, using a very fat fountain pen with some ostentation, and Abner watched the pudgy little hand curling slowly over the paper, almost unable to breathe. He'd done it; he'd made the first little log in the jam move. It might not be the big one, the one that started them all going, but it was a movement. The value of it was not whatever sum he was writing there but the fact that he was writing at all. Now Abner had some money and that meant he also had a lever. He caught his breath and said as casually as he could, 'Mr Venables, I'm delighted. Monty will of course negotiate the percentage' – and that, he thought with a wicked little spurt of pleasure, will force Nagel on board, like it or not; some real cash to handle – 'while I arrange the next stages.'

'I like vell kept books, my boy,' Venables said and reached for a rocking blotter of the sort Abner remembered Hyman having on his desk in the corner of the living room in Newark, and set it carefully on the cheque. 'Vether it's a stemp you buy or a camera, it's all got to be in the books, you understand?'

Abner lifted his brows, feigning hurt. 'Do I strike you as the

sort of man who doesn't run an efficient operation, Mr Venables?'

'From now on it better be Alex.' The fat man coughed then
and spluttered a little. 'Alex, tha's me. Friendly is my vay, yah?'

'Alex, then,' Abner said and reached out his hand and the little
man looked at the cheque for a moment, almost regretfully, and
then handed it over.

Abner glanced at it swiftly and could have wept with gratitude. Five thousand pounds; not a vast sum, but enough to be
worth taking seriously. A small lever to shift a bigger one to shift
the biggest of all, that was what this was; and he folded it
carefully and put it in his pocket book and then reached into his
document case for a sheet of paper.

'A receipt, Mr Venables,' he said. 'I do business the tidy way.'

'Ah, receipts, who cares receipts? So long as it's in the books.
Put it in the books and send me after receipts. Anyway, like I
said, you're Monty's boy, so you're all right by me.'

Abner felt a pang of guilt. 'Don't forget, we haven't signed
anything yet, Mr Ven – Alex. I wouldn't want to mislead you.
But I know he will – it was Monty, after all, who sent me to you.'
He grinned then and leaned back in his chair. 'Mind you, he sent
me to a few people. The only one I haven't seen yet is Milner –
Barney Milner. But I'm holding back on him for a while.'

'Of course,' Venables said. 'Equipment, hey? Cameras, lights,
the *megillah*. This you arrange later. Right now it's money – and
Monty knows what he's doing, who he sends his boys to. He sent
you to me, so signed with him or not, it's OK by me. Receipts you
can give me if you like. For my part, I ain't got no big worry
about you. Not for five thousand.' And he beamed again with the
simple pleasure of the rich man who was once very poor.

It was a look Abner had seen often enough in his years of
hustling money for his films; the man for whom the real pleasure
was not to be part of a major artistic endeavour, which would
have been Abner's own reason for investing in anything as
chancy as a film, were he rich enough, but for the pleasure of
handing out cash as though it didn't matter to people to whom it
mattered a great deal. And he relaxed a little, and realised as he
did so that he had become suspicious suddenly. But there was no
need. This man was straightforward enough. No mysteries here.

Just joy. Because he had the first real bite on *Postscripts* and it had only taken him just over a week to do it.

He went back first to Simmy Gentle. The man had seemed interested enough in the project; said he'd talk to his partner. Well, Abner now had the first nibble, he had a way of leaning on him, and there was no point in wasting time. Gentle had been seriously interested, he knew that. It was almost certain that by the end of the afternoon Abner would have the guarantee of more of the underwriting of his film that he wanted, and he moved fast through the crowded streets towards Wardour Street, elated at being at last on the way. With money from Gentle – and to add to it, it might perhaps be worth leaning on the Rossily woman too, which was an attractive prospect – he could leave the money angle alone for a while and concentrate on research.

The best bit that was, and he hugged to himself his childish excitement, revelling in it. When he'd been a kid he'd always saved the best bit of his dinner till the end, leaving all his mashed potatoes in a heap so that he could gobble it all at once, and here he was thinking in the same sort of way. Crazy, and he whistled softly through his teeth as he walked, letting his thoughts mill around his head uncontrolled, till they melded into a comfortable sense of well-being; mashed potatoes and Venables' cheque and Miriam Hinchelsea and old Etting and behind it all the image of his film actually growing, taking form as an entity, something real and not just a hope, a mere dream, a distant project. A real film, reels of celluloid, entries in the reference books, and people talking about *Postscripts* when they heard his name instead of *Uptown Downtown* all the time.

But his euphoria dwindled and vanished when he got to Gentle's office. The man was there, he knew he was, for he could see his distorted shape through the dimpled glass on his office door, but the girl outside steadfastly denied he was, standing in front of the door and staring mulishly at Abner as she shook her head at everything he said.

'Mr Gentle told me to come back after I made some other contacts,' he said, trying to keep his voice and his temper in check. It wasn't the girl's fault she had to tell lies. The bastard should come out and tell his own, if he wanted to. 'Is he saying now he doesn't want any part of my project? Because if not, that's fine by me. There are others who do. But I need to know where I am. When a man shows interest and tells you to come back and then refuses to see you, you get sore, you know? For all I know he's one of these rip-off guys who knows a good project when he sees one and wants all of it instead of just a little bit of the action. I left him with one of my sets of pages and I don't go out of here till I get 'em back. Or find out what he's doing with 'em.'

'I really can't say, Mr Wiseman,' the girl said and looked almost piteously at him and Abner glared back and thought, the kid's terrified. And tried to remember her name, some damn fool name too – and then it came to him.

'Listen, Tiffany,' he said winningly and perched one buttock on the edge of her desk. She was standing with her back to Gentle's office door, protectively, and Abner knew it would help to give her space. 'Listen,' he said again. 'I'm not a difficult man, but you have to understand my situation! I offer him a really hot property, one that interests him enough to keep the details with him, he tells me he likes it and that he'll talk to his partner. Says come back Friday. OK, it's Friday and here I am. And now he won't see me. Why not? If he's decided he doesn't want in, fair enough. If his partner hates the whole deal, fair enough – but he doesn't have to treat me like I'm some sort of walking pesthouse, does he, hiding in his office? Do me a favour, Tiffany. Phone in there, tell him I'm not going to bite, ask him to let me have back my treatment even if he doesn't want to speak to me, and then I'll go.'

She stood there and looked at him for a long moment, doubt in every line of her body, and then, unwillingly, walked round the desk to get to her phone and intercom. Deliberately he didn't move, so that she couldn't reach across her desk to get to it from the side she was on, and he knew she wouldn't come closer to him than she had to. He hated using tactics like this, but after the years he'd spent in this business he knew how to handle the tricky ones. And Gentle, he felt all the way through to the middle of him, was very much a tricky one.

He waited until she had reached the phone on the far side of the desk and picked it up. It was an odd thing he'd noted a long time ago; people could never just drop a phone hand-set when they were in a hurry. They always had to hang it up properly and he used that knowledge with all the timing skill he had. As she tucked the phone against one ear and reached for the buttons, he got to his feet smoothly and moving very directly but not seeming to hurry, had Gentle's office door open and was inside before she could stop him.

Gentle was sitting behind his desk, watching the door with an odd expression on his face; not precisely scared, Abner thought briefly as he saw the face smooth out in reaction, but still very uneasy.

'Hi, Mr Gentle,' he said affably. 'Good to see you. You said to come back Friday.'

Gentle stared at him, nonplussed, as Tiffany, her face twisted with anxiety, came running into the room to stand beside Gentle's desk and glare at Abner. She was half her employer's size but was clearly ready to defend him physically if she had to, and Abner smiled at her more cheerfully than ever, as she cried, 'Oh, Mr Gentle, it wasn't my fault, honestly it wasn't. I tried to stop him but he said just to phone you and I couldn't get to the phone from the front and – '

'It doesn't matter, Tiff,' Gentle said and got to his feet. 'Er – cup of coffee, Mr Wiseman?'

'Great,' Abner said heartily. 'Always like talking business over coffee. Feels civilised, you know?'

He felt better. There was no way he'd take a penny of involvement from this guy now, but there was equally no way he was going to leave here without knowing why the man had behaved like such a shit. To hide in his office and refuse to see him? Crazy!

'So, Mr Gentle,' he said and settled himself in the chair in front of the desk. 'Here I am, coming back as you said I should. How did you get on with your partner then when you showed him my project?'

Gentle flushed and sat down heavily. 'That man,' he said with sudden savagery, 'is enough to make you spit.'

'Oh? Why should that be? I thought he was just – what was it you said? A sleeping partner. The money man, was all. You're the one that runs things. That was the way you put it across to me when I was here.'

Gentle looked uncomfortable. 'So, all right. Maybe I – Listen,

I don't know what it is, or why it is, but my partner says lay off, so lay off I got to. I run a good business here, and I make a lot of successes. The money's coming in big and there's more to come, but when I started it wasn't so good. I had to have a lot of backing. You know the way it is in this business! You don't start with peanuts. And like the man said, you pay peanuts, you get monkeys, and me I always wanted the best. Commercial, you understand, but the best. We may do blood and guts movies, but they're the best guts.'

'I believe you,' Abner said, still affable. 'Why shouldn't I? You seemed like an honest guy when we met,' and the emphasis he put on 'seemed' was slight but unmistakable.

'Listen, Wiseman, what can I do? Sure, I liked your project. Sure I thought I'd like a piece of it. We could have worked well together, but there it is. The man didn't like it, and there's not a thing I can do about that! You think I didn't try to find out why he didn't like it? Of course I did! The more I thought about your project the more I reckoned you're on to a good one. As long as I could have persuaded you to open the thing out a bit, get a big bankable name up front – maybe Streep or even Streisand – God knows she's got the looks for it – we could have had a winner. A class movie that'd make money, better than *Sophie's Choice* but with that sort of feel about it, you know?'

Abner stared at him, loathing him with every part of himself. This was the sort of film man he most hated, who had about as much subtlety and sensitivity as a crack Panzer division and all the intelligence of a flock of sheep on a dull day. To have made *Postscripts* with any involvement from such a one would have been sickening. He was well out of it. But he was intrigued now. He needed to know why the chance had been taken away from him. It would give him enormous satisfaction to tell this guy what he thought of him and his judgement and to walk out of here taking his property with him and leaving him begging for it. But he wasn't being given that chance. The bastard was turning him down, so he needed to know why. *Postscripts* might not yet fully exist, but it was his baby all the same, had its own personality and integrity, and he'd protect it as fiercely as he knew how.

'But there's an end of it,' Gentle was saying. 'The man didn't like it, won't have any part of it. And there's not a thing I can do.

Here's your treatment. I was going to post it back to you. I don't
like seeing a man I've got to turn down, I can't pretend I do. That
was why I told Tiffany to say I wasn't here. But there it is, you
made me. So here's your pages and I wish you all the luck in the
world with 'em. Believe me, I wish I was part of the deal. It could
be a good one if you do it the way I said.'

'Oh, believe me, Mr Gentle,' Abner said earnestly and with
mock deference as he got to his feet and took the pages from the
man's hand. 'There's no way ever I'd do it your way. You can be
sure of that. And as for your partner – I don't know who the guy
is, but it's my guess, he's an Arab, right? You should have told
me that in the first place instead of talking bullshit about toning
down the Jewish angle. I'm not bigoted, you know. If a man has
his own religious attitudes that make him hate Jews and not
want to be involved in – '

'No!' It seemed to matter to Gentle that Abner understood and
he leaned across his desk, shaking his head hard. 'It's not like
that! Heller, an Arab? Do me a favour! He's as much a Jew as
you are!'

'Heller?' Abner had put the pages away and zipped his bag and
turned to go and now his chin came up and he stared at Gentle
with startled eyes. 'Heller? Would that be – ' And he stopped
and trawled his memory for the name and then it came up. The
man Garten had spoken about. 'Would that be Victor Heller?'

Gentle stopped and then sat down again, and bent his head
over his desk, fiddling with some pieces of paper there. 'Listen,'
he said. 'It really isn't important. Like I said, he's a sleeping
partner, and now I really have to get on. Goodbye, Mr Wiseman.
I'm sorry we couldn't do business, but you see how it is. Win 'em,
lose 'em is the way the business runs. Goodbye. Tiffany! Show
Mr Wiseman out!'

And Abner was too surprised and confused to refuse to let her
do it.

Fourteen

He bought himself lunch in a pub, needing time to think, and a noisy smoky room was as good a place as anywhere to do that. He ordered bread and cheese and beer (and it wasn't a patch on the same meal eaten that day in Oxford with Miriam Hinchelsea, he thought with a moment's pang), and as he chewed his way through it tried to put some order into his view of his situation.

Why on earth should the man Heller – and he tried to visualise him from that one brief moment in Nagel's office when he had seen him, and totally failed; all he could recall was a dark overcoat and an old-fashioned homburg hat – why should such a man block his project? Because that was how he saw what had happened in Gentle's office. His efforts had been blocked, hard. Gentle had been almost sewn up as a backer; he would have been hell to work with and Abner might eventually have rejected his involvement, but it had definitely been on offer, until this friend of Monty Nagel had screwed it up. *Why?* It didn't make sense, because hadn't it also been Heller who had put the man Garten in touch with him to help with the project?

He closed his eyes and tried to remember exactly what Garten had said. He could see the cruddy room in that cruddy club, could smell the sourness of the cheap wine, hear the rattle of the music coming from an old phonograph, and the man Garten rose before his eyes, sleek and oily in manner beneath his shabby ill-kept appearance.

'Heller?' the creamy voice murmured again as clear in Abner's memory as though it were speaking in his ear now. 'Who does Heller deal with most? We'll try a few names on you – Benson the distributor, no? Or Sampson, his colleague and – not that one either? Jimmy Brandon, Joe Mandelson, Lee Capetelli, Monty Nagel – ' And Abner's eyes snapped open.

It had been Nagel who had been the link there too. He had sent Heller to Garten and Garten to Abner to help him with the research for *Postscripts*, yet now it seemed that Heller had also stepped between Gentle and Abner to prevent the financing of *Postscripts*. Had Nagel been instrumental in that too? There was no logic in it at all.

He sat brooding over the remains of his bread and cheese, reviewing all that had happened since he had arrived in London. Was he getting paranoid, seeing mysteries where none existed? Because he saw them everywhere. It was a mystery that Venables had handed over five thousand pounds so easily; because now Abner thought about it, pushing aside his euphoria, it had been too smooth altogether. On the one hand the fat little man had talked about the importance of being businesslike, yet on the other he had refused a receipt for the cash and even more significantly had agreed to hand it over before negotiating a percentage of *Postscripts* for himself with Nagel, acting as Abner's agent. Who behaved like that in a sensible world? To have let himself be dazzled by the ready offer of a cheque, Abner told himself bitterly, had been positively juvenile. He should have known better; and reached into his pocket and took out the cheque and looked at it.

It seemed all right; the date and the sum of money were properly written in and the signature was clear, written in rather childish round characters that almost ran off the sheet. What would happen, he wondered, if he presented the cheque? Would Venables claim he had bought Abner's property for that sum? Was that why he'd refused a receipt and been willing to pay up before negotiating his share of profits? If Abner sent a receipt later, unless he sent it with a messenger and got a signature for it that made it clear it was a loan against a percentage to be agreed and not for an outright sale of his project, it could lead to losing control of his own film. And where was the guarantee that he'd ever get the sort of signed document he needed out of Venables?

He held the cheque and for a moment contemplated tearing it up. There was something very odd going on here and the safest way had to be to get out of the deal altogether, badly as he needed money to start work on the film; but he stopped just as he was about to make the tear. No, that wasn't necessary. As long as he didn't cash the cheque, no harm was done. But he could still get some use out of it, as a lever to get money out of others, and of course as evidence. In case someone else came along to try to set him up.

He moved sharply on the sagging old leather bench in the corner of the pub and stared at the people clustered round the bar in front of him. Was he going out of his mind and getting as suspicious and hostile as Frieda was, imagining dangers round every corner, being secretive and remote just to make himself feel safe? That was a horrible prospect; he had turned his back on Frieda because she was like that. It couldn't happen to him. Could it?

He paid for his food and left the pub to stand in the street outside, uncertain of what to do next. Nagel was out of London till Monday. Abner would be at his office first thing that morning to find out what he was up to, but right now he felt useless, and that was a dreadful feeling. There must be something he could do today, right now; and he stared round at the crowded street where the wet road gleamed with patches of rainbow colours from oil-leaking cars and vans as though it would somehow answer his need for him.

And, incredibly, it did. A man who was hurrying along with his head down against the cold wind almost ran into him as he stood on the kerb and lifted his head, startled, to apologise, and then stared at him blankly and said, 'Hey – Who'd ha' thought it! Abner Wiseman? What the hell are you doin' here, for Chrissakes? I haven't seen you since Christ knows when and I run into you *here*? Whatdya know about that? Abner goddamn Wiseman!' and he shoved a large hand at Abner, grabbed one of his and began to shake it furiously as Abner stared at him, memory struggling to place the face now beaming at him. It was maddening; there were times when he had total recall to an uncanny degree and yet here he stood, staring at a man he knew well and totally unable to put a name to his face.

The other man laughed at him, pleased as a child who has played a successful Hallowe'en trick. 'Jeez, you've forgotten me! Makes a guy feel really good, that does. Listen, try thinkin' of barbecued ribs and rice'n'peas, hey? If that don't make you remember . . . '

It worked. As the memory of the smoky taste filled his mouth it was as though he were there again, in that bar in the South

Bronx, with the whole crew sitting around him and shouting and laughing and teasing and knocking back the beer, cold pale American beer, and he was sitting in the middle of them flushed and bursting with excitement. They'd finished the last day on location, got all the film in the can, as clean and neat a wrap as anyone could hope for, and ahead of him stretched the months of editing and all the rest of the post production, and he knew he had a good film; *Uptown Downtown* was going to be a winner all the way.

'Dave Shandwick!' Abner cried and wrung the man's hand as though he would never stop. 'Dave goddamned Shandwick, what in hell are *you* doing here?'

'Same as you, pal, shaking hands with a right bastard – say, it's good to see you! How long's it been? Ten years, eleven?'

'Don't ask,' Abner said. 'Too long altogether. How are you doing these days?'

'Very nicely, old friend, very nicely indeed.' Shandwick winked, and Abner grinned indulgently. He was remembering more now; Dave had been the sound man in his best camera crew, but also an incorrigible wheeler-dealer. He'd learned how to be that in the army, he'd told them all blithely, when he presented the crew with a free crate of beer or offered brand new Swiss watches for sale at crazy prices. 'In Korea, who asks where it comes from, baby, who wants to know? Take it an' be grateful for the gifts life has to offer!'

Looking at him now in a London street in 1989 Abner could see the way he had been in 1979 in the Bronx and how he must have looked in 1951 as a perky young soldier in battledress with a gift for liberating useful items; a crew-cut scalp, round face split into a permanent grin, and the big cheek muscles that came from his interminable gum chewing. He was still the same man, even now in his well-cut English suit and aged – what? It must be close on sixty, though the crew-cut head was now covered in a greyish stubble and the cheek muscles had sagged a good deal.

'Still making movies, you old devil?' Shandwick said then. 'That was a great job you did on those street kids. I knew when we were making it you were on to something big, but you edited that film like a dream, take it from me, like a dream. I saw it in Cannes, you know, when you got the award? Cheered you to the

roof I did and knocked back a pint of champagne to you. And
now to run into you here! It's crazy. So what are you doing?'

Abner laughed. 'What do you think I'm doing? What do I
spend most of my goddamned life doing? Setting up a film deal is
what.'

The other nodded sagely. 'There's money here for your sort of
stuff. They got taste here, and don't get so frantic over big bucks.
What's the movie, then?'

Caution slid into Abner like a worm. He'd been so delighted to
see this memory of his past that he'd forgotten for a moment just
how tense and threatened he'd felt, and now it all came back to
him and he stared at Shandwick for a moment and said nothing.

The man grinned. 'So, listen, do I look like the sort who'd try
to rip you off? It's me, old Dave Shandwick, for Chrissakes! I
wouldn't even go after you for a job on it. I got myself too nicely
set up, believe me, to go around with a box of mikes and
permanent cans on my head ever again!'

Abner relaxed. 'I'm sorry, Dave. It's just that I've been having
a few problems with people here.'

Dave raised both hands in a gesture of despair. 'You don't
have to tell me. Dealing with these Brits is like swimming in
horse shit. I've been in business here long enough to know.'

Abner sharpened. 'You're in business here? What business?'

Dave tucked a hand into his elbow, 'Listen, come and see, if
you've got the time. My place is only just over there, round the
corner – in Bateman Street, see? I can get you a sandwich or
somethin' if you ain't eaten. I've just come from lunch or I'd say
let's go eat some place and – '

'Me too,' Abner said hastily. 'I'd be glad to see your place.
Time we got out of this anyway.' The wind was colder than ever.
'Lead the way, friend.'

Shandwick's office was small and cluttered, with a desk
dominated by a personal computer screen and its assorted
attachments and Dave patted it affectionately as he pulled a
chair up to the desk for Abner to sit down.

'This little beauty was the start of it all. Won it, you know?' He
winked heavily. 'I was over here working on a Superman movie,
and this sort'a fell into my hands and just to make use of it, I
started listing the names and the addresses of the guys I was
working with – sound men and camera guys and props, the

whole crews. Met a lot, too. That movie went on and on. And then I started hearing about jobs and those I couldn't do I passed on to the guys on my list – for a small consideration, you know what I mean? – and then I thought, hell, I'm not here on this earth for my health. There's a living to be made outa this! So I really got to work on it and here we are. The best agency for top crew on the patch!'

'You're an agent?' Abner said slowly, staring at him. 'For films?'

'And TV,' Shandwick said happily. 'Cover Britain and big chunks of Europe too. All that cable and satellite, believe you me, there's plenty of meat and gravy for everyone. I got the best freelances anywhere this side of Vladivostok, so when you're ready to start shooting, give me a whistle. I'll see you get the best, and check the prices.' Again he gave one of his outrageous winks. 'For you there's no padding the pay sheet, you know what I mean? I got arrangements with a few of the production managers, and one way and another – a bit of back scratching here, a bit there, and one hand washes another. But for you, none of that. You'd get a straight deal.'

'Could you get me some freelance work?' Abner said baldly, not even realising he was going to say it till he did.

Shandwick stared and sat down. Now he was watchful behind the *bonhomie*, though he still looked friendly.

'I thought you were setting up a movie of your own?'

'I am. But it's not as easy as it ought to be. Things fall through.' Abner shrugged. 'You know the way it is, better than most.'

'Not for you, pal,' Shandwick said bluntly. 'You've got a track record and – '

Abner sighed. 'For art house movies, Dave. Not for money spinners.'

The other pursed his lips and nodded. 'Just shows you, don't it? Here there are people getting money thrown at 'em, one way and another, and you can't get what you want. Even though there's a lot of Middle East oil cash going begging and venture capital from the City and – '

'If I hear any more about Arab money I'll spit,' Abner said. 'Take it from me, Dave, this idea isn't the kind the Arabs like, and I seem to be barking my shins on some sort of – ' Again he shrugged. 'I can't explain. Just believe me I'm having trouble and could do with a job. Of course I've no work permit.'

'Oh, that.' Shandwick leaned back in his chair. 'I don't worry about things like that. It's not so difficult these days, with so many European crews working here.'

'What difference does that make?'

'A lot. Who can check who's working for British companies, and who's working for European networks? And there's plenty of Europeans – they come here to make commercials for TV because they like London locations. You know the kinda thing – the Japanese make whisky, the Germans bottle it and label it as Scotch and they come and film a French guy jabbering about it in front of the Houses of Parliament or Buckingham Palace so they can sell it in Indonesia. They're doing that sort of thing three times a week, and I find the crews for 'em. To drop in a few guys who've left their work permits back home in Minnesota or Alaska's no big deal.'

'I could do with a couple of jobs to tide me over,' Abner said, thinking of the rent he'd paid for his apartment. 'This is one expensive town. Almost worse than Manhattan in some ways. I've got this one room apartment and they pulled my teeth for it.'

'Don't I know it,' Shandwick said feelingly. 'I've got this place over in Docklands – very classy, by the river, but I had to print money to get it.' He laughed then. '*Kinda* print it. You know me, Abner!'

'Listen, I want work, but I can't risk getting into any shit,' Abner said sharply. 'I do want to do a film here myself, eventually – when I get the goddammed funding right – and if I fall over the law or the unions before I start it could really screw things up.'

'Trust me,' Shandwick said. 'I've got my own interests to think of and there's no way I'd drop you in it. On account I'd fall in too. I'll get you work.'

He leaned across to his computer and began to hit buttons with great gusto. Clearly this was the part of the operation that pleased him most and Abner watched him, amused, enjoying the memories of the old days the sight of this pug-faced, sixty-year-old, eager kid brought back. He hasn't changed at all, he thought. Me, I know I'm older, know I look different, but he's still the same way he was in high school. He's that sort.

'OK,' Shandwick said at length. 'I can get you out on a shoot for dog food at Battersea Dogs' Home – just down the other side of the river, no travel costs, so that's OK – for two days next week, Thursday and Friday. It's a black one – no names, no pack drill, you get my drift? So I can't get you the rate for the job, but there'll be two hundred and fifty in a brown envelope at the end of the week. I know the union rates are way over that, but that's the size of it, pal. Take it or leave it.'

'That's one hell of a choice,' Abner said a little bitterly, knowing perfectly well how much more a fully fledged director, even of a lousy dog food commercial, should get. 'When you're as strapped for cash as I am, it's no choice. Do I have to work with live dogs?'

'Only in cages in the background. No shots of the bastards actually choosing to eat the stuff. Just a girl with a lot of hair and a low blouse spouting how great the stuff is. In Icelandic.'

'Icelandic? Christ! I don't speak a word of it!'

'Neither do the dogs, but they manage. It's OK. The girl's experienced. She does a lot of naughty stuff for me, too, you know? Not the hard core, just a bit of nice and naughty – and she speaks top rate English. She'll take care of you. Believe me, it's an easy two and a half.'

'You're on, Dave,' Abner said. 'Like I said, I need the money. Got the script?'

Dave shook his head at him amused. 'What do you think this is, *War and Peace*? It's a lousy two bit commercial, sweetheart, just a lousy commercial. The client'll turn up on site with it. He's putting it together now. All you need worry about is camera angles and the sound levels. I'm sending a good couple of guys as crew who'll do a great job, you have my word for it. The client'll stay till around twelve the first day, and then he has to go off to a meeting in Reykjavík or somewhere, so you'll be on your own after that. If you get on with it you should be able to clear that evening and put in a half day in the editing suite over at Charlotte Street. I'll give you the address. Get on with it ánd you can be out of the job in a day and a half for two days' pay.'

'Half day's pay, Dave, if that,' Abner said and Shandwick grinned unrepentantly.

'So what do you expect, working illegally? I've got to get my share of the ante. And because I do I get you more work when you want it. Believe me, I can keep you in rent the whole time you're here. One promise though. When you start shooting your own movie, I expect to be there on the ground floor, looking after your crewing.'

'You're on, friend.' Abner got to his feet. 'How do I contact these people, then, for next Thursday?'

Shandwick scribbled on a piece of paper and pushed it over the desk at him. 'Here's the place. I'll mark it on a map for you, too.' He busied himself at the photocopier for a while, using one of the maps of London that Abner himself carried and then shoved the marked page at him. 'See? Just turn up there and you'll see the crew van. It's marked "Shandwicks", very tasteful, in a blue and white logo. None of your garbage around me these days, eh, pal? The real stuff. I got six of those vans and they all work all the time.'

'Sounds like an unnecessary trimming, if you're a crews' agent,' Abner said, tucking the map away carefully. 'Why give yourself the trouble?'

'To keep 'em moving,' Shandwick said promptly. 'I really hustle for my dough, and that means making the sons of bitches work. No charging me hours of travelling when they've been playing pinochle. The van drives 'em, and I lay on flasks of coffee and sandwiches. It's called enlightened self-interest.' Again the gargantuan wink. 'The crews like it, on account it's different from the treatment they usually get and most of 'em don't see what's in it for me. You're unusual. You saw it right away. But then you always were a smart bastard.' He slapped Abner across the back affectionately. 'It sure is good to know you're in London, fella. I've been working here seven years now and still not got that many real buddies around. We must see more of each other.'

'Sure, Dave,' Abner said, and got to his feet. 'When I have time. I'm here to work too, remember. I'll take all the work from you I can have to keep the ice box full of beer, but after that I'm hustling too. But where can I get you? Got a phone number for that Docklands place? What's special about Docklands, by the way?'

'Only a quarter of a million for an apartment is all,' Shand-wick said with studied casualness. 'It's the place to live, where the money goes. And I'm making it – OK, Abner. Here you go. Great to have run into you, and enjoy the job!'

'I'll try. But not as much as you will, you old devil. You and your quarter million dollar apartment!'

'Dollars nothing.' Dave beamed broadly. 'Pounds, old pal, pounds. Come by again soon now, promise me. And I'll give you cash in hand on that job this time next week, OK? Bring the edited tape with you from Charlotte Street – that's the second address on that sheet I gave you – and make it look good, baby. These Icelanders got a lot more work they could put your way if they're happy.'

'I will,' Abner said and went clattering out to the street again, feeling better than he had an hour or so ago. He might have lost out on his high hopes for financing his film just yet, but at least he could now see a way of keeping himself above water on a personal level. Even if he had to do it illegally. And he wondered uneasily for a moment just how stringent the British authorities were in the matter of work permits, and then shrugged it away. That was Dave Shandwick's problem and it certainly didn't seem to make him lose any sleep. That's one hell of a successful set-up Dave has there, he told himself as he went on down the street back to the tube station to get a train back to Camden Town. There can't be many people in this business he doesn't know a good deal about, after so many years supplying crews for so many projects.

It wasn't until he was in the shower that he thought of it. If Shandwick knew people in the film business in this town then maybe he'd be able to give him some information about the people Abner had already been dealing with. Perhaps he could help find out more about Nagel and Heller and Venables? And – the thought drifted unbidden to his mind – the man called Mayer. He still puzzled Abner more than a little.

But by the time he'd got out of the shower and dressed and made for the phone he was too late. The office number Shandwick had given him didn't answer and neither did the home one. Well, there was always tomorrow. He'd call him over the weekend and really get the lowdown on some of these people. And he put on a heavy sweater and went out again to find a movie house showing something he'd enjoy, feeling rather better than he could have hoped he would at lunchtime.

Fifteen

Saturday was a frustrating day and yet ultimately he enjoyed it. Frustrating because he failed to reach Dave Shandwick; there was no reply from either his Bateman Street office or his apartment in Docklands, and not even an answerphone, which surprised him, and he frowned, all his suspicions surging up again. No way was he going to do that job at Battersea until he'd spoken to the guy again, he told himself. Now Abner needed more than just to pick Dave's brains about the people that he, Abner, had been dealing with; he needed more reassurance that Shandwick himself wasn't going to screw him. He'd always seemed a decent enough guy to deal with, totally honest about his dishonesty in a very disarming way, but you never knew; maybe he'd turned into a complete crook now and would let Abner do the work for him and then not pay up?

And as that thought shaped itself into words in his head he made a grimace at his own stupidity. Christ, he really was getting ridiculous. There'd be no percentage in Dave trying that. Of course there wouldn't. He'd made it very clear to Abner he'd get his money in exchange for the edited film, so no money for Abner, no film for Dave. There was no need to get so suspicious, and he let his shoulders relax and set out to make the most of the weekend that he could.

And did well. He left his apartment after breakfast to walk around his new neighbourhood and when after wandering in increasing gloom down one dreary street after another he suddenly found himself in a wildly busy street market, where bunches of silver balloons bounced over the heads of itinerant sellers, and stalls full of plants and clothes and antiques and sculpture were set hugger-mugger amid the reek of doner kebabs and falaffel frying which filled the air with hunger, while the water from the canal glittered in the afternoon sunshine as faces of every colour and type and voices of every pitch drifted by, his mood lifted to a crazy degree. This, he was told when he asked a passer-by, was Dingwall's, also known as Camden Lock, and as he stared around he felt a rich and agreeable vein of nostalgia open up inside him. This was life, this was fun, this was *terrific*; and he plunged into the hubbub, wandering from stall to stall and through the crowded alleys in a state of beatitude. For the first time since he had arrived in this town he was living for the here and now; he wasn't bedevilled by memories of the past and anxieties about the future. There was just the impact on his senses of the sounds and sights and smells of the place, and he loved it all.

He emerged hours later at the end of the afternoon as the short day dwindled into indigo and the lights over the stalls flared into the sky and those from the windows of the antique shops on the other side of the main road spilled out to make elegant patterns on the sidewalk, feeling great. He'd bought a crazy sweater in patchwork which he now wore knotted by its sleeves across his shoulders over his denim windcheater, and he'd eaten a bagful of crisp falaffel as good as any he'd ever had at home in Manhattan, and was content. But he was thirsty and stopped to buy a can of lager at a stall, then stood on the edge of the road dreamily watching the last people drift away homewards as he drank it.

Now what? It was too early to go home, too late to do any further sightseeing. In Manhattan he'd have called a friend maybe, gone to a movie or an off-Broadway show or found a good jazz bar to end the evening there, but who was there in London he could call? No one at all; and now a vein of melancholy threaded itself into his sense of well-being, but it wasn't a disagreeable sensation. It fitted the colours of the darkening sky and the increasing chill in the evening air. He was alone and lonely in a great city, and there was an elegiac element in his awareness of it that he enjoyed.

He dropped the empty lager can into a bin and turned and began to walk, not really caring in which direction; until he lifted his eyes to look across the road and saw the underground station and stopped. Chalk Farm. A great name for a station, that, and he tried to imagine what sort of place had been here before to leave such a label behind, and then blinked; for into the frame of his vision a memory had drifted up, a clear visual image. He could see the map of the Underground, that angled, diagramatic and curiously satisfying pattern, superimposed on the reality of the station across the street, and his eyes seemed to travel along the lines until they reached the Northern Line. His home station, Camden Town, was behind him. This was the next one along – and further up, going north, he read off the other station labels; Belsize Park and Hampstead and Golders Green, Brent Cross and Hendon Central and Colindale. And then he blinked and shook his head and the image vanished, but not before he had identified the next station down the line, and he grinned at the logo of London Underground sitting so perkily over the entrance and went plunging across. The next station up the line after Colindale was Burnt Oak, and that was where he would go. He'd go buy some more supper for Cyril Etting. They'd talk and he'd end the day as such a day should be ended. In the company of a good old guy. And he went whistling into the station to buy a ticket and push his way into the malodorous depths, delighted with himself, and not least because he had regained for a moment at least that goddammed photographic memory that he'd been so afraid he'd lost.

He bought plenty of Chinese food at the restaurant near Burnt Oak station, remembering the old man's tastes; spring rolls and prawn chow mein, and added this time a quarter of Peking duck, hoping the pancakes that went with it would survive the walk to Silkstream Close, and added lavish quantities of chilli beef and noodles and bean sprouts. They would have a lovely greedy evening and they'd talk and relax and share; exactly what Abner needed, and what Cyril was certain to enjoy too. And he carried his carefully packed paper carrier, feeling the heat of the little foil containers in it comforting against his leg and stepped out sharply through the now frosty evening to Etting's house.

There was a light burning over the porch of the little house and he grinned at the sight of it. There was no way, he was sure, that the old man wouldn't be in; where would he go on a cold winter's evening, after all? But it was comforting to see for himself that the house was occupied; and he used the knocker over the letter box to make a cheerful 'rattattat' sound that wouldn't alarm the old guy, but would bring him out of curiosity. He might be shy about answering the door after dark; a lot of old people were. But Abner would get him out; and he stood there on the step whistling softly between his teeth and waiting.

He didn't have long to wait; the square of the glass in the middle of the door sprang into soft multicoloured light as the lamp in the hall was switched on and Abner could hear heavy footsteps thudding over the carpet, and grinned again. Vast old Cyril, no way could his progress be silent.

Then the door opened and almost at the same moment the hall light went out, and a bulky figure came out and pulled the door almost closed.

'I'm coming, I'm coming already! So what's the hurry? You said half-past six and it's not quite that yet — what's the rush?'

'Cyril?' Abner said and reached forwards to stop him closing the door. 'You're not going out, are you?'

The old man peered at him over his shoulder. He was wearing an old homburg hat, and a thick yellow muffler was wound round his neck over a heavy rusty black coat, which was cut on generous lines but which still bulged over his back.

'Why shouldn't I go out?' he said pugnaciously. 'Where is it written I can't go out? And what are you doing here? They sent you to fetch me?'

'Of course you can go out,' Abner said. 'I just never thought that you — someone's coming to fetch you?'

'Sure they are! You think I can get there on my own? Half-past six, they said, they'd send one of the ladies, and I heard the knocker and I think, silly cow, she knows I'm not deaf and — '

Behind them a car drew noisily into the kerb with a crash of gears, and someone wound down a window. 'Oh, Mr Etting!' The voice was high and commanding. 'You shouldn't have come out yet, you'll freeze! It's a dreadfully cold night. Do come along, the car's all warmed up for you.'

'Ah, shit!' Abner said, his voice full of disgust. 'It never occurred to me you'd want to go out, for Chrissakes! I got Peking duck in here, too!' And he held out the bag from the Chinese restaurant.

Etting looked sharply at the bag, and then at Abner's face, and then over his shoulder at the car outside the gate, in one sharp bright eyed movement.

'So give it here,' he commanded and seized the carrier bag from Abner's hand. 'I'll put it in the fridge. It'll do me nicely for tomorrow.' And he went back into the house in a rapid shuffle leaving Abner standing on the step and the woman in the car calling plaintively, 'Mr Etting? Are you coming, Mr Etting?'

The old man was back remarkably quickly and again he pulled on the door, closing it this time, and shoved one thickly gloved hand into the crook of Abner's elbow. 'Come on,' he said briefly and made his way ponderously down the path and Abner shortened his step to match and went with him, too bemused to do otherwise.

'Who is it? So, Mrs Lipman? Oh, yes, Mrs Thing – '

'Greener, Mrs Greener,' the woman at the wheel of the car said brightly, reaching to open the car door. 'Cynthia Greener. Remember? Can you manage to get in on your own, or shall I – '

'My friend here, he'll help me. He's coming too.' Cyril took hold of the top of the car in both hands as the rear door swung open, and prepared to insert himself into it. 'He's Abner Wiseman, from America. He's making a film for the telly. He wants he should come with me tonight, I said you wouldn't mind.' And with a grunt he shoved himself into the car, disappearing into it rather suddenly as Abner held the door and pushed at his back to aid him.

'Wants to come with?' Mrs Greener said, clearly confused and excited at the same time. 'For the telly? What sort of – I really don't know, Mr Etting. I mean, I'm on the committee, but I can't speak for everyone, I really can't say.'

'Abner,' the throaty old voice commanded from the depths of the car. 'Come round the other door. I can't get over. Come round already. It's getting cold in here.' And Abner, ignoring Mrs Greener's fluttering, obeyed him. He felt as bewildered as the woman at the wheel of the car, but there was no gainsaying the masterful Cyril, it seemed, and he settled himself in the car at his side, noticing as he did so that it was a handsome Jaguar, smelling of expensive leather upholstery as well as Mrs Greener's even more expensive perfume.

'Uh, good evening, Mrs Greener,' he said. 'I don't want to impose, of course, but Mr Etting here seems rather – '

'Listen, I told you Abner, for research for your telly, the ladies at the *schul*, they'll be glad to help. They take care of me, you take care of me, we all take care of each other, eh, Mrs Greener? So, are we going already?'

Mrs Greener, who had been staring helplessly at the two of them in the back of her car looked startled and muttered, 'Oh, yes. Yes. Of course.' And with another crash of the gears put the car in motion. And beside him Abner felt Cyril Etting give him a sharp dig in the ribs with his elbow.

'You see?' he said serenely. 'Like I told you, Abner, any friend of mine is welcome. Our *schul*, they take good care of people. So, Mrs Greener, the ladies are keeping well, hey? Doing a lot of good work, hey? It's good, the dinners they bring me.'

'Oh, I'm glad you enjoy them, Mr Etting. We do work hard to make sure you all get the sort of meals on wheels you need.'

'The soup could be a bit thicker, you know?' the old man said judiciously. 'It's not bad, you understand, but for my part, a bit more barley would've been better, yesterday. Maybe tonight'll be good, hey?'

'Well, I'm sure it will be, Mr Etting,' the woman said, clearly nettled. And then went on. 'I mean, we don't get that many complaints about the food we provide.'

'From Jewish people you're giving to, you don't get no complaints?' the old man said in astonishment, and then laughed thickly in his throat, a wicked little sound. 'So who do you think this is, Mrs Greener? Another greener, hey? Sure they complain! They all complain. Me, I don't complain. I just make useful comments. Like the soup could do with a *bissel* more barley in it. But it's good soup, very good.' And again he nudged Abner's ribs. 'Me, I don't complain.'

Abner was beginning to enjoy himself. He had no idea where he was going or why, but the old man's clear delight in his machinations had communicated itself to him, and he looked sideways at his companion in the dimness of the car, as its now thoroughly demoralised driver manoeuvred it past a set of traffic lights and then left into a large car park in front of a red brick building, and again the old man winked at him in the dimness.

'Right,' Mrs Greener said with extremely artificial cheerfulness. 'Here we are! Almost the last, I see!' And she looked out at the almost-full car park. 'The ladies have all been out for all their people and I've still one more to fetch! You'll have to hurry a little, I'm afraid, Mr Etting!' And she got out of the car to bustle around it to help him out.

'It's all right, Mrs Greener,' Abner said hastily and shot out of his side of the car. 'Please, do let me – I can manage fine. Come along now, Cyril – that's it – hold on to me – great – out you come.'

With a good deal of grunting and shoving Cyril Etting emerged from the car like an unwilling cork from a wine bottle and Mrs Greener came round to his other side.

'Well, here we are!' she said brightly. 'I'll just see you inside and then I'll go and get Mrs Snyder and we can start things going for everyone.'

'Oh, don't you worry, Mrs Greener,' Abner said hurriedly. 'I'll see him in, as long as Mr Etting knows the way and – '

'Know the way?' rumbled Etting. 'Does a bird have wings?'

'Not all of 'em use 'em,' Abner said and firmly tucked his hand into Etting's elbow. 'I'll take over, don't you worry, Mrs Greener – and, uh – who should I talk to about staying to – uh, as Mr Etting said, my research.' Why not? he was thinking. The old boy's just having fun stringing her along, but why not? If the place is full of old people like him, who knows what else I might pick up?

Mrs Greener seemed to relax. 'Oh! Well, that's very kind of you, Mr – er – Mr – and if you just have a word with Marilyn Cowan – she's our Chairman this year, you know, it'll be me next year, but this year she's in charge, you just have a word with her. I'm sure she'll – er – do all she can to help. Tell her I've gone for Mrs Snyder, would you? She'll be wondering.'

She went away gratefully and Abner, with Cyril Etting holding on to his arm with fingers that were hard and almost painful against his biceps set out to cross the car park in the direction to which the old man steered him, looking round to see what he could in the darkness.

It seemed an ordinary enough building, like every synagogue hall he'd ever seen at home, the sort of nondescript place that seemed to grow out of the ground without benefit of architect and that slowly degraded into shabbiness from the day it collected its last roof tile. There was a familiar smell too, of dust and old sports shoes and sick children inside it, as they came through a large pair of double doors into a dusty cream and green painted corridor. Just like the *schul* at home.

The old man was laughing beside him, a slow agreeable rumble deep inside him, and Abner said, 'You can be a bit of a bastard, can't you?' And Etting laughed even more.

'So what else is there to enjoy these days? You think I look forward to these silly Saturday evenings they give us once a month? Them and their Friendship Club! I come for the food, not for the company, take it from me. A bunch of grizzling, old — who needs such friends? — Pfui!' And he gave a comprehensively dismissive noise with his tongue behind his teeth. 'All they can talk about is the way their feet hurt and how they're their doctor's sickest patients, he tells 'em so all the time, and seein' they all go to that same doctor, the man has to be one hell of a good liar. Listen, you stay with me. We'll eat what they offer — and it's all right, believe me — and then see if there's one or two of the more interesting ones here. They're not all stupid — just most of 'em. And if there ain't, then you can take me into the town in a cab and we'll have a coffee an' cake at one of the places there.'

'Town?' Abner said, startled. 'That's a bit of a way — '

'Nah, just up the road! Edgware! That's the shopping centre and they've got these places you can get coffee and cake and why not? You can't afford it for me? After all the talking we've done? And still will do?' And he looked sideways at Abner with a very intelligent glitter in his eyes.

'After buying all that Chinese?' Abner was amused again.

'So you grudge me? That I'll have tomorrow, and very nice too. Only don't say nothing about it to these *yachners* here. They think it matters, kosher. You can tell they never went hungry, the fuss they make about kosher — this way. Push the door there. That's it.'

They came into a big open hall full of people and arranged with carefully set supper tables round which groups of elderly people sat glowering at each other in deep hostility, while large numbers of extremely well-dressed women rushed around from one to the other, bearing dishes and baskets of bread and shouting loudly to each other all the time. And Abner stood there with old Etting on his arm, and grinned from ear to ear. He couldn't help it. He was three thousand miles away from home, and here he stood in precisely the same sort of room and with precisely the sort of people he knew best. This might be Edgware, a London suburb, but it was also Newark, New Jersey. In every possible way.

Sixteen

The sense of being at home in a foreign place persisted, rather to his surprise, for in his experience hitherto nostalgia was a fleeting thing. No sooner are you aware of it than the experience has gone.

But that didn't happen, and he sat and watched and listened, having been given gracious permission to do so by the loudest and busiest of the bustling ladies, and wallowed in it all.

They had organised their evening well, he thought. At each of the big round tables there were half a dozen or so elderly people, for whom the supper was ostensibly being held, but in addition to them there were also middle-aged and younger people, members, Abner discovered, of the Ladies' Guild of the synagogue, and their relations. Husbands had been brought along (some of the clearly unwillingly), and sisters and brothers too, and even a few teenagers, who looked very sulky in spite of maternal prodding, and Abner grinned sympathetically at one boy who looked thunderous as his mother urged him to 'Hand round the chopped herring. Simon, you're here to help, not to look like a lost weekend!'

'Here,' he said to the boy quietly. 'Let me. If you slip away I'll tell your Mom you had to go to the phone.' And the boy lit up and handed over the plate and fled, and Abner took himself round the table 'being useful' and thinking how pleased with him his teacher, Mrs Coburg, would have been. She liked her pupils to take care of their elders.

The food was good and plentiful, massive plates of salads and rolls, pickled cucumber and olives, smoked fish and cheeses, and then platters laden with cakes and biscuits. Little changes among Jews, wherever they live, Abner thought, as his plate of chopped herring was emptied with dispatch; he replaced it with a bowl

of coleslaw and made his way round the table again with that.
Give them masses of food and they feel safe and right. No
alcohol in sight anywhere – orange juice and coffee, tea and
Coca-Cola, of course, but alcohol? Who needs alcohol when
there's nosh? In fact, food enough for twice the number of people
who were here. And Abner looked across the table at Cyril Etting
who was steadily chomping his way through a plate piled so high
it was almost spilling off the edge on to the flower-printed paper
tablecloth, and could have laughed aloud. The old guy had all he
needed to make him happy; clearly it was no wonder he was so
willing to come here, even though he plainly despised the
conversation around the table.

Abner couldn't blame him for that. There were three large
middle-aged men, obviously husbands of the ladies of the Guild,
talking loudly over each other about business and working hard
at proving they were the sharpest and most successful of the lot
of them. Abner dismissed them as classic bores and looked at the
others; three old women, with their heads together, gossiping as
hard as they could about everyone they knew; and Abner
dismissed them too. They were having a great time, but it wasn't
one in which he could share. That left, apart from Cyril and
himself, just two others and he looked at them with covert
interest.

One was a tall thin man of indeterminate age; he could have
been one of the elderly to whom the Guild were doing so much
obvious 'good' in inviting them to their supper, or he could have
been a middle-aged relation of one of the ladies; he had a face so
long and thin that the skin seemed stretched over it, and the
bones almost shone through at their high points beneath the eyes
and around the jaws and chin. He had thick, iron-grey hair and a
neatly clipped, grey moustache that looked as though it had been
stuck on as an afterthought, and deep eyes hidden behind thick-
lensed glasses that made him seem quite inaccessible. He had
eaten sparingly and was now sitting with his head inclined
towards his neighbour, the last of the table's complement, a
round-faced and very eager little woman who was talking busily
at him. She had hair of an unlikely red, beautifully arranged in
waves and curls, and was wearing what were obviously very
expensive clothes. The diamond brooch on her collar was just
that, diamonds and not an imitation, and her make-up had the

smooth perfection that came only from application by an expert. She could have been thirty-five in a good light, but her neck, plump as she was, gave her away. About fifty or so, Abner estimated, and watched as she stopped for a breath, giving the thin man beside her a chance to speak.

His voice was louder than hers, and Abner could hear clearly what he said above the underlying rumble of conversation and dish clatter that filled the big room, and he found his ears straining in their direction as he realised just what they were talking about.

'She always said all she wanted was to get her hands on him, make him suffer the way he should,' he was saying. 'God rest her poor soul in peace. I told her it didn't help, that sort of feeling. Revenge, what good does it do you? I was in Israel when they executed Eichmann. Did it make me feel any better? I thought it would, but it didn't. The memory was still there – that don't go away so easy.'

'She told me, after, what he did to them.' The red haired woman shook her head. 'All those years and she never forgot.'

'How could she forget? The child – you saw what the child was like. It took me all the time there was to persuade her to let me arrange a decent place for him. In the home he's better off than he ever was with her. Especially now. She did her best, but how could she do all that was needed? She was ailing herself – I never thought she'd last so long, to tell you the truth.'

'It was hating him kept her alive,' the red haired woman said and sighed. 'I tried to get her to explain to me what it was that she found out, but would she say? Maybe she couldn't say. Her speech was gone, to tell the truth. You know how it is with these stroke people.'

'It was a blessing she went when she did,' the man said. '*Ala va shalom.*'

'I have to agree.' The red head shook dolefully. 'Bad enough she suffered in the camps the way she did. To carry such a load of anger as well – terrible.'

'You can understand it. She knew who he was, remember? Said to me that one day she'd be able to prove it, bring him down with a crash like a tree. That was what she said. Like a great big evil tree. A funny way to put it, I thought. Trees, evil? It don't make sense.'

'She didn't make much sense at all the last few months,' the woman said. 'One way and another. She told me she knew who he was too, but I said to her, so what if you do? What good will it do you to start a great fuss? Get your name all over the papers. Will it make your David, bless him, a different person? Will it make any difference at all? And those were bad times. Maybe he wasn't so wicked as she thought.'

'Not so wicked?' The thin man seemed to rear up as he turned his blank pebble lenses on his companion. 'He sold seventeen people for a bag of apples, for God's sake! How can you call that not so bad?'

'He was sixteen years old,' the woman said. 'Wasn't he? Sixteen years old. A child himself.'

'A man.' The pebble glasses glinted again. 'A man. Listen, did she ever tell you who he was?'

The woman shook her head. 'Tell me? Did she tell you? Sure she didn't. It was the biggest thing she had in her life, that she knew and no one else did. Well, maybe the others that'd been with her.'

Cyril Etting was sitting on the other side of the tall thin man, and Abner, who had been listening as hard as he could, moving his eyes from one to the other to follow the conversation as though he were at a tennis match, suddenly caught his eye. The old man was grinning, leaning back in his chair and grinning sardonically.

'Told you, Abner, didn't I? There's stuff here for you. Eh, Sam?' he said gruffly and nudged his neighbour who turned sharply and glared at him. His eyes shone hugely behind his lenses now, and gave him an ominous air.

'Eh, what?' he said.

'You see my friend over there?' Cyril said, not taking his eyes from Abner's face. 'He makes telly programmes.'

There was a sudden little *frisson* of excitement around the table as they turned to stare at Abner and he frowned, furious with Cyril. This was all he needed!

'He's doing research,' Cyril went on, still staring owlishly at Abner. 'All about the bad years, you know?'

'The bad years?' Sam said, and took off his glasses to polish them. His naked eyes peered helplessly at Abner, small pallid eyes, weak and watery. No menace there at all now.

'The camp years,' Cyril said. 'And the after years, the DP years. The *bad* years! What else could it be?'

Sam put on his glasses, and with them his air of importance and strength.

'Telly films about that? Who needs 'em? What good do they do? They give the anti-semites something to feel good about, and make a lot of our own people cry. I've seen 'em crying, when they thought all they was going to get was a bit of entertainment, a laugh or two. What do you telly people think you're doing?' He glared accusingly at Abner. 'People buy TV sets and licences because they want entertainment. And what do you give them? Holocaust pictures! A fire on your Holocaust pictures! Who needs 'em?'

Abner took a sharp little breath in through his nose. 'Television isn't just an entertainment medium, sir' he began and Cyril said with an odd air of malice, 'Call him Sam. He's Sam Hersh.'

'Mr Hersh,' Abner said after a moment. 'As I said, television is used for a lot of things. Teaching and informing and – '

'And upsetting.' The thin man stood up and his height seemed to dwindle; he wasn't as tall as he'd seemed when he was sitting down. 'Who needs it? Me, I got better things to do.' And he went away, moving across the room towards the corner where a gaggle of the Guild ladies were busily arguing over something.

'What sort of television is yours then?' the red-haired woman demanded and then with a sudden, very sweet smile leaned forwards and held out one plump hand. It was barricaded in rings and when Abner took it, it felt like a toy. 'My name's Singer, Mrs Doris Singer. I'm the past Chairman of the Guild. Just a guest tonight, you understand. It's a pleasure to have you here, Mr-er . . . '

'Wiseman,' said Cyril and beamed proprietorially at Abner. 'My friend, Abner Wiseman. We eat together.'

'With Cyril, you can't get closer than that,' Abner said, with a sudden need to be sharp, and Cyril stared at him and then laughed.

'You got something there, Abner, believe me. A full belly's a full belly. Don't knock it. So tell me, Doris – I can call you Doris?' Mrs Singer inclined her head graciously. 'So tell me, who was this you was talking about? I was listening, you understand.'

He showed no compunction at his admission and Mrs Singer tried to look disapproving but then shrugged.

'Oh, it's no secret,' she said. 'One of our Friendship Club members. Mrs Lippner, Libby Lippner. Died a couple of days ago. The *lavoyah* was yesterday. They're sitting a week's *shivah*, but I was at the *lavoyah* and – '

'*Lavoyah*?' said Abner, struggling a little with the word. He knew he knew it but it refused to identify itself in his memory.

'You're not a Yiddisher fella?' Mrs Singer said with sudden suspicion.

'Of course he is! Look at him! But he's an American. From where do they know?' Cyril said. '*Lavoyah*, Abner. Funeral – what else?'

Abner nodded. 'I'm sorry. I was just a bit – I got the impression she – this lady, rest her soul – I got the impression she'd had a bad time in the war?'

Mrs Singer leaned forwards, rested her round elbows on the table and shook her head dolefully at Abner, clearly all set to enjoy herself greatly and equally no longer interested in being told what sort of television programmes he made. The old women on the other side of the table had stopped paying any attention to them and were again sitting, heads together, gossiping, and the three businessmen, equally bored, had got up and wandered off to smoke cigars in the corner, ignoring the NO SMOKING signs everywhere. There were just the three of them talking, knotted into a tight little group, and Cyril was nodding a little drowsily in the warmth, Abner noticed. Not surprising after eating as much as he had.

'Did she have a bad time? So tell me, who had a good time?' Mrs Singer went on. 'Unless they were lucky and lived here in England or like you, in America.'

Abner blinked. 'Er – I was born in 1956, Mrs Singer. Well after the war.'

She peered at him and then smiled apologetically. 'Of course you were. You get to my age, you begin to forget. For my part, I was just a child at the time myself, a baby. I don't even remember VE day. I was told about it, but I was just a baby.'

There was a little silence and then Abner said tentatively, 'This friend of yours, the one who died – she was in the camps?'

'She wasn't a friend, you understand.' Mrs Singer looked a

little uneasy. 'A member of our Friendship Club is all. But we'd looked after her a long time. She was old – getting on for eighty.' She sighed then, gustily. 'Amazing. All that she went through and then to live to such a good age. Amazing. If it hadn't been for the stroke, she'd be alive still.'

Abner's lips quirked. If it hadn't been for the fact her heart stopped beating, she'd still be here, he thought absurdly and then said, 'What happened to her in the war? She had a particularly bad time, did she?'

Mrs Singer looked at him a little worriedly and then at Cyril, who was now frankly asleep, his chin resting comfortably on his chest, and his breath coming in regular little gusts that made a thick soughing sound. Around them the room still buzzed with chatter, and Mrs Singer threw a comprehensive glance around and then gave herself up to the luxury of an attentive audience.

'Libby Lippner,' she said, with a portentous air, 'was one of the Jews of Cracow.'

Abner looked puzzled. 'There were a lot of Jews in Cracow,' he ventured, after a moment.

'Ah, yes – but only seventeen of them got that special label. Some people called them the "Rats", complimentary you understand, nothing nasty, but all the same, the "Rats of Cracow". Seventeen of them there were. In the end. A few more to begin with, but there were losses. It's understandable, losses.'

'Yes,' Abner said, picking his way carefully, needing to hear more, scared of showing any reaction that might stem the flow of talk. 'Of course. Er – why Rats?'

She opened her eyes wide. 'Because of the sewers, of course! What else should they call them? They called *themselves* that. At first – '

'Ah!' Some light was beginning to dawn. 'They hid in sewers?'

'Then you have heard of them!' she said triumphantly.

'Er – not directly. It's just that – there were other people who hid in sewer systems that I've heard of. In Lvov – '

She nodded vigorously. 'Of course! That was where it all started! They hid in the sewers in Lvov and they did well there! Lots of them got away – lots got caught, of course, but more got away. Came out all pale they did, eyes gone white, couldn't look at the sun. There was babies in the Cracow ones, you know. Born in the sewers they were, and never saw daylight, and when they came to get them they cried more with fear of the light and the sun than of the Gestapo.'

'And this lady, Mrs Lippner, she was one of them?'

Mrs Singer nodded. 'She was one of them. The one who had a baby first. There were three babies born there. That was why they let them in the group. Because they were pregnant and they said the Germans treated pregnant women worst of all. So they took her and her cousin, Leah, and her next door neighbour, Mina — I never knew her other name, Libby never said — and a few others, and they went underground. Can you imagine? Down into the sewers with just a few bits and pieces.'

Abner tried to imagine and couldn't. 'How did they live there? I mean, I've never been in a sewer. I supposed it to be all waterways, but clearly it isn't.'

Doris Springer shrugged. 'I never asked her that. I suppose there were places that were dry. She told me, they had to sleep on the concrete, only she'd managed to wrap a blanket round herself so she had something to lie on.'

She stopped then and her eyes seemed to go blank as she stared back at her memory. 'She told me it was warm,' she said then, unexpectedly. 'Even in winter, it was warm. Damp and dark, she said, but never really freezing. That surprised me.'

'Yes,' Abner said. 'It does sound odd.'

There was a little silence and then he tried again. 'Did — did she tell you how they managed for food?'

Again that emphatic nod. 'Sure she did! It was the first thing I asked her when she told me what happened to her. How did you get to eat, I asked? And she said there was men in the group. Men and boys, you understand. Seven of them were men, six were women, and four were children. Under ten, that is. The men, some of them were children by my reckoning, but by theirs, they were men. Sixteen, seventeen, no more — '

'And what did they do, these men? These boys?'

'Food finders,' Doris Springer said. 'They used to get out, Libby said, using a different manhole each night, and out they'd go and they'd wander around the city, seeing what they could find. There wasn't a lot to be had, anywhere, believe you me, she said. But these men, they found a turnip here, a bit of fish there — sometimes a couple of candles for light and a bit of fuel. Then they could cook it. A bundle of wood and a bit of fish and a turnip and a potato, she said, you get wonderful soup. You know what she told me? She'd had the best sense of them all, because she'd filled her pockets with salt and pepper when they went under the sewers. That night, she wrapped herself in a blanket, she put on six pairs of knickers, she put on two dresses and in all her pockets, salt and pepper. She'd had sense that one, hey? She said to me, she thought – we'll be all right. We'll find food. We'll cook and when the stinking Germans are gone, we'll come out. A few days, weeks maybe, she said, that was what she thought.'

'How long was it?' Abner asked and she looked at him blankly, and then shrugged.

'Till the Germans went away? Never, as far as she was concerned. She had her baby, and so did the others and then it must have been when her baby was about six months old, thin and hungry and she herself, like a stick, still breast feeding and she had no breasts left, like bags of skin, you should forgive the expression, that was what she told me. Empty bags of skin.'

Again there was a little silence broken only by the sound of Cyril's contented breathing, which made an obbligato to the steady rumble of sound from the rest of the room. 'Bags of skin,' Doris repeated, and then without any self-consciousness reached in her bag for a handkerchief and blew her nose.

'What happened when the baby was six months old?' Abner asked quietly and she looked at him and said, 'Hmm?'

'What happened when Libby's baby was six months old?'

Her eyes slid away from him. 'They got caught.'

'Caught – ?'

'The Germans came down and got 'em out, didn't they? Sent 'em all to Auschwitz. Every one of them.' She shook her head, almost in wonderment. 'And she and her baby – they lived, would you believe? There were others, she said, came through as well, but to me it was a miracle. She told me, herself and her David lived through all those months starving in the sewers and then in Auschwitz and lived to get out and be sent to England. It was amazing.'

'And she lived to be almost eighty?' Abner said. 'That's what's so incredible. After so much.'

'Her son, of course, the baby. He didn't do so well.'

'What happened to him?'

'He's in a home, *nebbech*. Sam got him into a home. It was the best thing for him, poor devil. She tried, you know? Libby, she tried to make him right, took him to doctors, got money from us, from the Board of Guardians, from all the funds for the Victims of the Holocaust. Oh, he saw so many doctors! But what can they do? He was marked for life by being a rat in sewers. How could it be otherwise? He takes fits, you understand, and when he's not having fits, he's not – ' She made a face and shook her head. 'It's not nice to talk about. Don't ask.'

'He must be quite old now,' Abner said.

She shrugged. 'Forty-five or so, I suppose. It was all in the Forties, you understand, this happened. Around 'forty-one or two – who knows? Libby had forgotten dates. She never forgot some things, but she forgot dates.'

'Tell me about the man with the apples,' Abner said then, and leaned forwards. 'The man you said was a boy.'

'Just sixteen he was, Libby told me,' she said after a moment. 'Oh, but she hated him!'

'Tell me what he did,' Abner said, and his voice was insistent now. 'Tell me what he did.'

'It was like Sam said.' She looked at him sharply from beneath her brows. 'Do you think it was so terrible? It wasn't right, but a starving boy of sixteen, offered a bag of apples. Probably they never even said they'd do the people any harm – they used to be like that, the Germans. They could put on the charm, you know? The boy, what must it have been like to him? Offered a bag of apples, in the winter-time? Wouldn't you do something bad for such a prize, when you were starving?'

Abner bent his head and stared down at the table-cloth. He was shredding the soft paper beneath his fingers, trying to think honestly about what he would have done.

'I don't know,' he said at length. 'I can't imagine myself in such a situation. Can you?'

She grinned a little crookedly. 'You think I've always been rich, like now?' Unselfconsciously she stroked her expensive dress, and touched her diamond brooch. 'You think I was born to this? Believe me, we were poor, my family. When I was a kid, we were bombed out of the East End, had nothing. My father had to drag us back after the war. A cabinet maker, he was; ended up with his own furniture factory in High Wycombe. I did all right in the end – but I remember well enough, I remember. I can see that a starving boy would do a lot for a bag of apples.'

'He told the Germans where the people were?'

She shrugged again. 'Libby said they caught him. Told him, either we shoot you now or you tell us. What's more, you tell us where the people are you find food for, and we'll give you apples. What sort of choice did the boy have?'

'Libby Lippner didn't see it that way.'

'She said he should have let himself be shot,' she said. 'It's understandable, I suppose. She had a bad life, Libby. What with her David and all. She had no one but him and what was he? Nothing but misery.'

'What happened to the boy? The one who took the apples.'

Again she gave him that sharp little upwards glance. 'That was the thing of it. He went to Auschwitz too, and got out. He's here somewhere.'

He felt the authentic chill of excitement move through his shoulders, down into his chest and into his hands, making them shake, and he slid them off the table into his lap and leaned still further forwards. 'Here? In London?'

'So Libby said. She was always trying to find out what happened to him. She wanted to curse him dead or alive, but she had to know. And somehow she found out. Don't ask me how. She found out, is all I know, so she said. And she said he was doing good for himself. Very good. But she was going to do something to bring him down. Like an evil tree.' She shivered suddenly and then sat up very upright, her chubby shoulders and her round chin with its own ghost beneath it quivering a little. 'Such a subject! I don't want to talk of it any more. Go ask Sam – see what he'll tell you! For my part it's enough – eh, Cyril?' And deliberately she poked the old man in the ribs, and he woke sharply and stared at her blankly and then at Abner.

'You got some good stuff, eh, Abner?' he said then and yawned. 'I told you you would. Listen, how's about that cab and the visit you said you'd take me on, hey? It's getting on, time we was on our way.' And he got to his feet heavily and nodded at Mrs Singer and then at Abner.

'Enough's enough already. It's time to go.' And he turned and began to make his way to the door.

'No!' Abner called him back. 'Not yet. I want to talk some more here – '

Cyril turned and looked at him, and then shook his head. 'They don't want to talk to you, Abner. Leave it alone, already. It's enough for one day. Another time, I'll fix it for you. Maybe. Right now, I want to go to Edgware for coffee. And you can't stay here without me, can you? An' I'm going.'

And he did.

Seventeen

'I'm beginning to have a clearer idea about how it was you survived what happened to you, Cyril,' Abner said, watching the old man demolish a massive slice of strudel. 'You're a stubborn bastard, you know that?'

'You only just realised? Of course! Stubbornness gets you a long way further than heroism.' He pushed away his empty plate and leaned back to look around at the crowded restaurant. 'Now, this I like! The Ladies' Guild, they lay on a nice supper, I grant you, but if you want a bit of life this is the place to be!'

Abner looked round too, at the tables filled with prosperous-looking people, gobbling cake and ice-cream and sucking in buckets of tea and coffee and then back at Cyril, and felt guilt seep into him. If this suburban coffee shop, over-decorated with antiqued mirrors and crystal lights, was his idea of high life, how empty were his days? And he remembered the stuffy, cluttered, chilly little house and looked again at the ersatz brightness around him and felt ashamed.

'I'm glad you like it,' he said. 'And we can do better than this. I'll take you to a few other places, too hmm? What do you say?'

'Is the Pope a Catholic?' Cyril said and lifted his eyebrows at him. 'Sure, I say yes! Mind you, I don't think I got much more for you. To tell you the truth, that stuff Doris Singer was telling you – I never knew it. That was an extra.' He laughed then. 'Like the boy scouts say, you do good deeds, you get paid back. You turned out tonight to bring me some supper and get a bit more out of me, and look what happened! But I can't promise you no such extra rewards another time.'

'I don't do things just for what I get out of it,' Abner said, stung. 'Believe it or not, I made the offer out of – out of – because I just wanted to. Not everybody's out just for themselves, Cyril!'

'No?' the old man said and again gave him that raised-brows stare. 'Prove it.'

'Oh, for God's sake!' Abner almost snapped at him. 'You should know better than anyone! Didn't you come through that hell of a life in the camps, didn't you see how – how heroic people were? And can't you see how much people care for each other, even in little ways? Those women there at the synagogue hall tonight, working their butts off to give a bunch of thoroughly miserable old people a night out, a bit of supper. How can you say that people – '

Cyril leaned forwards, moving ponderously. 'Now, just you listen to me, mister. You got a lot of notions that are very pretty in a boy, not so clever in a grown man. The women at the *schul*? Sure they're good to us old people – us poor things they can patronise, and why shouldn't they be? Never think there isn't as much in it for them as there is for us. They ain't just doing us favours, you know. We make their lives worth living! They've got comfortable husbands they're bored out of their heads with, and grown-up kids who never have time for 'em no more, and no jobs to fill their days, no way to feel important. So what do they do? They start a committee and have officers and elections and chairmen and secretaries and the whole schmear, and suddenly, punkt! They're important, they got something to be busy about. They raise money and they make food – and what can anyone enjoy more than getting food ready for a party? – and they collect us all up and they bustle about, busy busy *geferlich*, the big "I Am" they're being all the time, and we have to be grateful. And you say they're doing it just out of the goodness of their hearts? You're a baby, Abner. I thought better of you.'

'Now, just a minute – ' Abner began, but Cyril would have none of him.

'Nah, it's your turn next. Right now, just you listen to me. You talk about how I saw heroism and goodness in the people in the camps, right? Well, let me tell you there was about as much heroism as that – ' and he spat over his shoulder, a minute bead of saliva that seemed to disappear in the air before it reached the floor. 'There was no heroism! There was scheming and managing and struggling and getting by and doing your best for yourself and your own and to hell with everyone else, take it from me. Do you think all those people in the camps didn't steal from each other, didn't push other people in front of them to get out of the gas chambers, out of the work, out of trouble? Of course they did! That's what survival's about, Abner. It ain't like the movies, where people make monkeys of themselves for stinkin' principles! You people in the films, you want nobility and self-sacrifice and virtue – well, to hell with all that! In real life you do what you have to do to stay alive and to get your share and anyone else's you can get your hands on too, and to the fire with anyone who gets in your way. And if this film you're making don't show that, then you're just another liar, looking for his own glory and using other people's lives to do it. And you're a fool, too. Because if you tell the story the way it really was, and the way it still is, at least you'll get some respect from people like me. If that matters to you. Though why it should I don't know. What the hell good did respect ever do anyone? It's a luxury – '

He caught his breath and then began to cough and Abner moved towards him, alarmed. There were patches of hectic colour in the hollows of his cheeks and his lips had a faintly bluish tinge; but he looked satisfied, even though he was coughing till his eyes watered and people turned to stare.

'Here, have a drop of water,' Abner muttered and Cyril took the glass and sipped and then gasped and relaxed; and slowly the sick colour subsided and his eyes lost their redness and he looked normal again, and he managed to smile at Abner and shake his head ruefully.

'Why can't I keep my mouth shut? I get so busy tellin' other people how to run their lives I nearly finish my own. Making a liar of myself, eh? Being self-sacrificing. Only I'm not. There's something in it for me, of course – proving to you you're wrong. Very satisfying, that is.'

Abner had to laugh and the old man sat and glinted at him and there was suddenly a bubble of accord that seemed to wrap them round in comfort. Abner thought, Hyman, why wasn't it ever like this with Hyman? And at once the bubble burst.

'Well, I'll prove you're wrong. I'll take you to a few other places, just for the fun of it. Not yet – I'm short of cash. But next week I've got a job to do and that'll help. Do you have any special places you'd like to go to?'

'Theatre,' Cyril said promptly. 'I never get to see the theatre. I see on TV all right, but the real thing – '

'TV's real as well, for Chrissakes!' Abner said and then shook his head. 'Goddamn you, Cyril! You have a real gift for making me mad.'

'Then I'm good for you,' Cyril said with great satisfaction. 'Getting mad keeps your circulation going. All right, we'll go to the theatre as soon as you can manage it. Me, I'm free any time. And an Indian restaurant, maybe? There isn't one near enough to my place to get takeaways and I'd like to have some of that – '

'Indian,' Abner said, with resignation. 'OK, I'll see what I can do.'

All through Sunday morning he chewed away at it all in his mind; the story that Doris Singer had told him went round and round in his head as he tried to see how he could use it; for there was no question but that he had to use it. It was too real, too vivid, too true; and then as he was sitting hunched over a cup of coffee at his big round table in the window staring sightlessly out into the street, it hit him. The whole story stank. It had been offered to him secondhand for a start; and that always made everything dubious. There was no way it could be otherwise, of course: Libby Lippner was dead and the only way to get her story was from someone else, but the tale he'd been given had a huge hole in it. And he'd only just seen it.

How the hell did she know what the boy had been offered to shop the people for whom he was finding food? It made a great story, the image of the sixteen year old pretending to be a man, but a scared boy at heart, letting the Germans talk him into revealing the hiding place of his group in exchange for a bag of apples, but it didn't ring true. They didn't have to bribe him into telling all he knew. They just had to threaten him.

And anyway, how could Libby Lippner have known what the Germans offered the boy they'd apparently caught? Did he come back down to the sewers and tell them all, 'Hey, you lot, better get packed up. The Germans are coming to get you all. I swapped you for a bag of apples'? No, it didn't make sense.

But there was something there, of that he was certain. He thought again of Doris Singer and all she had told him and knew as surely as he knew that the coffee in his cup was cooling that she had been as honest as she knew how. She had told him exactly what old Libby Lippner had told her. There had been no guile in that over-dressed, plump little red-head. She had been told the story, believed it implicitly, and passed it on in the way she had got it. And even though he had never seen the dead woman, had never heard of her before last night, Abner was seized with the conviction that she had believed her own story completely. She had somehow become convinced that the boy, whoever he was, had sold her and her child and the rest of her friends for that bag of apples. And because she believed it she had made Doris Singer believe it. Yet he, Abner, could not.

And then he remembered; could hear Doris Singer's voice again, rather thin and nasal, trying to be polite but displaying its raw backstreet origins in every vowel. A comfortable pleasant voice, an honest voice: *That was the thing of it. He went to Auschwitz too, and got out. He's here somewhere . . .*

He's here somewhere in London. That had been the only thing that kept Libby Lippner going until she had her stroke. She had wanted to find out who he was, and she had managed to do just that; and she had wanted to bring him down like an evil tree.

He had to find him, too. Whoever it was that Libby had found, Abner Wiseman had to find. But how? That was the huge barrier that stood before him. How the hell could he get the information he needed from a woman who was dead? A woman who had had only one relation in whom she might have confided, and who was – from all accounts – inaccessible? Damaged in some way. *He takes fits, you understand*, Doris Singer had said. *And when he's not having fits he's not – it's not nice to talk about. Don't ask.*

Well, he was going to ask. Somehow he'd have to, because that was the only way he could see to find out what he needed to know. And that he needed to know it was undoubted. His film was growing in his mind, spreading and shapeless in places, and with ill-defined edges, but at its heart two hard stories. Miriam Hinchelsea's grandfather David, walking all over Europe to find his daughter Barbara; and this story, the tale of the Jews who were the Rats of Cracow, delivered into the Gestapo's hands for a bag of apples. Or so it had been said.

*

He stood in the doorway hovering, and pulling awkwardly at the bow tie he had managed to dig out of his luggage. It wasn't the evening suit they had demanded – who the hell travelled tuxedos these days? – but he'd have to get away with it. It was a very sober bow tie after all, and the suit was a good dark one.

All this had better be worth it, he thought now grimly, looking round the place. One of the medium level London hotels, he decided. This was no Waldorf Astoria or Hyatt Regency; this was a place that people who lived suburban lives imagined was glamorous, a larger version of the Edgware coffee shop to which he'd taken Cyril last night, but no more than that.

But it was full. The ballroom strewn with silver balloons and festooned with blue and white paper streamers had been arranged with tables set for dinner and there was a small area left for dancing. The band on the dais was small and dispirited, playing big band numbers with just three instruments and sounding as tired as they looked, but the people milling around beneath them seemed contented enough. There was a good deal of glitter about the women; hair had been sprayed with it and cheeks and eyelids painted with it, and most of the dresses were sequinned. The men in their well-creased tuxedos, Abner decided, looked as though they'd all put on a good deal of weight since they'd first invested in them; bellies held barely in place with cummerbunds argued with shirts with bulging buttons, and again he tweaked his tie and felt a little less uncomfortable than he had feared he would. He at least had the advantage of being younger and better built than most of this lot.

His eyes moved as he looked around, trying to find the man, and then he spotted him and moved through the crowds towards the glint of his glasses. He'd been less than helpful last night, but who knows? Here clearly he's a big noise, an important person – and he grinned at himself, remembering Cyril's pithy account of the fire that drove the Ladies' Guild – and maybe that would have softened him.

Abner touched his sleeve. 'Mr Hersh? Thank you for leaving the ticket for me.'

The pebble glasses turned and gleamed at him for a moment and then the man managed a thin smile. 'Oh, yes. Mr – Wiseman, wasn't it?'

'Yes. As I say, it was good of you to fit me in.'

'Listen, for this cause I can always take a man's money,' Hersh said, and the smile seemed to grow a little. 'There's no way I get involved with films about the bad times, but I'll get involved with anyone for this cause. It's a *good* one. Listen, I can't pretend you've got the best of tables. A long way from the band, I'm afraid, but you booked late and there's not a lot I can do – '

'That's fine,' Abner said fervently, deeply grateful to be well away from the band. 'It really doesn't matter. I – ah – there aren't many people I know here, being a stranger in town and all . . . ' He smiled winsomely, hating himself for putting on such an act, but it was necessary, after all. 'I'd be glad of the chance to talk to you about this charity. I didn't manage to get all the information when I called you this morning – '

'You were lucky to find me in at all,' Hersh said reprovingly, as though Abner had been pestering him. 'The day of the Ball, you understand. It's the biggest event of our fund-raising year. The money we make tonight keeps Roseacres going for three months at least. The rest we struggle for with covenants and so forth – so as I say, I'm usually gone very early. I had to go back to fetch something my wife managed to forget – ' He looked malevolently over his shoulder at a small woman who looked as though she had been upholstered in acid green sequins – 'So you were lucky.'

'Very lucky,' Abner said, thinking of the forty pounds he had just had to pay for the ticket Hersh had bullied him into buying. He'd only tracked down his phone number and called him to try to find out the name of the home where the son of Libby Lippner was, but Hersh had been implacable. First resistant but then highly opportunist, he'd made it very clear that he only talked to people who needed information of any kind if they supported his pet charity and there was an end of it; and Abner, thinking bitterly of Cyril's dictum that no one ever does anything out of real altruism, had been caught in his trap. If he wanted to know more about the boy and the apples, this was the road he had to go down. Goddammit.

'There's a tombola,' Hersh said now, very brightly, and began to turn away. 'I have to organise things for the raffle – we'll be coming round the tables to sell tickets, so you needn't worry you won't get your chance – so go now and see what you can win. It's all good stuff. It ought to be. We worked hard enough to get it.

You bought one of the brochures? They were hard work too. Melinda! Come and sell Mr – ah – Wiseman here a brochure – ' and he went bustling away leaving Abner to take one of the glossy magazine-sized booklets which were clearly loaded with advertising, and dig out of his wallet another five pounds for the pretty painted teenager with her collecting box held ready. Tonight was going to be ruinous; he'd end up needing every penny of the lousy fee he was getting for that dog food commercial. Dave Shandwick had better come up with some-thing else, soon, he thought bitterly, and moved across to the corner table indicated for him on the table plan, carefully avoiding the tombola where men were waving ten pound notes around with some ostentation, and began to read the brochure. There seemed little else he could do as that awful band went grinding on and on.

'Roseacres,' he read. 'A real Home from Home for the Unfortunate Ones who need constant care. Every Facility, Physiotherapy pool, Expert staff, Single rooms, Kosher food,' – he turned the page gloomily and read on – 'at least a hundred thousand pounds needed every year to make up the deficits left after inadequate local authority funding. We try to charge the lowest fees we can and for some people of course, there can be no fees. Such as long-stay resident Mr David Lippner (see right) a survivor of the Holocaust who – '

Abner sat bolt upright and stared down at the page. The picture was clear enough; a tall thin man in a wheel chair, a blanket over his knees, staring dispiritedly into the camera. The eyes looked blank, but not because they were unintelligent. It was boredom, Abner thought, not stupidity that glazed them. If I can talk to him, maybe I'll find out more. Surely, surely, *surely* his mother talked to him more than she talked to the well-meaning but essentially rather silly Doris Singer? He'd have to make him talk, that was the thing. Make him.

He looked again at the brochure and then smiled. The address of the home was clearly marked. Better than that; there was a small road map to show exactly where in the leafy Cotswolds it was, and a phone number. And he tore out the page and folded it neatly and put it in his billfold, and then slid the remains of the brochure under the table. That had been well worth a fiver, he told himself, and looked then at the menu that was set out on the table in front of him. It read fancy and French, but he knew with every fibre of his being that it would be repellent. He'd rather have a hamburger any day.

And, he decided, he would have just that. He'd got what he'd come for without the trouble of talking more to Sam Hersh, who was now busily marching around on the dais in front of the bored musicians, arranging the table for the raffle and generally looking very important. He was getting his rewards in spades for what he did, clearly, Abner told himself. And I've got mine. Forty-five pounds was a lot to pay for a name and address, but never mind. If it got him what he needed, he'd be on his way. As soon as possible.

Eighteen

As soon as possible turned out to be longer than he'd hoped. First on Monday morning he had to see Dave Shandwick. There were not only too many unanswered questions about the guy himself, there was also information on other matters to be sought, and as much as he ached to get on with the research for the film, he had to get the matter of the funding sorted out first. Or at least, in tandem. So, at nine sharp he was standing outside Dave Shandwick's office door in Bateman Street.

The place was locked fast and a woman sweeping the dirt around on the stairs in a desultory fashion, looked at him owlishly when he asked where Shandwick was.

'Don't ask me, I just clean here. I never sees none of 'em. They just leave snotty notes.' She sniffed unappetisingly and put on a high nasal imitation of a middle-class English voice. ' "Make sure you clean the lavatory well." Bugger 'em and bugger their lavatories. Don't ask me where they are. But I'll tell you this much – none of these lazy sods knows what work is. None of 'em turns up till ten, so far as I can tell. And later.' And she went on stirring up the dirt and making no attempt to actually clear it away.

Abner swore under his breath and went clattering down the stairs again. In New York at this time of day offices were buzzing; in LA they started even earlier, coming in as early as eight-thirty in their jogging clothes or damp from the pool, well before the sun got too hot for comfort. Would he ever get used to the way they did business in this town?

He sat in a sandwich bar in Greek Street, watching the steam from the coffee urns coalesce into greasy droplets on the window, drinking thin coffee and trying to keep his temper, but by ten to ten he had to admit defeat. He was in a foul mood and not fit company for anyone. He'd have to work hard at not getting right up Dave Shandwick's nose.

But all his resolve melted away when he got up the stairs again, because the office was still locked; and he stood there, steaming with irritation, for ten more minutes before at last he heard the whistling below him and saw Dave's stubbled, grey head appear round the bend of the stairs.

'And where the goddammed hell have you been?' he shouted wrathfully as the man arrived at the door, digging in his pocket for keys. 'Christ, man, how do you make a living if you don't start work till the day's half over?'

'Hey, now cool it, cool it!' Dave said good naturedly. 'Where's the sense in me turning up all bright eyed and bushy tailed at nine a.m. when there's no one else ever crawls out of the woodwork till ten? Do me a favour, Abner. What's got into you? I thought we'd got that job all sorted out for Thursday and Friday. What are you doing here now? Not crawling out are you?'

'I don't know,' Abner said, still angry, but simmering down a little. 'Christ man, do you go into hiding over a weekend? How come you've got no answerphone at that fancy pad of yours?'

'Because I don't want to be driven *meshuggah* by guys calling me when I've got my feet up. I reckon to work hard all week and play hard all weekend. I'm not into killing myself for a buck, you know. I choose to take the time – here, listen, Abner, what's bugging you? You look the way you did the day the Mayor's office got shitty, remember? I thought you were going to kill someone – anyone. I don't know what's happened to you today, but don't come taking it out on me. Not an old pal like me.'

They were in the office now and he had snapped on the lights and hit the switch of a coffee maker, after filling it with water from a cooler near the door, and Abner stared at it and thought, that's the first I've seen in an office since I got here, and felt again one of those deep pangs of homesickness. Shandwick caught his eye and laughed.

'Just like home, hey? I can't be drinking the warm tap stuff these people go in for, and as for that French bottled water – Christ, the buggers probably make it themselves. It sure as hell tastes like piss. Listen now, Abner. Calm down and tell me what's got under your skin. You look like you need a bit of attention from a shrink, one way and another. And I'm a good shrink for this business.'

He began to run a coffee grinder and the scent filled the air with even more homesickness and Abner did as he was told, sinking into the armchair at the side of the desk with relief. He was, he discovered, so uptight he could have cried. In fact, he was as close to tears as he could ever remember being since he went into long pants, and that startled him. To get this mad about being kept waiting – it was crazy. It wasn't as though he had any other urgent appointments to go to; why the hell was he in such a state?

Shandwick was clearly telepathic. 'So, why the hell are you in such a state, fella?' He shoved a beaker into his hand and it was full of hot and strong coffee. He sipped it gratefully.

'Jesus, I don't know. It's this whole – I feel like I'm sinking into a bowl of spaghetti, and if I could just get hold of one end I could unravel it, find my way to the edge and be OK. But I just thrash around, falling over names and people, and crazy goings on and – and there's that goddamn girl, and Saturday night Etting made me feel a real shit. I'm not doing this movie just for myself, I swear it. Only I suppose I am. Oh, I feel like hell!' And he leaned back in the chair and closed his eyes against the suddenly very bright light, amazed at his own fluency and the way churning emotion was pushing at his throat, needle sharp.

'Start at the beginning, baby,' Shandwick said. 'Forget this is England where the bastards never talk. This is a corner of the Big Apple and here people say what they mean when they mean it. Here we ain't afraid to let it all hang out, the way the man used to say – start at the beginning.'

Abner took a deep breath. He'd trust him; he'd have to. He needed to talk desperately; hadn't realised till now just how lonely and abandoned he felt, and he sat there with the comforting hot beaker held between his hands, his eyes closed and his head back on the cushion behind him and let the words flow.

He told him all about it. The idea for the movie. The way he felt about what happened to his parents, and particularly about his rage at having been excluded from it for so long.

'They robbed me, Dave,' he said. 'That was my life as well as theirs. I was well fed and comfortable. I had a bed to sleep in at nights and they never did, not in the bad years, and they never let me share the pain. It was mine as well as theirs. They wouldn't share it, so they shared nothing. No pain, no love, not *anything*. I have to make this lousy movie to get it out of my guts. And it won't be a lousy movie, for God's sake. It'll be the best I've ever done, if I can get it going. But everywhere I turn there are mysteries, there are guys here who – who – I can't explain it. They seem to fit together like those dolls from Russia, you know? The babushkas, one inside the other, and every time you think you've reached the big one, there's another on the top they all slip into. I need to know who they all are, and why they're so interested in me and why they don't just put up money instead of wriggling round like eels and – '

'And the girl?' Shandwick said, and Abner opened his eyes.

'The girl?'

'You mentioned a girl. I think maybe that's even more important. It usually is.' Dave grinned crookedly so that his sagging cheek muscles bunched and he looked like a chipmunk. 'That's why I gave up love, Abner. I go in for sex in a big way – a very big way, take it from me – but love? Forget it. You don't just hit a bit of trouble when you get into love. You hit the mother lode.'

'The girl,' Abner said after a moment, trying not to tell him, but knowing it was too late for discretion. 'Miriam Hinchelsea. Lives in Oxford. Her mother was in the camps. It's the craziest thing – I wanted to talk to this very high-toned English Professor of History and what do I find but a fellow traveller. He'd married a girl from the camps, so her mother had a lousy time too. But she told her daughter all about it. And the girl is one screwed-up lady – '

'And you're leching after her,' Dave said and lifted his brows at him cheerfully.

'That's a hell of a way to put it!'

'OK, I'll try the English way. You fancy her. You want to get into her pants.'

'That', Abner said, 'is sure as hell not English. Shut up!'

'Oh boy, but you've definitely hit that mother lode,' Dave said and got up to pour him some more coffee. 'It's worse than anything I said. You're in love, mister. God help you.'

'Yeah,' Abner said, and closed his eyes again. 'God help me.'

There was a little silence and then Dave said, 'Who's Etting?'

Abner pulled himself up, slopping the hot coffee on to his thigh and ignoring the pain. 'What the hell do you know about him? Ye gods, it's getting worse! Now *you* know about people that . . . '

'All I know is that you mentioned him a few minutes ago,' Dave said mildly and reached for Kleenex and gave a sheet to him, jerking his chin to indicate the wet patch on his trousers that needed rubbing. Abner took it and bent his head to pad away at the damp, not because he cared about it, but because he was so ashamed of his sudden surge of suspicion.

'You see how it is?' he mumbled. 'I've got so I'm watching my own shadow to make sure it doesn't screw me. Etting's a crazy old guy – I like him a lot. I got his name from a list my mother sent over from the club she goes to in Newark. It's for Holocaust survivors. I went to see him and – well, I fell for him. He's an incredible man. Greedy as all get out – hoovers up food like a gannet – and as sharp as they come. Saturday night I was with him picking up another incredible story and – he said things that made me feel bad.'

'Like you're exploiting your folks because you want to make this film?'

Abner lifted his chin sharply. 'I don't think he meant that, exactly – ' he began.

'But you've been thinking something like it ever since, hmm? What did the old guy say?'

Abner put down the Kleenex and began to sip at his coffee. Already he was feeling better, more relaxed. 'Oh, it was general stuff really – about there being no such things as heroes or martyrs, that everybody does what they do out of self-interest. That no one, but no one, ever acts with true altruism. He didn't say that in so many words, but it was what he meant. I felt like a shit. Still do. Look at how I was last night. Went to a charity fundraiser, complaining inside my head all the time because it was costing me money I can't afford, and as soon as I got the information I wanted, to see me further on with my research, I got the hell out of there for fear I'd have to spend more money.'

'That's not the only reason you skedaddled,' Dave said. 'I can't think of any normal guy who spends more than five minutes at a charity fundraiser unless his wife has made him do

it. Or unless he wants to show all the other fellas on his patch
how much richer and more generous he is than they. You're
getting too soft, Abner. Christ, it was because you were so soft I
loved you. That movie you made, *Uptown Downtown*, that was
real bleeding hearts stuff, but you believed it, so it worked. It
didn't stick in my throat like cheap candyfloss. It's the best thing
you've got as a movie maker, that tender skin of yours, but hold
on and don't peel off any more layers. You'll get too soft and
make yourself useless. It's no sin to skip out on a fundraiser. It's
no sin to make a film because you want to do it, and to make
yourself feel better about your folks. What sort of movies do
people make when they don't have anything they care about to
say? They make "Who Killed Roger Rabbit?" and "Superman" – '

Suddenly Abner laughed, choking a little into his coffee. 'They
make money, you mean?'

'Yeah,' Shandwick said a little wistfully. 'They make money
like a horse makes shit. But all the same – there's more to life
than money.'

'Is this Dave Shandwick I'm talking to?' Abner managed to
sound ironic. 'The guy who spent all his time liberating this and
that because he couldn't bear to put down hard cash for it?'

'Ah, that! That's for fun, not for profit! At least, not just for
profit. It's the wheeling and dealing and making it happen I go
for. If it was only money I was in for, wouldn't I have an
answerphone at home, be in here crack of dawn every day to
make even more? Sod that for a life! I go for balance, baby,
balance. I have fun making it happen, schlepping the shekels my
way, but it don't figure that big in my life, whatever I might
pretend. You, you get your rocks off on opening up your heart
and emptying it on to celluloid and you make sonofabitching
magical movies because of it. Don't ever knock the reasons you
have for doing what you do. It's no crime.'

Abner stared at him. Dave's crumpled face had gone pink and
his eyes were bright as he stared back and Abner felt his own face
redden.

'Well, hell, Dave, thanks a lot,' he said at length. 'You've been
– well, you were right. I needed to talk. Thanks a lot – '

'Same hour next week, leave the check for half a grand with

my nurse, send in the next patient *if* you please!' Dave said, but he was pleased, and they both knew it.

'Listen, Dave,' Abner said then. 'This isn't why I came to see you, you know. I had other things I wanted to talk about.'

'Sure,' Dave said, assuming an air of businesslike alertness. 'Talk away.'

'These guys I keep barking my shins on — maybe you know more about them than I've been able to find out. OK, if I run a few names past you?'

'Sure! Glad to help,' Dave said promptly. 'I know most of the people in the trade in London. Not all, mind you. There are some very funny ones. Porn and so forth. Not my scene, never was. Even when I was a kid. I like my sex personal, know what I mean? Can't be doing with these one-handed movie merchants.'

Abner nodded 'OK. Monty Nagel.'

'Agent. Straight up guy, got a great list. I should be half so successful as he is and I'd be twice as happy,' Dave said promptly.

'Really straight?'

'I never heard otherwise. Doesn't take on a client he can't work good for, you know? Some of 'em take anybody and leave them to rot if nothing happens from it. Nagel's not that sort. He's got the reputation of putting himself about for his clients.'

'What about his financing?'

'How do you mean?'

'What I say. Does he use other people for finance at all? Is the business he runs all his own? Or does he have sleeping partners?'

Dave grimaced. 'This I can't know. How could I? You'll have to ask him. Are you joining his list?'

'I'm supposed to be. If he agrees. I reckon he will. I'll call this afternoon. He's been out of town — '

'Then ask him. In my experience he's an honest enough guy. Ask him right, and he'll tell you.'

'He's been good to me so far,' Abner admitted. 'Gave me other contacts to use even before we had a deal. I could screw him easy.'

'Exactly,' Dave said. 'That's the sort of reputation he's got. You could go further and fare worse, take it from me.'

'OK. Victor Heller.'

Dave sat silently for a while, staring at him, and then said slowly, 'Heller's a round-the-edges sort of guy. I've bumped into him here and there. Always seen with people in the know, you understand me? I've never heard of him ever actually doing anything direct. But there he is at the BAFTA awards every time, and at all the industry events. Looks nothing much, but he's always around, you know? Tell you what, you find out anything about him and I'll be interested to hear. He's a puzzle to me too.'

Abner nodded and then said, 'Eugene Garten,' watching Dave carefully.

The result was a dead blank. He turned down the corners of his lips and shook his head. 'Doesn't ring any bells with me.'

'Says he's a film publicist.'

'Oh!' Dave's face cleared. 'Then maybe. The town's crawling with *them*. They're the fleas on the industry's ass.'

Abner laughed. 'They're not all bad news,' he said. 'Are they? Someone has to get a movie talked about to get the mugs in.'

'Oh sure, but there's talking and talking. There're one or two big companies in the business I like, and I'll recommend 'em to you when the time comes. Just ask me. But watch out for the solo operators, the little guys. If this is one of them, he's the last thing you need.'

'That was my reaction. And then, of course, there's Jo Rossily. I liked her – do you know her?'

Dave nodded. 'Everyone does. Great distributor, gets involved in all sorts of things other people don't like. Feminist, you see. All those red hot bra-burning movies, that was how she got started. Now she deals with a lot of rather more sophisticated stuff.'

Abner frowned. 'When people say sophisticated they usually mean porn. I didn't take her for one of those.'

Dave threw his head back and roared as though Abner had made a great gag. 'Jo Rossily and porn? Christ, that's the funniest idea I've ever heard! No way, baby! I mean *sophisticated* – stuff from Czechoslovakia, France, Germany – the sort of movies that get their BAFTAs at the start of the evening before all the interesting stuff gets going. Last year she had a winner with a Japanese movie they say made a fortune. In Japan. Here it was zilch. But she gets by.'

'That makes sense,' Abner said. 'I didn't see her as at all – as anything but straight up.' He frowned then. 'That reminds me.

There was one name that I wanted to ask you about – not anyone I've met but it seems to keep coming up. He turned out to be her partner, Mayer – Matthew Mayer.'

Dave looked at him sharply. 'What about him?'

'Well, yeah. *What* about him? Like I said, I keep on hearing his name, seeing it too. Monty Nagel had this great list of contacts on his computer and I saw it and over and over again this guy was there. Never a principal, always in the second row, you know?'

'It's not unusual in this business,' Dave said, and bent his head. 'In fact it's – um – common.'

'Well, sure. Lots of people have sleeping partners. But not all the same one! This fella seems to be sleeping with Jo Rossily and God knows who else besides. I don't suppose he's the only one though. There was this guy Venables – '

'Alex Venables?'

'You know him?'

'Oh, sure I know him. Front man, no more. Deals in financing films. But never acts on his own.'

'That's what happens with all of them,' Abner said disgustedly. 'I saw a guy called Gentle, Simmy Gentle. I reckoned I had him on toast and what happened? He backed down all of a sudden because of his money man. Said he didn't like it – and it turned out that his partner, the guy who didn't like the project Gentle thought was great, was Victor Heller.'

Dave shook his head. 'Oh, come off it! He isn't Simmy Gentle's man! Everyone knows who that is.'

'What?'

'I said, Simmy Gentle's partner ain't this Heller. I told you, he's just a schlepper, a hanger on, a gofer. No, the real one's someone quite other.'

Dave seemed to be beginning to enjoy himself and Abner felt irritation rise in him. He wanted straight answers, not this runaround.

'Well, who the hell is it, then?'

'The same as Jo Rossily's partner. The same as more businesses in this town than you can shake a stick at. Matthew Mayer, that's who.'

Nineteen

'Just make sure you get to that dog food shoot on time,' Dave said. 'It's all I ask. And when you fill up, use unleaded. Me, I'm one of your up-to-the-minute guys. Had the engine fixed soon's I could. You got a map?'

'I'll get one,' Abner said. 'Listen, Dave, this is very good of you – '

'Good, hell! Like the man said, what's a pal for? You need a break. I don't need the car for a couple of days, so it's all easy.'

'And thanks for fixing the date with Mayer,' Abner said, and got into the car. It felt odd to be sitting on the wrong side, but he'd get used to it. He was getting used to a lot in this country. 'Maybe *he* can help me get *Postscripts* moving properly. It just doesn't make sense. People get interested and then they – '

'Yeah. You told me,' Dave said, and slammed the door on him. Abner rolled down the window. 'Now listen. You make a left on to the roundabouts and you don't get priority on the red lights for a left. Don't forget that. And – '

'Dave, I've been driving more than half my life. It can't be that different here. If it's going to worry you, then I won't take the car.'

'Aw, shut up. Take it and enjoy it. I was just trying to tell you, is all! I hope this guy in the Cotswolds comes up with useful stuff. No harm even if he doesn't. It'll give you a chance to relax. It's a nice sort of area to see. You'll like it. Looks like an ad for Hathaway shirts, know what I mean? Cute. On your way, buster. See you when you bring the dog food home.' He stepped back and very carefully Abner started the engine and moved the car out of the cramped little car park and made for the exit, very aware of its anxious owner watching him. And he couldn't blame him; the car was a handsome black Rover upholstered in thick crumpled leather and with a polished wood dashboard; not quite an antique but a much-cherished old one. It was extraordinarily good of the guy to let him have the use of it for a couple of days; and he took a deep breath as at last he was out into the street.

A crazy sort of morning, he thought, as carefully he made his way through the heavily clotted traffic towards Shaftesbury Avenue. That seemed the right end of Soho to aim for and he'd stop off as soon as he got home to Camden Town and get a road map and work out how he was to get out of London to the Cotswolds, wherever that was. And maybe pick up some chocolate; he'd forgotten how much he liked eating chocolate while he drove, and he had a sudden memory of pushing a car through the grid of Manhattan in much the same sort of heaving reeking traffic as this, and felt a surge of excitement; he was here in Europe, in London. He was at the wheel of a car in the middle of one of the greatest cities of the world. It made him feel sophisticated and aware of himself in a way that was new to him. And it was comforting. Because he'd sure as hell had made a fool of himself this morning with Dave. To have lost his temper so crazily – who needed that sort of behaviour? He must have lost his marbles there for a moment; and he grinned as the British expression slid into his mind. Another few weeks here and he'd be speaking the local lingo like a native.

At his apartment – and he took an almost juvenile delight in the way he'd managed to work out the route without going too hopelessly astray – he collected a few things to take with him, shaving gear (and again memory pushed at him and he thought – Miriam. Maybe I can use the car to get down to Oxford, too? That was a very pleasant thought) and a clean shirt and some of his dwindling supply of cash. He'd have to contact his American bank and draw on some of his special reserves. He hadn't intended doing that when he'd come to London for that National Film Theatre lecture. He'd had it all worked out that with them paying his airline ticket he'd be able to keep his costs low. He'd been pretty confident that he'd have his business sewn up fast, and have a budget he could work with. He hadn't been certain he'd get his film set up, of course he hadn't. But he'd been *almost* certain, and it rankled now to think how wrong he'd been.

But he brightened then as he locked up the apartment and went down to the street, then stopped, thought and went back up again, and picked up the phone.

'Mr Nagel's in a meeting,' the girl said in a bored voice. 'Perhaps you could call back later – '

'No.' Abner said firmly. 'Going out of town. Tell him Abner Wiseman. He wanted me to call him today.'

The girl sniffed and there was the usual electronic music on the line (God, but he hated that) and then Nagel's voice, a little thick and slow.

'Well, Abner! I hear you've been putting yourself about a bit!'

'How do you mean?' At once Abner was alert.

Nagel laughed. 'What should I mean? Just that I know you've been busy, a real credit to yourself. People have told me. Taking up all the suggestions I gave you.'

'They haven't done me a lot of good,' Abner said a little bitterly. 'I got hopeful there once or twice but when it came to it there was always a reason why people pulled out. Listen, Mr Nagel – '

'Monty. Why so formal?'

'OK, so Monty, I'm getting a bit sore, you know? Everywhere I turn there's obstacles, and I can't see why – '

Nagel made a tutting sound. 'Oh, come on Abner! You're no baby in this business. You know as well as I do, these things take time. How many deals get to the edge after years of finagling and then go down the tubes? More than ever get finished, that's for sure. You should know that better than most.'

'Of course I know it. But I also know the difference between deals that fold from natural causes and those that don't.'

There was a little silence and then Nagel said, 'How do you mean, natural causes? And what's different about what's happening to you?'

'Oh, it's hard to explain!' Abner said and shifted the phone to his other ear, suddenly aware that he'd been pressing it so hard against his head that he ached. 'It's just this feeling I keep getting that people are deliberately holding me back. That there's interest in the idea – a hell of a lot of interest – but that for whatever reason there are some people who just want to make it difficult for me. Gentle and Venables and – '

'Imagination, old boy. It's just that people have to be careful with their money these days! Times are hard, you know that, and getting harder – '

'And yet at the same time everyone's saying there's lots of money about and plenty of opportunity on account of the way the satellite channels are opening up and – '

'Well, yes. But isn't this the most paradoxical business in the world? Isn't that why we love it so much? We're not making hammers and nails and mousetraps, you know. We're making movies, bits of people's hearts.'

'Very poetic, Monty,' Abner said. 'At the same time we're in a business which wants to make money. It has to make money, for God's sake. You as much as anyone – are you still interested in taking me on?'

'Are you willing to work with me is the question,' Nagel said. 'You sound pretty angry one way and another. You seem to think the people I sent you to are some sort of – I don't know – swindlers, maybe. I can't say I feel that – '

'Oh, hell! I'm not blaming you.' Abner fanned the pang of compunction that had lifted in him, wanting to be ashamed of his suspicious feelings. Maybe this was just the way people were in this town. 'I suppose I'm getting a little dispirited. Still, it's getting a bit better. Met an old friend from the States. Working here as an agent. He's – ' He stopped himself just in time, remembering the possible illegality of working without permits. 'He's put a bit of useful stuff my way. And he's fixing a meeting for me with Matthew Mayer.'

Again there was a little silence. 'Is that a fact?' Nagel said then. 'Who did you say fixed that?'

'I didn't. But I will. His name's Shandwick, Dave Shandwick. Runs a small agency in Bateman Street.'

'Shandwick – oh, yes, I know. Crew guy, yes.'

'You got it. He was my sound man on *Uptown Downtown* years ago. Very good too. It's not easy on these city locations. Noisy – and he was a great fixer.'

'From all I hear he still is. And if he fixed for you to see MM he's a pretty good fixer indeed.'

'MM? Oh, Mayer. Why?' Abner sharpened. 'Is he so big a noise that – '

'Oh, no, it's not that.' Abner could almost see the shrug. 'Hell, no. It's just that he's a real background man, you know? Never got involved in making a film in his life, not really. He just handles money and the background stuff. I can't see why you'd bother to meet him. He can't do you any good. And why he'd use time for you. He's just a number type, you know. Doesn't give a damn about what the product is – he's just a buyer and seller. That's all. He likes money, not movies.'

'Then why is he involved in so many film businesses? I saw his name on your computer over and over again. If he's into money, he should be selling those hammers and nails and mousetraps. You know where you are with that sort of stuff. Not like this business – you can lose a fortune overnight.'

'And make one,' Nagel said drily. 'I reckon that's the attraction. Anyway, like I said, seeing him won't get you anywhere.'

'Well, I'm not so sure. Gentle told me his partner was Victor Heller, but according to Dave it's really this Mayer guy. So, since Gentle turned me down when he'd started out being all interested and excited and then tells me it's because of his partner, and lies to me about who this partner is, well, naturally I'm interested.'

Again that invisible shrug. 'Well, it's up to you if you want to waste your time – '

'What else can I do?' Abner said. 'I don't seem to be getting anywhere with anyone else. Maybe this one can make it work for me.'

'You don't need him,' Nagel said. 'Not if you join my list – and I'd be happy to have you.'

He felt better; he couldn't help it. 'Well, thanks. It certainly is useful to know someone takes me seriously.'

'Oh, they all do, believe me. It's just like I said, these things don't always work out so easy to start with. Then they will. Listen, let me see you, hmm? Come in, let's go through the people you've seen, work out where you stand and we'll go on from there. When can you make it?'

'Well, Dave Shandwick's lent me a car and I want to make the most of it, do some research, talk to someone who lives in the Cotswolds. I've only got it for today and tomorrow, returning it Wednesday morning. Could I come in then? I'm – er – tied up Thursday and Friday.'

Nagel gave a little crack of laughter. 'One of Dave Shandwick's little jobs on the side, hmm? Well, make sure he pays you at least half the rate for the job. When are you seeing this Mayer guy?'

'Wednesday afternoon.' Abner stopped then, a little puzzled. 'You don't actually know him? Mayer, yourself? The way you said that made it sound like – '

'Mmm? Oh, I've met him. There aren't many people in this business I haven't. But I don't have much to do with him. Why should I? Like he said, he's only the background for the people who really do the work. No big deal.'

'Oh.' Abner felt a little crestfallen. 'I thought maybe he'd be a source of funding. After all, he's Gentle's partner as well as Jo Rossily's and – '

'Oh, Abner, Abner! You really don't have to believe all you hear! Dave's leading you on, you know? I dare say MM's got a few bob in Gentle's operation, but it's Heller who's the real power there.'

'He's a friend of yours, isn't he?' Abner said then, as casually as he could. 'I met a guy called Garten and he told me that you knew him.'

'Who told you?' The voice was sharp.

'Garten. Says he's a film publicist. Contacted me, told me he'd be glad to help in my research and said he'd been tipped off about *Postscripts* by Heller, and then said Heller was a friend of yours.'

'Jesus, this sounds like a telephone directory you're reading to me,' Monty said fretfully. 'What do I know of this Garten? I never heard of him.'

'Never?'

'Well, possibly! Ye gods, Abner, what do you want of my life? I've told you, I know a lot of people in this business and even more of 'em know me. I'm a big noise, you know? Not exactly Morton Janklow or whatever that big New York guy's called, but big all the same. Is it any wonder people push my name about? Why put me through some sort of third degree over it? So, you're having troubles setting up your movie. Stick with me and you won't find it so tough. I make no promises, of course, but I have good hopes for you. It's a good project and it'll work. But don't go giving me any *mishegass* nagging. I can't take it.'

Abner stood silent for a while and then nodded, knowing it was an absurd action as part of a phone conversation, but still doing it. 'OK. Maybe. I guess you're right. I'm sorry, I've just got so – '

'Yes, I can tell. So stop it. Go down to do your research, whatever it is, what is it, by the way? What sort of information will you find about the camp people in the Cotswolds, for pity's sake? That's real Ye Olde Englishe countryside, you know? Can't imagine any camp survivors living there.'

'Oh, you'd be surprised. There's a Home there. For people who are handicapped one way and another. There's a fellow whose mother went into hiding in a sewer, gave birth to him there. He's been so damaged by it all that he's in this Home now. It's an extraordinary story. I heard about what happened to the mother – it's got to be a major strand of the film. But the woman's dead and I can only talk to this son. I'm just hoping he won't be too damaged to be of some use. Hell, I don't mean to sound that cynical – '

'I'm sure you didn't. Listen, take it as read. You're a decent guy with an honest heart and no intention of ripping anyone off. OK?'

Abner felt himself go pink. 'Hell, you see what's happened to me? I've got so defensive, I just don't know. Anyway, I'll let you know Wednesday how I got on. And Monty – '

'Yeah?'

'Thanks for taking me on. You won't regret it.'

'I don't intend to,' Monty said. 'Wednesday then. Have a nice day.' And the phone clicked in Abner's ear.

Twenty

He drove out of London via the Marylebone Road, climbing to the crest of the motorway at its western end with a sense of elation that made him feel like a boy again, and settled down for the long straight run the map had shown him lay ahead. He had found the radio on the dashboard and was playing BBC Radio Three, and the Haydn concert that it was offering added a sense of peace to the elation, so that he felt better than he had for a long time. He sat there behind the wheel watching the roofs beside the road flash by and thought, Dave was right. It did help to talk about bad feelings. He was still ashamed to remember how badly he'd behaved this morning, but it seemed like another life now. Everything had changed since then. Now he was one of Monty Nagel's clients officially, and the combination of the sense of real involvement, at last, that that gave him and the relief that had come from pouring out all his feelings worked as powerfully in him as the gas did in the Rover's engine. And, of course, he had wheels. That was almost the most exhilarating thing of all. In his teens he'd been crazy about cars and though he'd outgrown the passion, there were enough remnants of it left to make this trip in a powerful, elegant vehicle through the early afternoon of a hazily sunny February day feel good.

The suburbs came and went, streaming past him in a very North American way; this could be any of the turnpikes at home, with factories linked by low cost housing and used car lots and service stations, all sewn together into a continuous necklace with billboards; but then the buildings became more occasional and fields began to show themselves between naked spidery trees and rough bushes and he could see the shape of the land itself, and it was not at all American, and his sense of well-being moved up another notch. He'd seen hardly anything of

England yet but London, he told himself; this should be a great afternoon, whatever happened when he got to Roseacres, and he looked around as carefully as he could, consciously registering all that he saw, carefully storing it into his memory. Maybe he'd need it one day for a movie, another movie, the one that might emerge long long in the future, post *Postscripts*.

He glimpsed a tall obelisk with a carved eagle on it, a surprising object to find at such a place, he thought, and on an impulse took the next exit so that he could pull off the road to look at it; and was almost unbearably moved. It was the Polish War Memorial, a record of the men of Poland who had died as serving members of Allied forces during the war; and he read all of the names aloud, one after the other, stumbling a little over the pronunciations, and then got back into the Rover and made the complicated turns necessary to get back on to his road, feeling even more certain that his film had to be made. And made well. He owed that to so many people. He wasn't going to make any reference in it to dead Polish pilots or navigators, but all the same, they were part of it. A war from half a century ago still affecting lives today, he told himself. That's what it's all about. My piece of it is the people of the camps. Theirs was what happened when Germany invaded their homes. The difference is huge, but negligible too. I must make my story *right*. Please God, let this fella at 'Roseacres' have something to tell me.

The road went on swooping between grey-green fields dusted with the thin gold of the sunshine and past muddy green pastures where cows wandered and he felt the shape and look of it all seep into him. Such small fields; such neat little houses. He had seen something like it before here in England, of course he had; how could he have forgotten the train journeys to Oxford? But this looked different; better, because the sides of the road were clean, not littered with garbage and wrecked buildings the way the sides of the railroad lines had been, and he whistled softly between his teeth as the road dipped into a miniature chasm and then opened out to a sprawling softly curving landscape again. He was having a wonderful afternoon.

The road he was on bypassed Oxford, taking him west towards Cheltenham, according to the signboards, and he relished the sound of the name of the place on his tongue, murmuring it aloud, Chel-ten-ham. It was a way of keeping his mind away from how close he was to Oxford and, therefore, to Miriam. It would be very easy to go back to the last roundabout, which had indicated Oxford off to the left, and take that road. He'd find her at home, sure to, and then they could . . .

But he pushed all that aside with resolution, and again said the name of the place the road was going to; Chel-ten-ham, and after a while, pulled over to the side to consult his map again.

'Roseacres' was just outside a small place called Burford. He peered at the map and worked out the road numbers and then set off again, and less than half an hour later pulled over again to stare at the place he had found.

Burford ran before him in one long street falling gently from a small hill, a street that was wide and handsome, lined with greyish-yellow stone-built houses and shops that were quite the most pretty he could remember seeing. This place looked like some sort of calendar, for God's sake, or those jigsaw puzzles the grandfather of one of his childhood friends had been addicted to. The trees that lined the street were tall and elegant; the shops were attractive, the people walking along beside them comfortably dressed in warm country clothes and he took a deep breath of sheer pleasure as he looked at it all.

He stopped at a pub halfway along the main street of the town and ordered a half pint of beer and one of those ploughman's lunches he'd learned to enjoy, and they brought it to him beside a big, open log fire. Abner sat there and ate and drank and let himself think of Miriam. How could he fail to think of her, when they had shared just such a lunch the first time they'd met? Around him the pub murmured gently as the few people there talked quietly, and the fire crackled a little and then hissed in a companionable fashion; his sense of contentment increased and bubbled in him until it reached his head, and he thought, I can call her. I can't be this close to her and not call her, can I? And it was as though he heard Dave's voice again: *Oh boy, but you've definitely hit that mother lode*, it said cheerfully, *It's worse than anything – you're in love, mister. God help you.*

Yeah, Abner had said. *God help me.*

Well, was he? He didn't know. He'd found girls before he'd cared about, a great deal for one of them. Frances had been – well, never mind. But this girl was different. How could you tell if you were in love with someone as sulky, as awkward, and altogether as unpredictable as Miriam Hinchelsea? And he closed his eyes against the brightness of the fire and tried to reach the inner side of his mind, to find the answer there, and couldn't.

Instead he got to his feet and went to find the phone. Calling her was a must. He had to do it.

'Where?' she said when he tried to explain. 'Oh, God, Burford? Right in the middle of the tourist trap.'

'It's a lovely spot,' he protested. 'Pretty and charming and – '

'I've heard people say the same about Disneyland,' she said. 'Still, if you like it.'

'I didn't come for the scenery,' he said then. 'I'm doing research. I've discovered that there's a camp survivor – well, in a way, though he was a baby. Anyway, there's someone who may be able to give me some information. He's in a home, the other side of this place. I'm on my way there. I thought, could we meet afterwards, and have dinner? Here, perhaps? They seem to have a restaurant.'

'In Burford?' she said, and there was a jeer in her voice. 'No, I don't think I can handle that. I loathe Burford. I know somewhere that's even more Disneyish, if you fancy it. More like Brigadoon, really.'

'Brigadoon?'

'My father always said that it was too pretty to be true. That it probably disappears when no one's there, and only turns up again when people look for it. I could see you there, maybe. That's got a pub with a restaurant.'

'Anywhere you say.' He was absurdly elated. And grateful and excited. 'Anywhere at all.'

'It's called the Old Swan. At Minster Lovell. Anyone'll direct you if you can't find it on the map. It's *old* Minster Lovell you want, by the way. There's another place, same name, not so fancy. The pub's at the start of the village street. I'll call them and book a table. See you there around seven-thirty or eight. I'll pay for myself.' And the phone clicked and went dead even as he opened his mouth to argue with her.

Well, he could sort that out later; right now he had an exciting few hours ahead of him dealing with David Lippner and then he'd meet her; and he whistled softly as he paid his bill and went out into the amber afternoon.

*

'Roseacres' managed to look even better than the photograph in the charity brochure and that cheered him. He knew only too well how creative photography could make the dingiest of places look passable. This place, however, looked genuinely attractive, whereas the photograph of it on the torn sheet that Abner held in his hand was bleak and rather uncompromising. He parked the car cheerfully and made his way round a crunching gravel path to the entrance.

The woman who answered the door showed no surprise when he asked to see David Lippner. She opened the door wider and invited him in with a silent inclination of her head and then said, 'If you'd wait here a moment please,' and went padding away, leaving him to look about.

Some of the charm he'd felt outside at the sight of the rose-red brick building sitting in the middle of its well-trimmed lawns dissipated. There was an undoubted institutional air about the place; wheelchairs were parked against one wall of the hallway in which he was standing, and there was a long set of hooks on the wall on which coats and walking sticks were hanging untidily. The floor was covered in a heavy oilcloth, which looked scuffed, and the stairs were carpeted in the sort of heavy, dark drugget he remembered from his school days. There was a smell of disinfectant and urine in the air, a queasy mixture that was again familiar. The latrines at summer camp had been a bit like that.

A man in a high-buttoned white coat that made him look like an advertisement for toothpaste came bustling along the corridor into which the woman had disappeared, and nodded affably at him.

'You've come to see one of our residents? We don't usually have visitors except at weekends, but, of course, we don't make any restrictions. Only too glad when people take an interest – some of our people sadly never see anyone from outside.'

'I should have called first, maybe,' Abner said, a little alarmed. Surely there'd be no problems over seeing the man? It hadn't occurred to him that there might be. 'It was just that I happened to be in the area and – '

'You're an American,' the man discovered and beamed, and Abner smiled back, glad to use his status as a foreigner in any way that was useful. 'Well, fancy that! It's so exciting when one of our residents hears from relatives from so far away.'

'I'm – er – ' Abner began and then stopped. If that was the assumption the man wanted to make, why argue with him? He'd let something like this happen before, after all. 'I'm grateful you don't mind me coming at an awkward time.'

'Oh, it's not awkward,' the man said sunnily. 'All of the older ones like a little *schloof* in the afternoons, you understand. But for a visitor from America – well, I dare say whoever it is won't mind. Who do you want to see?'

'David Lippner,' Abner said. 'If he – '

The man's brows snapped down at once. 'David? But no one ever visits David! I mean, not since his poor mother died, *ala va shalom* – I thought he didn't have any relations apart from her.'

'Oh, you're right,' Abner said hastily. 'I didn't say I was related. But his mother, rest her soul indeed, was ah – ' He swallowed. Why was it so hard to tell a lie in such circumstances? One of these days he'd learn to be as crooked as everyone else.

He didn't have to lie. The man's face cleared at the obvious distress he recognised on Abner's face. 'You were a friend of his mother? There, there, don't upset yourself. It happens to us all, and it was for her a happy release, they tell me. David took it bad, I can't deny he took it very bad. He had one of his turns that first night he was told and after that, well, it happened several times a week. It's a bit easier now. Mind you,' – the round brow crumpled a little – 'maybe talking about her again will upset him.'

'Oh, I'll try not to,' Abner said earnestly. 'It's the last thing I want to do. I just want to talk to him to – to – well, to talk to him.'

'Listen, don't worry. We've looked after David Lippner over ten years now. No one knows his turns better than we do. Come along then. He'll be in the garden room, I dare say. He usually ends up there!' And he laughed cheerfully and led the way down a long corridor that smelled this time of floor polish and bleach as well as the disinfectant and humanity of the hallway.

The garden room was at the far end, a small afterthought to the main building, made of glass and white painted wood and filled with plants. It smelled different; of damp earth and a slightly cloying scent and as Abner looked round he saw the source of that; a tub of flowering lilies set in one corner.

'We used to get the gardner in to look after these, when he had finished in the grounds, you know? Until we found out how good David was at them,' the man said brightly. 'He really has a great gift for plants – some of them do, you know. They seem backward but they have special gifts. God can be good to the afflicted.' He said the last sentences in a piercing whisper that made Abner cringe as he looked across the green-tinted room to the wheelchair at the far side. A thin bent man was sitting there with a rug round his knees and lying on the rug was a pair of secateurs and a roll of green raffia together with a few small garden tools, a trowel and a miniature fork, on the top of them. He stared at Abner blankly and then at the round man in the white coat who smiled brightly at him, as though he were a child rather than a man on the way to being fifty.

'See, David? You've got a visitor all the way from America! Isn't that nice? Now you sit down Mr – er – and I'll go and fetch a nice cup of tea for you both, hmm? Then you can talk nice and comfortable.' Again he produced the piercing whisper loud enough for someone halfway along the corridor to hear, let alone the silent man in the wheelchair. 'There's a bell here, if you get worried. He's all right most of the time, but if he has one of his turns, just you ring that bell and we'll come running. Now, here's a chair.'

At last he went away and Abner sat down in a gingerly fashion and looked at the man facing him. Thin, certainly, with bony cheeks and temples and neck as scrawny as a half-starved chicken's. I hope they feed them well enough, Abner thought uneasily. I hope this fuss they're making of me isn't just for show – and then pushed the idea away. The little round man may be a bit on the pretentious side, dressing himself up in a fancy white coat so that he could look vaguely medical, but his goodwill seemed genuine enough. David Lippner had shown no sign of any fear of him, and surely he would have done were he being ill treated. And anyway, he looked well cared for; his face had been carefully shaved and his sparse hair neatly cut and arranged. He was wearing a white shirt under a dark red open-necked sweater, which showed the whiteness of the shirt clearly, and the shoes on his feet, arranged on the step of the wheelchair, had been well polished. Abner looked at his hands then, knowing what a giveaway they could be and relaxed even more. The nails were short and properly cut and though there was peat on the fingers, David Lippner was clearly usually very clean.

The man in the chair stared at him for a long time with apparently blank eyes and then opened his mouth. The voice that came out was rough and deep and that startled Abner; for some reason he had expected it to be thin and reedy.

'Who are you?' he asked. 'I don't know you.'

'No, you don't,' Abner said. 'But I'd like to know you, if you'll let me. My name is Wiseman. Abner Wiseman. I'm a film maker.'

He braced himself, waiting for the usual television inspired excitement, but the man said nothing, just looking at him, and now he was getting used to that seemingly blank stare, Abner could see that it wasn't as empty as he'd first thought. There was a lively intelligence and a sharp awareness here and he relaxed his shoulders, which had tightened with anxiety, and tried a smile.

'I've come to ask you for some help, Mr Lippner,' he said then, as formally as he could. 'I'm researching for an important new film and I need to talk to people who have experience of the sort of material I need to use.'

David Lippner stared at him in silence and then the thin lips seemed to curve a little. He wasn't precisely smiling, Abner thought, but there was something there. And then as the words came out, he knew what it was. Scorn.

'You're making a film about epilepsy, are you? About people who have disgusting fits and bite themselves and mess their clothes and then get attacks of fury they can't handle, is that it? They've sent you to talk to me about that?'

The anger in him was unmistakable. He was furious and Abner warmed to that. It was something he understood.

'No,' he said firmly. 'Absolutely no. I know you have epileptic fits. I'm sorry to hear that. But I don't want to talk about that. I do want to talk about your life, though. A long time ago.'

He watched carefully, not sure how far or how fast to go. They'd left him alone with him, but maybe there was a major risk? What would he do if the man suddenly had a fit, one of his turns, whatever they were? And he remembered the fear that had filled him once at college when a girl in his year had suddenly started to convulse and had bitten her tongue and bled all over the floor and made the most dreadful noises.

'How long ago?'

He had to take a chance. There would be no point in being here if he didn't

'When you were born,' he said very deliberately. 'I need to know how life was for your mother in the sewers in Cracow. I need to know of your first memories after you came out of the sewers, and when you were in Auschwitz. I need to know what your mother told you about the boy and the apples.'

There was a long silence, and all Abner could do was look at the long face and deep eyes staring at him and think, will he tell me? Or will he turn his back on me?

It happened all at once. Just as the round man in the high-collared white coat came bustling in with a tray on which stood two beakers of tea David Lippner started to laugh, not moving in any way but opening his mouth and letting the sound come out in great rolling waves, laughing as though he'd just heard the most exquisite joke of all his life.

'There,' said the little man with great satisfaction as he put down the tray on a low table beside Abner's chair. 'There, isn't that nice? It's lovely to have visitors to cheer you up, isn't it, David?'

But David said nothing. He just sat there and went on laughing as, beaming with pleasure, the little man went away, leaving Abner to wait until the laughter stopped. If it was ever going to.

Twenty-one

———⧓———

They never did drink the tea. It sat ignored in the beakers, with its milky surface congealing into broken patterns that stained the sides of the cups, as they sat shrouded in leaves and the scent of lilies and talked in the dwindling light of the February afternoon. Because once David Lippner started he seemed unable to stop.

At first a good deal of it was disjointed, a flood of words that leapt from one topic to another as a fly swoops round a table full of food. It was as though he had never had the chance to talk before and again the doubts about the quality of care the man was getting came back to Abner; and then suddenly Lippner said, 'They tell me to shut up, the others, the empty heads, when I start to talk to them, stupid they all are, stupid, and they say "Shut up", so I do sometimes, but it's not stupid. It's good to talk, good when people listen. I'm glad you came to listen. Who did you say you are again?'

'Abner Wiseman. I'm making a film.'

'Oh, yes, a film. We get them here Saturday nights, in winter, Sunday nights in summer, because of *shabbat*, it goes out too late on Saturday in summer, they say, to start showing films, but we watch the television, or they do, the empty heads, they do, so why not watch films which are better? It's them, the white coats, they like to take it easy the summer nights, too much trouble to show us films on the proper screen, the big one, not that stupid little box of a telly. What sort of film?'

'About the war. About what happened to people who were in the labour camps,' Abner said steadily, watching him all the time. 'About the things that happened to you and your mother — before you got there — and after — '

The bony face seemed to go smooth, as though the few lines

that were there had been steam ironed and Abner stared, a little puzzled; and then saw the eyes again, and they seemed to him to be darker. That hurt him, he thought. Oh, God, what do I do? Not talk about her because it hurts? But I need to.

'She died,' Lippner said abruptly. 'She was old and it was time and she died. But the idiots here, they say she passed on – it makes me so angry I could scream. I do sometimes. "Passed on!" Dead, dead, she is, dead. Why can't they say it?'

'Oh, yes,' Abner said with fervour and for the first time smiled with real pleasure. That was one of his own *bêtes noires*, people who couldn't use honest words for honest experiences. 'Oh, yes indeed. My father died last year and when people tried to wrap it up in fancy language I could have screamed too.'

'Did you?'

'What?'

'Scream.'

'No.'

'You should. It surprises them and they get all fussed. Interesting really. They call them my turns but it's just for the change really.' And Lippner smiled, a narrow-lipped wicked little grimace and Abner relaxed, letting his shoulders sag into a more comfortable posture. They'd been very tight and his head ached a little in consequence.

'Hey,' he said, a little less carefully. 'Hey, you're a bit of a bastard – '

'What else can I do, stuck here in this chair?' Lippner said with sudden savagery. 'I can't exactly go and work it off on a run around the countryside, can I?'

'Why the chair?' Abner asked, feeling more and more comfortable with the man. 'I know people with epilepsy – they don't need wheelchairs as a rule.'

'MS,' Lippner said. 'And why should I bother to keep on trying? No point, really.'

'MS?'

'Multiple sclerosis. I get shaky, can't walk right and though it's a bit better sometimes, I prefer the chair. In my room on my own, I get out of it, walk about a bit but not anywhere else. What's it to do with them? Anyway, they feel better feeling bad about me this way. So, let 'em. Much I care.'

Abner shook his head slowly. 'Like I said, a bit of a – but I'm sorry about the MS.'

Lippner shrugged. 'So? What's the difference? I'm not fit to live on my own because of the epilepsy. For all their drugs they can't stop the fits happening and they happen a lot, and I think they're why I got the MS, though they all say I'm wrong, but it's my body. I know what goes on in it and I think it's the fits that started it, and they were started by the doctors in Auschwitz, so there you have it. And what does MS matter when you're epileptic? Anyway, is that what you came to talk about?'

'No. I – it's about the story I heard about your mother. The Rats of Cracow . . . '

The thin mouth twisted. 'Oh, yes. The Rats. It's a good tale, isn't it?'

Abner blinked and stared at him and David Lippner stared back and there was a sardonic look about him and Abner said, with a sudden sinking sensation deep in his chest, 'Are you saying it's not true? The story Mrs Singer told me about the small group in the sewers of Cracow, about you being born down there, isn't true?'

'Oh, it's true all right,' Lippner said. 'It happened all right.'

'Then why that – why did you say it "made a good tale" that way?'

He shrugged. 'I heard it too often, maybe. All the time I was growing up, I heard it. Over and over. She never stopped telling me. It was her way of dealing with what happened to me. Afterwards.'

'Afterwards – in Auschwitz?'

'Yes.'

'What did happen? Christ, that was a stupid question! I mean, what in particular to *you*? You said the fits were started by the doctors in Auschwitz – in what way?'

Lippner sat silent for a long moment and Abner thought, I've found the worst bit. I've gone too deeply into the part that hurts most. But then Lippner said in a dreamy sort of tone, 'I was two years old, you know? And the incredible thing is I can remember. Not all of it, but some of it. Two years old, and it's all there, like it's wrapped in cling film, all stretched over the lights and me and the trolleys and the machines – '

'Machines?' Abner prompted gently, for the silence lasted even longer this time.

'Mm. Well, I call them machines. I don't know what they were. All I know is it hurt. They had me on a bed, and I was tied there with straps. I remember the way they felt. Hard and a little bit of stretch, not much, but I remember lifting my arms and thinking I'd lifted them high and they hadn't moved at all. I'd just felt the leather stretch a little, you know? And they put hard cold pieces at the side of my head and held them tight so I couldn't move and then they took my hair off. I saw them, you know, because there was a light over the top of the bed, a light with mirrors, lots of little ones, and I could see them and I could see lots of mess, on the bed, and the woman with the razor, cutting all my hair off. And then the doctor brought the machines close and started cutting where the hair used to be on my head, and then I shouted, I remember that, shouting and screaming – ' He stopped then and smiled at Abner, and it was an extraordinarily sweet smile. 'It helped then and it still does. Shouting and screaming. So why not do it?'

'Yes,' Abner said. There was nothing else he could say.

'That's all I remember, though. Just that time, all covered over in cling film so that it never changes inside my head. I don't remember anything else, much. But the fits started afterwards, I know that. I don't know how I know, but I know it, and I've had them ever since. Couldn't go to school properly, couldn't do anything except stay at home with Mama. And she cried a lot, Mama. So I screamed a lot. That was when they sent me to the school in Surrey.'

'You and your mother went to live in Surrey?'

'Not Mama. She stayed in Edgware. She was all right in Edgware. They took care of her there, the women, the *schul*, they took care, so she stayed there. No, it was me. She said it was boarding school to them all. But it wasn't. It was a place for kids like me, who screamed a lot and had fits. Or such things.'

He sat in a brooding silence for a while. 'I don't know what was worse. Going back to Edgware for the holidays or going back to school. Wherever I was it was awful.'

'I'm sorry,' Abner said without thinking.

'Are you apologising or pitying?'

There was a silence and then Abner said, not daring to lie to him, 'Both. Please forgive me.'

'Well, at least you said the truth,' Lippner said. 'And you should apologise anyway. Look at you – you're a Jew, aren't you? And you're all right.'

He managed not to do it, managed not to tell him of Hyman and Frieda, managed not to hide his guilt behind their pain. He just sat and looked at Lippner.

It was almost dark now as the colours outside drained away to leave a monochrome landscape, and after a moment, needing to be active in some way, Abner got up and went to the door to find the light switch. The place was prettily lit, with lamps with yellow bulbs hiding among the plants. The glow they threw made both of them seem warmer and softer and that helped Abner relax again. He came back to his chair and sat down and said, 'Your mother. She had a bad time.'

'She lived to be eighty and gone,' Lippner said. 'More than I will.'

'In the early days. In Cracow,' Abner said and didn't look at him, afraid to see the anger in his eyes. 'They must have been dreadful days.'

'Oh, yes.' He sounded bored. 'Dreadful. Living in a sewer and all.'

'Did she tell you a lot about it?'

Lippner laughed. 'Every bloody detail,' he said. 'What they ate and when. Once she chewed a candle end and felt so bad and it wasn't because of eating the beeswax, she said, it was because of having to be in the dark. But it wasn't always bad. Sometimes they had good food, she said. They used to steal it from the best places.'

He gave an odd laugh then, a low cackling sound. 'She made me laugh about the first time they ate ham, Westphalian ham, she said. They had it raw, the right way to have it, and she didn't know what was worse for them all, eating raw meat or eating pork meat. I liked that, and laughed at it every time she told me. Me, I get the gardener here to get me bacon crisps from the pub. I give him money and he gets them and he laughs because he doesn't like Jews much and I laugh because I'm eating bacon and they'd go crazy if they knew.'

'What else did she tell you, David?' Once again Abner was aching to use a notebook, once again he knew he couldn't.

'Oh, all of it.' He began to sound bored. 'The way they slept all day and only moved around at night, and had to stay in the deepest galleries in case their candle-light shone out round the manhole edges. The way they had to use the water channels for a lavatory, and sometimes fell in, and getting clothes washed was almost impossible. That sort of thing.'

'Did she tell you about the boy and the bag of apples?'

'Oh, that – well, yes, of course she did. Once she knew about it.'

Abner tightened. 'Once she knew what?'

'It was after they got here. After the camps were opened and they got to the displaced persons' camps and then got sent here. When they found each other.'

'You'll have to explain more if I'm to understand,' Abner said, and leaned forwards a little to try to make the man look at him, for he had been sitting for some time with his head down, turning the loops of green raffia from the bundle on his lap between his thin fingers.

He did look at him. 'You're as bad as the rest of the empty heads,' he said scornfully. 'All right, so listen. So she comes here to England with me, right? And they get all excited about us because I'm still a baby and the hair has grown back, golden it was.' He lifted one hand to touch his thin dust-coloured hair and the green raffia dangled from his fingers like spiders' legs. 'They fussed over us, wrote articles in the papers – she showed them to me and they were so stupid, full of fancy language. I tore them up and threw them all away once when I was having a turn, and she got so mad, but I felt better. Stupid stuff it was. Anyway, they found us a flat and money and tried to send me to school, only I screamed a lot and they sent me to Surrey, and she started going to the club and she met this man who was one of the Rats. Came down to Surrey specially to tell me, she did, and to fetch him to see me. Nasty he was. I hated him. I didn't like his face, and I hated him and screamed at him, so he only came twice. She was all excited and pink about him, silly it was. Excited and pink. I hated him.'

Abner sat silent, afraid to stop the words, which had started to come in a rush now. Lippner was staring over Abner's head at the lilies in the corner, and seemed to have forgotten Abner was there. He just went on talking.

'I told her he was a rotten one, but she wouldn't have it. She went off with him and it was three weeks till the holidays and I had a lot of turns then, screamed and shouted and broke the windows.' A reminiscent smile curved his lips and he looked pleased with himself. 'Nice windows, with coloured glass in them and not only a small bit. A lot. Ruined them I did, into tiny bits, with the hammer, and I got the bits in my thumb and it went septic. Oh, those were nasty days. And then the holidays came and it was time to go home and she said she couldn't if I was ill and screaming so they sent me to hospital and he was there, making her pink and excited – the stupid – I ask you! An old stupid woman and a creature like that, looking like a bluebottle. All shiny and ugly.'

The hatred and jealousy of the small boy who had been David Lippner came echoing down the thin man's years of brooding past and the venom in his voice made Abner's shoulders tighten again. And then Lippner stopped staring over his shoulder and focused on him and seemed to like what he saw in his face and produced a thin smile.

'You'd have hated him too. It wasn't jealousy. I know you're thinking I was just a jealous kid but it wasn't that. I just didn't like him. A bluebottle.'

'You've never seen him since?'

'I won't. He tries sometimes, sends presents, sends cards. I make them send them back, the white coats. They stand there and they bleat at me and I tell them I'll scream, so they send them back. Food and books, all sorts. Why should I take anything from him?'

'Why not?' Abner said, and lifted his brows at him. 'Maybe he felt he owed you something.'

'Why?'

'Because he came out of the sewers better off than you did. He doesn't have epilepsy and MS, does he? Maybe he feels bad about you.'

'Good!' David Lippner said after a moment. 'If he does, good. No, he won't though. It was my mother he was interested in, not me. Old fool.'

'How old? As old as your mother?'

Lippner shook his head. 'That was what made me so angry. It wasn't right. He'd been a boy then, only sixteen. Twenty years younger than she was. And he comes buzzing round her like a bluebottle, telling her tales – '

'What sort of tales?' Abner felt his skin prickle with excitement. It was here, almost here. He was getting something special. This was the authentic thing.

'Oh, such tales!' Lippner said scornfully. 'You'll like them, you make films, of course you'll like them. That one about the boy and the apples – it was him told my mother the story of the boy who sold them all for apples. How could she believe him? He told her and she believed him! I told her, if it's true why doesn't he say who he is and where he wound up? It was him, the bluebottle, he told Mama that the boy lived here in England now, that he was very comfortable, had a good position – such lies! If it were true, why didn't the bluebottle tell everyone, get him strung up? "Oh," she said. "Believe me, he's got good reason not to tell yet, but one day he will, one day everyone'll know. But not yet – he's got his reasons." And she'd laugh and – faugh – it makes me sick to think of it.'

His voice had started to rise, the deepness in its tone thinning to a tight shrillness and again Abner's skin crawled, but this time with apprehension. Lippner was getting excited, he was going to start screaming, he knew it, and that meant he had to stop questioning him. There were more questions to be asked, but not now. And perhaps there were other ways to find out more. He'd think about that. But right now he had to get away from this man who was, frankly, now frightening him. And he got to his feet and leaned over the wheelchair and held out a hand.

'David, I'm very grateful to you. May I come and see you again?'

The thin man blinked and lifted his head to stare at him and then slowly his face changed and the settled sullen look came back.

'If you like,' he said. 'Much I care.' And bent his head to the raffia again. Abner took a deep breath, grateful to hear the voice return to its usual level.

'I'll be back soon. Is there anything I can get you?'

Lippner looked at him and then laughed, a flat dull little sound that emerged from lips curled back over surprisingly white teeth.

'Go to that Body Shop I'm always reading about in the magazines, tell 'em I'll have another one like this only new and working properly, with a decent trade-in price, all right?' And he reached down to the wheels of his chair and twisted on them and the chair turned and he rolled away towards the lilies in the corner. 'If you can do that, I'll be happy to see you. If you can't, don't waste my time.'

'I'll be back,' Abner said. 'And thank you.' And he went quietly out of the garden room and along the corridor, which had now added the smell of frying to its other odours, looking for the man in the white coat.

He found him hovering in the hallway, ostensibly arranging some flowers on a window sill, but Abner felt he'd been more than interested in trying to hear what was going on in the garden room. For all he knew, he may have been listening outside the door and had only come scuttling back here when Abner had shown signs of leaving. Certainly he seemed a little flushed as he peered up at Abner now.

'He's all right then?' he said brightly. 'Didn't start one of his turns? I thought perhaps he might.'

'No,' Abner said firmly. 'He's fine. Er – one thing though. I want the full name and address of his other visitor.'

'Other visitor?'

'Well, he doesn't come here, I gather, but tries to send things. But Mr Lippner sends them back, he tells me. I think perhaps I might be able to – uh' – he was improvising wildly now, and wasn't at all ashamed of his own deviousness; sometimes lies were so necessary they were moral and this was one of the times – 'uh – persuade David to see him. So, I need to get in touch with him, but I lost his address a while ago. You know how it is, time passes.'

'But no one ever visits Mr Lippner,' the man said and his round face creased worriedly. 'Not since his mother, rest her soul, passed on.'

Abner bit his lip and then said carefully, 'This man sends him gifts sometimes, and David insists you send them back. You must have his name and address so that you can send them, surely?'

The man in the white coat went a sudden and very fierce pink. 'Listen, I can't help it if people send things and residents don't choose to accept them,' he said, his manner full of bluster but with a whine in his voice. 'It's not my fault if people are so . . . '

Light dawned on Abner and he put out one hand to touch the other's shoulder and said winningly, 'Oh, it's all right. Of course it was right to keep the things here for the other residents to enjoy! The man meant the stuff as a gift, so why send it back and insult him? I quite understand and he would too, if he knew. Not that I intend to say anything to him about that, of course. I just want to get in touch to see if I can heal the rift between him and Mr Lippner, you know how it is.'

Slowly the red flush subsided and the little round man stared at him uncertainly for a while and then nodded and turned and went bustling away to a door at the far side of the hall.

'You'd better come into the office,' he muttered. 'As long as it's understood that whatever comes here is used for all the residents, no favouritism.'

'Of course not,' Abner said soothingly. 'It's a matter of no importance at all – just the name and address is all I need.'

He was leafing through a folder and then stopped, and at last, still a little unwillingly, picked out a card and handed it over to Abner.

'Harry Brazel,' he read. 'Financial consultant.' And there was an address in Swiss Cottage, and a phone number.

'I'll copy this down,' he said and reached for a pencil and a scrap of paper from the cluttered desk. 'Then I'll give it back to you. That way no one knows I got it from you, or anything else, right? I just want to get in touch – a blast from the past – you know how it is.'

And he scribbled the note and then escaped gratefully into the rawness of the February evening and took a deep breath of it. The air tasted of woodsmoke and horses and winter. It was marvellous. He made for the car, patting the scrap of paper in his pocket as though it were a piece of treasure, which in a sense perhaps it was.

Twenty-two

The air at Minster Lovell smelled of woodsmoke, too, and
though he was a little late, since he'd had trouble finding the
place, hidden away as it was in the valley of the River Windrush,
he lingered after he'd parked the car outside the Old Swan.

The front of the building had been carefully lit and there was a
wealth of old Cotswold stone, naked roses and creepers (which
must look superb in the summer and autumn, he decided) and
well-tended grass. Ahead of him, up the dark village street, he
could see a receding avenue of lamps that showed thatched
cottages as pretty as any chocolate box cover, and somewhere a
dog was barking mournfully. The lighted windows of the hotel
spilled warm squares on to the ground and there was a drifting
smell of good food and beer added to the woodsmoke as
someone came out of the low front door, shouting cheerfully
behind him, and Abner grinned with delight. Ealing comedy,
here I come! he thought, and went plunging across the dark grass
to the front door.

Inside it was even more picture-book. A vast log fire burning
sumptuously in an ingle-nook, polished stone-flagged floors,
shabby comfortable chintzy furniture and pleasant people sitting
about, who gave him a casually curious look as he bent his head
to get under the low lintel and then returned to their conver-
sations; he looked around and almost laughed aloud at it all.

'I told you it was like Brigadoon.' Her voice came from behind
him, and he turned swiftly and smiled at her. She was wearing a
dark green dress, high in the neck, and again fitting her long body
smoothly; she had pinned her hair up on her head in that elegant
fashion that so suited her, had even, he suspected, applied a little
mascara, and that warmed him even more. Had she gone to that
sort of trouble, just for him? An exciting thought.

'It always feels like a special event when I come here,' she said, providing instant deflation. 'Geoff thought of it as a place to celebrate, so we did and I always made a special effort to look right.' She looked him up and down a little censoriously. 'I suppose you'll do.'

He looked down at his jeans and sweater and reddened. 'Hell, I didn't even think about it – it's not a thing I ever do worry about much, the way I look and – '

'I said you'll do. It's just a country pub, really. And I was being sentimental to fuss at all.' She gave him a sudden grin, wide and appealing. 'I've only just got here myself. Shall we have a drink?'

'Sure.' And he followed her round a big, square stone pillar to where a long and cheerful bar winked against the far wall.

'What'll you have?' she said.

'No,' he protested. 'I'll do this and – '

'I told you – I'll pay my way.' She gave him a look over her shoulder that was so severe that he blinked and closed his mouth, unable to protest further; and then was amused at himself. After the years he'd spent working with and knowing American women, he should fuss about who paid for what? He must be crazy.

'Is there a local beer? I'm getting to like this stuff,' he said, and she laughed and lifted her brows at the barman, who nodded and reached for the handle of a beer pump.

'Me too,' she said. 'And find us some bacon rinds, Peter, if you can. I can't stand these greasy nuts.'

There was another log fire tucked around the corner with chairs set in front of it, and no one else there, so they took their drinks and the dish of crisp bacon bits the barman found for her and settled down to read the menus that had been handed over. Abner drank his beer and watched the way the firelight picked out the shape of her face as she concentrated on what she would order for dinner as though there were nothing more important in the world.

'Right,' she said at length and looked up at him. 'I've decided. What about you?'

'Tell me what you've chosen,' he said. 'Let me be lazy.'

'Mushroom soup – they get wild ones from the fields around here – and a grilled trout with almonds. The fish comes from a farm just a few miles away. All very local. And they grow their own vegetables too. Or used to. I shan't ask them if they still do. I couldn't bear it if they didn't.' She smiled again, a little shyly this time. 'As I said, I'm being sentimental. It was always special, here.'

'Is that why you chose it? For old times' sake? Or because I was coming with you?' He knew he was being daring and didn't mind. The beer was a strong one and in the heat of the fire had reached his brain rather quickly, making him reckless.

She shook her head. 'I can't remember why.' And she looked at the fire. 'It just seemed like a good idea at the time, I suppose. And – ' She looked back at him then. 'And I need to celebrate. I got some money this week.'

'Oh? What sort of money? Legal, illegal? Prize or earned?'

She laughed. 'Oh, strictly legal and very much earned, though not by me. It was a book of Geoff's. Believe it or not, some Hungarian publisher wants it, though he wrote it twenty years ago. They sent me a cheque for masses of forints. It works out to about two thousand pounds!'

'Wow! That's big bucks!'

'Isn't it just. Have some bacon rind.'

He reached for the dish, and as he put one of the frizzled scraps in his mouth laughed. 'I wonder if that's what he meant by bacon crisps?'

'What?'

'The guy I saw this afternoon. Lives in a special Home run by Jewish charities and sends the gardener to buy him bacon crisps. He does it to annoy the people there, though I suspect they don't know, so how can they be annoyed? But it pleases him.'

She considered for a while. 'Sounds like my sort of chap. Bloody minded. Was he useful?'

'Oh yes, he was useful. So once again I'm eaten with guilt. What right have I to go upsetting people, reminding them of what they need to forget, just to provide film fodder? It doesn't stop me, mind you. No way. If I'll need it I'll go for it. But I still feel guilty.'

'That's an occupational hazard for Jews,' she said with an air of lightness. 'There's always something to have to feel bad about.'

'If it's only the fact that someone else has a better recipe for chicken soup?'

'Very funny,' she said. 'And anyway, maybe. In case you don't know, it's called displacement activity. The thing you feel really bad about is so unspeakable it's easier to feel bad about chicken soup. So you do. It helps a lot.'

'What do you feel bad about tonight then?'

'Hunger.' She got to her feet. 'Let's go and sit in the restaurant and make them hurry up.' And she led the way, the big menu tucked under her arm, towards a door beyond the bar.

'Oh, this is ridiculous!' he said, as he ducked in under the doorway and looked round. The roof of the restaurant was a network of vast wooden beams set against white plaster and another ingle-nook at the far end of the long table-filled room had been stacked with dusty bottles of wine. The windows were small and pretty, the place was lit by candles, and even the waiters looked venerable. 'This *is* Disneyland, surely.'

'It's authentic,' she said and laughed. 'That's the trouble with it. It's so old and so real, it looks phoney, doesn't it? But it's been here, this great room, since sixteen hundred and something. Hello, Sam.'

The most grizzled of the waiters had been peering at her and now his round face split into a smile so wide that his skin looked as though it were made of creased parchment.

'Well, if it isn't Miss Hinchelsea! I haven't seen you since, well, I don't know when – how's the Professor?' And he peered shortsightedly at Abner as though he might just possibly be a transmogrified Professor.

'He died a few weeks ago, Sam,' she said, and he looked up at her with milky blue eyes and twisted his mouth into a gentle grimace and said comfortably, 'Well, I'm sorry to hear that. A good kind gentleman, the Professor. But he did good work, and had a good life. Will you have your usual table?'

'Please,' she said and Abner followed her, marvelling a little at the old man's equanimity. Was that the compensation you were given when you reached old age, the ability to be nonchalant about death? That was a comfortable thought; that the fear receded as the reality came closer. Had it been like that for Hyman? He hadn't thought about that before, and he looked at the fragile old waiter now holding a chair for Miriam in a courtly fashion and wished he hadn't thought about it now.

'Don't have the kipper pâté,' Sam was saying to Miriam. 'I saw the kippers he used. Nasty dyed things, not the Loch Fyne we usually get. A stubborn man, the second chef. But the mushroom soup's well up to the mark and the trout are as plump and pink as you could wish.'

'I'd already decided on that, Sam,' she said and leaned back so that he could arrange the napkin on her lap. 'And a bottle of that Chablis Geoffrey always liked – '

' – And our own sesame bread. I know,' Sam said, and nodded at Abner as he sat down opposite Miriam. 'The same for you, sir, I've no doubt.' And went creaking away without waiting for an answer.

'I've always heard you get the best value at the restaurant you're best known at,' he said. 'But this, really it's a bit – '

'Yes, I know. Over the top and all that. Well, so what? I like it.'

'So what, indeed.'

There was a little silence as they waited for Sam to bring the wine and go through the ritual with it; and it amused Abner that the old man made no attempt to defer to him, as he might have expected from so traditional a sort of person. He offered the bottle to Miriam, so that she could inspect the label, showed her the drawn cork and poured the regulation quarter inch of wine into her glass so that she could taste and pronounce it drinkable and then, to Abner's total delight, bowed slightly and went away to fetch the food.

'Too much,' he murmured and buried his nose into the glass of icy wine, which tasted superb. 'You called up in advance and arranged to pay them to blind poor ignorant visiting Americans with their All British Style, of course.'

'Of course,' she said equably, and drank too, taking a big mouthful, and he liked that. Her appetites, he decided, were strong and deep and – No. Not permitted thinking, that.

'Tell me about your afternoon,' she said then. 'This man and his bacon crisps. What else did you discover?'

He told her, in all the detail he could, adding graphic description to an attempt at imitating the man's voice, and she listened, drinking her wine and watching his face and saying nothing, and that helped a lot. It fastened all the memories of the afternoon into his head even more firmly, and he knew he wouldn't forget a single word David Lippner had said, even though he'd made no notes at all.

'This man you say told Lippner, or his mother, about the boy with the apples,' she said at length. 'What did you say his name was?'

The mushroom soup arrived then and he didn't answer, letting Sam set the lidded silver bowl in front of him and proffer the garlicky croutons and then the sesame sprinkled bread, all done with an air of careful ceremony that would have amused him more had he not been eager to get back to Miriam; but he waited as patiently as he could, and at last the old man went away and he said, 'I didn't say.'

'Mmm?' She had started her soup and was clearly delighted with it, and she made a gesture at him with her spoon to tell him to start too, so he did, and she was right; it tasted superb, rich with the scent of wild mushrooms and with an undertaste of good chicken broth. Frieda would have approved, he thought then, and took another spoonful to drown the memory of her kitchen.

'You asked me the name of the man who was David's mother's friend. The one who sends him presents he won't accept. He's — ' He put down his spoon and reached into his pocket. 'Here you are,' and he set the scrap of paper in front of her. 'I'll try to see him as soon as I can. I've got to spend the next two days making a dog food commercial, heaven help me, but once that's done I'll try to see him.'

She peered at the piece of paper without stopping her attack of her soup, and then frowned and for the first time set down her spoon and picked up the paper.

'Brazel,' she said and narrowed her eyes slightly. 'Brazel. I know that name from somewhere.'

He lifted his chin sharply. 'You do?'

She sighed and pushed the piece of paper back over the table to him and started on her soup once more. 'I thought so, but I can't be sure. It rang a sort of bell somewhere, but I dare say I imagined it — why should I know, after all?'

He put the scrap of writing back into his pocket and returned to his own soup, thinking hard. 'Maybe he came to see your father's stuff sometime? Doing research?'

'Hardly,' she said dryly. 'Not a financial consultant. Whatever else people talked to Geoffrey about, it surely wasn't money. Poor Geoff, he was even more stupid than I am about it.'

'I don't entirely believe that,' he said. 'That you're stupid about money, that is. I think you pretend not to care. That's quite different.'

She stared at him with her brows down sharply and he grinned and said, 'No, don't look at me that way! It'll get you no place – not the lady who sat out there cheering over her fistful of forints.'

She relaxed and made a little face. 'Well, I suppose so, but I'd have to be mad not to be glad I've got it. You've no idea how close I am to the edge when it comes to cash.'

'Tell me,' he said and she looked at him sharply. And then shrugged.

'I own the house, but it's a wreck. Ought to be worth a good deal – not as much as it was a few months ago, what with the market falling the way it has – but it's in a dreadful condition. Needs a lot spending on it to get its real value. I'll have to sell it, of course, but I'd like to be able to get enough to get a decent place of my own somewhere. A small flat.' She looked yearning for a brief moment. 'Somewhere small and warm and centrally heated without open fires to be lit and cleaned and – ' She caught his eye and reddened. 'Well, why not? I dare say you think a house like mine's picturesque and all that, that open fires are real cute and that I ought to be glad to live in such a heap of old – '

He shook his head. 'I think nothing of the sort. I have a healthy respect for comfort and clean plumbing and hot water and radiators. Open fires are attractive, sure, in other people's places, like here. At home you need something more sensible.'

'I always needed something more sensible,' she said. 'You can't know what it was like coming back to that house on a cold day after school. He'd be there, so busy he hadn't noticed the cold, though he'd be blue with it, and I'd light the fire again – though I always did it for him before I went to school, he always forgot to put any coal on. Then I'd do what I could about supper, and that was it. Till school again.'

'Was it always like that?' he asked, needing to encourage her, for she had stopped and was staring sightlessly down the long room.

'Mm? Oh, pretty well. He tried in his own way – we'd go out for a meal sometimes, walk a bit, but mostly it was just his work he needed. He was old. Work was more than enough for him.'

'Oh, Miriam, you poor lonely – I mean – ' He changed tack

hastily as he caught a sharp glance from her. 'Didn't anyone notice how deprived you were? People at school, neighbours?'

'Did anyone notice how deprived *you* were?' she retorted and he caught his breath sharply.

'I take your point. So you had it hard in that house.'

'Yes.'

'Is that one of the reasons you want to sell it? Only bad memories there?'

'Such stuff!' she said with some scorn. 'I'm more practical than that! If the house was comfortable, I'd stay in it. But it isn't. It never has been. And as soon as I can get Geoff's stuff safely into a library somewhere, I'm going to sell it – I must.'

And then she shook her head in some irritation. 'I don't know why we're talking about this – '

'Because I asked you. OK, so you'll sell the house and get a flat, a nice, small, really comfortable flat. What then? Will you have enough money left over to live on from selling the house?'

'Oh, that's very likely, that is!' she said scornfully. 'Of course I'll have to get a job. Though what kind – I'm not trained for anything except looking after old historians. There's not a lot of demand for that as far as I can tell.'

'Ever thought of being a researcher? In films?'

She stared at him. 'A what?'

'You heard me. A researcher.'

'I don't even know what a researcher does in films. How could I have thought of doing it?'

'A researcher digs out information. Checks on backgrounds, the history of the piece, and all the details the script writer, the designer and costume department need. Some of the people in those departments do their own basic research, but there's always need for some more. Researchers work close to directors and writers, to make the film authentic – with your experience you'd be a wow, I think.'

Her face lifted into a wide jeering grin. 'I see! Because I've spent all these years looking after an old man, you reckon I'd be good at looking after you, hmm? You want someone to run around after you and make sure you've got your slippers or whatever, and dig out a bit of information from time to time, just to keep my hand in and make me feel I'm more than just a house servant – just the way I used to do for Geoff. Is that it? Thanks for the offer, but no thanks.'

He had flushed a brick red. 'I wasn't offering you a job.'

'No? It sounded bloody like it to me.'

'Then you should listen more carefully and try not to be so full of yourself,' he retorted. 'Goddammit, I don't have a production set up yet! I'm the only person working on this lousy project right now and I'm getting zilch for it. I'm as broke as you are – more, because I've got no house to sell. That's why I have to make dog food commercials. So don't come the acid with me, lady! I tried to make suggestions, is all.'

She shook her head at him as Sam arrived to remove their soup bowls and set trout in front of them with a shaky flourish, and he watched in frustrated fury as the old man fiddled around and piled his plate with creamed cauliflower and mashed potatoes as well, impatient and feeling horrible. What had seemed charming a while ago was a nuisance now. The pleasure he had been finding in the evening had vanished and a prickly irritation had taken its place. For two lousy pins, he thought savagely, I'd get to my feet and walk out on her here and now, the sour bitch. Why does she have to be so – ?

'I'm sorry,' she said as soon as Sam was out of earshot. 'I really am sorry. That was rotten of me.'

His head snapped up and he stared at her, as the irritation slid out of the ends of his fingers and left only a comforting glow behind.

'I do it all the time. I don't mean to. I hate myself for it. It's just that whenever anyone's kind to me I get so angry and – and suspicious. It's so stupid. I've sent away so many people I might have liked, and I don't want to do it again. Please, do accept my apology. And the idea's a super one, really it is. I mean, if you think I could learn how. Would you help me, find someone who'd give me a job maybe?'

He shook his head in confusion, dazed still, staring at her. She was looking at him very directly with eyes that seemed to glitter in the candlelight, and there was a nimbus of light around her dark frizzy hair that gave her skin a golden colour. She was quite the loveliest thing he'd looked at for years, he thought confusedly, and knew he was gaping at her stupidly.

'If I do that again – get nasty, I mean – tell me off, for pity's sake. I really — ' She bent her head and picked up her knife and fork with a sharp little movement. 'Well, I wouldn't want to make you so angry with me that you went away. This fish smells awfully good, doesn't it? It'd be an awful pity to let it get cold. Bon appetit.' And she set to work on it as though they had talked nothing but small talk all evening, and there had never been that flare of anger in him.

So he ate his dinner too. There seemed little else he could do. But good as it was, he didn't taste any of it. All he could think of was the words she had used — *I wouldn't want to make you so angry with me that you went away* — because they really were the best words he could ever remember hearing anyone say. Ever.

Twenty-three

Afterwards, standing in the road outside the Old Swan, feeling the agreeable nipping of the cold air on his cheeks, he had to bite his tongue not to ask her to stay longer; to talk more, to just be with him. But to do that would be to court disaster with this one; he knew that as well as he knew himself to be full of good food and wine. And somewhere at the back of his mind he thought gloomily, hell, how am I ever to get anywhere with this lady? Like Shandwick said, I've hit the mother lode, and I don't dare to touch it.

'Are you in a hurry to go?' she said abruptly and he turned and looked down at her in the dim light and lifted his brows.

'At half after ten! I shouldn't say so. I was even thinking of maybe seeing if they have a room here for the night. I don't have to be back in London till Wednesday morning. Seems a shame to waste the car.'

'There are ruins at the end of the village,' she said. 'Rather magnificent. And there's a moon, so you'll be able to see. If you like.'

'Yes, please,' he said, not believing his good fortune, and she nodded and started to walk up the village, her hands pushed deep into the pockets of her coat. She had her collar up and above it her profile was sharp and agreeable to look at. He looked at it a lot as they walked up the gentle incline that ran between the cottages.

But not all the time. He had to look at the village too, and with each yard they covered it became more and more like a film set. He was seized with the notion that if he walked behind any one of the cottages he'd find it was just a canvas front with struts holding up the back and held in place with braces and weights.

He said as much to her, and she nodded. 'I told you it's too pretty to be true. The people who live here, they're the same. There was a time when it was a real place, I imagine, but now it's mostly retired people and second-homers so busy being authentic and countrified it's like they're made out of plastic. The real life of the place is somewhere else. But it's a good place to come. I like the peace. And the ruins are – well, you'll see. Come on.'

At the top of the street she turned right into a road where the houses petered out and then left, and there ahead of them loomed the bulk of a church, and he let her lead him between the tilted moss-grown gravestones, feeling a certain guilt. Was it decent to march over people's graves this way? But she seemed insouciant about it, so he said nothing.

And then, on the other side of a small gate and a patch of mown grass she stopped. 'Here's the old road, you see?' she said in a matter of fact voice. 'This section of stones – built in the sixteenth century, or thereabouts.'

He looked down and saw them, the patterned rocks set into the ground like cobbles, and put out a foot and stood on one and it felt hard and painful through his shoe.

'Jesus, they walked on this?'

'Mostly rode on it. It was built for traffic. Horses and carts and so forth. Walkers went alongside on the soft verge. Look, through that arch there. That was the way it went.'

He looked and caught his breath for at the same moment the cloud cover, which was moving fairly swiftly across the sky, thinned out towards the east where a late-rising moon sat absurdly full and grinning, and the archway was clear against the indigo of the sky. The arch was massive and led into a dim covered way and she turned and made for it, and he followed, letting the dimness swallow him up, and came out on the other side.

All round him was grass, smooth cut and even, grey in the moonlight, and dotted about were piles of old stones, open-roofed enclosures and great soaring ruins that came straight out of an old Victorian monograph, an effect that was heightened by the silvering of the moonlight. Somewhere ahead of him he could hear water chattering angrily and he lifted his head to listen.

'The Windrush,' she said. 'Shallow here but wide and busy. It's heaven here on a hot day – you can sit with your feet in the water and pretend you're almost anywhere but in the real world.'

'What is this place? Or what was it?'

'Minster Lovell Hall. Remember the old saw? "The Cat and the Rat and Lovell our Dog ruled all England under a Hog." That Lovell.'

'Oh,' he said, and she laughed.

'Sorry, I should remember what a foreigner you are. All right. Richard the Third, King of England in the late fifteenth century. His banner carried a boar's head insignia. He's had a bad press over the years, but all we know is he took over the throne when his nephew Edward the Fifth was pronounced illegitimate, and from then on it's a bit shifty. Edward and his brother were put in the tower and were murdered there, and there are people who say Richard did it. That was the belief for years. I don't think he did. Anyway the boys were killed and Richard was made King and eventually he was killed at Bosworth by Henry Tudor, who was a Welsh usurper, and that was the end of Richard. But one of his closest supporters was Lovell. There were two others called Catesby and Ratcliffe who were ill-thought of by Richard's opposers, so they came up with a rhyme about them – the "Cat" and the "Rat" and so forth. When the trouble started for Richard, Lovell fled, so the story goes, came home here to his manor and was hidden by his trusty manservant – have you noticed, they're always labelled "trusty"? – Anyway this chap tucked him away in a secret hiding place that only he had access to and then got himself killed, so Lovell couldn't get out and died – walled up in his own home. They say they found his skeleton years later – it's probably an apocryphal story, but it sounds interesting.'

'Ye gods,' Abner said, overawed. 'One hell of a story! How long ago did it happen, do you say?'

'Well, Bosworth was in 1485, so I suppose around five hundred years or so.'

'You say that like it was just last week.'

'So it was, in someone's mind. This is rural England – memories run deep here. There's a bedroom at the Old Swan with a wall painting in it that's supposed to date from the other Richard's time – Richard the First. And he was three hundred years earlier. I don't believe that myself, but lots do.'

He stood there on the dim monochrome grass, staring at the grey and black of the stones lying so elegantly thrown around him and then laughed. 'Jesus! I thought I was into history, working on what happened forty years ago. And you people here think in hundreds. You make me feel a bit stupid.'

'Tens or hundreds, it's all history. It all matters,' she said. 'Geoff was an historian and knew damn all about what happened before the nineteenth century. He stuck to his period. You're sticking to yours, that's all. And someone has to record what really happened. Here we get stories with no evidence to back them up. You're looking for evidence for your history, aren't you?'

'I am?'

'Of course you are! You went to talk to that man this afternoon – that's good historical research. You're getting the truth from the prime source of it, people who were there.'

'Not really. Not with him. He doesn't remember.'

'He remembers what his mother told him. That's better than just stories handed down over centuries. You don't realise how important the work is that you're doing. It's good stuff.'

She turned to move away, but he couldn't stop himself from taking hold of her arm and pulling her back.

'What did you say?'

'I said you were doing good stuff.' She looked up at him in the darkness and pulled back in an attempt to get out of his grip but he didn't let go and she stood there letting him hold her and keeping her eyes fixed on him.

'You've changed your mind – you don't think I'm wasting your time when I go through Geoff's stuff then, for just a *film*?'

'I told you. No, I don't. I'm sorry I was so rude the first time.'

He couldn't help it. She looked too good to be true and there was such elation in him that it just happened. He let go of her arm, took her shoulders and kissed her hard. She stood very still and her mouth was like a trap, shut tight, and then she softened and her mouth opened and he felt a leap of excitement that made him shake. Just for a kiss? Ye gods, it was like being a child again and smooching behind the bicycle sheds with one of the girls in the sixth grade, and he felt the laughter brimming in him to threaten the excitement.

And then she pulled away and said in a flat voice, 'Well, I hope you feel better,' and turned and went back to the archway and the old road and he stood and watched her go as the excitement dwindled and died. And then sighed and went after her.

He caught up with her on the other side of the churchyard.

'Am I supposed to apologise like one of your milk and water heroes in an old movie?'

'You must do as you please,' she said, and her voice was still flat. 'It's not important to me, either way.'

'Oh, boy, what a putdown!'

'Really?' she said. 'I don't see why.'

'If you don't see why then there's no way I can explain it.' He was angry now and the feeling warmed him as they went rapidly along the smooth tarmac of the road, the slap of their heels echoing sharply against the houses as they passed. 'So I don't apologise. Why should I apologise for being a normal man, for Christ's sake?'

'Ah, I see,' she said. 'I'm not a normal woman, is that it?'

'You're a goddammed peculiar one,' he said and then as they reached the Old Swan put out a hand and held on to her arm. 'Oh, come on, Miriam! What the hell. So, I got a bit elevated and got fresh with you. It's no big deal.'

'Isn't that what I said?' She looked up at him. 'It's not important to me. I'm not fussing. You are.'

He let go of her arm and stood there, feeling flat and stupid. 'Yeah. Well, I suppose so. OK then. I'll take you home.'

She lifted her brows at him. 'And what do I do about my car?'

'You really have a gift for it, don't you?' He shouted at her, luxuriating in a loss of control. 'Making a man feel like a little heap of something really nasty! What's in it for you, this sort of — are you coming the liberated lady or what? It's not liberated to be bitchy. It's just bitchy.'

She kept her cool remarkably. 'I only pointed out that I'd driven myself here, and if I let you drive me home, I'd have to leave my car behind.'

'Oh, go to hell,' he said furiously and flung away from her, digging in his pocket for his car keys. 'Do what the hell you like. I try my damnedest with you and much good it does me.'

'I don't know why you're so angry,' she said. 'Is it because I'm not angry? So you kissed me. So what?'

'That makes a guy feel really great, that does. Me, I get emotional, I show it. You, you're just as – '

'I'm just what I am. Damaged goods,' she said quietly and turned and left him, walking into the car park that stood alongside the Old Swan, and he stood beside his own car, uncertain what to do next, until he heard the cough of her engine as she switched on the ignition. And he knew he couldn't let her go that easily.

He flung himself into his own car and switched it on and threw it into reverse and shot backwards just in time; the lights of her car came bumping over the gravel of the car park just as he reached the entrance and stopped, almost blocking the way.

He got out of the car and walked round to the driver's side of hers and tapped on the window. At first she sat stonily staring ahead and then with an impatient movement wound down the window.

'I'm sorry,' he said. 'I was a bastard and I'm sorry. It's just that – you have a bad effect on me. A great effect, but a bad one.'

She took a deep breath and looked at him and then tried to stare ahead again. 'Yes, well. I'm not sure what I'm supposed to say to that.'

'You're not supposed to say anything. Can't you just be normal? Simply react like – just the way you want to? Do you have to think about everything, plan it, make a whole scenario out of it?'

'Yes,' she said. 'I don't know any other way to be.'

He stood there silently for a long time and then sighed and stepped back. 'I see,' he said. 'Well, I guess we've got a lot to teach each other, one way and another. I can see you again?'

'Why not?'

'You're not too angry to allow that then? You're not going to send me away for ever for getting fresh?'

Now she turned and looked at him again and this time she was smiling. 'Oh, God, do I really come across as so wet?'

'I'm not sure how you come across. You're umpteen different things all the time. I no sooner think I'm getting to know you and you're something else again. I get so goddammed confused with you. I never know where I am.'

'Is that so bad?' She seemed genuinely interested but remote, like an intelligent student quizzing her tutor.

'Well at least it's not boring,' he said after a moment and then they both laughed and it was as though the spurt of anger between them had never happened.

'I'd better go,' she said then. 'I've got a long drive back. Thanks. It's been — I've had a good evening.'

'*All* of it?' And she looked sideways at him and then slid her eyes forwards once more to stare out of the windscreen ahead.

'Well,' he said. 'If you've no answer, I'm going to take it as an affirmative. Goodnight, Miriam.' And very deliberately he bent and shoved his head in through the car window and kissed her cheek. And she said nothing, but put the car into gear and rolled forwards slowly.

'Goodnight,' she said. 'I dare say I'll see you again soon. You'll need to do some more digging in Geoff's files, won't you?' And the car reached the gate and went through, manoeuvring carefully past his own car slewed half across the way and then turned right to the road leaving him standing in the vast country darkness and watching her red tail lights diminish and then vanish.

He was reckless enough to ask for a room at the Old Swan, and they had one ('a slow time of the year, sir, so we can just squeeze you in') and though it was pricey and his budget was dwindling fast, it was worth it. He ate a vast breakfast of eggs and bacon and sausages in the coffee- and woodsmoke-scented dining room before taking to the road again. He'd be a tourist, he decided. He'd done it in London and to an extent in Oxford, and now he'd do it in the Cotswolds. What better way to stop himself thinking about Miriam Hinchelsea?

It didn't work. By early afternoon he was sick of driving through one picturesquely named place after another — Stow-on-the-Wold, Bourton-on-the-Water, Moreton-in-the-Marsh — sick of thatch and golden stone and sweet little tourist shops and most of all sick of himself. He plotted a route back to London that would take him the harsh way along an ordinary motorway, and got back just in time to be snarled heavily into the evening rush hour, to sit and steam furiously for an hour from the western end of the Marylebone Road to Camden Town.

There was a message on his answerphone from Dave, reminding him of his appointment with Matthew Mayer.

'He doesn't take kindly to being kept waiting, so do me a favour and be on time,' the tinny voice grated. 'It'll be my ass that's on the line on account I was the one who fixed it. You're wasting your time, though. The guy's not about to hand out handfuls of gelt just for the asking.'

He swore and switched off and went and took a shower, and then, wrapped in a bathrobe, sat at his table in the window and began to make notes of his conversation with David Lippner. And his appetite for work thus whetted, pulled a foolscap pad towards him, and began to work on a storyboard for his film. And to his joy it came easy. It was shaping up in his head so fast it was unrolling like a reel of film already in existence, and his pen could hardly keep up with it. Briefly he thought of using the typewriter to put it all directly into print, and then abandoned it. He was afraid to stop the words that were now pouring out of the ends of his fingers; it might halt the flow as suddenly as it had started.

He would begin with long shots of each of them as they now were, Cyril and David Lippner and Miriam. Establishing footage would show them, real people living their real lives now. He'd take them in among crowds to get the establishing shots, and then slowly pan in to concentrate on each of them, like that old silent movie *The Big Parade*. If it was okay for King Vidor, it was okay for Abner Wiseman.

He chewed the pen for a moment and then scribbled on. Each would tell his or her own story in voice-over. The *real* voices, as unscripted as possible. He'd record them all in interviews, cut them to make a continuous narrative and then, using actors, would recreate each scene as they described it. And – here his pulse began to beat faster as the idea formed, and he knew it was a good one – the actors would not be heard. They'd be filmed improvising the action, speaking when they felt it right to do so, but all that would be on the sound track was the voices of the real people living now. Cyril and David and Miriam. No music, no sound effects, just those real honest voices.

And then what? He didn't have to stop to think about that. His hand and pen moved almost without his volition, as though he were experiencing automatic writing. Back to the present, to Cyril in his cold house and David in his wheelchair, and Miriam with her father's papers and books. And his own voice, completing the voice over, telling the audience the sort of lives lived by the children of these survivors, as the camera pulled back again from shots of his three main protagonists in a crowd. Once again, a direct reference to that old silent movie he'd always admired so much.

When he'd finished, he leaned back and stretched and let the deeply agreeable fatigue that followed a job well done seep out of him as he looked over his notes, and then set them aside ready to be typed. He'd done well, and he knew it.

But he felt restless now, and in need of action of some sort, and on an impulse, reached for the phone. He'd call Harry Brazel now, why not? The man could have more to tell him to fill out his storyboard.

'Who?' The voice was querulous and female, and Abner said as patiently as he could, 'Mr Brazel won't know my name. I'm a friend of David Lippner. I'd be grateful if he could come to the phone. I have a message for him.'

'He doesn't see many people,' the querulous voice said.

'I just want to talk to him,' he said, holding back his irritation almost physically. Christ, but why did people have to make such a drama out of everything in this stinking country? 'A few words is all.'

There was a long silence and then a voice said carefully, 'May I help you?' It was a very soft voice and the accent was very precise, very English, but he could hear the sound behind it, his father's voice, his mother's too, though it was a shadow of both. This man had worked at his accent, but still hadn't been able to eradicate all traces of his past.

'Mr Brazel,' Abner said heartily, trying to sound relaxed and easy. 'I'm so glad to have this opportunity to talk with you. I visited with David Lippner yesterday and he asked me to call you.'

'Now that isn't true, for a start,' the voice said, silky now and with a note of amusement in it. 'There is no way that man will ever have anything to do with me, even through a third party. Try again, mister.'

Abner was silent for a moment and then laughed. There seemed little else he could do. 'OK. He didn't. He hates your guts and clearly you know it. But I'm interested in talking to you about him all the same.'

'Why?'

He sighed. It was getting wearing, this constant explanation. But he had to do it and he launched himself on his usual spiel, trying to make it sound interesting, worthwhile, exciting. Damnit, it was. Why was it getting so difficult to keep explaining it to people?

'I see,' the smooth voice said when at length he stopped. 'And you want to put the story of poor Libby and David Lippner on the screen?'

'Something like that,' Abner said. 'It won't be them, in the early days, you understand. I'll need actors. It'll be a dramatised documentary. I make that clear in the credits – I never claim that it's – '

'I'm sure you don't,' the voice said. 'But why do you need me for this? David, I have no doubt, let you know all you needed to know.'

'Not entirely. There's a story about a boy who sold them all to the Gestapo.'

'Ah,' Brazel said consideringly. 'Ah. That story.'

'Yes. That story.'

There was a long silence and Abner held on, praying it would work. It often did; just staying quiet made the other person feel driven to talk.

'Why ask me about it?'

'David said I should – ' Abner began.

There was a soft sound, a laugh Abner thought, but he couldn't be sure. 'Mr Wiseman, you're lying again.' The voice sounded almost playful. 'David Lippner may have told you about me, but he'd never tell you to *ask* me anything. No, let me have the truth, hmm?'

'Oh, dammit,' Abner said. 'OK, Mr Brazel. He didn't. He said there was this man who was a friend of his mother – he doesn't like you, you're right about that. Hates your guts, frankly. But he said you told his mother about the boy and the apples and I want to know that story in the worst way. So I managed to get the information to find you from the home. OK? Now, will you see me? I'm a persistent man, Mr Brazel. I'll go on trying so you might as well say yes now.'

'Why shouldn't I say yes? Now you've come clean. Isn't that

what you Americans say? Now you've come clean. Shall we meet then?'

Abner caught his breath. 'Well, sure. Where and when?'

'How about tonight? At the Savoy? I can manage a little supper at the Savoy. I'll be there at around nine or so. They'll show you to my usual table. *Á bientôt*, Mr Wiseman. So interesting to talk to an honest man – ' And the phone clicked as he hung up.

Twenty-four

———◇◇◇———

Even the glitzy hotels in this country are unique, Abner decided
as he stood in the lobby of the Savoy hotel. He'd stayed in hotels
in a good many different places, and always the expensive ones
had smelled the same, looked the same, been the same. He could
have been anywhere from Maine to Albuquerque, Rio de Janeiro
to Toronto, in them. Only the cheap and doubtful places ever
had any individual personality, like the little joint in Bayswater
he'd stayed in when he'd first arrived here. But this was different.
This looked old and genuinely elegant, smelling of coal fires and
cream cakes and hot tea. Abner relaxed, took off his leather
jacket to hook over his shoulder on one finger and made for the
main lounge, which was where he'd been told by the hall porter
Brazel was waiting. Small low tables with peach coloured lights;
a central wood framed bandstand where a bored pianist pretended to be Cole Porter as the soft hum of well-bred voices
competed with his desultory notes, and people hugely pleased
with themselves combined to create an aura that was, to Abner,
pure cinema, and he relaxed even more, felt more than ready to
enjoy the meeting ahead of him.

But his anticipatory pleasure withered fast, as an impeccably
tailcoated head waiter came and looked at him consideringly,
taking in his open-necked shirt and jeans, and was clearly about
to send him away as unsuitable to occupy his domain, even
though Abner said firmly that Mr Brazel was expecting him,
until a soft voice on the other side of the bank of flowers that
flanked the entrance to the lounge said something and the man
looked over his shoulder, lifted his hands in a way that clearly
relinquished any responsibility and turned away. And Abner
followed the sound of the voice and went round the flowers.

In the very centre of the sofa that was fitted into the embrasure

there, there sat a small man in a very precise pose. His hands
were neatly folded on his knees and his head, which was sleeked
with dark grey hair, was held slightly to one side. He had very
large, very bright dark eyes, and they glittered at Abner above
the smallest and neatest line of black moustache Abner had ever
seen off a Thirties movie screen. He was wearing a suit of so deep
a black that the fabric almost shone and his shirt was as white as
a TV soap ad. And Abner thought: My God! David was right.
He does look like a bluebottle, a shiny bloated creature with a
tough and gleaming carapace, which, for all its odd beauty,
looked menacing – and the thought filled him with a sudden
gloom.

The man on the sofa smiled, showing incredibly even white
teeth and lifted one small and obviously well manicured hand to
indicate the armchair to the side of the long table that stood in
front of him. It held a bottle of champagne in a dewy ice bucket
and a couple of glasses, one of them already filled with amber
fluid, and as Abner sat down Brazel leaned forwards and lifted a
finger; a waiter came at once and filled the other glass.

'Well, well, Mr Wiseman. You will have even my status at this
establishment called into question, dressing like that. We seem
old fashioned here, I dare say, to you Americans, but – '

Abner glanced round at the other people there, in their neat
grey flannel suits and carefully knotted ties over polite white
shirts, and lifted his brows.

'Half the people here are Americans, I'd say, looking at 'em,'
he said a little scornfully. 'A stuffed shirt is a stuffed shirt in any
country. Me, I dress comfortable. Always have.'

'And a very estimable choice that is. I was not criticising.
Merely making a point. And it amuses me to have so – *louche* a
guest. It pleases me to show the staff here that they make rules
for other people, not for Harry Brazel. Well, now, you are
making a film.'

'Indeed I am.' Abner took a deep draught of the wine, and it
was agreeably smooth with a hint of sweetness that he liked. The
man has taste as well as money, he thought, noting the label on
the bottle – Moët et Chandon, and a vintage year. Very nice too.
He drank some more.

'And you are, of course, fully financed? We are not wasting
our time here just talking about projects? I like projection, you

understand, but I also like to know to what I am committing my time.'

Abner scowled. He couldn't help it, feeling the lines digging into his cheeks without his volition.

'Not yet,' he said. 'Not quite yet.'

'I see,' Brazel said comfortably and sipped his own champagne. 'Not at all, that means. Well at least we know where we are. You wish to do the research and write your script first and then seek the money? This is after all the usual manner.'

Abner glanced at him sharply. 'You have some knowledge of the film business?'

The man's smile widened, again displaying those even white teeth and Abner thought: Capped Teeth and Caesar Salad, hearing the song's melody in his head. Was this guy really a Californian in disguise, after all?

'Of course I have,' Brazel said. 'In my business it is necessary to have a smattering of information about all sorts of activities. Especially those which use a lot of money and make even more, sometimes. Very much the film business, that, wouldn't you agree?'

'Very much,' Abner said and looked at him directly, staring into the big dark eyes as though he were looking for words written there. 'Will you help me?'

'With money or just with information for your script?'

Abner caught his breath. 'You could help with . . . ' and then shook his head. 'No, that'd be too easy altogether. Information was what I came for, though later perhaps we could talk money.'

Brazel made a small grimace. 'It's up to you to do as you think best. So, you want information about the Rats of Cracow?'

'Yes. You were one of them, I understand.'

Brazel smiled again, that same glittering smile and Abner thought; he's hiding behind it. The more amiable he seems, the more watchful he's being, and settled down to a fencing session. This man was going to be a difficult one.

But he didn't seem so after all. As they talked he displayed such an air of disarming honesty that Abner had to work hard to prevent himself being beguiled. David Lippner had hated him, he reminded himself, and Lippner was no fool. He'd had very good reasons, surely, to be as filled with rage at this man as he so clearly was.

'It is a story that is both uplifting and very unedifying,' Brazel was saying in his smooth but precise voice. 'The image of human beings having to hide like rats in a reeking network of sewers — this cannot but disgust a fastidious mind, and this I always had, coming as I did from a family of some standing in Poland.' Again that wide smile. 'My father, you understand, was an academic, a Professor at the University of Cracow.'

'Indeed,' murmured Abner and thought somewhere deep in his mind — like hell he was. This is pose, pose, pose. The father of this one was lucky if he was a gate porter at a university. There was, for all his elegance and veneer of expensive clothes and cologne — for Abner could smell him from where he sat — a vulgarity about Brazel and a guttersnipe sort of self-assurance that came from a quick mind rather than a thoughtful or original one. And for a moment he was amused at himself; in England so short a time and yet thinking of such matters as vulgarity?

'But the Germans — the Herrenvolk, the Master Race — they were lower than the rats, all of them. When you are overrun by one species of vermin where better to hide than with another set of them? And I preferred those with four naked feet to those with two in jackboots.'

He's enjoying this, Abner thought. He's telling this with such smooth ease — he's told it often before. Suddenly Abner could bear it no longer and gave in to his irritation.

'All this sounds very practised, Mr Brazel,' he said, taking the risk boldly. He wanted information, but if all the man was going to do was trot out some sort of party piece, forget it. He needed the real stuff, the original feeling, something of the sort that David Lippner had given him. And as he thought of the man in his wheelchair, glaring at him from among the leaves and lilies in the garden room in Oxfordshire, a wave of affection rose in him that startled him. 'Let's get to the point,' he went on sharply. 'David Lippner told me you were one of this group of people who had to hide from the Germans in the sewers. He told me that you, together with other men of the group — '

'Men?' murmured Brazel, still smiling. 'Did you say men?'

'Boys, then. Boys,' Abner said a little impatiently. 'He told me you were a food finder and that you knew how it was the group were betrayed to the Gestapo. That someone sold them for a bag of apples.'

'Tell me all he told you. I really can't give you all you need until I understand where the gaps are in your information, hmm?' The smile didn't waver and Abner felt growing dislike for this smooth creature crawling through his veins. Bluebottle, grinning, buzzing bluebottle.

'He told me that you knew who it was. That you'd found his mother after you'd all got back here after the war – well, not all, but those of you who did – and told her the story and after she'd heard it she got very – I have the impression she became – obsessed with it.'

'Wouldn't you? If you'd had a child born in such a place who had suffered as that child did? If you yourself had suffered as Libby Lippner had suffered, wouldn't you want to know about why it happened? About who made it happen? And wouldn't you want to get your own back? Excellent reasons for an obsession, I would have thought.' Brazel's voice had sharpened with a sudden flash of fury, and it took Abner aback, though it vanished as fast as it had appeared.

'Yes,' Abner said after a long moment. 'Yes, I suppose so.'

'Well, that was how it was with Libby. However, her son, David, he was different.' The man shook his head then and for the first time his attempt to replace the smile on his face wavered. 'That child, that David, that staring, screaming object – he was like a tapeworm to that woman. He ate her alive. She could give no sustenance to anyone but him or he screamed obscenities for hours on end. If she sought respite for herself, again he screamed and shouted and – do you think she would have allowed them to take him from her, to put him in that school, if he hadn't been so evil, so – '

'Evil?' Abner's brows had snapped down. 'You call him evil? How can you – the man went to hell in a hand cart, for Christ's sake! You sit here as sleek as a cat drinking your champagne in a place that obviously costs megabucks in anyone's currency, and which you use like your own goddamned kitchen, and you tell me he was *evil*? That's as wicked a – '

'Mr Wiseman, Mr Wiseman!' Brazel lifted his hands. 'You must contain your emotion, credit though it does you! You are here to make research, hmm? Do you want information for your script – or do you want confirmation of your own gut reactions, as you no doubt would call them? I tell you that the way that boy treated his mother was evil. She had a dreadful time, an unspeakably dreadful time, and when at the end of it all there was a possibility of happiness for her with me, what did he do? He pushed his own jealousy down her throat and screamed her to exhaustion and spoiled it all. She could have been happy in her last years. The twenty years of age between us was as nothing. I was the only one she knew, the only one who had known her in her good years – the only one who remembered her as she was and cared for her and would have gone on caring for her. But would he allow that? Would he give the poor woman any joy in her life? Not him.'

Brazel leaned back on his sofa now and stared at Abner with those great dark eyes over what were now red cheeks, so that for a moment he looked ludicrously like a painted Dutch doll, and Abner could almost have laughed. But, amazingly, pity welled up in him and took away the amusement and he could only say, 'I'm sorry.'

'You should be. What can you know of what is true of that man? Yes, he has suffered too, I grant you this. Yes, dreadful things were done to him. But isn't it still possible that somewhere underneath all that he was an evil person? To assume that all the people who suffered in Europe were good people, that they were innocent of any stain of any kind, is a nonsense. Yes, the Germans were wrong, God knows they were wrong and wicked and did devilish things. But not all the Jews who suffered were angels, my friend! They too were greedy and selfish and acquisitive, some of them. They too were abusers of opportunity, lacking in generosity, less than perfect, some of them. Many of them. You must not be sentimental if you are to make any sort of honest film of this story. And me, I value honesty so highly that I will not help anyone who does not intend to be as honest as it is in him to be. There is no such thing as complete and absolute truth – this any intelligent man knows – but as long as we attempt it, try to show the world itself as we believe it to be, then truth emerges. Don't cover the Holocaust in tears of sugar, my friend – you insult all of us if you do that. I tell you that boy Lippner was born to be selfish and cruel and so he was, whatever happened to him later. His mother was a great deal nearer the angels than he was.'

'And you loved her a great deal,' Abner said, watching him,

fascinated by the man's smooth face and wide dark eyes, trying
to see beyond the surface into his head. 'This isn't just a story – '

'Ah, faugh!' Brazel looked as though he were about to spit, but
instead took up his glass and drank again. 'If you cannot see the
reality of truth in me, how can I ever waste time on you or your
film?'

Abner took a deep breath. 'Yes,' he said after a long moment.
'Yes, I believe you. You loved her. Though she was, surely, much
older than you.'

'I told you, twenty years. Ah, Mr Wiseman, you should have
seen her as I first saw her! A ripe woman, so round and ripe – so
lovely! She had the richest of yellow hair, even richer than her
child's, later on. And God knows he was beautiful enough. But
she, with her eyes as darkly purple as plums in chocolate, and her
hair in great sheets down her back – even in those sewers she
bloomed. And her body so round, at first, so rich, until the
hunger took over. But in those days when we first arrived down
there, she was so – ' And suddenly he lifted both hands and with
the heels of his palms wiped his eyes, and Abner felt his own
nostrils tighten with unshed tears.

'I was sixteen and she was thirty-five,' Brazel said then, 'and I
loved her so much I wanted to die for her. It was she I went out
for with the others. Nothing else could have got me out of that
dreadful manhole, into a great empty street, nothing else could
have made it possible for me to go through those roads and into
those warehouses and get what we had to get. I was sixteen, Mr
Wiseman, a skinny boy! Sixteen – and she was warm and
generous and still had room for me in the middle of all her horror
and fears, still had it in her to see me weep in the night and take
me close to her and make me know what it was to be a man. She
was so good to me . . . ' He shook his head and now the wide
smile had finally vanished to be replaced by a tremulous lower lip
as he looked back down the bleak vista of forty-five years to the
boy he had been and wept again for him. 'Of course I loved her. I
still do. Not the frightened old woman I found here, of course
not. But the woman she had been in Cracow, I'll love her for
always and fight for her for always. Of this you can be certain.'

'Yes,' Abner said and didn't know what else to say.

'We need more champagne,' Brazel said then, briskly, as
though he had been speaking only of the weather. All traces of

his emotion had vanished, and Abner watched a little stupidly as the man crooked an imperious finger and the waiter came scurrying across the wide lounge to fill the glasses from a bottle that had been standing just inches from his hand.

'So, you wish to know of the boy with the apples,' he said then as he lifted his glass again. 'Ask and I shall be glad to tell you. I think that for all your occasional ineptitude you are an honest man. Honest enough, that is. I do not ask the completely impossible.' And again the wide smile was back in place, as fixed and bright as ever.

'Is it a true story?' Abner said abruptly. 'I first heard it second-hand from some woman Libby had told it to, before she died, and then again from David, but it sounds so ridiculous to me when I think about it. How could the people in the group – the Rats – *know* what happened? If he, whoever he was, had done such a thing he would hardly come back down the sewer and say to you all, "Here – get packed – I've made a deal with the Germans and they're on the way. I got a bag of apples for telling 'em of you, by the way." It's ridiculous.' He looked at Brazel very steadily then. 'Unless of course it really was *you* and you're telling the story now, afterwards, when it's safe.'

Brazel lifted his brows. 'Safe? When is safe? No one is ever safe, believe me.' He laughed then, a soft fat little chuckle. 'Ask Simon Wiesenthal if safe ever comes. Ask the dead soul of Eichmann. Ask any of the ones that were caught. It's never safe. No, I was not the one. But I can tell you it's true!'

And he laughed again, a louder sound, full of real humour and a sumptuous pleasure. 'I've been living comfortably on that truth this past forty years. I have built of it my own comfort and that of many others. Of course it's true.'

Abner frowned, and shook his head.

'I don't understand.'

'Why should you?' Brazel said and drank again, watching him over the rim of his glass. 'You are a good simple man, with no knowledge of these things of which I speak, you with your comfortable American life behind you, and your rich successful film-making life ahead of you – for believe me, you carry the stamp of achievement in your face – how can you understand?'

'My parents were in the camps,' Abner said, and his voice was loud and he didn't care. He felt no guilt at saying it, no shame, only anger at the man's assumptions. 'I understand more than you know.'

'Indeed,' Brazel said easily. 'Indeed? So you think this gives you understanding? You think it was like being there? Where did you first find love, first find the joy of a woman's body? In a warm bed or in a rat-running sewer? You think you understand? Listen and learn, my friend, before you make such claims on others' backs. Even those of your own parents.'

Abner felt his leg muscles tighten, was almost on his feet ready to hit the man first and get the hell out of this soft, rich place right afterwards, but Brazel, seeming to know, shook his head at him. 'Such anger! Don't be a fool, Wiseman. You need my story and I intend to tell it to you. But I warned you I am an honest man, and that means I say what I think. And I cannot care about the suffering of the children of those who survived the camps, whether they be people like David Lippner, or people like you. What does my scorn matter to you? Why should you care? Isn't it the story you want, the story you've got to have?'

'Damn you,' Abner said softly and had no stronger words to use. 'Oh, damn you.'

'You think your curses can hurt me more than my own already have?' Brazel said and the eyes glinted dark and deep and the smile returned to fix itself in place. 'You flatter yourself.'

'The hell with all this,' Abner said roughly. 'I can't listen to any more of your fancy talk. I just need to know if it was true that there was a boy who did this. If so, I want the story. I want to know who he was and what happened to him afterwards, and – '

'As to who he was, that I am not at liberty to tell you. In detail, you understand. I can tell you he is here in England. He escaped with a whole skin as well as a reasonably full belly – he got more than apples, believe me – and came here. Now he is a respected successful man. He is comfortable, rich – not as rich as he would be if it were not for me, of course – but rich enough. And – '

'Not as rich as – ?' Abner said and stared at him and Brazel laughed.

'You amuse me, Mr Wiseman, you really do. So innocent and so surprised by such obvious things! What do you think I have been living on these past many years but my memories of the boy with the apples? How do you think I have the finance to do all the things I do?'

'You blackmail him.' Abner said slowly and shook his head to try to clear the confusion that was there. 'But – I don't see how. Surely, *surely* he'd have found a way by now to stop you, to – '

'To get rid of me?' Brazel shook his head. 'Of course, he must have thought of it, prayed for it, but how can he dispose of me? He doesn't know who I am, you see. We haven't spoken of what happened since that last night in Cracow when I was there and saw what I saw and heard what I heard, and they sent the Gestapo down the manhole. He was outside and I was outside and me, I ran, God forgive me. I ran and left her there.'

His face suddenly distorted into a grimace of extraordinary pain and then smoothed almost immediately. 'I ran and remembered. And when I got here to England at last I found him. I looked and I found him. I knew it was here he would go. Not America for him. A European in every way, he was.'

'He doesn't know you? But you know him and you get money out of him – '

'We communicate by bank account,' Brazel said and giggled.

'Yet you're telling me about him? What's to stop me discovering who he is and telling him that you're the man who – '

Brazel laughed again, with genuine amusement. 'My dear Mr Wiseman, leaving aside the question of whether you would protect such a man against someone who suffered as a result of his actions more than was necessary, leaving aside the way you clearly feel about Mr David Lippner, who suffered even more, leaving aside your memories of what was done to your own parents, there is no way I am going to tell you who he is, is there? I can and will tell you the story – but I shall not yet say who it is about.'

He bent his head then and picked up his glass and after a moment looked sharply at Abner from beneath his brows. 'But I will eventually.'

'You will? – Well, why not now? If you're ready to tell me at all – though I'm not sure I understand why – then what's the point of – '

'Oh, there's every point in the world,' Brazel said. 'I have nearly enough for my purposes, you see. I have had something in excess of a million pounds from him over the years – I am not greedy, you understand; I have left him with ample for his own needs – and I have used it well. Soon I shall, as it were, retire. I doubt I have many years left, you see. But I intend to enjoy my share of *schadenfreude* before I go. So I shall bring him down when I am ready. It won't be long now, and that is why I am speaking to you. You are the piece of good fortune that shows me I am planning it all as I should.'

Abner shook his head, hopelessly adrift again, and Brazel sighed with a slightly theatrical patience.

'Your film could help me in my plan to expose him, for heavens' sake! The time will come when I will tell all I know of him, and he will stand there accused and no longer be able to hide himself behind his seemingly innocuous occupations. The time will come when all will know of all his ways and of all his evils, and I will have your film to show them. Because I will be part of it, part of the story you will tell. Hmm, Mr Wiseman? You agree I would be worth including? And you had better make sure it is a good film, Mr Wiseman. I need it, you see. And so far I've always got what I needed, one way or another.'

Twenty-five

'I hardly slept, Dave,' Abner said. 'Would you have done with a story like that dropped in your lap, and you can't get hold of the best part of it?'

'I don't see why the fuss,' Dave said. 'Listen, you ain't some sort of detective, are you? You're not here to dig out some guy and string him up. Leave that to the FBI or Scotland Yard, or whoever. You want to make a movie, and you're doing the research, OK. You've got a cracker of a story, love interest, the lot – and what love interest! A boy of sixteen and a luscious broad of thirty-five – it'll grab 'em all by their excitable bits, that will, men as much as women. Like I say, why beat your brains out about who the guy is? He's not the same one that did it anyway.'

'What?' Abner looked at him sharply. 'You know something about this? Don't hold out on me, Dave!'

'Christ, you're getting a real obsessive, you know that?' Dave said and shoved a fist at his shoulder in a friendly but definite fashion, so that Abner had to subside again into the armchair. 'Of course I don't! I just mean, the kid who did this betrayal bit for his bag of apples, he was a *kid*, right? Sixteen, seventeen, whatever. A starving kid – and I have to say, to have a villain in a movie who's as pitiful in his own way as the hero, that has to be a great stroke – anyway, that isn't the guy this Brazel was talking about, was it? He'd be – what – sixty odd, now? A different man! Are you today what you were at sixteen? Am I?'

Abner grimaced. 'Well, I know what you mean; but all the same – and anyway, yes, I am the same. Inside I'm not even sixteen, sometimes. Twelve, maybe.'

'Sure, twelve years old and just starting to learn how to beat your meat. Come off it, Abner! Leave it alone already. You've got a good story, so use it and leave the revenge scenario to the sequel. Right now you have to raise the money for this project and you've got yourself an appointment with one of the guys in this business who might help you, and he ain't a guy any one of us ever likes to play around with. He's an impatient fella. You want to do business with him. And you have to do it in his time. So give me those car keys and get going, for Christ's sake.'

He fielded the car keys that Abner threw to him and dropped them into the drawer of his desk and then leaned back and put his feet up on the edge of it. 'So tell me, did you score? Get to see your pretty lady in – where was it – Oxford? You weren't that far away.'

'Mind your lousy business and your dirty tongue, big mouth,' Abner said as lightly as he could, and got to his feet. 'Listen, thanks for loaning me the car. It made a difference. I've got some great stuff – the guy Lippner as well as this Brazel.'

'My pleasure. Make sure you send me in a decent piece of work tomorrow – Friday, I mean. I've got a few more jobs here I can put your way, make you a living if not a luxury bankroll. You'll have to wait a month or two yet to get on *Lifestyles of the Rich and Famous* but I'll see meanwhile you don't go without the beer that keeps body and soul together. Listen, you've got to move. The man's waiting and taxis are thin on the ground this cold weather – '

'I'm not due there for half an hour. I'll walk it.'

'Who'd ever think you were a guy from Manhattan? Walk it? It's in Mayfair, the other side of Piccadilly.'

'I looked on the map. I can walk it. Listen, I'll see you Friday, OK? And Dave, thanks for everything – I suppose you're right. Why get so excited about who the guy is? It doesn't really matter, I've got the best part of my story.'

'I always knew you were a clever guy,' Dave said heartily and got to his feet to come round the desk and throw one arm over Abner's shoulders. 'It makes a pal feel real good when his advice gets listened to. And I wouldn't give you the old three card trick, believe me. If I know what's what, I'll tell you. If I don't, I just call the cards the way they fall. On your way, buster. See you around.'

As he pushed his way through the crowded streets of Soho on his way to Shaftesbury Avenue so that he could weave a route on through Piccadilly to Shepherd's Market, he went over it again and again, just as he had during the night when he'd woken from fitful sleep to see Brazel's grin glimmering at him in the darkness and heard his silky voice repeating it. *I'll bring him down when I'm ready – when I'm ready – when I'm ready.* But now the edginess that had filled him half the night had gone. Dave was right; what did it matter who the man was now? He wasn't trying to do a Wiesenthal and hunt down quarry to wreak revenge on them. His task was elucidation, not blind vengeance. He had to tell everyone what had happened and why it had happened and how it had hurt the children of the people it had happened to. People like Miriam.

That helped a lot, thinking of Miriam. He had shied away from conjuring up her presence in his mind during the night. He didn't know why, except that somehow it had felt wrong to do so, but now it felt right and he re-ran their conversation at the Old Swan over and over again, against the background of Piccadilly's crawling traffic and the reek of diesel. *I wouldn't want to make you so angry with me that you went away – I wouldn't want you to go away.*

He hugged it to him, that memory, wrapping it round his fatigue to ease it, and soothing his hot eyes and slightly aching head with it. Soon he'd call her and see her again, and they'd move a little further along their tortuous path. It was like playing that silly game his grade teacher had shown him, 'Giant's Footsteps' where you had to get across the schoolyard without being caught by the guy who was 'It'. 'Two steps forward, one step back, that's the way you win in this game,' she'd told them. 'It's true in life too, sometimes, never forget that.'

Well, it was certainly true with Miriam and though it was maddening in some ways, it was exciting too; and he held the thought of the excitement warm in his belly as he reached Half Moon Street – such names these places had! – and turned into it. From now on Miriam belonged safely tucked away at the back of his mind together with Brazel, in a different corner, of course; while he concentrated on the meeting ahead of him.

And then, as he reached the corner of Shepherd's Market, he stopped and stared blankly ahead. Miriam had reacted to Brazel's name, he remembered now. She knew it from somewhere, she had said, and that had to be looked into. A good reason for contacting her, he thought joyously. He'd call her tonight, this afternoon even, as soon as he'd got this meeting over; and whistling softly between his teeth he went on along the narrow street, looking for the building he needed.

The office was perfect, he decided, just what an office should be. It was in a small and inconspicuous building that was clearly part of an old dwelling house. The room he was shown into was a perfect cube, as high as it was wide as it was long; the walls were panelled with plaster in beautiful satisfying shapes, and each one bore a small but elegantly made light-fitting in crystal and gilt. Everywhere had been painted in pale blue and white, except for the ceiling on which a number of highly unlikely plump women and cherubs, all with carefully flowing draperies arranged over groins and at least one breast, gambolled amid pink and gold edged clouds under the benevolent eyes of a large bearded man in a long white robe sitting on a throne with his legs spread wide. It looked innocent and lascivious in equal measure and Abner was straining his neck to look at it all when, at last, the door opened and the man came in. He would cheerfully have waited longer for him if he had had to, for there were other things to look at and enjoy; the sound of music, coming from some hidden source, and filling the room with rich orchestral cadences, above which a violin wept and laughed deliciously; shelves full of books that looked as though they were actually read, and a painting on an easel that was a riot of colour and excitement. But he jumped to his feet as the door opened and looked at the arrival expectantly.

A small man, he thought, small and dapper, with a mane of thick white hair that looked as though it had been carved out of alabaster which was why, surely, he made Abner think of some sort of sculpture. But then as the man moved into the room and closer to him Abner saw what it was; he had a massive head and shoulders and a broad chest, but then his body dwindled away to the most delicate of hips and legs and feet, so that he looked rather like a bison; and the thought amused him and made him more hearty than he meant to be as he thrust out his hand.

'Hi, Mr Mayer. It's good of you to see me. I appreciate it.'

The man seemed to flinch a little from his *bonhomie* but held out his own hand and shook Abner's with a fastidious air and then went to sit down behind his desk, an elegant affair of mahogany and brass, on which was arranged a blotter and pens in red Florentine leather, also brass studded. It was all so very tasteful that Abner felt like an oaf straight off a Kansas farm as he sat down again in the Chippendale chair into which he had been shown by the quiet secretary who had greeted him. He didn't know for sure it was Chippendale, but it certainly had that air, he told himself. The whole place looked too cultured to be true.

'I trust the music doesn't bother you?' the man said, and Abner shook his head at once.

'Oh, not — it's great. Really. I'm not sure I know it.'

'*Symphonie Espagnole* — Lalo. That's Henryk Schering on the violin. Splendid, isn't it?'

'Great.' Abner said and tried to think of what to say next. Mayer seemed to understand and smiled slightly, a faint movement of the lips that went as soon as it arrived.

'So, Mr Wiseman, you are a friend of Dave Shandwick.'

'Known him for years,' Abner said, trying not to sound hearty again. 'He was my sound man on a film I made called *Uptown Downtown* — ' Shut up, he thought then, for Christ's sake shut up! You're showing off, making a complete ass of yourself. And went on, 'It did rather well — '

'Oh, indeed, you don't have to remind me, Mr Wiseman. I remember the film well. As well as *Yesterday's Babies* and *Wall of Silence*.'

'Oh!' He was nonplussed and then was annoyed with himself. Why should he be surprised this guy knew his work? Wasn't he supposed to be interested in the film business? Didn't he have partnerships in all sorts of firms that were in the industry? 'Well, it's no secret,' he said then, a little ungraciously. 'I guess I'm in most of the right reference books.'

'Ah, but I remembered you before I looked you up,' the man said and smiled widely.

At once Abner felt better. He was a pleasant enough guy, for heaven's sake. The problem was he'd been told so much about the man that he'd built him up in his mind to some sort of ogre, and impulsively he said, 'It's good to meet you, Mr Mayer. I've been very curious about you.'

'Oh?' The neat eyebrows made circumflexes over intelligent eyes. 'For any special reason?'

'I saw your name attached to so many companies, it seemed to me that everywhere I looked there you were, and – '

'Everywhere?' Mayer murmured.

'Well, Jo Rossily and then Simmy Gentle and – oh, dozens. I saw a list on Monty Nagel's computer – your name cropped up over and over.'

'Dear me,' Mayer said mildly. 'Monty Nagel has me on computer? I wonder why?'

'Oh, it's not just you. It's only because he's got lists of all the people he deals with and how the companies are made up.' It seemed suddenly vital to explain, to reassure this man that there was nothing underhand in his knowledge. 'The thing is, I have this crazy eidetic memory. Well, sometimes it is – it's not entirely reliable. But quite often I can see things and then remember them in every detail, and it just so happened when I looked at the computer screen I retained it in my head and I could see your name bobbing up on it, over and over.'

'An interesting gift to have,' Mayer said.

'Oh, I'm not so sure. It kinda clutters you up sometimes, you know what I mean?'

'Not entirely, but I can imagine,' Mayer said with great courtesy. 'Well, here we are. You've come to see me, and you can see, I trust, that there is nothing odd about me!' He waved his hand comprehensively round his office and Abner smiled.

'It's a beautiful place to work,' he said. 'It's more like a sitting room than a working area.'

'I like to treat my work as a hobby, and my life as my work,' Mayer said. 'I spend more effort on music and painting and books that I read for pleasure than I ever do on the things that matter to most people. Like money making.' He sighed. 'That is why it is so wise for me to join forces with eager young people who are very interested in money making. They need cash, which I like to provide, they do the work and enjoy it, and then my share of the cash they make buys another painting for me to relish, or perhaps, just perhaps, a new partnership somewhere to help another eager young would-be money maker. It's an excellent system, I do assure you, and I've been using it for a long time.'

'That would mean you do get involved in a lot of companies,' Abner said, and couldn't keep the eagerness out of his voice. 'More than actual film makers might — if you've just the financial involvement and not too active — '

'Precisely,' Mayer murmured and smiled at him over hands which he now held clasped in front of him. 'And I have the distinct impression, Mr Wiseman, that you want to persuade me to get involved yet again, hmm?'

Abner reddened. 'Hell, I didn't mean to — '

'My dear chap, it happens all the time. I do my best to save as much of my time as I can for my real work — the music and paintings, you understand — but sometimes someone bursts through the fences and I think, ah well, here we go again!' He turned his head slightly to the side towards the easel and its painting. 'Tell me, Mr Wiseman, could your project bring me enough for a companion piece to that?'

Abner looked at the painting and its profusion of reds and yellows and greens, almost bursting off the edge of the canvas.

'It depends on how much it costs,' he said cautiously.

'It's a Dufy. Raoul Dufy.' Mayer got to his little feet and at once the massiveness of him dwindled to a manageable size as he crossed the room to stand in front of his easel. 'Such joy, such love, such blood there is in this! Don't you agree? Is it worth over a million pounds, you might ask? But me, I ask you, what else could you buy with your million that would have the richness that this has? And now I own it.' He looked over his shoulder at Abner and said almost shyly, 'Tell me you envy me.'

'Anyone would,' Abner said. A million pounds? This guy must be gold dust. Oh, Christ, come on Abner, sell yourself, get yourself in there with Dufy!

Mayer came back to his desk and sat down and once more became a version of Mount Rushmore, solid and reliable and above all massive. 'But enough of this; you have no time to waste on such nonsense, have you?'

'It isn't nonsense!' Abner said. 'It's just that — '

'I know. You're one of the eager hungry ones. Like my dear Jo, and Simmy Gentle and all those other people whose names run alongside mine on Monty Nagel's computer. And you would rather talk of money for your project than about my paintings.'

'No – I mean, dammit, yes. But not at the moment,' Abner said and shook his head ruefully. 'Hell, I can't win at this one, can I? Whatever I say I'm in shtooch. Look, I can enjoy paintings as much as anyone else. Goddammit, I'm a film maker! How could I be otherwise! I prefer Renoir and Manet to Dufy, mind you, but all the same – '

'Ah!' Mayer took a deep breath and positively beamed at him. 'I couldn't be more delighted to know that! So, you understand the importance of balance and scale in a picture, have a taste for richness of surface texture as well as content of subject, understand the importance of the depth of lighting and the careful use of colour – your films show this, but it is good to know that you use a trained eye and not merely an instinctive one. Instinct is useful but it badly needs the moderating influence of education. And I am happy to know that if I do get involved, as you express it, with your project, whatever it is, I shall be with a man who understands the difference between Renoir and Dufy. I am indeed comforted.'

'Ah, well, I'm glad to hear it,' Abner said and stopped, unable to say more. After that, he thought, how can I get back into mundane matters like front money and budgets and –

'Well, shall we spell it out, Mr Wiseman? What is it you want to do, and how much money do you need? Have you any development money up front? Have you a working script? Tell me what there is to tell. I'm listening.' He glanced at his watch. 'For perhaps ten minutes or so more. After that I must go to a very important sale of music manuscripts.' He smiled. 'There is rumour that it may contain an unattributed but very likely autographed Mozart piece – very exciting. Ten minutes, Mr Wiseman. Think concisely.'

He took a breath and did just that. 'Guilt, Mr Mayer. That's my theme. The guilt of those who survived the labour camps is my first step. But I want also to tell a story – the story of pain suffered by their children who never saw a gate with 'ARBEIT MACHS FREI' over it and who never smelled the reek of the ovens. For them the guilt can be even more overwhelming in its own way. I've uncovered two – no, three – real life stories that will be the basis of my film, using actors who will improvise after spending intensive time – perhaps a month or more –

being with me and the material, talking it, living it, breathing it. That's it, the core of the film I want to make. *Postscripts*. The thoughts that come after the main story is told and done.'

There was a long silence as Mayer stared at him and then nodded, never taking his eyes from Abner's. 'So tell me, what are the real life stories?'

He told them, carefully and simply, using no names, but speaking of Barbara and David, of the way Miriam's grandfather had walked all through Europe looking for his child, of the painful legacy of loneliness and hatred that had been left in Barbara's daughter. And he spoke too of the Rats of Cracow, of the boy and the apples and the man in the wheelchair, though he said nothing about Brazel. To admit dealing with a blackmailer would be difficult to say the least. He could consider how to use Brazel's story later; right now he'd better be kept under wraps. And all the time he talked, Mayer watched him and showed no reaction.

When Abner had finished he stirred at last and then nodded slowly. 'You tell an elegant story, Mr Wiseman. Perhaps you should write it down. It would make an excellent script of the usual sort, I'm sure. With it you could raise your finance without too much trouble, I'm sure.'

Abner shook his head with some vehemence. 'I don't want elegance. I want truth.'

'Ah, truth. Is that to be found in the inventions of actors more than in the written words of a man as passionate about his theme as you seem to be?'

'Well, thank you for that. Yes, I'm passionate. And I'm convinced I can do it with actors better than I can if they have to learn lines. And I'll use the voices of the real people, too. A voice-over technique. You get real emotion that way – it's not impossible.'

'Oh, I know, I know. John Cassavetes, wasn't it? And others – no, not impossible. Interesting. Indeed, Mike Leigh does it on stage as well as on film, as do so many others. Well, now, what do you want of me?'

'Money,' Abner said after a moment. 'As much as I can get.'

Mayer laughed. 'My dear boy, how can I just give you money? It is, I grant you, an enthralling theme when you tell it, but I need more than that! The story of the Rats of Cracow for example, unfinished! You have not completed your research, have you? I need to be sure the story is complete before I can offer finance.'

Abner felt hope deflate as surely as if it had been a real substance that had been filling his chest and belly as he had talked to this man. He had seemed so urbane, so thoughtful, so real a thinker, with his paintings and his music, and yet now he was talking like any of the fat cats in LA or New York, and the sour taste of disappointment made him twist his lips.

Mayer laughed. 'I'm not turning you down, you know,' he said gently. 'Far from it. Just asking for a little more. I can give you a little support while you complete your research, but my further financing depends on what you get. You understand?'

Abner blinked. 'You're – what did you say?'

Mayer sighed, deeply amused. 'I said, I can finance the research stage – and am willing to do so – as long as you let me know what you find. I don't want to be faced with a *fait accompli* that is not what I would be proud to be involved with. Continue your search for these people – the story of the Rats of Cracow fascinates me. I want to know who the boy with the apples was, for example. I can't imagine a film being made of that story that doesn't include the end of it. Can you?'

'I don't know,' Abner said. 'I – it was – the other story was what I found most painful. The suffering of the girl who was born to the child whose father had sought her all over Europe.'

'Perhaps the boy with apples has children now too,' Mayer said. 'Had you thought of that? No, I can see you hadn't. You'll have to find him then, won't you? So, I will open an account for you, which I expect you to service with receipts and information and so forth, with great care. I will discuss with your agent – Monty Nagel? Yes, of course, Monty – to get a reasonable deal made. And I look forward to seeing you again soon. Come and see me when you can.'

He looked at his watch and lifted his broad shoulders above his fragile legs to stand and smile up at Abner, who was also on his feet. 'You can stay and listen to the music a little longer if you like. I, sadly, must leave it. Mozart's manuscript calls. It will cost a great deal, but what more could a man ask than to own that? *A la prochaine*, Mr Wiseman. My secretary will deal with details — '

And he was gone, leaving Abner alone with the music of the violin, crying heartbreakingly all around him and wanting to burst with excitement. He really looked to have cracked it this time.

Twenty-six

He called Miriam three times that afternoon with no joy, and that first irritated him – what right had she not to be there when he called? – and then alarmed him. She had said she hardly ever went out. But then he shook his head at his own childishness. She couldn't sit over the phone all day, after all; and anyway, Miriam being Miriam, she was very likely not bothering to answer the thing when it rang. It would be just like her.

So he couldn't share his excitement with anyone except Dave, and he was not totally satisfactory.

'Oh, great!' he boomed down the phone when Abner told him that he had the offer of some research money. 'Glad for you. But it doesn't guarantee he'll take any more equity in it, you know. Depends on how much he gets out of Nagel. I wouldn't cheer too loud until I knew the actual deal. But it's great you're not as strapped for cash as you were. You'll still do my commercial, of course.'

'A deal's a deal. Of course I will.'

'And after that? I've got one or two nice little jobs here that'll bring in a buck or two.'

'I want more than a buck or two for my time now, Dave.' Abner grinned at his own reflection in the glass of the phone booth, imagining Dave's crestfallen face at the other end of the line. 'You're one hell of a chancer, man! I'm working for coffee money tomorrow – why should I do more? Not exactly a union man's dream, are you?'

'The day I am'll be the day they take me out of here in a wooden overcoat. Listen, we can make an arrangement. Good directors aren't exactly falling out of the sky right now, know what I mean? I got a nice little one here – just a sixty second job – half in London, half in Amsterdam, would you believe. Nice town Amsterdam. You can get stoned out of your skull just smelling the air when you land at Schiphol airport. That place really is Pot City – legal there, it is.'

'I know, I've heard. Listen, let me see what Nagel does with Mayer, OK? If I get enough cash, I'm obviously going to concentrate on the research for the film. If not, I may be glad enough for a coupla days in Amsterdam. At a decent rate, mind you. None of your – '

Dave ignored that. 'Lots of interesting stuff about Jews in Amsterdam, Abner. Did you know that? Ann Frank house and the museum and all – '

His interest sharpened. 'Museum? Ann Frank, of course, I know about – '

'Knowing and seeing are two different things. I was raised a good Catholic boy and I'm here to tell you I came out of that house choked to my eyebrows. Couldn't talk to anyone for half an hour. The museum, it's in the old Jewish quarter of the town. It's one hell of a place for sightseeing. Old buildings full of hookers hanging their tits out of windows. It's the red light district now, but they say there's a great museum there now, all about what happened to the Jews of Holland – me, I never went, but I was told. So, listen, make my commercial and you can see it for free.'

'Some free! What's the product?'

Dave laughed fatly. 'Wait for it. Condoms.'

'Come again?'

'Rubbers, Johnnies, prophylactics. Here they call 'em French letters. In any language they're real passion killers.'

'They have commercials on European TV for them? Jesus! I never knew.'

'Not yet, but they will eventually. We've had 'em here in the UK already. AIDS and so forth. But this isn't for a terrestrial station. It's satellite. They're having a go. They want a voice-over scenario so they can use it in every language, the whole schmear, lovers in romantic places, flowers reflected in water, girls' hair blowing in the breezes on canal boats, all ending up with hotel windows and lights going out – really original stuff and I don't think! Not tricky for you though, believe me, but it needs to look good.'

'Why Amsterdam? I thought your people all worked here and

made commercials for foreign companies. How come the reversal?'

'Condoms, that's how. Scares the shit out of the UK companies. Me. I like to be a fixer, you know that. So I said I'd fix the London end and got the whole job as a reward. You can have five hundred smackers and your expenses. As long as you travel cheap and don't stay in no fancy joints,' he ended hastily.

Abner laughed. 'I'll think about it. After I've talked to Nagel. And, Dave, thanks for fixing the meeting with Matthew Mayer. It's paid off and I truly appreciate it.'

'Forget it. I said I'm a fixer. On second thoughts, don't forget it. Go to Amsterdam for me. Quid pro quo.'

Abner laughed. 'I'll let you know. Tomorrow when I see you. Maybe,' and hung up.

He tried Miriam again with no success and stood there in the phone booth listening to the distant ringing, imagining the sound echoing through those dusty manuscript filled rooms and a worm of anxiety crawled into him. But he stamped it down and called Nagel. Who came to the phone at once.

'Hey, hey, Abner, you done good with a vengeance, hey?'

'You know already?' Abner said, amazed. 'About Mayer?'

'Of course I do. He's one of the most efficient people you can deal with. Rowena's been on the blower already and – '

'Rowena?'

'The secretary. Tall thin woman with legs like a piano. You didn't see her?'

Abner laughed. 'I saw her. So she's the power behind the system, hmm? I should have thrown her a line, maybe.'

'No need. She's just Her Master's Voice. Never thinks a thing for herself, but deals tough for him. He wants five per cent, in exchange for funding up to script stage, or working storyboard stage, whichever you use, as monitored and accepted by him. Not to exceed fifteen thousand pounds.'

'Five per cent of the – Christ! That sounds a lot. For a lousy fifteen thousand.'

'He also wants you to use designated companies for the filming once you start and – '

'Oh, does he?' Wrath began to bubble in him. He'd been so pleased with himself but now it was all beginning to go sour.

Again. Was this project ever going to get off the ground? 'And what else?'

'The option to carry all the finance if you get to the script stage with his approval and start work. He'll cover all costs and – '

Staring out of the phone booth into the street, and the traffic roaring past him, Abner shook his head in disbelief. 'He'll carry the whole film? Can he do it? Has he got that sort of money?'

Nagel laughed and the sound was thin and clattery in Abner's ear. 'M.M.'s forgotten how much he's got. He's a money man, Abner! He makes it big. And he spends it big when he does – it's up to you now. If he likes what you come up with, you're in business. If he doesn't, well, forget it. No one else'll pick up anything he leaves in this town. And if you find the finance overseas, he'll still be in for the five per cent, remember. But face the facts, Abner. Once you've asked M.M. you're on a roller coaster.'

Abner squinted a little through the dirty glass, staring sightlessly at the lumbering red buses.

'It feels like it. How much of the equity does he want for all this, for Christ's sake? Do I get anything at all for my efforts?' And he put all the heavy irony he could into the question.

'I did my best, for you, Abner. And, with M.M. it's a good deal. Rowena said seventy per cent – '

'Seventy!' Abner howled. 'The man's a piranha! How can we get any sort of distribution deal, any sort of – '

'Will you shut up and listen, Abner!' Nagel shouted back and Abner took a deep breath and said grimly, 'So, I'm listening.'

'I got her down to sixty-five. But that's the end of it, because he handles distribution, marketing, the lot. Through his own people, of course. Jo Rossily, Simmy Gentle, they'll all get a piece of the action. But it's out of his cut, not yours, get me? You're left with thirty per cent of the profits, remembering to add on his five per cent for script research cash. But it's a clear and clean thirty per cent of the gross. There are guys making movies on the West Coast don't end up with that much of their own properties once everyone's had a nibble. M.M. doesn't nibble, he takes one big bite, but at least you know where you are and you don't bleed from a dozen different wounds. And as long as you get yourself a really good production accountant and make sure you don't do yourself down with sloppy budgeting – even arrange for a bit of creative bookkeeping – you'll do fine.'

'It all sounds a bit dubious to me. I know it'd make life a lot easier to have just one financial set up, but sixty-five per cent? Seventy, I mean – Christ! Can't you chop that at all?'

'I could try, but it's my guess he'll lift his shoulders and smile graciously the way he does, and just walk away. He's not hungry, you see, Abner. You need him more than he needs you, and he knows it.'

He stood there for a long moment, thinking hard and then said, 'Listen, Nagel – Monty – this is a hard one to ask. But I have to. You're not giving me any sort of runaround, are you? Is he – ' He stopped, and then went on with a little rush, 'I get the impression M.M.'s into every part of the business in this town and I can't help wondering if he's part of you too. He wants me to deal only with his companies when I get going. Is he already dealing with one of his own in dealing with you? And if he is, aren't there laws in this country about that sort of thing? Cartels and so forth?'

He felt the sigh as much as heard it. 'Listen, Abner, this is no time for me to give you a lesson in the facts of life. Let me just say this much – controlling interests are what matter, and yes, we have laws about that and no, they're not being breached, OK? When a guy has a slice of a company he naturally tries to help it any way he can – but having a slice and being in control are two different things. I can assure you that M.M. is not controlling anything he shouldn't be. It's all above board.'

'You haven't answered my question. Is he involved with your company!'

'Christ, you're a suspicious bugger! No, he isn't. He has no money in my business. I bought it back when – '

'What? You mean – '

'I mean just what I say. It's no secret in the business. He once did help me out. He's a good guy and he helped me out. I'm bloody grateful to him. But I'm straight with him and he's straight with me. Once I got going again, got a coupla big earners in pop music, I bought my equity back and no arguments from M.M. But I won't deny that I like to do business with him now. He was good to me, I'm good to him. Why not? One day I might need him again, and anyway, it'd be a lousy business if you only ever dealt in money alone. It's personalities too, it's goodwill, it's *trust*, Abner!'

'Yeah,' Abner said and stood there still staring blankly out at the street. 'Yeah.'

'So tell me, what's the decision? It's still your movie. You can still pull out, tell him you don't want him, go elsewhere to find cash. If you can get it.'

'I've got a clearer picture now, Monty. I don't think there's any place else I can go to where I won't find M.M. Am I right?'

'Pretty much,' Monty said cheerfully. 'He's not the only one like him, mind you. There are other people involved in films around but – '

'I know. M.M.'s the one with the muscle.'

'You got it. So what do we do? I think it's a good deal. I can go through the contracts with you line by line, with any lawyer you care to bring along if you don't trust me, and you'll see what I mean. You'll still be better off at the end of the day than you would with the usual sort of bits and pieces deals people make. But if you can trust me . . . ' He left it dangling in the air.

'I trust you,' Abner said wearily. He was suddenly tired of it all, and anyway what did it matter? He had the chance to make his film and that was what came first. The whole project could still founder, he could still lose it – and even if he made it and it was released, it could still bomb at the box office. Mayer stood to lose a hell of a lot more than he did himself, in money terms. For himself, it was passion and conviction and the need to make the film that he had to put in the pot. M.M. was the one with the real weight, the one putting in hard cash. So why make a drama out of it? And anyway, didn't he always say money was a secondary consideration? Making the movie was what mattered – but it still rankled that he might be the subject of a rip-off.

Dammit, he thought then, dammit. Let's make the film. To hell with the rest. And he turned his back on the street to stare at the graffiti on the notice board behind the phone and said, 'It's OK, Monty. I won't do any checking. If I can't trust you, who can I trust? You're in this too, after all.'

'Am I ever. And remember I'll get my cut out of your share, my friend. It pays me to get the best deal for you that I can if I want any sort of deal for myself. And I'm well pleased with this, well pleased.'

'Then it shall please me too, my lord,' Abner said.

'Eh?'

'I was quoting Shakespeare at you, my friend. The French Princess and Harry Plantagenet, who's just raped her country – never mind. Maybe you didn't see both the movies the way I did.'

'I'm not into classics. OK. Come into the office as soon as you can. The documents'll be here, we'll sign and there'll be a bank account for you. Doesn't it make you dribble?'

'It sure does,' Abner said and laughed. 'OK, Monty. We're in business, at last.'

'Almost,' Monty warned. 'Remember he insists on stage reports on the script's progress. Wants to know what research you do and what you pick up. He's really interested in this one.'

'I won't forget. And Monty – thanks a lot.'

'Well, well!' There was a rich irony in the voice. 'He noticed!'

'I noticed. You did me well, I think.'

'I did the best possible. See you soon then.'

'Yeah. Very soon. I've got a job to get out of the way first and then I'll be in – '

'Ah, yes. One of Shandwick's little ventures. Have fun and remember to count your change. If you think I'm a chancer, watch him! 'Bye, Abner.'

He could have enjoyed working on the dog food commercial more if he hadn't been so concerned about Miriam, who still wasn't at the end of her phone. In the end he had sent her a letter last night, marking it urgent and asking her to call him, and then gone grimly to work in the morning, doing his best to get what he could out of it.

It wasn't that difficult. The dogs were agreeable enough, if smelly, the people in the Battersea Dogs' Home friendly and co-operative and the crew was clearly very experienced and blessedly taciturn. And his star, he decided, was a riot. A tall girl with an unbelievable bust of cliff face proportions, which she displayed to the best advantage she could in an incredibly low cut dress even in this cold weather, she had the yellowest and most abundant hair he had ever seen. She knew precisely what he wanted almost before he asked for it. Even as he squinted through his viewfinder, while his cameraman stood mutely sucking noisily on an empty pipe beside him, she turned her body so that her breasts seemed to obliterate half the background and stared at the camera with sleepy lasciviousness that was very beguiling if, as Abner told the sound man, who guffawed, a bit of a waste on dog food. Her voice was high and easy to hear and, as far as Abner could tell, she got the intonations and emphases right in her piece to camera. She'd learned it well before she arrived, and Abner liked that. A true professional, he told her cheerfully, and she nodded and laughed and said with a sidelong glint at the cameraman, whom she clearly fancied, 'And not only on a film like this,' in heavily accented English. The cameraman ignored her but Abner, delighted, laughed a lot and went on setting up his shots in a better humour than he could have hoped he'd be in.

The client, a small fussy man clutching a briefcase which he never opened, and clearly comprehending no English at all, arrived after they'd done the first shots and had to be shown them all again on the monitor as the presenter – who, it turned out to everyone's amazement, rejoiced in the name of Magnolia – talked volubly at him in a great Icelandic waterfall. But he seemed happy enough with what he saw, and for the rest of the time stood behind the camera watching unblinkingly the way Magnolia's breasts heaved and rolled with every breath, seeming perfectly happy.

It started to rain hard just after twelve and they had to retire to a small shed to one side of the area they had commandeered for their set and sat, watching the water trickle across the courtyard and listening to the dogs snuffle and whine while the crew drank cup after cup of stewed tea and did the *Telegraph* crossword. They ignored Magnolia and the client whispering in the corner, and left Abner to his own thoughts and devices, too, as he stared at the pouring grey sky, trying to estimate how much more time he needed to get the last of these fiddly shots in the can and himself out of this malodorous place. If the rain stopped within the half-hour he could do it, he decided, as long as they made sure there was no ground in the frame, for continuity's sake; the concrete had been dry when they started.

His thoughts began to drift away from the job in hand to his own affairs, and he sat and stared at the water trickling down the window of the hut and thought again about Brazel. That the guy had been honest according to his own lights there was no doubt in Abner's mind now. A nasty piece of work, but for all that, he said what he meant. There was a man in this country who had once sold seventeen of his own people to the Gestapo, a man who was now doing very well indeed. He had to be for Brazel to be getting so much cash from him. And he thought about that for a while and to his own amazement found himself smiling. There was something so very brazen about it – and then he laughed aloud so that the cameraman looked up at him briefly with a sympathetic glint in his eye. Brazel the brazen; it had a satisfying ring to it.

Maybe he could talk to Brazel again, find out what sort of business this man was in. If he was rich he had to be making his money somewhere because he clearly hadn't inherited any and the logical place for that surely would be The City. London's Wall Street. Or so he imagined. He'd seen enough of British television news now to know just how powerful the City of London was, and it made sense to seek the man there. A stockbroker? A commodities dealer? Who could he ask for information about such people? He knew no real financiers here, no one whose brains he could pick.

And then he thought – the man's a Jew. How many prominent Jews are there in the City, with the sort of money that makes it possible for them to be blackmailed of a million and still be left with ample for their own need? Wasn't that what Brazel had said? He had a hazy notion that he'd heard somewhere that, as in the States, Jews did not fit as comfortably into the hierarchy of the Stock Exchange as they did into others, like manufacturing industry. Old-style antisemitism, he thought wryly dies hard. Just like the new kind. Perhaps he should look elsewhere.

Manufacturing industry; again he was floundering. How could he possibly know who were the really fat cats here with shadowy pasts that could just possibly be rooted in Eastern Europe during the war? He had heard of some tycoons since he'd been here, of course he had. There were Australians, he knew, who were cutting swathes through not just this country but his own as well, and he thought about the best known of them and then shook his head at himself. They had always been written about exhaustively, with their cricket interests and their television connections and their newspapers and their airlines; no, none of them. There must be others, less forthcoming in public and, therefore, better able to keep their pasts out of scrutiny.

And that, he thought bitterly, was the bind, the true catch. The visible tycoons were by their very visibility absolved of guilt in this case. They couldn't be the Boy with the Apples unless they'd totally fabricated their stories of their origins, and to do that successfully in a country with a gutter press like the one in Britain, Abner thought grimly, was very unlikely. And any tycoon who kept his light turned low and well shielded would be by definition unknown, a hidden creature. So how could a stranger like Abner find him?

No, it had to be up to Brazel. Somehow that man had to be persuaded to disgorge his information. Because if he didn't, there was no way Abner could get M.M. to disgorge his real money and get *Postscripts* on the floor.

At which point the rain stopped and the crew finished their crossword and the client woke up and began to fuss. Having to go back to work again on a dog food commercial was, Abner discovered then, not such a bad thing after all. It sure beat worrying himself sick over his film. And, of course, over Miriam.

Twenty-seven

He went back to Camden Town as full of pleasure, as he told himself gleefully, as a monkey is of nuts, glowing with the grunted approval of the cameraman ('It makes a nice change to work with a bloke that knows what he's doing. Hope to work with you again, mate,') and triumphantly clutching his can of film under his arm. He'd brought the thing in in one day's shooting, in spite of the rain, in spite of the sudden attack of fussiness on the part of the client who had decided at half-past two that he needed to talk at length in an incomprehensible babble about everything to do with his company's precious dog food, and in spite of Magnolia's increasingly blatant attempts to make the cameraman, and that was one hell of an achievement.

He walked from Camden Town station with his head down against the rain, which was back with a vengeance and had become the spiral sort that seemed hell bent on getting into every aperture of his clothing, rehearsing in his mind what he would say to Miriam as soon as he got her on the phone. He'd try again as soon as he got in, he promised himself. She might just have got his letter by now and be ready to answer when the phone rang and he actually ran up the steps to his flat, ignoring the humped shape of someone sitting on the bottom step just inside the dark hallway. There usually were people there, waiting out of the rain for the bus that stopped just outside, and he'd learned to behave like any Londoner and pay them no attention. It was like being back in Manhattan, really.

But as he put his key in his lock the shape came up the stairs after him, and he turned, suddenly alarmed. Maybe Camden Town was more like Manhattan than he knew, with muggers and all.

'I'm sorry I didn't answer the phone,' she said. 'I got bored with it and switched it off. We had one of those silencer things fitted when Geoff was ill and I just used it and then forgot to switch it on again.'

He stared at her, dumbfounded. She looked totally different, and he couldn't see how at first, and then realised. She had cut her hair; the cloud of dark frizz had gone and been replaced by a cap of small tight curls, and she was wearing a black and white checked coat with the collar pulled up about her ears in a way that made her look vulnerable and a little lost.

'Miriam? Ye gods, Miriam, how the hell – what are you doing here? I thought – what have you done to yourself? I've never seen you looking so – hey, come on in, for God's sake! I'll make some coffee.'

She followed him into the flat and suddenly he felt as awkward as a schoolboy on a first date, and dropping the film can on his desk with a little clatter rushed around the room to tidy it, thrusting discarded shirts and socks into drawers and ineffectually pulling at the covers of the bed he hadn't bothered to make and stow away before he left that morning. She watched him for a few moments and then laughed and untied the belt of her coat and pulled it off.

'For pity's sake, Abner, will you stop coming on like Chicken Licken and settle down. Make the coffee. I'll straighten up here.' And she pushed him aside with a friendly roughness that pleased him enormously, and set to work on the bed, converting it back into a sofa, with the covers and the pillow neatly stowed in its bottom, in a matter of moments. And then went about the room moving odd things, tidying papers and generally making it look agreeable as he made the coffee, taking the time to use real coffee and a hot jug.

'No dust and water for us,' he said and grinned at her. 'Real Colombian stuff. There's a place over the road roasts its own and grinds it fresh for me.'

They sipped in a companionable silence as he sat perched on the edge of the big pine table and she sat composedly in the typing chair he had in front of it, until he couldn't keep it back another moment.

'You look incredible. What have you done to yourself? It's – well, incredible.'

'You mean I looked like a dog before?'

He flushed crimson. 'Jesus, no! You can be so — listen, you walk in here wearing a whole set of new clothes, as smart as goddamm paint, and with your hair cut to the scalp and a fancy make-up on — I make films, for Christ's sake, so I notice things like that! — and you don't expect me to react? You looked fine to me before. Now you look great. All right? Not that it matters either way, of course. I guess I forgot myself there for a moment. I've been around enough modern women to know it's the greatest insult to say good things about their appearance. So, I'm sorry, forgive me, grovel, grovel, I take it all back. Happy?'

She smiled up at him then and shook her head. 'Not in the least. I don't want you to take it back. I want to be told I looked fine before, but now I've spent some money I look fantastic. I wasn't being fair to tease you. So I take it back. It's my turn. Have I done a good job?' And she put down her cup and stood up and went pirouetting across the room and he watched her, delighted.

'The dress I got in a sale so I don't feel quite so wicked,' she said gaily. 'I never wore a red like this before, but it cheered me up.'

'Me too,' he said fervently, because indeed it was a splendid dress, in vivid scarlet that was enough to make anyone laugh aloud at the sight of it. She was wearing red shoes too, and above them very sheer black tights that made her long legs look even longer, and which seemed to go on for ever since her skirt was remarkably short, well above the knee.

But it was the haircut that had done it. Her neck looked long and beautifully curved and above it her chin made a perfect line with her throat; her ears were small and well set back and the make-up she had on — put on by an expert he judged — gave her a whole new glow. He knew then that he was past redemption and so far involved with this girl there was to be no way out, ever, and laughed aloud at the joy of it.

'The mother lode,' he said. 'Oh, are you ever the mother lode!'

'I'm what?'

'It doesn't matter. One of these days I'll explain. If you give me the chance. We'll see. You look a million dollars, Miriam, you really do.'

'Not quite,' she said. 'A fistful of forints, is all. I told you, I got money from Hungary — '

'And you couldn't have spent it better,' he said and held out both hands to her. 'Let me be the first to congratulate you on your brilliant business sense. I never saw money better spent.'

'I'm going to spend some more of it too,' she said and there was defiance in her voice now. 'I know I ought to be sensible and put it into fixing up the house to make it a better proposition for buyers, but it's been so long since I spent anything on myself I thought – the hell with it. It's my turn.'

'Is it ever! What are you going to do?'

'Travel,' she said and glowed. 'I'm going to buy a ticket and get in a plane and go somewhere – '

He laughed, caught up in her joy. 'Where?'

'I don't know. Somewhere. Anywhere. Paris, maybe. Or Rome? Not Rome. Too ugly, Rome. Anyway it's a place for the summer time. Amsterdam, maybe, to look at the pictures or – '

'Amsterdam?' he said and lifted his chin almost exultantly. 'I have to go there next week. I've got a job there. Making a commercial – '

She had stopped her twirl around the room and was standing staring at him. 'You have? Really?'

'Really.'

'Doing what?'

'I told you. Making a commercial.'

'What for?' She was looking suspicious now.

He grinned from ear to ear. 'Condoms. What is it he said you call 'em here? French letters.'

Her face cracked. 'God, that has to be true! You could never have invented it.'

'Why should I invent it? I'm telling you. The job I did today was for dog food. Another commercial – ' He flicked his forefinger at the can of film on the table beside him. 'The same man I made this for wants me to go to Amsterdam to do this other job. All expenses paid as well as a fee. And it's the chance for me to do some research, too. May I come with you, Miriam? Please may I? It'd make one hell of a difference to me.'

'Why?' she said then, still standing there and staring at him. 'Why should it make such a difference?'

He was silent for a long moment. This was, he knew, important. It was like being at an exam and facing the last question, the one which would either pass him or fail him. He had to get it right. And he took a deep breath and stared at her as directly as he knew how and said simply, 'Because I'd rather be with you than anywhere in the world.'

They ate dinner in a small Greek restaurant around the corner, and he let her pay for it. She had said with an air of studied casualness that she would give him dinner this time and he knew better than to argue, though he wanted to; but, at least, he could steer her towards a place he knew wouldn't cost too much, well aware of how furious she would be if she realised it. But she didn't, because the food was plentiful and good and she enjoyed it. They ate quantities of *houmous* and grilled *halloumi* cheese and salad and a massive *kleftiko*, fragrant with herbs and as tender as butter and drank a good deal of the rough Cypriot wine. There was some music, too; a boy with a bazouki which he played with great panache if small skill, and that made them laugh a lot. The whole evening made them laugh a lot and he sat opposite her in the soft light, watching the way her head was set on her neck and the movement of the muscles of her cheeks, which he found particularly beguiling, and tried not to think of what the feelings he was battening down might lead him to.

It could be hell, he knew; at present she was being wonderful, approachable, even affectionate and enormous fun, but at any moment she could be plunged back into her depths again. Could he handle that for always? At this second he knew he wanted her company for always, but that was as she was now. How long could always last when she went back into her miserable mode again? He simply didn't know.

They were eating sticky Turkish delight with their almost equally sticky Turkish coffee, when he started to tell her of what he'd been told by Brazel and she listened, her eyes bright in the soft light but a little distracted as though she were watching him more than listening to him and that pleased him, for it meant she was as happy being with him as he was with her, he thought. That's why she looks like that. But he pretended he hadn't noticed and talked on about Brazel.

' . . . whoever the man is now, or wherever he is, I've got to find him,' he was saying. 'Because without that information Mayer won't part with the rest of the money for the film. It really is like playing craps with loaded dice.'

Her eyes sharpened suddenly and she was staring at him. 'I've remembered,' she said abruptly. 'I was thinking about Amsterdam while you were talking about Brazel and I remembered. He wrote to me – '

'He wrote to you? Are you sure?'

'I told you I knew the name. I tend to remember silly things and I remember that one. It was the signature and such pompous prose, you know? And then he signed it Harry Brazel, so casual and – it just seemed odd. Not Harold or Henry or Harvey, a proper name, but the diminutive. It didn't seem to go with the sort of careful English of the letter.'

'He's European, Polish. I didn't ask him what – but he had a different first language. That's why he now speaks – and obviously writes – perfect English. What did he want?'

'Hell, I can't remember.' She frowned hard, staring at him blankly as she dug down into her memory. 'I just know I came across the name. But what did he want? Oh, damn it all, why can't I remember?'

'Close your eyes,' he said with some urgency. 'Maybe you can do what I do and – well, close your eyes. See yourself opening the letter. Look at the signature, Harry Brazel . . . '

She had obeyed him and now her lips curled, and she sat there very upright with her eyes tightly closed, and smiling. He could have leaned across and kissed her. He almost did.

'How odd!' she said. 'I can see it, you know? All very flowery – easy to read but lots of curly bits on the letters.'

'Now read what's over the signature,' he said softly. 'Just look at the page and read it. It's only a trick – you can do it.'

'Typewritten,' she said. 'It's typewritten.'

Inside his head he swore. He knew how much harder it was to remember a typeface; he didn't know why but it was. 'Try, Miriam. Try to see what it is he wants from the letter.'

There was a silence as she sat there with her eyes closed and he sat opposite her with both hands curled into fists on the table, watching eagerly. And then she sighed and shook her head and opened her eyes.

'I can't,' she said. 'It was odd, though. I was sitting at the kitchen table and there was a pile of letters in front of me and this one was in a thick white envelope. I *saw* it – isn't that odd? But I can't manage anything else. I'll tell you this much, though –

whatever it was, I didn't do it. I mean, he wanted something and I didn't want to do it so I sent him one of the cards.'

'What cards?'

'Oh, the ones we had printed: "Professor Geoffrey Hinchelsea regrets he is unable to accede to your request. His documentation is available only to historians. The information you require should be available elsewhere in established libraries." I use them a lot.'

'Then what he wanted wasn't to do with your father's period or research?'

'It could have been that. Or just that it wasn't real history.'

He flashed a grin at her. 'Like me?'

'Like you,' she said and grinned back and again he had to stop himself leaning across the table to touch her. She looked wonderful. Goddammed wonderful.

'Or it could have been something you didn't want to let him know about?'

'It's no use trying to wheedle me, Abner. Honestly, I can't remember. He wanted something that I knew wasn't what Geoff's stuff is for so I said no. That's all I can tell you. Why not ask him?'

He was struck by that. 'I suppose I could — '

'Well, do it. And let me know what it was. And now, it's time we went — I've got a long drive home.'

At once Brazel and his interests, the film, everything, vanished from Abner's mind and he looked at her and then picked up his cup of coffee to pretend to drink the thick cold dregs. I mustn't say it, he was thinking. I dare not say it. Oh, Christ, how can I not say it?

'Do you have to?' He said it as casually as he could.

She was looking over her shoulder, trying to catch the waiter's eye to ask for the bill and she sat very still, her head still turned away.

'Go home? Of course.'

'I just wondered,' he said, still very casual. 'I could offer hospitality of a sort and you could go and see about your trip to Amsterdam tomorrow, couldn't you? I'll be able to phone early to sort out when I'll be there and — '

'Stop it, Abner,' she said and turned back to the table as the waiter arrived. 'Just stop it. I haven't even agreed to Amsterdam yet.'

He swallowed. 'You have. You must. I've set my heart on it.'

She managed to laugh at that. 'Oh, I see. You've set your heart on it, so that means it has to happen?'

'Yes,' he said quietly, and she stared at him and he looked down at the table.

'I'm going back to Oxford. Now,' she said abruptly.

'If you prefer,' he said then. 'It was just a suggestion. I'm trying to make things easier for you.'

'Nothing's easy for me,' she said with a sudden savagery in her voice. 'Things that are so simple and normal for other people are hell on earth for me. I thought you understood that. Or some of it.'

'I do,' he said. 'And I'm – no, I'm not sorry. I'm sad. There's no need to be afraid of me, you know.'

'I'm not afraid of you, damn you,' she flared. 'You ought to know that by now! It's nothing to do with you. Let me have that bill, for God's sake!' And she almost snatched it from the hand of the slightly startled waiter who had been hovering.

He said nothing as she reached into her bag and pulled out a wallet and the notes to pay; it was touching to see she used neither cheque book nor plastic, and that underlined for him the narrowness of her life in a way that made his throat tighten. She had had a dreadful time before him; and was still having it, was still a frightened child who needed nursing through her bad dreams.

'It's all right, Miriam,' he said gently. 'Everything's going to be fine, I promise you.'

She looked up at him briefly and he saw her eyes were glittering with the threat of tears. 'Is it?' she said. 'Is it really? How can you promise anything?'

'I can and I do – and what's more I'll make it all come right. Believe me. Tonight go home to Oxford. Drive like an angel, please, and get there safe. And next week Amsterdam. Hang on to that, Miriam. Because that you really are going to do.'

'Yes,' she said. 'Yes. I am, aren't I?'

Twenty-eight

―――――――――――――――

Not until the plane actually took off and was banking steeply over the reservoirs and ticky-tacky houses around Heathrow did he believe it would happen. The whole project had been so fraught with uncertainty that he had almost lost sight of why he had wanted to go to Amsterdam in the first place.

Sorting out the job with Dave Shandwick had been no trouble at all. Abner had taken in his edited film, after a fruitful morning in an editing suite in Charlotte Street, and Dave had run it through his playback and grunted his approval.

'Can't beat a pro, can you, Abner? They'll love it. What's more, they'll want more. I'll dub in music tonight. I thought for the dog shots, we'd use a bit of "William Tell" – hunting and all that you know? They'll like that. And we can take it down behind the girl's spiel – and that's some pair of tits, for Christ's sake, ain't it just? You should see her in some of the blue stuff she does – incredible!'

' "William Tell",' Abner said and almost groaned. 'Come on, Dave, can't you think of an even bigger cliché than that?'

'Good, ain't it?' Dave said complacently. 'Think like the common man, that's the whole secret of success. Well done, my old friend. Here's the cash I owe you and how about a bit more?'

'Seven hundred and the Pulitzer Hotel and you're on for your rubbers commercial,' Abner had said and then grinned at him. 'Come on, Dave, it's a bargain! Apart from anything else, I thought about the brief, and you don't even have to use paid presenters or performers.'

Dave's eyes had brightened. 'I don't?'

'No – opportunistic stuff, that's what we need. Wander round the place with a good crew and your eyes open and there'll be lovers, lots of 'em. Just film the bits of scenery they happen to be in, is all. As for the flowers on the water, the breeze in the trees and the rest of the schlock, who needs any extra cash for that? And I can cod a light in a window without paying for the privilege! I'll be cheap at seven hundred. Anyone else'd want actors, for God's sake.'

'Anyone else wouldn't get 'em. Make it six hundred.'

'Six seventy-five and that's my last. And I want to do Amsterdam first, London later. OK?'

And Dave had sighed a deep lugubrious sigh and then they'd laughed and the deal was on. And Abner went off with details of where he was to meet his crew in Amsterdam and a handsome advance on the job in his wallet. He was beginning, he told himself, as he clattered down the stairs into the street, to feel like a real man again. And had whistled softly between his teeth as he loped off towards Monty Nagel's office.

There, all had been very smooth. The secretary had greeted him by name with a wide smile and showed him through into Monty's inner sanctum and he thought sourly of the way money made a man visible. Last time he'd come in she'd had scant use for him, but now there were smiles all round. And he looked at her coolly and refused her offer of coffee and felt better.

The contract Monty had waiting for him was all he'd promised; a model of careful detail and, as far as Abner could tell, very well thought out. Every time he remembered some detail he ought to look for, drawing on his memories of previous tussles over contracts, there it was in a sub-section to a paragraph somewhere, and he took out his pen at last and initialled and signed wherever Monty pointed; and then shook hands with him and leaned back in his chair.

'Well,' he had said. 'So far, so almost good. Now I have to make sure I come up with the sort of story he wants, and that I want.'

'Finished stories,' Monty had said, and rearranged his belly surreptitiously over his too tight waistband. He looked to have gained a few pounds even since Abner had seen him last, he thought. A rich life, being an agent. Beat directing hands down, if it was money you were after. 'He was very hot on that, was M.M.'

'What sort of guy is he?' Abner had asked curiously. 'All I

know is he's got a lot of money, and seems good at making more and likes painting and music.'

'And theatre and books.' Monty lifted expressive brows. 'He's always been a pushover for companies that deal with the arts. So he's got fingers in a lot of pies. But I'll tell you this: he never puts a foot wrong. If he takes over a publishers and chooses the books, then he gets bestsellers. Not schlock, you understand. Heavy stuff. Booker winners, the whole bit. You got to admire him.'

'Oh, I admire, I admire!' Abner had said. 'But tell me, where does he come from?'

'Come from?' Monty was puzzled.

'Yeah, where was he born and all that?'

'I don't know,' Monty said. 'Why should I? The guy lives here, so I imagine he was born here.'

'Like hell! Even I can see that London's as big a melting pot as Manhattan ever was. I've met enough people here to know that half of them come from some place else and the rest are immigrants.'

Monty had laughed. 'You're right there. My lot came originally from the *haim* – you know, the Pale. My father always said he was a son of Neptune, born on the boat between Hamburg and here. They meant to go to America, the grandparents, but they got this far with a sick premature baby so they waited till he was fit to make the rest of the journey and there it was – they never got no further. So, punkt! Here I am. And to think I could have been one of your real high priced LA agents – enough to make you cry.'

'You're doing all right,' Abner had said dryly. 'Was M.M. like that?'

Monty looked slightly shocked. 'One of the old timers, the ones that came over on the onion boats? Never think it! He's a real top drawer type. Old fashioned, you know? Very cultured. Real public school stuff.'

'I thought with a name like Mayer, he was a Jew, too,' Abner said. 'But it –'

'You can't tell a thing from names,' Monty said. 'Why do you ask? Is it important?'

'No, it's not important,' Abner said. 'I suppose. It's just I'm a curious guy. I like to know all I can about the people I work with.' He grinned then. 'I know a bit more about you now, don't I?'

'Yeah. And I take size eleven in shoes and a seventeen and a half in collars and I dress on the right. Satisfied?'

'Satisfied enough. I'll get to know the rest some other time. Over dinner, maybe.'

'Sure. You can afford it now, right? I've sorted out the business side with my own bank. Tania will give you the information – you can shift it to your own bank if you like but believe me they give good service and there's a branch only just round the corner, which is handy. So what's the next step?'

'A bit of combined operations. I'm going to Amsterdam to make a sexy commercial for Dave Shandwick and while I'm there I'll do some research.'

'Oh?' Monty said and looked at him sharply. 'Why Amsterdam?'

'Why not? I'll be there anyway and Dave tells me there's a great museum there. The Jews of Holland had a bad time in the war. Enough of them went to the camps. I might pick up something useful.'

'But you've no specific lead there?' Monty seemed eager for an answer and Abner looked at him, his brows raised.

'Not anything special. Why? Does it matter?'

'Oh, not at all, not at all,' Monty said. 'I was just interested. Listen, enjoy it there. Don't smoke too much funny tobacco and keep away from the Waterlooplein – '

'Where the ladies offer their wares in the windows, yeah, yeah, I know. If anyone else tells me about that, I'll spit! In the coffee shop this morning where I had my breakfast I said, "Amsterdam" and they were all drooling, and then a guy in the train I got talking to – everyone seems to think I'm sex-obsessed to be going there.'

'We can all have our dreams,' Monty said and grunted to his feet. 'So, listen, good luck. Come back as soon as you've got some stuff for M.M. and we'll fix another meet. Get back soon's you can, now. You've got some real work to do – not these tuppeny-ha'penny commercials.'

'Just a few days,' Abner had promised. 'Just a few days.' And had gone away to make some highly satisfactory arrangements at the bank, and then to buy a couple of new shirts and a pair of light trousers and phone Miriam. So far, so good.

The plane settled down to a steady grumbling roar and he turned his head and looked at her. 'They'll fetch coffee and drinks soon,' he said. 'What'll it be?'

She shook her head, peering down at the ground through the window beside her, clearly absorbed in all she saw, and he looked at the line of her cheek and tried to relax. They were here, and considering how hard she had wriggled, how strongly she had at first denied that she had ever really intended to go, that was amazing. He had had to go down to Oxford and almost drag her out to the travel agents so that together they could book the flight and their hotel rooms; and she had protested hard all the time. But not hard enough. He had been determined, keeping firmly in his mind's eye that moment at the Greek restaurant in Camden Town when she had replied to his question about really going to Amsterdam. 'Yes,' she had said. 'I am, aren't I?' and had reminded her of it every time she tried to protest.

They had bought the tickets, and he left her to pay for her own, feeling not only that it was important for her own self-esteem that she do so, but that it carried a form of insurance that she would go. Parting with that much money added a compulsion of its own; but he could have cheerfully strangled the girl behind the desk who, when she handed over the packet of tickets had said brightly, 'There's a twenty-four hour cancellation facility – they can always shift these tickets to stand-by passengers, you see.' But then Miriam had looked sideways at him and burst into laughter, enjoying the look on his face, and that had been a good moment.

Booking a hotel had been a little more difficult. The girl had taken it for granted they wanted a double room, making Abner almost spell out in words of one syllable what they wanted, but at last understood and with elephantine tact said she'd look for hotels that offered single accommodation – 'though there aren't many, not these days.'

'It doesn't matter that much,' Abner had said then between tight teeth. 'I'm not that hung up on saving a few bucks. Just telex the Pulitzer, will you, and see what they can do?'

He'd heard of the hotel from the man in the train that morning. He'd stayed in Amsterdam often, he'd told Abner, full of traveller's excitement, and waxed lyrical about the hotel made out of several of the old Amsterdam merchants' houses, on the Prinzengracht.

'They've got these concentric canals, you know,' he'd said earnestly. 'The King's canal, that's the Kaisergracht, and the Princes', the Prinzengracht, and the Gentlemen's – and that's the Herrengracht. The Pulitzer's on the Prinzengracht just down from the Ann Frank House, and really it's super. All "olde worlde", you know?' In spite of that gut-wrenching description, Abner took the risk; it was the only hotel name he knew of outside the ubiquitous Hiltons and their ubiquitous coffeeshops and blank anonymous rooms, and anyway, it had a glorious sound full of good omen. Pulitzer, the prize for excellence. So, he had signed the booking form and then handed it over to Miriam, mute at his side, and she had signed it too, and he had watched her anxiously. It was important she wanted to go, important that she enjoyed this. If she only made the trip out of some sort of obligation to him it would be hell for both of them. And as soon as they were out of the travel agents and standing in the bright wintry sunshine of Carfax he said so to her.

'This is supposed to be fun for you, Miriam. You're carrying on as though I'm trying to get you to book seats on a tumbril, Madame La Guillotine next stop.'

She had stood there with her hands in the pockets of her new coat, her collar up about her ears and stared out across the bustle of Carfax to the other side, her face long and still.

'I'm doing my best,' she had said then. 'I really am. Don't ask me to go dancing and singing as well.'

'I'm not,' he said, and risked sliding one hand into the crook of her elbow. She tightened against it but didn't move away, and he left his hand there, resting gently, not moving. 'I promise I'm not. Just assure me you want to go. That this is just – just stage fright.'

She looked at him sideways. 'It's stage fright,' she said. 'I'm doing my best, Abner. I told you that. I really am.'

They stood there a while longer as the people eddied round them, ignoring them as a brace of lamp posts would have been ignored. 'Is it me you're scared of, or the – or what?'

She considered that. 'All of it,' she said at length. 'I've never flown, you know that? This is the last decade of the twentieth century, and I've never been in a plane. It somehow never happened. When I was small they never went anywhere and after she died . . . ' Her voice dwindled away and then gathered strength. 'And there's you. I don't know where I am with you. You seem to – you're very kind.'

Now she did look at him and he couldn't help his hand tightening on her arm. 'I'm not so stupid that I don't know when men fancy me, and I think you do, and that scares the shit out of me. Other times, with other people, it just makes me mad. I'm not mad, but – ' She shrugged.

'So get mad,' he said as flippantly as he could, though it wasn't easy. To have this girl admitting this much about her feelings for him in the middle of Carfax at the busiest time of the day was an impossible situation to be in. 'If it'll help.'

'It won't.'

'Then don't.' He had smiled at her. 'Just do what you want. As for me – I'm no trouble to anyone. House-trained, haven't jumped up and bitten the neighbours since I was a pup. Trust me.'

'I'm trying to,' she had said, and then had turned sharply and started to walk in long strides along the pavement, almost dragging him behind her, and pushing people aside as though she hadn't seen them, appearing to be totally unaware of their occasional protests. And then they'd gone to have lunch and not another word had been said. But he hadn't stopped worrying about whether she would actually show up at the airport when the time came.

And he hadn't stopped wondering, either, about how he would cope. Was he setting himself an impossible task, staying with her in a hotel in a romantic city well away from home, wanting her so badly? Was this whole trip going to turn out to be the most disastrous mistake he had ever made?

The plane banked again, making his ears tighten against the change in air pressure and suddenly she turned her head to stare at him and it was as though she had been changed by some sort of magic. Her eyes, which had been shadowed and dull, avoiding his gaze ever since they met this morning in the lounge at Heathrow, were glittering with excitement, and she seemed to be glowing.

'Abner, I've just remembered! It's the most stupid thing! I was looking down there and I was thinking – that's Amsterdam. I'm really looking down at Amsterdam though it's all cloudy really and then it just popped out. That was what Brazel wanted to look for. That was why I remembered him the other night when we were in that restaurant, only I forgot almost as soon as I remembered. You said Amsterdam and that made Brazel pop up and then just now, I remembered again.'

He was staring at her, as excited by the way she looked as much as by what she was saying, until the import of her words really sank in and then he took hold of her elbow and said urgently, 'What have you remembered? Oh, quick, Miriam! Before you forget again! What was it?'

She laughed, a high happy sound that was clear, even above the heavy noise of the plane's engines. 'It was the silliest thing to ask an historian. He wanted to know about the people dealing in diamonds in Amsterdam in the Forties. I ask you! As if Geoff would have had lists of such things as that! But that was what he wanted. So, of course, I sent him one of the cards, because I didn't have the information he wanted. Does that help, Abner? Because I do hope so.'

He smiled at her and shook his head. 'I don't think it does, honey. But what the hell! You've remembered – and that means that at least we've got that out of the way. I guess it's nothing important, and natural enough – just a money man looking to make a bit more. So it won't help my film at all, will it?'

'But, of course it could!' she said. 'I told you! It was diamond merchants in the *forties* he wanted to know about – not the ones there are now. If he was just wanting to make some sort of money arrangement now, he'd want people who were dealing now, wouldn't he? But he was quite clear. It was the forties he was interested in and nothing more. So maybe it's got something to do with our research after all.'

And he couldn't be sure which made him feel better; the fact that she was, of course, perfectly right and Brazel's interest could be worth following up after all, or that she had referred to 'our' research. Either way, here they were in Amsterdam, and her new excitement seemed to have banished all the hesitancy that had been so worrying him; they had nothing to do but enjoy themselves. And that was precisely what he intended they should do.

Twenty-nine

It was, he decided, wonderful. The city was all it had promised to be; busy, self-absorbed and yet welcoming, it lay beneath the wide opalescent skies of early March, glittering with water and the chrome of its myriad bicycles, smelling faintly of fish as well as marijuana — which was indeed well in evidence — and, of course, of flowers. They were spread out on the cobbles at the top of one of the most attractive streets, great banks of yellows and reds and blues, interspersed with exotic glowing plants with vast leaves, pots of decidedly obscene looking cacti and tubs of dried leaves and grasses; and when they came to it on their first long walk through the city, it made Miriam stand stock still and just stare.

'Flowers are so corny,' he said after a moment. 'They always look the same, they always smell the same and yet every time they grab you by the collar and choke you with sentimentality. Look at those flaming things over there, see? I'm not sure I believe them. They look like an angry tannoy.'

'Amaryllis,' she said dreamily. 'There are some there too, see? Lemon and orange and cream — '

'What are those, then?' He pointed to a trough filled with yellow and green spikes and her lips curved.

'Fritillaries,' she said. 'I used to think with a name like that they'd be able to fly away. Like butterflies. They're sometimes called fritillaries, aren't they?'

'I don't know,' he said. 'Here, let me be corny too. Please let me be corny.' And he darted towards one of the stalls and bought a small bunch of deep purple violets and came back to pin them on to her coat. 'There. Now I feel like a real tourist. All we have to do now is eat pancakes over at that place there and we're fully paid up members of the rubbernecking class.'

'Then we'd better do it,' she said gaily and led the way to the rickety row of iron tables on the pavement outside the eating house on the corner and plumped herself down. 'I want coffee, a great big bowl of it, and one of those things over there.' And she craned her neck towards the next table where a small child was ploughing her way systematically through a sugar dusted confection that was oozing cream.

'We'll make that two,' he said and gave the order, and then they both sat staring over the crowded flower market towards the glitter of the canal that backed it, and which just showed in places between the slats of the stalls, comfortably aware of the agreeably cool air on their faces and the scent of coffee, which now added itself to the cocktail of smells around them.

'When do you have to work?' she said, turning to look at him. 'You're not just here for fun, like me.'

'I hate you,' he said cheerfully, and licked the last of the cream from his pancake off his upper lip. 'Talking about work when people are eating this sort of thing is downright disgusting.'

'Still and all,' she said and grinned wickedly. 'You have to work and I don't. Did you see that bit on the notice board by the concierge's desk at the hotel? About Keukenhof.'

'I did,' he said and made a face. 'Flower gardens. I want to go there in the worst way. Maybe we could – '

'I thought I could do that while you were working,' she said. 'I'm perfectly capable of making a trip like that on my own, you know.'

'I'm sure you are. I'm not worrying a tuppenny damn about you – how do you like that? A "tuppenny damn" – I'm learning English as she is spoke from the cameraman. He's Dutch, so, of course, he speaks it really well and, naturally, perfectly idiomatically. Like I say, I'm not worried about you making trips. I'm worrying about me missing 'em.'

'Well, you can't do everything I do,' she pointed out reasonably enough. 'You do have to work, don't you? Your advert.'

'Tomorrow and the next day. That's the deal. And you could come with me. All I'm doing is filming pairs of lovers. I could do with a spare pair of eyes to share the spotting. Why don't you come and – '

'Trying to find me a job again?' she said, and he heard the tightness in her voice and threw up both hands.

'There you go again, coming the old porcupine! OK, so don't come with me. I just thought we could manage the flower gardens – where is it again?'

'Keukenhof.'

'Yeah – well, I thought we could do some work there. It's sure to have lovers leaping around. And then in the evening, one of the tours in the canal boats. That'll give me some nice atmo shots, water reflections – the whole bit. And then the next day we could – '

'The next day I'm going to the Rijksmuseum,' she said firmly. 'And the Van Gogh and any other art gallery I can find. And I don't want to go with a TV camera hanging around.'

'You're on,' he said at once. 'Come with me to the flower place and on the canal boat, and then I'll get on on my own.'

She thought for a moment, and he watched her as she did it, enjoying the shape of her mouth and chin and the way her hair fitted her head so well now. I'm a goddamn fool, he thought, digging my hole deeper every minute, and I love being that way. I love it. Dammit all to hell and back.

'All right,' she said then. 'You're on. But don't expect me to take the job as seriously as you will. I'm here to have fun.'

And they did. Next morning, the camera crew, a small bustling Dutchman in a battered leather jacket on camera and the most taciturn of sound men Abner could ever remember working with, arrived to prove themselves efficient and agreeable, not fussing whatever Abner asked for, and coming up with useful suggestions of their own (or at least Willem, the cameraman, did) and they got good stuff in the can early in the day just from walking along the canal sides, and over the little humped bridges. Amsterdam seemed alive with photogenic couples who posed in obliging postures against the best backgrounds and then wandered off, seemingly unaware of their important roles as film extras, and Abner was exceedingly pleased with himself when they stopped for a casual lunch at one of the roadside stalls, eating *matjes* herring and chips with mayonnaise ('Disgusting!' said Miriam and ate them greedily and with great gusto) and said so to Miriam.

'If this is all there is to film making, I'm not surprised you like it,' she said, and licked her fingers for the last of the salty fishiness left by the herring fillets. 'I can't imagine why so many people make a fuss about it. It all looks very simple to me.'

'The art that disguises art,' Abner said, refusing to rise to the bait. 'Listen, Willem says he can get us all in his car. It's a battered old Volvo estate, I have to tell you, and the back of it's littered with cameras and gear, but it'll get us to Keukenhof. OK by you?'

'It's better than paying for a bus,' she said. 'We go now?'

'We go now.'

'No time to go somewhere else first? I want to see – oh, I don't know. So much. I don't want to waste a moment.'

'Glad you came?'

She threw him a glance, looked sour and he knew it was meant to hide her shyness. 'You know bloody well I am. And if you dare come the I-told-you-so bit, I'll – '

'You'll what?' he said, because she had stopped and was staring across the canal, but she shook her head.

'I'll think of something. Look, must we go to the Keukenhof right away? Can't we go to a museum or something now? I really do want to see something – well, solid.'

'I could get this stuff back and into the system,' Willem offered. He had been watching them with a benevolent smirk on his face that Abner tried not to see. Was his obsession with this girl so visible that it made total strangers smirk indulgently at him? A dreadful thought. A great thought. A thought not to be thought at all. 'And if we don't go to Keukenhof for another couple of hours that'll still be time enough. You could go back to Prinzengracht, go to the Ann Frank house before we leave, if that is what Miss would like – '

'Miss would like it very much,' Miriam said abruptly and turned to leave. 'I'm going anyway, Abner. You don't have to.' And she began to walk swiftly up to the bridge which led to the Prinzengracht.

'OK, Willem,' Abner said hastily. 'Where do we meet?'

'Pick you up in Dam Square, by the Royal Palace, three o'clock,' Willem said. 'Go, run after your bird. She's escaping.'

'She's not my bird,' he called back over his shoulder as he ran after her, needing the man to understand, but he just grinned more widely than ever and waved, and Abner, irritation moving in to flatten the morning's euphoria, tried to pretend he hadn't seen it.

They walked in silence along the canal side, her heels rattling on the stones, and his own trainers flapping against them in a regular padding rhythm. He tried to talk to her, but she was silent, gone away into one of her sudden darknesses, and he sighed and gave up. She'd be back, eventually. She usually was, after all; and it was odd to realise, he thought then, that he could think of what she 'usually' did. They hadn't known each other long, but it was all beginning to feel like a real relationship, the sort where you cope with each other in all sorts of moods; and then he grimaced at himself. Such a word, relationship. It meant everything or nothing, he hated it.

The bells began a deep humming as the Oude Kerk's and then the softer sound of the Nieuwe Kerk's lifted on the midday air, and then other bells came singing in. At once his heart lifted; a joyous place, this city, ringing and glittering in the spring sunshine like a happy dream. And he glanced at the girl beside him and the moment of happiness shrivelled and died, for she was scowling furiously and he couldn't understand it. And said more roughly than he meant to, 'For Christ's sake, Miriam, what is it? One moment you're fun and then — what the hell's biting you?'

She took a sharp breath in through her nose so that her nostrils flattened, giving her face a drawn middle-aged look. 'I don't know,' she said after a long moment. 'It suddenly seemed – ' And then she stopped. 'It was the old man and the woman there, by the stall where we ate lunch. You saw them?'

He was puzzled. 'There were lots of people there. I saw no one special.'

'They must have been – oh, I suppose, eighty, maybe. I'm good at judging ages, because of Geoff. After looking after him, being old is something you understand. And I saw them and suddenly, it was not now any more but the way it must have been then – in the war. They were young and the Germans were here and I thought – did they collaborate? Were they the ones who helped the Germans shift the Jews out of here? Did they shoot them or were they the other kind? Did he work on the docks and go on strike with them, the others, did she support them, take them food?'

He shook his head, mystified. 'Miriam, I can't see where you're going – or where you're coming from. The docks? What's all this about docks?'

She stopped walking and turned abruptly to lean on the railing beside the canal as a loudly ringing set of bicycles flashed past, bearing young men in football strip off to some remote playing field, shouting at each other about football scores and goals, as far as Abner could tell. It didn't matter what they were saying, of course, but he needed to hear and listen to them as their high young voices receded into the traffic din, knowing all that he was trying to do was blot out the way Miriam was behaving. She had been so different for so long, he'd thought the sharp and angry Miriam had gone for ever. Yet here she was again.

'You call yourself a researcher,' she said now, her voice scathing. She didn't look at him, staring down instead into the murky water below the railings. 'I made sure before I left that I read up all I could about what happened here, from Geoff's notes, but you, you've done nothing to find out. The dock workers, here in Holland, were the only people in all occupied Europe who stood up to the Germans, and you should have known that. In the other countries the workers knuckled under and did as they were told, but here, they went on strike. You hear me? They actually went on strike. They were complaining about something to do with shifting out Jews by train. They wouldn't do it – so some said. Not all agreed that was why, but enough said it. Anyway, they went on strike. And the Germans just turned guns on them. Can you see them? Can you hear it? They were shot. Not all, of course, but enough. And now there's a great statue to them, the Dock Worker. Maybe we'll see it, maybe we won't, but you ought at least to know the bloody thing is here.'

'Well, I didn't and there's an end of it if I didn't. I'm grateful to you for the history lesson and now can we go and see the Frank house? Then you can give me another lecture about what I didn't know, and didn't have the wit to find out in advance, and you can feel good.'

She threw him a blistering look, but straightened her back and turned to start walking again, and they were striding side by side along the road like strangers, her hands deep in her pockets, and he, equally grim, marching alongside her.

The house, when they found it, very near their hotel, in fact, was quiet. 'Lunchtime,' Abner said and looked at her, almost hopeful. Perhaps the energy of the walk had softened her? 'People are eating. We'll have it to ourselves, maybe.'

She said nothing, just staring up at the house. It was like any one of the hundreds that lined the canals. Tall, rich in windows and generously gabled, but very narrow, with a front door that looked as though it would barely admit one body moving sideways, let alone two side by side. High up beneath the gables was a great iron hook and tackle, ready still to haul up goods and chattels that couldn't make it through the door. The place looked innocuous, dull even, and after a moment Abner walked to the door and pushed it open.

Ahead of them a narrow staircase climbed uncompromisingly in a steep cliff face, and an old woman sitting at a table in a little booth to one side peered at them over her embroidery and held out her hand for their fees. Abner paid and was given a pair of tickets and the woman jerked her head at the stairs and went back to her stitching. And they began to climb.

At first it was all rather dull, silly in a way. A narrow house with rooms once full of furniture for the people living and working in them, now containing only ugly glass-fronted display cases full of sheets of paper bearing in many languages accounts of what happened to Holland in the War and during the Occupation; the sort of material designed to bore you into a state of shuffling quiescence. For all that, there were children in one of the rooms, running about and making a good deal of noise, and Abner looked at them and at their ineffectual teacher who was trying to hush them and thought – why shouldn't they make a noise? What possible meaning can this house have for them? Nothing here is meant to remind them, to move them, to be anything at all really. It just makes a gesture to the past, not a real homage to it.

But then, as obediently they followed the terse instructions pinned on the doors that took them from room to room and ever higher in the house, pausing to read and stare at the exhibits as they passed them, awareness began to creep over him. It was in this very house that those Jews had hidden. It was here, and only here, that it had all happened, those events in that book he'd been made to read in the ninth grade – who was the teacher who'd given it to him? He couldn't remember, but he could remember the book. Oh, he could remember the book, and now, as they climbed the last set of rickety stairs to the attics in the annexe where the Frank family and their friends had hidden for so long, it all seemed to move into place at last. And he was as silent as Miriam and as locked inside himself as they stood and looked.

Pale faded wallpaper. A small sink in a corner. Markings on a wall, near the jamb of a door, faint pencil marks that showed where they'd measured the children's growth. Ann's and her sister's and the boy Pieter's. And without looking for Miriam or for anything else he turned and went, stumbling a little, back towards the exit, away down the stairs and out through the big room below, following the carefully organised one-way system, until he stood outside in the chill light of the early March afternoon, watching the boats move along the shifting canal waters and not knowing when he would be able to speak again.

He hardly noticed she was beside him, hardly realised when he started to walk that she was keeping him company until, after they'd gone a few yards, she slid her hand into the crook of his elbow. Together they walked the long way back to the Dam Square where they stood, their backs to the Royal Palace, watching the changing throng and the traffic and the people and waiting for Willem. And at no point did they say a word to each other.

Thirty

———————— ∞∞∞∞ ————————

Nor did they discuss their visit to the house later. It was as though there was nothing to say, Abner thought, and then amended that. It was because there was too much to say, and it was safer to say none of it.

All through their journey to the Keukenhof, bouncing in Willem's battered old Volvo along the neat Dutch roads, through the neat Dutch towns, he stared out at the now grey afternoon and tried to put order into his thoughts, but order demanded words rather than pictures and all he could get from his head were images. The house as they had seen it, but also as it might have been almost fifty years ago; people moving in shadowy patterns through those rooms, people hiding behind the hinged bookcase that disguised the annexe, measuring the children's growth against a wall, the children laughing and preening at the way they were reaching nearer to the sky than they used to, and the adults looking at them with their faces carefully blank. And Abner felt the cold apprehension that had filled them slide into the back of his own neck.

'Did they say Faffenheim?' The sound man, who was driving, leaned towards Willem who was crouched beside him with his precious camera balanced on his knees. 'I know the road as far as Haarlem and I know Lisse – but wasn't it Faffenheim next?'

Willem grunted something and under cover of their conversation Abner leaned across towards Miriam, sharing the back seat with him.

'Thanks for coming with us this afternoon,' he said. 'It wouldn't have been the same without you.'

She looked at him and lifted her brows briefly. 'It wouldn't have made the slightest difference,' she said. 'You know that perfectly well. There's no need to stroke me, you know. I'm not a ruffled bird, whatever Willem may call me.' And she looked sharply at the cameraman who had lapsed into silence again and was staring out of the window.

'I'm not stroking. Just telling you how it is. I'll remember not to bother again,' he said savagely and almost threw himself back into his corner. Why the hell did he put up with this? Maybe she had been stirred up by the visit to the house, maybe it had made her feel bad, but hadn't he been there too? Hadn't he had the same experience? She had no monopoly of pain, goddamnit, though the way she carried on you'd think she had. In Miriam's world only Miriam had cause to grieve over the past, he told himself furiously, no one else could, and he glowered into his windowed reflection and tried to hate her. It would make life much less complicated if he could.

After a while she reached out and pulled on his arm. 'Sorry,' she said.

'You always are.'

'I know. But that doesn't make it any the less real. I truly am sorry.'

'They why do you – oh, never mind. Let it go.'

'I'll try harder,' she said and turned her head away to look out of her window, and so they remained the rest of the journey, each with one shoulder turned against the other. But she had left her hand on his arm, and he made no attempt to remove it and he thought – that shows how it is with us. Half and half. Neither one thing nor another. Half and half. Will it always be?

The Keukenhof undoubtedly saved the day. Even in the dreary light of the dwindling afternoon, the flowers glowed richly, and in the greenhouses they moved from banks of orange and amethyst azaleas to crimson rhododendrons, from massed purple tulips to sheets of creamy hyacinths, half choked with the scent and dazzled with colour; and outside in the grounds they walked along sleek watersides and through wide, wet green lawns where couples behaved in engaging ways, seemingly oblivious of the camera that Willem trained on them to very good effect. Even a pair of pigeons put on a strutting mating dance that Abner persuaded Willem to catch on film.

Willem had stared at Abner as though he were mad when he pointed out the birds and had shrugged and taken the film but had talked all the while of the waste of it. 'Pigeons use condoms now? If they did, believe me we'd be grateful, the mess they make of the cars. Who needs so many pigeons? But condoms? This I'd like to see. But you want pigeons, so pigeons you can have.'

Miriam had caught Abner's eye at this and her face had creased with the effort of controlling her laughter, and after that all the animosity that hung around them in the car melted away. She knows how to laugh, he told himself, joyously, as they moved on to get the shots of flower heads floating on the water that Abner wanted; she can laugh. We can sort this out yet, if she can laugh at the same things I do.

They came back to Amsterdam in the twilight, just in time to take their booked seats on the canal boat that plied its candle-lit ways through tourists' Amsterdam, and this time she sat away from him, against the rail, her coat wrapped warmly around her against the bite of the wet air, watching the water slide by as the crew got their last shots; and Abner stopped worrying about her. She was relaxed and comfortable now, he knew, and afterwards, when the boat came back into its little harbour and Willem and his silent sound man had packed themselves into their Volvo and gone away, they went to one of the Indonesian restaurants on their hotel's recommended list.

'We can't be in Amsterdam and not eat at a Reistafel,' Miriam said gaily. 'I read it all up and I know exactly what we have to eat and what it tastes like.'

And that was fun too, with apparently innocuous-looking dishes proving to be so fiery that Abner, disbelieving her warning and taking an unguardedly large mouthful, was reduced to choking tears, much to Miriam's amusement; and a good deal of banter from the waiter looking after them about the aphrodisiac effects of what they were eating, which managed to combine a startling explicitness with a total lack of any offensiveness.

'A great tourist experience,' Abner said as they got back to their hotel. 'I wouldn't have missed that for the world.'

'Nor I,' she said, and looked up at him, laughing again. Her face seemed to have changed its very shape, he thought; the cheeks looked rounded beneath the wide bright eyes, and her mouth had a softness that nearly dissolved his bones, and he had to clench his fists in his pockets to stop himself hugging her; to do that here, where they had adjoining bedrooms, would be asking for trouble, he knew that. He was beginning to know which of Miriam's eggshells that he walked upon were the most fragile.

'Tomorrow I'll show you the dock workers' statue,' she said then. 'And perhaps we could go to the Jewish Museum. You could find it useful – '

'Anything you say,' he said and smiled and stepped back. 'Goodnight, Miriam.'

'Goodnight,' she said and they moved like a somewhat under-rehearsed pair of dancers to unlock their bedroom doors. It wasn't until he was inside his room with the door closed behind him that Abner dared to think of what he thought he'd seen on her face; had she looked, just for a moment, disappointed?

'It's too much,' Abner said. 'Just too goddamn much. How can anyone take all this in? It's like – oh, hell, I don't know. Like over-eating, you feel sick and nothing tastes of anything any more and you don't really care anyway. And that's the worst part of all.'

She lifted her brows, but didn't look at him. She was still turning the pages of the album of photographs in front of her. 'You're a novice,' she said with that familiar note of scorn in her voice. 'That's your trouble. If you'd had Barbara for a mother, you'd be used to it. I've been dealing with this stuff for ever.'

Suddenly he couldn't bear it any longer. He slammed shut the album of pictures he had himself been going through and slapped his hands, palms down, on top of it.

'Listen, Miriam, this has to stop! You can't go on and on like this.'

'Like what?' She stared at him, her face blank with amazement, for he had shouted it.

'Competing! Jesus, it's like no one else is allowed to feel any – any reaction that you don't sneer at! No one else is allowed to look back on what happened to them and feel bad about it without you making it plain that what happened to you was much, much worse and much more important. I feel you thinking it, as well as saying it, for God's sake! It isn't like that. It can't be like that. There are hundreds of thousands of Miriams and Abners, hundreds of thousands, and more to come – it won't be all that much easier for the grandchildren than it's been for the children of these people we're reading about here, believe it or not. Are you going to rubbish what they say too, and rubbish their feelings simply because they aren't yours? It's got to stop, Miriam, it's got to.'

She stared at him with her face seeming pinched and he realised she had gone pale. 'Rubbish?' she whispered. 'Do I do that? Rubbish – oh, God, don't say that, Abner! I didn't mean to be – oh, hell, why can't I get through to people? It's like no one can hear what I'm really saying. I – I thought you understood, but you're the same as everyone else.'

'No,' he said, wanting to comfort her, wanting to hold on to her and reassure her and knowing he dare not. 'I'm not the same as everyone else. It's you who're always the same when you talk about this, about what happened to you and what happened to these people.' He slapped the album lightly with both hands. 'You're the one who's trying to take all the pain on to yourself. Maybe you do it for right reasons, Miriam, but it's coming out wrong. If everyone else is out of step with you, couldn't it just be your problem and not theirs?'

There was a long silence and then she said, still almost whispering, 'I beseech you, in the bowels of Christ, consider it possible you may be mistaken – '

'I beg your pardon?'

'Cromwell,' she said drearily. 'Talking to the English parliament. Oh, Abner, what am I to do? How can I get it right? I want to get it right!'

Around them the museum was heavy with silence. At this time of the morning, the curator had told them, there weren't too many people around.

'They seem to cope better with it all in the afternoons,' he had said dryly. 'I can understand it! It's a difficult matter after all. The Holocaust collections? Over there. Those are the relevant cases. And if you wish you can see the collections of photographs we have, as you're Professor Hinchelsea's daughter. We don't show those to ordinary visitors.' And he had smiled at Miriam, a wintry smile, but the first he had produced since he'd met them, and gone away to fetch the albums and then left them alone in this small room to go through them. And now she sat with her head down, staring at the page open in front of her, which was, as far as he could see upside down, of a row of crematoria ovens of the sort he had already seen so many times this morning, and let the silence grow.

'You will,' he said at last, as gently as he could. 'You'll get it right if you work at it. At least you accept that there's a problem.'

She looked up at him then, her eyes glinting. 'My God, you sound so American! You'll be dishing out the psychobabble next.'

He relaxed. This was better; the spurt of anger mixed in with her distress cheered him absurdly, as though she were a patient and he her doctor, elated to discover her temperature had dropped by a half degree, even though it remained dangerously high still.

'And you sounded so English back there I thought I'd choke! "Ai'm Miriam Hinchelsea. Mai father, ai think, has had some correspondence with you in the pa-a-st . . . " ' And he dragged out the long 'a' like a wail.

'If you don't want to use any help I might have for you, then that's fine with me! You don't have to. I just wanted to be useful and – '

'Oh, shit,' he said and closed his eyes. 'Here we go, fighting again. I don't think I'm strong enough to handle it any more.'

Again a silence and then she said a little gruffly, 'Nor am I. End of it, all right? No more arguing. Listen, I had an idea.'

He opened his eyes and stared at her. She nodded at him, sharply, like a school teacher. 'It was that business with Brazel. Wanting lists of Amsterdam diamond dealers in the Forties. I know you said we'd see what we could find out through the diamond bourse, but I was thinking – it's always been a very Jewish trade. Maybe they'd have the sort of information he wanted here? Maybe if we asked Mr Van Gelder whether he can think why someone would want that sort of thing – '

He blinked, trying to clear his head. 'Is that an apology?'

'I suppose so. I can't keep on saying I'm sorry, can I?'

'No,' he said and shook his head at her, rueful now. 'No, you can't, can you? OK, apology accepted. And yes, why not? Though I can't see that finding out'll make a lot of difference. Even if we get the information he asked for, we still don't know what he wanted to do with it.'

'Geoff always said, get the data first, then analyse it. You can't do a thing till you've got all the facts.'

'He sounds more like a kid's comic-book sort of professor every time you quote him. Wasn't he ever any fun?'

'I'm not supposed to complain about what happened to me, remember? We're playing this game Abner rules now.' She got up and made for the door. 'I'll ask Van Gelder.'

'I'll come with you.' He stood up and picked up the two big albums. 'I've had as much of this as I can take.'

They made their way back through the museum, now occupied by a few desultorily staring visitors, and found the curator's office. He was sitting very upright at his desk, hitting the keys of a computer set to one side, and Abner sighed. Even here in a museum, those ubiquitous machines; he was beginning to hate them and their faint scent of ozone and the greenish flickering of the screens.

'Mr Van Gelder,' Miriam said. 'We're grateful for the material we've seen but there's other information we'd find useful.'

She came and sat on the edge of his desk and the man looked up, faintly disapproving, and Abner looked up at her and found his own puzzlement growing; she could go from pomposity to laid back coolness so fast she almost left speed lines in the air, and he sighed and thumped down the heavy albums left, her to do all the talking. He stared round the room as she did so, noting the extreme tidiness of everything and wondering vaguely whether people became tidy in this obsessive fashion because they worked in museums among carefully tabulated collections, or whether they became curators of museums because of their passion for order. A silly surmise, for the answer was obvious, he told himself sternly and dragged his attention back to Miriam and her conversation.

' . . . so you see, we were just wondering if you were able to help our colleague with this. He had to go off and do another piece of work in the States, I'm afraid, so I couldn't check with him whether he'd been in touch with you, and, if he had, where the material was. So I just thought, you might remember?'

Abner blinked. That sounded like the end of a carefully fabricated tale and he caught her eye, and she stared limpidly back at him with no hint of a smile on her face and he shifted his gaze to the man, who was now hitting his computer again and peering at his shimmering screen.

'Oh, yes, here we have it. He is on the same piece of work as yourself, Miss Hinchelsea? I'm most interested. I said to him, now I recall, that I was startled to find anyone outside Holland showing as much interest in our wartime business, for it is a delicate area – yes, very delicate. But there it is. He wanted to add the material to the book he was working on about the survival of the internal economy of Europe during the war years. And that is your area of interest too? I seem to recall that Professor Hinchelsea was not so much interested in economics as in other aspects of the period and – '

'Oh, indeed he was,' Miriam said swiftly. 'But I developed my own interest in parallel, you understand, and I have always been quite fascinated by the economic factors. History of banking and so forth. So did dear old Brazel find the data he wanted?'

'Oh, yes.' The man nodded complacently at his pale green screen. 'Yes, we gave him his print-out and he gave us a generous donation to the museum's funds, you know, and – '

'Oh, dear,' Miriam said. 'If only he'd left it available to me before he went off to the States! I could have used it to make excellent use of our time here. As it is, I shall have to wait till he returns, I suppose.'

'I could give you a print-out again,' Van Gelder volunteered. 'It is no difficulty, I do assure you.'

She looked charmingly struck by the commonsense of his suggestion. 'Could you really? How very kind that would be! Brazel may not be back for weeks, you see – and well, I would indeed be grateful. So would my junior assistant here.' Once more she turned her limpid gaze on Abner, who looked blank for a moment and then hastily nodded. 'So if it wouldn't be too much of an imposition . . . '

Half an hour later they came out into the Waterlooplein where the gulls whirled and screamed over the flea market and stood there with the wind whipping their cheeks to crimson as Miriam stared down at the sheaf of computer print-out paper Van Gelder's secretary had put into her hands.

'Well,' she said with some awe. 'There it is, Abner. You've got whatever it was Brazel wanted. Now, can you work out why he wanted it?'

And then, as he held out a hand to take it from her she said, 'There are about three hundred names here. So we can hardly ask all of them if they know him and what he wanted, can we? Or can we?'

Thirty-one

———⚬⚬⚬———

'I can see the Rijksmuseum another time,' Miriam said. 'I've made it to Amsterdam once. I can do it again.'

Abner grinned. 'More Hungarian forints?'

'I haven't spent all the first lot, yet. Look, do you want me to help or don't you? If you don't, of course, then say so, instead of just – '

'Of course I do! There's no way I can sort this out on my own. And I suppose I do have to – '

She lifted her chin sharply, and pushed aside her coffee cup. They had been poring over the list of names on the computer print-out all through dinner, and this was the first time he'd sounded at all uncertain about what he wanted to do.

'Of course you have to!'

'Why?'

'Why? Because – well, it's all part of your film, isn't it? Knowing what happened and why and – '

'That's what I'm beginning to wonder about. I'm making a film using two parallel stories, yours and the Rats of Cracow. And maybe some of Cyril Etting too, though I'm not sure – anyway, that's my story. What has all this –' and he flicked his thumb at the sheets of print-out paper – 'got to do with any of that?'

'Maybe it's the way you'll find out about the boy and the apples,' she said. 'How else can you? You told me that Mayer will only finance you if you get all the story complete – and that means what happened to that boy. And for all you know the boy could be Brazel. He could have lied to you, you know. Hadn't you considered that possibility?'

He stared at her. 'Brazel? How could . . . ?' And then his voice drifted away as he sat and thought. 'The boy could be anyone,' he said then. 'Couldn't he? Anyone in England. Anyone I've met and haven't met – '

'I think you have,' she said and bent her head again to run her finger down the list of names spread before them. 'I don't know why, but I think you have.'

'But why should I have done? I mean, there's no logical reason, is there? It'd be a coincidence if one of the people I met in London turned out to be, wouldn't it? And coincidence – '

'Happens all the time,' she said. 'Read your Koestler again, if you doubt that.'

'I only heard about the boy by accident,' Abner said. 'If it hadn't been for Cyril taking me to that synagogue supper, if I hadn't been given Cyril Etting's name as someone who'd been in the camps at the same time as some of the people in my parents' Shoah club, if – '

'To hell with the "if"s,' she said and there was a newly robust air about her. 'And to hell with your dismissal of what you call coincidence. People are linked in all sorts of ways, and sometimes a new person steps into a pattern and then all the other people already in are linked with him. That's what's happened to you. You came to Europe to make a film and you've got entangled in other people's tangles. And this is one of the ways out of it, I'm sure of it.'

'Womanly intuition?' He couldn't resist the gibe.

'No,' she snapped. 'Years of working on historical documents with a highly experienced historian. This sort of thing happens all the time, take my word for it. You can't spend the time I've spent listening to an old man expounding theories of history and synchronicity without knowing how common such linkings are. And there's another one here, so that you simply *have* to use this list, somehow. Now, what do we do? Ask Brazel why he wanted it?'

'I hardly think he'll tell me,' Abner said dryly. 'Though it's a possibility, I suppose.'

'Well, leave that in abeyance for a bit. Right now we have two more days here, and you say you've got all the stuff you want for your advert already done or whatever it is – '

' "In the can" is the phrase you're looking for.'

'Jargon!' she said with a fine scorn. 'But if you insist, in the can. So why not use the time to get ourselves round some of the people on this list? The diamond people are all close together here, aren't they?'

'In a sort of stockmarket of diamonds, you mean? I think so – the Diamond Bourse, isn't it? But there'll be lots outside, I imagine. And anyway, these addresses are all over the city. We've already seen that, from the map.'

'You're being altogether too defeatist,' she said, in a scolding voice and he laughed and after a moment so did she. 'Yes, I suppose I do sound like a schoolmarm, but all the same, here we are. Tomorrow we'll take the list and we'll walk from one damned building to another till we find someone who's on it. Right now, though, we've got to plan it. We'll do it upstairs. There's quite a decent table in my room we can spread this on, and one of the big maps and we'll plot it out so that we can get to as many different people as possible in the shortest time possible. Fair enough?'

'Fair enough,' he said and laughed. It was one hell of a reason, he was thinking, to be invited to the bedroom of a girl he fancied as much as he fancied this one. A hell of a reason.

It turned out to be a prosaic task, after all. They sat with copies of the Amsterdam phone directories, and went through them painstakingly looking for name after name, matching the addresses of those they found with addresses given on the computer print-out. Most of the people on the list were not in the directories, of course; as Abner said, it would be little short of miraculous to find any at all after almost fifty years that had started out with a harsh Occupation; but they found some.

'Oh, wouldn't it be marvellous if we could go and see them all now!' Miriam said, crouching over the new list of some twenty names they had made, like a child with a treasured pudding.

He looked at her curiously. 'Are you excited because you're a natural researcher – sorry, historian – or because – well, why are you so excited?'

Because indeed she was; her eyes were glittering and she had more colour in her face than he could ever remember seeing there. She had an animation about her that was very new, and for a moment he recalled the image of the sullen girl with the cloud of frizzy hair who had greeted him that first time in Oxford, and marvelled.

She looked at him a little sideways and laughed, embarrassed, and some of the glow faded. 'Oh, I don't know. It's just that – there's a great challenge to it, you see. You get hold of a tiny piece of information and you tease it into a bigger one and then a bigger one still. Or you find one little hook and you go and find the eye that fills it and that has a hook on it and so it goes on. It – yes, I find it exciting.'

'I told you you ought to work as a researcher in films. That's exactly what the job is. That's just advice – don't fly into a rage, for God's sake! I'm not offering you a job, I'm just saying that when you get round to getting yourself one, that's the road to go.'

'I'll remember,' she said and got to her feet. There was no sign now of excitement. 'We'll start early tomorrow, I imagine. So, goodnight.'

'Oh.' He got to his feet, a little nonplussed. 'Yes, I suppose so. Goodnight, then.' And he bent to pick up the papers spread on the table.

'No, leave all that. I'll tidy it. I really do want to get to bed now.' And she almost hustled him to the door. 'I'll be at breakfast by eight,' she said as she closed it in his face. 'Sleep well and all that.'

And, of course, he didn't, tired though he was, not falling asleep until the small hours and then dreaming confusedly of all sorts of things, though never once of her, waking eventually with a sour taste in his mouth and the ghost of a headache. She, on the other hand, was as crisp and alert as a textbook secretary, sitting at the breakfast table in a neat dark suit and obviously comfortable shoes, waiting for him.

'I've been talking to the concierge,' she said without any preamble. 'He suggests we start with the group over around the Oosterpark – here, you see? We've got five there. Then we should come back towards the Weesperplein, where we've got two, and then the Albert Cuypstraat where there's just one, and end up here in the oldest part of the city where most of the rest are. That way, we clear up a lot in a hurry.'

'You told him what we were doing?' He stared at her in amazement. 'It might have been better to discuss it with me first, wouldn't you think?'

'Of course I didn't tell him!' She looked up at him in surprise.

'As if I would! I just said we were looking for a wartime contact of a friend in the RAF – people who helped escapers and so forth. That happens all the time in Europe, doesn't it? He wasn't at all surprised, or even curious.'

He hid his face in his coffee cup and mumbled something and she said sharply, 'What did you say?'

'I said, I'm sorry!' He almost shouted it. 'I should have known better. Listen, Miriam, can we stop all this? Dealing with you is like walking in a field full of thistles.'

'It takes two to argue,' she said coolly. 'All I was trying to do was find ways to make it easier for you and – '

'Well, great – fine, but stop being so – so masterful! It's not that I don't want help, it's just that I don't want to feel I'm being railroaded all the time.'

'Go on your own, if you'd rather,' she said icily and pushed the sheets of paper, all carefully collated in a clip, over the table to him.

'That,' he said equally coldly, 'is childish.'

There was a silence and then she laughed. 'I suppose it is. Fair enough. Maybe I was getting over-excited. It's just that – all this – it's the most interesting thing that's ever happened to me in all my life. I've spent so long just sitting around with Geoff. All this is a bit like something one reads in a book. So I was trying to get to the end in a hurry, the way you do when it's a specially good story, you know?'

'I hope it isn't one that you want to finish quickly just so that you can get on to the next,' he said and she looked at him briefly and then away.

'Don't take the metaphor too far. Listen, are you eating anything? Because really we ought to – ' And then she stopped short and bit her lip. And again he laughed.

'Bad habits take a long time to cure,' he said. 'It's obvious you've been bossing your father around so long that you can't stop bossing me. Well, you're trying to cure it, I'll give you that. I want nothing to eat, thank you and yes, let's go.'

Outside in the street, where the light glinted off the canal so brightly it made them squint, she held the small map of Amsterdam they were using in her thickly gloved hands and showed him, with a jerk of her chin, where they were to start, according to the concierge, and he bent closer to lean over and read it, and the smell of clean hair and soap again filled him with pleasure, and it was as though he were back in Oxford again, the first time they'd met. It was a good feeling.

'You agree then?' she said. 'We make for Oosterpark?'

'I agree,' he said and stepped back a little, looking down towards the end of the street where the bridge crossed the canal, carrying traffic into the centre of the city, and saw a taxi setting down a fare. 'Come on,' he shouted. 'We'll get that one.' And started to run and she followed him, so that they both arrived red-faced and breathless, one each side of the taxi, just as it was about to draw away; by which time the ruffles between them were smoothed over as though they had never been.

They developed a patter quickly, working together as though they had done so for years, and Abner enjoyed that; and looking at Miriam as they made their way round the fourth building on their list, he could see she did, too.

'You don't look as cast down as I'd have expected you to,' he said, as they climbed the steps of the house they wanted. 'Quite elevated in some ways.'

'I've more sense than to expect the first ones to come up trumps!' she said. 'Actually, I think I'd be a bit disappointed if they did. I mean, it's the looking that's the fun, it seems to me.'

They were in a small anteroom of the sort they were getting used to. Clearly the Amsterdam diamond trade plied its business in surroundings as shabby as it could find; this room was small and dusty and cluttered, and against one wall was a low table and above it a hatch, tightly closed.

Miriam stepped up to it with all the assurance in the world and tapped on it smartly. After a moment it slid open, and a round face with dewlaps looked out at them.

'Could I speak to – ah – ' Miriam looked down at her list. 'Mr Heine, please?'

'Mr Heine? You want Mr Heine?' The face looked suspicious. 'Who are you that you come here asking for a man dead these last five years? He died before I came.'

'We're looking into some events of the last war,' Miriam said smoothly. 'Historical research, you understand. My friend here, from America, represents the US forces who were escaping prisoners of war, and I'm here for the British group. We're looking for people who so bravely aided our boys in those dark days for a book we're writing, and we were told Mr Heine might be one of the people who was involved.'

The face cleared. 'I see. I see! Well, well, such a thing, after so long! But as I say he is sadly no longer with us. His son can help perhaps.'

'Oh! There's a Mr Heine junior?' Abner said.

The dewlaps wobbled as their owner shook her head. 'Nah, nah – I should have said stepson. He's Mr Kuyper. His mother married Mr Heine, as I understand it. He's in his office. I'll tell him. Wait there.'

Almost as soon as the hatch slammed shut the door on the other side of the room opened, and a little fat man popped out, rather, Abner thought, like a weather cock. He had clearly been listening behind the door, Abner decided, as he moved forward, hand outstretched in practised *bonhomie*, to greet him.

'You're looking for people who helped escaping Allied prisoners of war?' the little man burst out. 'Yes, yes, I was listening – of course I was! No businessman speaks to strangers till he hears what the strangers want! And I'm here to tell you that you've been given some crazy information. My stepfather, may his soul rot for ever in hell, was no helper of Allied escapers. If he had been, what a difference to my life! Oh, I could tell you – '

He stopped, almost choked with emotion, and Abner stood there, his hand still outstretched, as amazed embarrassment crawled over him. This little man looked so very unlikely, standing there and shaking with feeling, and for such an unlikely reason. And he put his hand in his pocket, trying to look relaxed and said awkwardly. 'I'm sorry, Mr Kuyper. We meant no harm in asking, believe me.'

The little man took a handkerchief from his pocket and mopped his face. He was getting his control back now and even managed a tremulous smile at Miriam.

'You must forgive me. I couldn't believe – after all this time. Let me tell you, my – er – well, let me tell you that man Heine was a monster. He married my mother when I was a child of seven and he gave her the hell of a life, you understand me? The hell of a life. He was a bully, a miser – I can't tell you. But now he's dead and the business comes to me because he didn't even make a will, the stupid old fool, and he left no relations but my mother, so it comes to me. And I can make her last few years what they should be. But he was evil, a bad one – he helped no Allied prisoners of war.'

'I see. Well, thank you, Mr Kuyper,' Abner said, almost despairingly. How could he ask this distressed little man now about Brazel, and why he might have been interested in his stepfather's business? He could see no way he could, and then Miriam said, 'Tell me, Mr Kuyper, was your stepfather a collaborator. Did he have anything to do with the fate of the Jews here in Amsterdam?'

Kuyper looked at her miserably. 'You know about that, then?'

'I'm sorry?'

'Someone has told you.' He sounded tragic.

'Told us what?' Abner said.

'About – oh dear!' And he almost wrung his hands, twisting them together as he talked. 'Listen, isn't it enough he's dead? I had others coming here after him, the Israelis, all sorts, years ago that was. I told you I hated him, but he was my mother's husband and if it all starts again, it'll kill her. She's over eighty, you understand, a frail old lady. Let me give her what sort of life I can in the days she has left. Leave it to rest now, after all these years.'

'If you'll explain, Mr Kuyper,' Miriam said gently. 'Then we'll be able to help, won't we? But until you do . . . '

He looked up at her, for she was a good deal taller than he was, and almost nestled against her, for she had put an arm across his shoulders and suddenly Abner could see the skill with which she was handling this distressed man. Geoff, he thought, was a lucky guy to be so cared for till his death.

'He was a Jew, of course he was a Jew,' Kuyper whispered. 'Belonged to a synagogue even, before the war, the same as my parents did. That was how he met my mother. My father, rest his soul in peace, died in 1937, when I was just a baby. That's how it was he came to ruin our lives. Yes. Sure. He was a Jew, a Gestapo Jew.'

There was a little silence, and then Abner said carefully, 'A Gestapo Jew?'

'It happened everywhere the Germans came. They'd find a local Jew, as many as they could in a big community, to work with them. Making lists, shipping them out, tipping them off who to get rid of first. They lived, the Gestapo Jews, and the others died. He was a bad man, my stepfather!' The voice trembled and rose again. 'I told you, bad, bad, but let it rest now! Please, please, let it rest.'

'Of course we will,' Abner said, but Miriam cut in, quickly.

'Just tell us, though, Mr Kuyper, did anyone else ever come to you to talk about him? From England? A man called Brazel?'

Kuyper seemed to shrink even smaller. 'I told you, I want it to stop,' he said. 'I told him, I tell you, it's nothing to do with me. After the war he went on dealing with God knows who, but me, I knew nothing of it. When he died, then I got rid of it all, all the papers, the boxes, the lot. I wanted no part of them, and I got rid of it all — '

'Rid of what?' This was Miriam again, still holding the man with a protective arm across his shoulders, but still as sharp as a needle with her questions. 'Just explain that and we'll be on our way.'

'All the stuff he left in the second safe. The stuff no one was ever allowed near when he was alive. Once he was dead, I was going to throw it all out, the papers, whatever. But there were boxes and bags as well and it made me sick, I didn't know what to do. And then Coenen came and he'd been the old man's partner, you see, so I gave it all to him and good riddance. And now I want no more of it, you hear me? Not another word. Jacob Heine never helped any Allied escapers, never helped anyone but himself. I want no more of him, now or ever. I never want to hear another word about — '

Miriam had let go of him and had been peering at the papers in her hand and now she lifted her chin and looked very closely at Kuyper.

'Your stepfather's partner was named Coenen?'

'What? Oh, yes. Coenen.'

'Isaac Coenen?'

Kuyper stared at her, and his nose, red now from his emotion, seemed to twitch.

'That is his name,' he said cautiously.

'Of Albert Cuypstraat — '

'Then you know all about him already!' Kuyper almost wailed it. 'So why come here and drive me mad? Look, I told you, I know nothing more than I've said and I want to know nothing more. Leave me and my mother alone. I'll want to hear nothing ever again, you understand me? Tell your friends, tell them all, next time I stay behind the door. I don't come out.' And he scuttled back through the door he had left open behind him and slammed it shut, leaving them both staring at its blank panels with equally blank surprise.

Thirty-two

———————∞∞∞∞∞∞———————

'Poor devil,' Abner said and pushed his hands deeper into his pockets. 'The poor bastard.'

'Why?' Miriam demanded. 'He'll get over it soon enough. It's not as though we're going to come back to him. All he wants is to be left alone, so we will. Won't we?'

'I didn't mean that. It's the guilt. Poor bastard.'

'Oh,' Miriam said, and stood still. They had been walking along the small street that housed Kuyper's office, towards the Ruyschstraat where they'd be able to find a taxi, but now she turned to look at him. 'I suppose so. He must have survived because of Heine.'

'That's how I see it. Other Amsterdam Jews were taken off to the camps or had to hide in attics and annexes or wherever. This man and his mother belonged to one of the Gestapo Jews so . . . '

'Poor bastard indeed,' she said after a moment. 'What a hell of a thing to have to live with.'

'And inherit. You heard what he said – the business is his now, through his mother. He has to look after her, so he hadn't much choice about the situation when she inherited. He had to keep it going for her, I guess. Her living, you see. But now she's old, won't live much longer, and then how does he live with his conscience? Throw the business away and start clean somewhere else? He's past fifty and not the most dynamic of characters, I'd say. He's as trapped in his stepfather's guilt now as he was as a child.'

She started to walk again, and he fell into step beside her. 'There's more than one way to break your heart,' she said then. 'Worse ways to grow up than we did.'

'Yes,' he said. 'Yes. I guess so.'

*

The taxi deposited them outside a narrow building on the corner of a small street that looked back down towards the park they'd skirted to reach it, and Miriam, looking at her map, said, 'That's called Sarphati Park, would you believe. I imagine it's the same as Sephardi?'

'I'd think so,' he said. 'Most of the Jews who were here in Holland were Sephardi, weren't they?'

'The ones who came early, from Spain and Portugal, the fifteenth-century ones, they were. But the later arrivals from Germany must have been mostly Ashkenazi. What are you?'

'Hmm?'

'Which are you? My mother took a great deal of pride in saying she was Sephardi through her own mother, not through David Novak. One of the grandee families, she said her maternal grandparents were. So what was yours?'

'How should I know? No one ever told me. I explained that to you.' He felt a chill creep between them, as the memories seeped in again, the old sense of outrage at never being told anything at all about himself that mattered. And here was yet another piece of the jigsaw that was Abner Wiseman having to be cut out by someone else. 'Does it matter?'

'Not at all,' she said and looked away, shy suddenly. 'I just thought – look, here's the place. Not like Kuyper's. It's a shop.'

It was a very small shop with the windows filled with tired trays of cheap jewellery, all of which looked to have lain there undisturbed for years, and twists of faded once-coloured crêpe paper at the front that were deeply depressing in their attempts to look cheerful. The door of the shop had a cracked glass panel in it, and when they pushed on it a discordant bell made a half-hearted attempt to ring over their heads.

Inside the place was even more dispirited. A path had been scuffed through the dust on the floor and led to a narrow wooden counter, where watch straps on curling cards and trays of tarnished silver earrings jostled for space with a lamp and a scatter of jeweller's implements. There was a very old man sitting with his head bent over a watch he was manipulating in the pool of light thrown by the lamp and he didn't look up as they came in.

'Mr Coenen?' Abner said. 'Could you spare us a moment?'

The old man stopped working, his hands remaining fixed in

the position they had been in when Abner spoke, as a child holds a rigid pose when he plays a game of statues. He did not lift his head.

'I've come here, with my colleague, from Mr Kuyper, over at Oosterpark, and we just wanted to ask you – '

The old man lifted his head then and sharply pulled his hands away from his work and the watch which he had been working on clattered as it landed on the counter. He looked at them with wide pale eyes, faded with age and with milky rims around the irises.

'Another one?' he said, and leaned back so that he was in the shadow outside his working lamp. 'How many more? I told him what he wanted to know. I can't do more. I told the man.'

'Told who?' Miriam said. 'Told what?'

There was a little silence and then the old man said in a guarded voice, 'So? You tell me what Kuyper sent you for. A watch repair? This I won't believe. This is what the other one told me, and I believed him. Why should he send work to me, that Kuyper, feeling as he does? But I believed the other man. You I won't believe. Why did he send you?'

'We're doing some research,' Miriam said, 'historical research, to help members of the Allied services who escaped from prisoner of war camps through Holland to – '

'No, we are not,' Abner said abruptly. 'I'm sorry Miriam, but we're not. I'm doing research for a film, Mr Coenen. I'm interested in the effects of the labour camps and the Holocaust on the children and grandchildren of the survivors. That's the theme of my film, but I'm exploring it via real stories of real people. And as part of the work I've done already I've heard about a man who, when he was a boy in Cracow, betrayed some hidden Jews for a bag of apples. One of the people who knows who this man is and won't say, recently collected information about the diamond dealers in Amsterdam in the Forties. I don't know why he wanted this information, but we now have it too. Your name is one of those on the list we got from the museum computer. So was Mr Kuyper's – or rather his stepfather's, Heine. We went to see Mr Kuyper, who told us something about his stepfather's dealings in the war. He told us you were Heine's partner and took over some of his papers and so on after Heine died. I don't know what the connection is between you and

Brazel – the man who was seeking this information and who knows the identity of the boy from Cracow – but since it's the only lead I have at present, I'm following it up. There! Now you have it all straight and true. Can you help me?'

There was a long silence and Abner's spirits spiralled downwards. He could have followed Miriam's lead, done it her way, with a devious tale of seeking Dutchmen loyal to the Allies during the war; that approach flattered, made people willing to talk. His own had clearly been a disaster. And he was very aware of Miriam silent at his side.

There was a scraping sound as the old man pushed back his stool and got to his feet.

'You'd better come in,' he said, and his voice sounded tired and a little shaky. 'I can't talk out here,' and he went shuffling off into the dimness behind him. After a moment, Abner, seeing a gap away on the left, followed him round the counter through a door that was just behind it, with Miriam on his heels.

The room the door led to was startlingly different from the dusty old shop outside. It was furnished with a mass of heavy, lovingly polished mahogany furniture and carpeted with a clearly costly Persian rug on which, in front of a large tiled stove that glowed richly with banked-up coke, a deep leather sofa was set. A vast marmalade cat was asleep in one corner of it, and it raised a sleepy head to stare balefully at them as they came in and then curled itself into sleep again. The old man moved one hand towards the sofa to invite them to sit down and dragged another chair from the far side to sit and face them.

'You want coffee?' he said wearily, and Abner almost laughed; the automatic offer of hospitality was so ludicrously irrelevant.

'No, thank you,' he said. 'Miriam?'

'No,' she said. 'Thank you. Look, Mr Coenen, we don't want to upset you, you know. It's just that we need some information to help us and if you have it, we'd be really grateful. There's no risk – we're not after you or anything. No one wants to hurt you. Just answer a few questions, and we'll go. That's all.'

She's gone into her nurse-to-the-old mode, Abner thought; the specially soothing voice with a hint of firm commonsense practicality beneath it to make sure the old man does as she wants. And he felt a pang of shame on her behalf.

'You think I'm frightened?' the old man said. 'I'm not frightened any more. Once I lived with it, there was nothing in my veins but terror, but now what does it matter? I'm old. It's too late now for anything like frightened.'

'So you don't mind talking to us?' Abner said, and a wave of gratitude slid over him. There was something so distasteful about harrying people, and yet it was so often a necessary function of honest research. Anyone who made it easier had to be loved, and for a moment Abner loved this tired old man who gazed at him with those pale eyes that looked as though they had been boiled.

'Mind? What does that mean to me? I'm tired, that's all I know. Very tired. Talking is work, so maybe – no, I don't mind. What is it you want to know?'

'Brazel came to see you?' Abner said.

'If that was his name. A small man, in black, like a suit of armour, it looked, black and shiny, eyes the same, and a little moustache,' and he ran a gnarled finger over his wrinkled upper lip in a gesture that was suddenly perky and which ended on a little flick of his wrist, and it conjured up the bluebottle nature of Brazel exactly.

'That was the man,' Abner said. 'What did he want?'

'The same as you, I imagine,' Coenen said dryly. 'Money. Or the way to get it.'

'We don't want money!' Miriam said with a sudden sharpness, and her voice was frosted with scorn. 'Do you think that?'

'Everyone wants money,' Coenen said. 'Until they get so old they discover it doesn't matter any more.' He shook his head, in an odd little gesture. 'Oh, to be born now, or to go backwards and take your knowledge with you! That would be the dream, hey? Such a dream. You're young and wouldn't understand, would you? And you want money, like everyone else.'

'I want to make my film honestly,' Abner said. 'And that's why I'm asking. What did Brazel want exactly?'

The old man took a deep breath and seemed to slump a little in his chair. 'I'll have to tell it all from the start, like I did him. It's easier that way. If I try to tell it backwards in answer to your questions it takes longer, and me, I'm *tired*. I don't have much time left for things that take too long. So listen and you'll see. Don't interrupt, all the time. The other one, he interrupted – '

'We'll listen,' Abner said and sat with his hands clenched inside his pockets as he leaned back in the sofa, prepared to listen with his mouth clamped shut. And Miriam looked at him and opened her mouth, and he gave her a minatory shake of the head and she too leaned back and said nothing.

'*Menschen*, yet!' the old man said with an ironic chuckle. 'Children who listen and, who knows, perhaps understand! Such *menschen*! All right, I'll tell you. But I need schnapps. You?'

Abner and Miriam shook their heads together and again the old man produced that faded chuckle and without getting to his feet leaned back and extracted a bottle and a small glass from the cupboard behind him and set them on the table at his side. He poured a drink with careful deliberation, swallowed it in one gulp and then poured another before he leaned back in his chair and stared at them both.

'All right. So, I'm Isaac Coenen and for the past hundred, hundred and fifty years, maybe, my family have been diamond dealers here and in Rotterdam. Not in a big way of business, you understand, but well established and well thought of in the trade. People trusted us. God, how they trusted us. That was why it all happened – my father, rest his soul in peace, was a man such as you don't find everywhere, if anywhere at all. So honest, you could lead him to your own diamond mine and he'd brush off the soles of his shoes as he left for fear of taking away something that was not his. So, when the bad times come and the Germans start their games, it's natural enough that people come to him to protect their fortunes, hmm?'

Abner felt Miriam stir beside him and he reached out and put a warning hand on her leg and she relaxed, and the old man glittered slightly at him and went on.

'They come with cash and convert it to diamonds and they say, "Joseph," they say. "I've bought these diamonds from you and now I want you to take care of them. Later, when it's safe, when I have my wife, my children, my old parents, out of Germany, I'll come and collect them. Take care of them for me." So he does. And after the first comes two more and then ten more and then a hundred more. People hear that you can leave money with Joseph Coenen, safe in diamonds, and one day you can come and get them back and you'll be sure it will be there, safe as you left it, not a fraction of a carat missing. And he didn't mind what he took. Small fortunes, no more than one or two decent diamonds and a handful of bits and pieces, or millions of marks in big stones, uncut stones, good stones. And by the time the Germans came here to Holland he had a big store of such fortunes, all pledged to be returned – and he will return them – because he's Joseph Coenen, and people trust him. Jews don't trust German banks and safe deposits. Or Dutch banks, either. They're no safer than Germans, and Joseph Coenen, he's safe.'

He stopped speaking then and after a moment reached for his second glass of schnapps and drank it in one sharp throwing back of his head, and then sat in silence for what seemed a very long time. But neither Miriam nor Abner said a word.

'They took him and my mother,' Coenen said eventually. 'I wasn't here, I was in the country. I had a girlfriend then, not a Jewish girl, and that upset my father. He wouldn't have her in the house, so I used to go and visit her in her father's house near Delft. In the country. And when I came back I hear what has happened, and in my father's special safe, which the Germans don't find – they'd emptied all the others, of course – I find the letter he left me and all the store of diamonds he's holding for people. There were accounts in a book, all listed so neat and tidy. He had a wonderful clear handwriting, my father, wonderful. Millions of guilders' worth there were. Millions. You can pack a lot of money in a small space in diamonds, my friend, you know that? And there I sat, a boy of twenty-five, my parents taken off to a labour camp, nothing left in the business I can sell, no way of making a living and afraid they will come and take me too. And I go to my father's friend, Uwe Heine, and I beg him to help me, and he tells me he will, and – '

The old man swallowed and tried to speak again and couldn't, and again reached for the bottle of schnapps. Abner watched him anxiously. If he drank too much, surely he'd stop being able to talk coherently? But even after three glasses he seemed unaltered in his manner, and was able to go on speaking.

'I did what he did. Why not? When times are bad, you do what you must. I was a good enough boy, no better, no worse than that, but I was twenty-five, I had my girl, my lovely girl, and I wanted to live, so I turned. All right, I turned. I wasn't the only one. My father's best friend, old Uncle Uwe I'd called him all my life, he did it, and others, many others. Why shouldn't I? I'd have walked over other people's dead bodies to stay alive, you hear me? Over dead bodies . . . '

And he leaned forwards and rested his head in his hands. 'I did,' he said. 'I did just that.'

Still Abner and Miriam said nothing. He looked up at Abner and said loudly, 'So? What do you say to that?'

'Nothing,' Abner said quietly. 'You said to say nothing. And anyway I don't want to say anything.'

'You don't want to tell me what a bastard I was? What a devil incarnate, what a criminal? A thief, murderer and robber of the dead? You don't want to speak of this? What sort of man are you?' And his voice became shrill.

After a moment Abner said, 'Just a man. Not a judge. What would I have done in your shoes? Not a great deal differently, I imagine. You weren't alone.'

Coenen looked almost as though he were going to weep then but he managed to restrain himself. 'Well, there it is. It's what I did. When I needed money, there were the diamonds in my father's special safe to lean on. I didn't care what would happen afterwards. If the owners came back to get it, what would I know? My father was dead. I couldn't help it if there were mistakes in what was left for them. You see how far down I went? Willing to lay the blame for my own evil on my father's back after he was gassed at Treblinka. Oh, yes, I knew what happened to them. The Gestapo made sure I knew. It kept me in line, they said. But I never told them of the special safe. They never ever knew what I had hidden. And there it stayed . . . '

Again his voice dwindled away and Abner ventured a question. 'You didn't go on drawing on it after the war?'

He shrugged. 'After the war, I started to think – maybe some of them would come back. A few. I used enough of the diamonds to restart my shop and the rest I locked away. What did I need it for anyway? There was only me. No wife, no children, no one who mattered.'

'The girl in the country?' Miriam murmured.

'The girl in the – phht! As soon as the Germans came her father beat her, told her what would happen if she didn't stop going with her stinking Jewboy, so, of course, she did. She's been dead this past ten years, anyway. Cancer. Married some lump out of the mud and had seven children and now she's dead.' And his eyes glinted with sudden malice that chilled Abner. 'So, like I said, I need little enough. The diamonds are still there − ' And he made a wide gesture with one arm at the rest of the room and Abner thought, the schnapps has affected him, after all. 'Or they were.'

'Were?' he said.

'Until they came and started to ask for them. And not only the stuff I had. The stuff Kuyper sent to me after Uwe Heine died. They went to him too, the frightened ones, before they were taken to the camps. All the other stuff I collected.' He looked dreamy then. 'It was a lot. If it hadn't been so long after, if I had been young enough to live with what I'd done, young enough not to care, like in the bad years of the war, I could have started such a business − I could have been bigger than any of them on the Bourse, any of them. But there it is − they came, the men, to get them − '

'Brazel came to get the diamonds people had left here in trust?' Abner was stupefied. '*Brazel* came and you gave him − ?'

The old man stared at him, his head up and his mouth a little twisted. 'No, of course not, you fool. Of course not. The other ones. Your Brazel, he just wanted to know what had happened to the diamonds my father had been guarding for the Jews in the camps, and I told him, they came and got them. They knew who were acting as bankers, here and other places too, and they came with names and addresses of survivors in England, they said, and I had to give them the stuff. They said as long as I kept quiet about it, they wouldn't say how much I'd taken for myself. That was all I cared. I didn't care they were taking it for people who − well, they didn't *prove* to me they had permission to get the stuff from me, that the people they said had sent them really had, but what did I care? An old man, getting tired now, a silly heart, what did I care? I still don't care. So that's it. Now go away. That's all I care about. That you should go away and leave me quiet. I'm tired. I'm tired of all of it. So go away and leave me to get on with what's left!'

Thirty-three

He slept little that first night back in his sofa bed in Camden Town. There was so much to think about that he felt that his brain was actually crawling inside his skull, making his eyes feel swollen and hot; he tried hard to get his thinking into some sort of order so that he could find the relaxation he so desperately needed to get to sleep. He ached for sleep, couldn't remember when he'd last felt so weary.

Miriam first. She had been so quiet all the way back to Heathrow that he had thought she had regressed to the old surly Miriam, and that had depressed him deeply. In Amsterdam she had been short tempered sometimes, inclined to snap sometimes, but she had shown him a whole new aspect of herself that had tied him even closer to her; she had been difficult, yes, but not the almost unapproachable creature she had been in Oxford.

And yet she had sat in the plane beside him staring out of the window at the featureless banks of cloud with an abstraction so deep that she could barely be roused for the breakfast that was served on the flight, and then refused it; and he drank his own orange juice and coffee in a state of deep gloom, trying to ignore Miriam's silence by going over in his head yet again all that he had discovered from Isaac Coenen.

But again she had surprised him, because suddenly she had turned and said with an air of urgency, 'Abner, I've been wrong, haven't I?'

'What?' he had said, startled.

'I've been wrong. About so many things. About you and about me, lots of things.'

'I'm not sure,' he had said carefully. 'I know you've been confused about the way you feel. I know that you're often angry when you don't mean to be, but – is that what you mean now?'

She had laughed then, a high cheerful sound. 'Abner, I don't think I know quite what I mean! Just – I've been thinking. It's been the most incredible few days of my life, this trip. It's not just that I never did it before. It's more than that. It's like I found a different person waiting there to get inside my skin when I arrived. I wasn't the person I thought I'd been all my life. It was a different me. I heard with different ears. Oh, hell, that sounds so pseudish! I'm sorry – or I would be if I hadn't promised I'd try to stop apologising. Just – well, thanks. Thanks so much for making me go.' And she had seized his hand so fervently he had spilled his coffee and they had to go into a lather of drying him and dealing with the stain on his jacket.

Which helped. By the time that was done they were back in an easier mode of conversation and although they said nothing at all important to each other, there was enough comfortable banter to make Abner feel very optimistic indeed as he saw her back to London and then in to her taxi to Paddington and the Oxford train. They made a definite arrangement for him to go down to Oxford at the weekend, to take her out to dinner, and she called to him out of the window of the taxi as it moved off, 'I'll talk to the estate agent about the house before then, I promise,' and had waved to him like a cheerful child going home for the holidays.

Where, he asked himself, turning over yet again on the rumpled sofa and getting tangled in his sheets, where do we go from here? Getting involved with a woman here in England had never been on his agenda. He'd found her as part of the work for the film, had become even more enmeshed with her as a result of the research and now – now what? He couldn't think about it. Somewhere ahead there lay huge and painful decisions about such matters as homes, and sharing and even, oh God, children. And somewhere deep inside he felt almost petulant and the thought drifted to the surface of his exhausted mind; it's not fair. I've got enough to worry about with this film. Why did she have to turn up and complicate everything this way?

And that was so wickedly ungrateful a thought (for wasn't she now a vital part of the film?) and so unpalatable that he turned instead to think of all that Coenen had told him as he had sat over him, refusing to go away until he had more information, hating himself for pushing the tired, clearly very unhappy, old man the way he had had to; but that was what had to be done if the film was to happen. So, he had done it.

And now he had all the information that he needed to finish the research for his script. He hadn't pinpointed the boy with the apples yet, but surely he was almost there? And he rolled over to lie on his back with his hands clasped behind his head, staring sightlessly at the pallid square of almost darkness that was his window, and tried to work it out logically.

It was quite clear to him who the 'they' were who had come to bully old Coenen out of the diamonds that had been entrusted to his father, who had blackmailed the old man and piled guilt on to his guilt to make him the wretched creature he was. The descriptions had been too clear, the little movements he had made as he described them too vivid for there to be any doubt. Just as a touch to his upper lip had sketched in Brazel, so had the old man sketched in the two men who had come to torment him over three long years. Listening to Coenen, Abner had hated them both. Yes, the old man had behaved appallingly, had been a betrayer of his own kind, a thief, a robber of the dead, all the things he called himself. And yet he was not as bad as the creatures who preyed on him, and God knew he had paid a just rate for what he had done so long ago in his frightened youth. All the years of misery Coenen had lived weighed on Abner as though he'd lived them himself, and he hated the two men who had come to Coenen with a rich hate that filled his chest so full it was tight when he breathed. But that did nothing to help him decide which of them was the boy with the apples, or even what he would do about his information now he had it. What, for example, would he do about David Lippner? Because he had to be thought about, too. And thinking of Lippner made him think of old Cyril Etting; again he rolled over in the hot crumpled bed, yearning to sleep, and kept from it by a head that was buzzing with conjecture.

He got up at six, weary and with eyes filled with sand and pulled on a sweater and jeans and went out into the dark empty street to do something he had not tried for years – running. He knew the way into Regent's Park, and got there before his breath ran out and then found his second wind as he loped between the trees, now blushing green in the early light. The smell of the dew wet grass, the shimmer on the muddy lake and the discordant shrieking of the water birds – disturbed too early by other runners – cleared his head wonderfully.

He showered in a long, leisurely fashion as soon as he got back to the flat, and then went down to the Greek café on the corner for breakfast, and wolfed a massive one, for the cook there had once worked in Chicago and understood pancakes; he ate a stack of them and that helped a lot. Eating pancakes was not just a matter of the calories, he told himself as he came out on to the street again, but was a reaffirmation of American citizenship, and for the first time since he had talked to Isaac Coenen his sense of humour stirred and made him feel better.

The decision about who to talk to first made itself. He went back to the flat to telephone, and started with Mayer. He had made it clear he wanted regular reports on progress, but it was more than that for Abner; the man had, after all, partly financed the trip to Amsterdam. He had a moral right to be told first. But the secretary – and as he heard her thin and precise voice he remembered how incongruously she was named – Rowena told him that Mr Mayer was out of London until the end of the week and would not be available on the phone before then, and could she help?

'No thanks,' Abner said. 'I was just reporting in. Make sure to tell him I did when he gets back with you.' And a fragment of one of the verses his English teacher in the eighth grade had been so keen he should learn came back to him. ' "Tell him I came, but no one answered, that I kept my word, he said." ' And Rowena, her voice as colourless as ever said, 'I will.' And hung up the phone sharply. He smiled at the dead phone and thought smugly, I may be an American but I know an English poet better than she does. One up to Abner Wiseman and Walter De La Mare.

So it had to be Monty, and he was puzzled for a moment at how uneasy he felt about telling Monty what he had discovered; and then shrugged at his reflection in the window-panes at which he was staring. So it would be tough telling Monty that people he was connected with might be – the hell with it. He'd have to know sooner or later; for good or ill he was part of *Postscripts* now. He was Abner's agent, had a financial interest in it all. He had to know.

He reached for the phone, then changed his mind and went out into the street and down to the Underground to take the tube to

Tottenham Court Road. From there he went striding along the people-clotted pavement to Monty's office. God help any snotty secretaries who tried to keep him away from the people he wanted to talk to, he told himself wrathfully, pushing past racks of jeans, shrieking T-shirts and giggling teenagers going through lewd cards in the stands outside the souvenir shops. God help them.

He need not have worried. It was clear that Monty's secretary had been trained to treat established clients very differently from mere supplicants for her great man's attention. She welcomed him warmly and apologised profusely because Monty was late in getting to the office, but definitely on the way because he'd called her on the Rolls' carphone (and that made Abner's lips twitch; why be at such pains to point out Nagel's ownership of such status symbols? Well, maybe they reflected on her). She fussed with coffee.

Abner stood there in the middle of the over-decorated reception room and looked at his reflection in the artificially antiqued mirror that covered the wall facing the door to Monty's inner sanctum and remembered his first visit here and the way the little wizened man in the corner had made Monty so alarmed that he had made faces at him behind Abner's back. Well, he'd have to find out, that was all, and he tightened his shoulders as the door to the reception room burst open and Monty came in a flap of cold air and heavy Crombie overcoat.

'Listen, Tania, get me – oh, Abner! So you're back! What are you doing here so early? I gotta lot to get through this morning, and I can't – '

'Yes you can,' Abner said firmly. 'Ten minutes, maybe. Or longer, once you hear what I've got. You can be the judge.' And without waiting to be invited he opened the door to Monty's office and held it invitingly so the fat man could go in.

Monty grunted and shook off his coat and, dropping it on to Tania's desk, and growling, 'Coffee!' at her, went into the office.

'This had better be important,' he said. 'I don't take easy to being pushed around in my own office, know what I mean, Abner? I got more than your project to deal with, you know. This is a major business I got here and – '

'Of course, I know,' Abner said, conciliatory now that he'd got the man where he wanted him. 'But I'm the impatient type, and this'll interest you. A lot. I know – or almost – who the boy with the apples is.'

The door opened and Tania came in with coffee on a tray that gave Monty something to fuss over, which he did, with saccharin tablets and demands for dry biscuits, before turning back to Abner. But Abner had seen the way his neck had stiffened at his words and was more alert than ever.

'What do you know?' Monty said with an air of studied carelessness that did nothing to convince Abner. When he'd set out to come to Monty's office he hadn't really given much thought to his possible involvement in the complicated scenario Abner had uncovered. But now every sense he had was up and alert, because the memory jogged by the sight of that bronzed mirror in the outer room had unloosed a flood of doubt. Monty could be – Jesus, had to be – involved in some way. Didn't he?

'There's a scam,' Abner said baldly, watching him over the rim of his own coffee cup. And waited.

'So? The world's full of scams.'

'Not like this one. Robbing the dead, this one.'

Monty didn't look at him, concentrating on a list of appointments on his desk, trying to sound abstracted. 'That doesn't sound as bad as robbing living people.'

'No? When the dead are the ones who died in gas ovens? Of typhus, of starvation, of beatings, of – '

'All right, already!' Monty lifted his chin and stared at him. 'You're not filming now, you know. I see no cameras, no sound booms. This is just a conversation, for God's sake – no need to come on like a – ' And he shook his head irritably, unable to find the word.

'I'm having a conversation,' Abner said. 'I'm trying to tell you. Were you listening, or are you more interested in that piece of lousy paper?'

'All right, I'm listening.' And Monty folded his hands on the list. 'So get on with it. I ain't got all day.'

'The scam involves diamonds. I found out that in the Thirties when Jews in Germany and Poland and Czechoslovakia – everywhere – began to realise they might be in trouble, some of them went to Amsterdam to convert their cash into diamonds and left them to be looked after by people they trusted.' He made a face then, letting the disgust he felt show. 'For some of them the trust was misplaced. The original trustee of their diamonds was taken to Treblinka and died there. His son turned into a Gestapo collaborator, and used some of the diamonds for his own needs. But he wasn't a greedy man – there was a good deal left at the end of the war.'

'So?'

'So, he thought maybe some of the people who'd left the diamonds with his father would come to claim. I gather one or two did in the very early days, but still there were a lot who didn't. So the stuff just sat there. And then, not long ago, just over five years or so as I understand it, someone turned up – two someones – with tales about how they had relations in England who were survivors of the camps, and who had left diamonds in trust to this man – Joseph Coenen. They wanted them. The son – his name is Isaac – tried to argue. He wanted better evidence than just their word for it that they were entitled to take the stones. But they were tougher than he was. Told him they knew he'd used some of the stones for himself and they'd make sure the whole world knew if he didn't co-operate.'

Monty was staring at him with his face impassive but his eyes were wide and dark, and he stirred as Abner stopped speaking.

'So what do you want me to say?'

'Do you know what's coming?' Abner said bluntly.

'How do you mean, do I know?' Monty put on an air of bluster but now Abner was overtaken with sudden rage, and he snapped at him.

'Oh, for Christ's sake, Monty, you must know! I saw one of 'em here in your office the first day I came here! You made a face at him behind my back – I saw it in the mirror – and it meant nothing at the time. I just thought it was odd. But now I want to know your tie-in with all this. Because the two men who went to Isaac Coenen – and have had Christ knows how much out of him in diamonds – were Victor Heller and Eugene Garten. And I repeat: I first saw Heller here, and Garten told me he'd been put on to me by Heller. So you have to be involved.'

'Why do I have to be involved? Don't I get the world and his stinkin' wife through that office out there? Don't they all come creepin' round me? I'm a top agent, for God's sake. Why should I be expected to know every crawler who comes in to – '

'This one you knew,' Abner said implacably. 'You made a face at him behind my back, which I saw in the mirror. You indicated me as someone he had to keep quiet in front of – and he did. So don't come the it's-nothing-to-do-with-me bit. You don't have to insult my intelligence or your own that way.'

There was a long silence and then Monty said, 'Jesus, why the hell did you have to choose me to get involved in your bloody film? Why me?'

Abner stared at him, taken aback. 'What's that got to do with – '

'Can't you see? I had to take you on, whether I wanted to or not, once I knew you were digging around for a film about what happened after the camps were opened. The children and the grandchildren, you said – you could have found out anything. The last thing I wanted to get involved with was that sort of film. Not that I don't think it'll be good. Dammit, I know it will. I'm torn in half by you, you know that? Torn in bloody half.'

And to Abner's total astonishment, Monty began to cry, sitting there behind his vast rosewood desk and making no move to check the big oily tears that came trickling down his wattled face.

Thirty-four

He recovered after a while, and pulled a large silk square of handkerchief from his breast pocket and almost covered his face with it, like a nun's veil, as he repaired the ravages and then emerged a little flushed and red-rimmed about the eyes, but in control of himself.

'So, what else did you discover?' he said huskily. 'Let me have all of it.'

'Oh, no,' Abner said softly. 'I'm sorry, Monty, but no. That'd be too easy, wouldn't it? I want to hear from you how it is you're involved with all this, and which of the two of them is the boy I'm looking for. Because I'm convinced one of them is.'

Monty stared at him for a long moment and then began to laugh. Not a frightened laugh, not one full of bravado, but one that was genuinely amused.

'Oh, Jesus, Abner, that's one hell of a jump to a conclusion, isn't it? Why the hell should it be one of them? It might as well be me.'

Abner took a sharp little breath in through his nose, hearing the hiss of air in the sudden silence that had followed Monty's attempt at flippancy.

'Is it?'

'Is – oh, be your age! Would I make a joke like that if I were? That has to be the most stupid thing I ever heard – '

'Why? All I know about this guy is that he's a successful man, well thought of in his business – I was told that way back, that he's in this business – and very well off. And now I think of it, you with your fancy offices and your Rolls-Royces and your – I guess you've got a fancy enough pad as well – '

'It's good enough,' Monty said, watching him beneath half lowered lids. 'It's good enough.'

'So it could be you – ' and indeed, the thoughts were skimming around in his head, rearranging themselves feverishly. He had assumed that it had to be one of the two men who had actually collected the diamonds, but did it have to be? Indeed, how could it be? Neither of them were well off or respected in the film business. Unless one of them was acting a part, which seemed unlikely, he thought; remembering how seedy and run down both of them had appeared to him. Surely, it had to be someone they worked for? Couldn't that be why he'd first seen Heller in Monty's office?

'OK, so there's a scam involving diamonds', Monty said, 'but where's the evidence that makes you think there's any connection between that and the Rats of Cracow? There isn't an atom of proof to link anything – '

'Oh, yes, there is,' Abner said very gently. 'Oh yes, there is, Monty.' Suddenly he was enjoying himself as the ideas and the information bits began to click into place. He'd stopped having any personal feelings at all about any of it. The springs of *Postscripts* that lay deep in his own childhood, in the experience of Hyman and Frieda, in the pain he had shared with Miriam, none of that meant anything now. All he was seized with was the joy of the researcher who at last has identified the significant log in the jam and is poised to release it to send the whole lot tumbling down river. He was a hunter, and the prey was there in his sights and he played, just for a moment, with life and death, delaying the exquisite second when he would fire his shot.

'So tell me. What evidence?' Monty said truculently. 'Not another word do you get out of me till – '

As suddenly as the pleasure of the hunt had hit Abner it evaporated and a sort of weariness moved into him to replace it. This was sickening. People had died horrible deaths and others had profited from their sufferings, and now all the two of them were doing was sitting here fencing with words. Sickening.

'A contact of mine found it out. Only it was Isaac Coenen who told me,' he said. 'One of the people who had left diamonds with Isaac Coenen was a woman who had been one of the Cracow Rats, Libby Lippner. Isaac had shown me all the lists of names of people whose diamonds had been collected, and her name was on it. In fact, hers were the first to be collected by Heller and Garten. The very first.' Abner managed a thin smile then. 'Isaac told me that had made him feel good, you know? He'd been given what he thought was a genuine document that made it possible for him to give back some of the property that was eating him away with guilt. It wasn't genuine, of course. Brazel came later with the one that was. It had been given to him by Libby Lippner. But Isaac thought it was, so he handed the stuff over to the pair of 'em. But it wasn't enough for them. They came back after that, over and over again, looking for more diamonds, and each time the evidence they brought to claim them was more and more flimsy. But he had to part with them – the poor bastard had to part with them – because of their threats, and now he's dying with the shame and guilt of it all.'

'You're sorry for him?' Monty said and his voice was loud now and full of scorn. 'You're sorry for that thief, that corpse robber? You dare to sit there and cry pity on that scum and tell me you're thinking ill of me? Why the hell you should think you've got the right to – '

He stopped suddenly and stared at Abner, and his eyes seemed to narrow as a thought hit him. 'How do I know what you're saying is true? This woman whose name this feller – who was it, Brazel – recognised. Who's Brazel, for Christ's sake? How the hell can he – '

'I've told you this before,' Abner said. 'He was one of the Rats himself, one of the boys who was there. He knows who the boy with the apples was. He's been shaking him down for years. Says the man doesn't know him by sight, hasn't seen him since they were both kids of sixteen or so – but Brazel knows who he is now. But he won't tell me. Not yet. I have to find out alone. And I'm beginning to think I have.' And he stared at Monty challengingly.

Monty shook his head. 'Not me, my friend. Not me. So, your Brazel knew the woman whose diamonds Coenen was looking after, the first ones you say that Heller and Garten collected?'

'That's it. I told you, her name was Lippner, Libby Lippner. She died recently. Her son is the man who lives in the Home in the Cotswolds I told you about. He's entitled to that money, to whatever those diamonds are worth – God knows he needs it and he has a right to it – and the guy who was the boy who sold his mother and her friends for a bag of stinking apples is the one who's got the diamonds. He's still in the business of betrayal.

Still selling people for his own profit. And I'm determined to get them from him and see that David gets them. So if it's you, you'd better hand them over. Now. I'm not angry enough yet to do you any harm, but I could be.'

There was another silence and then Monty said heavily, 'It makes me as sick as it does you, Abner. Believe me, it does. I'll tell you my involvement. It's honest enough in its own way. Listen, I need a drink. I don't often, but right now I need a drink. You?'

Abner shook his head and watched as the fat man lifted himself heavily from his desk and went to the elaborate drinks cabinet in the corner to pour a stiff brandy for himself. He looked like a wrinkled balloon that has been left out overnight tied to the doorpost of a house where children have had a party the day before, still recognisable, but soggy, without bounce or confidence of any kind. For a moment, the sadness in him transferred itself to Abner and he felt it almost physically, and wanted to get up and put his arm around the man's shoulders and tell him, *It's all right, Monty, take your time. It's all right. I know what it's like to feel ashamed, guilty, frightened, I know.*

Monty came back and sat down and drank slowly, in steady sips, not looking at Abner, and then began without preamble.

'She died in 'eighty-four, my wife. A good enough girl in her time, a good girl. A real Golders Green sort of girl she was, never thought of anything but the clothes on her back and the covers on the furniture, know what I mean? Well, maybe not. You don't live here, after all. But she was. A good girl, a bit greedy, but good. She'd had it hard. Her parents were refugees, got out of Germany just in time, when she was twelve. Lost everything, or so she was told. They were a secretive lot, her family – Solly had been a furrier – my father-in-law *ala va shalom* – but here in England no one wanted to know. He never got a decent job. Spent all his life here moaning and complaining. When I married Jessie – a boy I was, only twenty, such a boy – he told me one day there'd be a *nudden* for me, a dowry, you know? As soon as he could get his hands on it. But me, I never minded. He had a stroke not long after we got married in 'forty-five and then he died. His wife, Rivka, she died a little after – never got over him – and then my Jessie died in 'eighty-four. And going through her stuff after, I found this piece of paper and I couldn't believe it.

Her father had kept it in his socks drawer, or something – must
have done. I don't know how else Jessie got hold of it except after
he died and she cleared out their flat. She was only a girl herself at
the time – what would she know? Anyway, she had this piece of
paper I'd never seen, and I looked at it and I thought, I must find
out. So I asked Heller to help me. I've known him for years, a
schlapper he is, no more. I wrote letters to Amsterdam and got
nowhere, so I had to have a gofer, because me, I didn't want to –
well, I just couldn't go. Don't ask why, I couldn't.'

There was another silence and then he burst out, 'Shit, I
couldn't! Couldn't face a man and ask outright for the stuff listed
on that paper. I was entitled – Jessie left me everything the way
her parents had left her everything – but I felt sick and bad about
it. I wanted it but I couldn't go and ask myself, so I sent Heller.
Promised him a lot if he went, and that I'd find him and kill him if
he cheated me. Anyway, I knew he wouldn't. He's a real *nebbish*
that one, a gofer is all. He can run errands but he's got no nous to
do anything for himself. He's trustworthy because he's too
scared and silly to be anything else. So he goes and gets me the
stuff and there I am with stones worth – well, I don't know what
now.'

He got to his feet again and looked at Abner and then across
the room and then with an almost imperceptible shrug, as if to
indicate how little it mattered, went across to the other side with
a lumbering walk and pulled on the picture of the singer
Rousseau that simpered from its gilded frame. Abner turned in
his chair and watched and saw the safe that was behind it, and
with a sudden awareness of what it meant twisted back. He
didn't want to see him work the combination, would never want
to know how to have access to the thing. Not that he was a
potential thief, but he somehow felt safer if he didn't watch.

Monty came back and put a package on the table beside him.
'Have a look,' he said. 'You'll see your friend Coenen lied to you.
Or he chose to have forgotten what really happened. He gave
these to Heller for me five years ago. I was the first one to send
him there. So look!'

Abner stared at the package and then, as Monty said again,
impatient now, 'So look!', he reached out unwillingly to pick it
up and unwrapped the brown paper. It covered an old tobacco

tin and after a moment he opened it and inside there was cotton, which he pulled aside, still unwillingly, and there they were – half a dozen dull pebbles the size of hazel nuts. He gazed at them and Monty said, 'Uncut, they are. I took 'em to Hatton Garden, had a word with a friend there. He offered me a hundred and twenty thousand pounds for them. As a gamble. Said if I sent them for cutting myself and they turned out to be first quality stones then I might expect more. If not, a lot less. But he'd gamble if I wanted to sell to him.'

'You didn't do either,' Abner said and closed the tin. 'They're still here.'

'I didn't do either,' Monty repeated and took the tin and wrapped it and locked it away again, as Abner sat and stared down at his hands. 'I couldn't do it. You understand me? I couldn't do it. It would have been like – ' He came and sat down behind his desk again. 'It would have been like making a table to eat from out of Solly and Rivka's bones. If the old fool had told me before, or told Jessie, what the paper was – but then he was a secretive old sod. If I'd known when Jessie was alive I could have gone and fetched them with an easy conscience, could have sold 'em, bought for my Jessie all she ever wanted – ' Again his eyes glinted. 'Not that anyone could do that. Wanting was what my Jessie did better than anything. She died too young, rest her sweet soul. But now she's dead I can't use them. They've been there ever since, those stones. Five years, almost, now.'

There was another silence and then Abner stirred in his chair. 'I'm sorry,' he said at length. 'It wasn't till I started to talk to you here that I thought just possibly, it could be you. The mirror and all. But now – I'm sorry.'

Monty said nothing, lifting one hand in a sort of benediction and they both sat and thought their own thoughts. Until Abner sighed softly and said, 'But that wasn't the end of it, was it? For Heller, I mean.'

Monty's face seemed to settle into heavier lines. 'No.' Now he allowed himself the luxury of anger. 'That stinking little bastard can't keep his tongue between his teeth. He was paid enough to do that errand. The whole thing cost me money, a lot of money, seeing I never sold the stones. But can he keep quiet? Not him. Goes shooting his mouth off to Garten, and the next thing I know is they're back here, the pair of 'em, asking me who else I know who might have money in Amsterdam. They've got the whole list – all the names the man Coenen had in his notebooks. The old fool had let Heller look as much as he liked; so, using more sense than I ever thought the little toerag to have, he copied the lot. They wanted to go after all the names they could. "Bounty hunting", they called it. They kept coming to me, over and over. I know so many people, you see. But I told 'em I wanted no part of it – it made me sick. These things belonged to people who'd been gassed, tortured, how could they do it? Unless they were going to get the money out to give to Jewish charities maybe – but those two? They'd give to charity the way a drowning man hands over his lifebelt.'

'You let them get away with it?' Abner said. 'It didn't occur to you to tell other people – the police, perhaps? What they were doing had to be illegal, surely?'

'What's illegal? You think I didn't think of that? Nothing was illegal. They'd got information about property held by someone else. They're looking for the owners so they can claim for them and get a commission, maybe. They've got this idea there'll be children, grandchildren who don't know their lost relations had property they could claim. That's not illegal.'

Again a silence, and then Monty said painfully, 'I could have made a big song and dance, of course. Told the world what they were doing, especially when I knew they were forging papers, making up the names of the people they said were children of the owners and then holding on to the goods. That *was* illegal. But they had me over a barrel. Or rather, *he* did.'

'He did?'

Monty looked at him and then his eyes slid away. 'There aren't just those two in it. I told you, Heller's nothing more than a gofer. A guy who can do what he's told but never thinks for himself. Except that one time, the first time he went to Coenen. Don't you think I feel bad about it? Where did he get the idea from but me? It's hell to live with. But he couldn't do more than that, he has to have other people to help him – '

'Garten,' Abner said and shivered slightly, remembering the unpleasantness of the man Garten in his seedy club with his cheap red wine. 'Hasn't he the ability to run a scam like this?'

'Maybe. But I don't know – there's more to it than you think. It's not just in Amsterdam it's happening.'

' "Not just" – how do you mean?'

'Oh, it's all over the place. Jews stashed away goods and cash in so many places. Some got out and managed to get their possessions after the war. Lots didn't. In 'eighty-five or so, the money that was in banks had to be lost – after forty years it seems the banks no longer have to hand it over. It becomes theirs.'

'You're kidding!' Abner said. 'That can't be legal!'

'It seems so. Anyway, I've found out – God, but I found out! – it's been going on for years. You'd think by now they'd scraped the pot clean, but they haven't. Someone found a warehouse in Paris in 'eighty-six full of the most marvellous gear – Lalique glass and Gaillard ceramics and Grasset silverware that had been put away by one big French family. All of them died in the camps, and no one knew what was there till the land was sold, and the place opened up. As I understand it, they sent the money to Israel. Or some of it. There's more around no one ever hears of. Lots of it. And people have been scouring around to get their hands on it for a long time. Six million Jews died, Abner. Not all of them were poor people, believe me. The Germans took a lot of what they owned, but enough got hidden to make searching for it worth while. And they've been searching.'

'Heller and Garten – '

'And others. It's a – how shall I put it? It's been well orchestrated. Run by a clever man.'

'The boy with the apples.'

'If you say so. I don't know. It seems possible.'

'It has to be. He's the only one who could have known that Libby Lippner had property tucked away like that. Once Brazel found out from her about it he went to try to get it for her, but it had already gone, hadn't it? Someone had forged a document to get his hands on it, using Heller as his tool. He had to be someone who knew that she had it. Who else but the boy who'd been in the group? They must have talked about what they had, what they'd done – maybe he'd been promised payment for his efforts after the war from what she'd got put away in Amsterdam?'

'All this is surmise! Who can tell? But I suppose you could be right. I mean, that the man who runs this and the boy with the apples are the same person.'

He sat and stared down at his hands. Abner watched him, almost feeling the struggle that was going on inside him.

'I know who he is. The person who's running this whole thing,' Monty said at length. 'I've always hated it, always felt sick about it, tried not to think about it, but sometimes you have to – '

'Then tell me,' Abner said.

'You're asking too much! Jesus, but you don't know what you're asking of me! He can – he's got so much bloody clout he could ruin me, you know that? He can ruin anyone as easy as he chops the top off a boiled egg at breakfast. The man's got no concern, you know what I mean? He does what he wants, when he wants and he's got no concern. Not an atom.'

'Tell me who it is,' Abner said again. 'Take the chance. I'm not afraid to make sure the law is brought in. If he's lying and cheating and forging he can be got by the police.'

'Want to bet?' Monty said with the ghost of a smile. 'I'll believe that when I see the sun rise in the west for a change. No one stops this one from doing what he wants. He's too clever to get caught, whatever he does. He sold his own people and got away with it.'

'Not entirely. Went to Auschwitz, didn't he and – '

'And came out again,' Monty said. 'From all accounts the only boys who managed that did it by playing the whore for the guards there. What do you think of that, hmm? Boys of sixteen doing that for German guards. Jewish boys.'

'People will do a lot to survive,' Abner said after a moment. 'They'd walk over dead bodies.' And he saw Isaac Coenen in his mind's eye as brightly as if he were standing there beside him. 'Survival drives people along hard roads.'

'That hard?' said Monty. 'That hard?'

'I think so,' Abner said. 'The thing is, I don't know what I'd do in his situation. What would you do?'

'I sure as hell wouldn't go on cheating and lying and stealing long after it was all over the way this one does,' Monty flared at him. 'I sure as hell wouldn't use people the way this one uses 'em! He runs rings round everyone and doesn't give a shit. As long as he's got his stinkin' paintings and his music and – '

Abner froze and stared at him, saying nothing and Monty caught his stare and laughed, his mouth twisting a little.

'Don't look like that. Who else could it be? I don't know if he's your apple boy, but I can tell you he's the one who's scooping up diamonds and anything else the dead left after the Holocaust. Mayer, of course. Isn't it obvious?'

Thirty-five

———————————⌇⌇⌇———————————

'What the hell do I do, Miriam?' Abner said again. And got to his feet and began to prowl the room once more, moving jerkily between the piles of books and the fireplace where the flames flickered comfortably, and the cat slept on Miriam's lap as she sat on the hearth rug watching him.

'What can I do? If I go and tell him I know he'll laugh at me. Because what evidence do I have? Monty's right. Unless we have real documentary proof that this man is using forged material to get his hands on dead men's property, there isn't anything I can do. And Isaac won't help – you saw him. How can I expect him to help? He's a wreck. He blames himself for all of it. There's no way this side of the last trump he'll stand up to questioning about the sort of treatment he had at Heller's and Garten's hands. And what about them? Would they tell the truth about what happened? Heller might break down under questioning – the man's apparently a complete nerd – but the other one? I just don't know. And even if I do go to the police and start a whole drama, there's the matter of *Postscripts* – ' And he turned a face towards her that was a mask of misery.

She got to her feet in one swift movement, sending the cat hissing away in fury, and went over to him and took hold of him by his elbows.

'Now just cool down, Abner. You're tying yourself up in knots and that'll get you nowhere. Come and sit down.'

Obediently, he came with her, and this time she sat down beside him on the rumpled old sofa and sat there with one hand holding his upper arm, pressing it against his body so firmly he could feel the warmth of her hand through the sleeve of his jacket. He was very aware of it, aware too at some deeper level of how much pleasure it would have given him once, but now he was too preoccupied with the massive dilemma in which he found himself caught to give it the attention it deserved.

'I shouldn't care about it so much, but I can't pretend I don't. If I open up this stinking mess and show it to the world, one thing's sure – the film never gets made. It was to be Mayer's money that made it. He already owns a piece of it. How can I go ahead and make it under those circumstances? I'd be using money he stole from people who died in the camps. But how do I find the rest of the funding I need if I don't use his? Can you see anyone else taking up his leavings? Take it from me, no one would. I've leaned that much about the way the business works in this town to know that. So if I do what I ought to do I ruin my chances of making my film and – '

'If you do what you ought to do you'll make your film, no matter what,' Miriam said and he stopped staring at the fire with miserable eyes and turned to look at her.

'What did you say?'

'You heard me. Make your film. It's the most important thing you could possibly do.'

'The most important thing I have to do, surely, is make sure this man gets his – that he's stopped doing what he's been doing and gets punished for what he's already done. All the years of betrayal and all that money, all those people he robbed.'

'Dead people. Losing money can't hurt them.'

He shook his head at her, and almost pulled away in revulsion. 'I can't believe what you're saying! They're dead, so it's OK for anyone to come along and help themselves to their property? What about people like David Lippner? As destroyed by the Germans as his mother was, living on charity in a Home – what about him and what he's entitled to? Are you saying I should keep quiet about Mayer, and to hell with all the Davids he's found to rob, just so that I can make my film? How do you suppose I could live with myself if I did that?'

'You could live with yourself better if you stopped and thought a little more and emoted a little less,' Miriam said acerbically. 'Try hearing me out, will you?'

He opened his mouth to argue and then, seeing her face, closed it again. She looked extraordinary, he suddenly realised, a totally different person from the pinched watchful creature who had opened the door of this house to him a few short weeks ago. Her eyes were wide and dark in the low light of the room, for there was only the firelight and it was very dark outside the uncurtained windows, her cap of tightly curled hair seemed edged with a halo from the flickering of the flames and the expression on her face was one of such intensity that he had to listen to her.

'This film, it means a great deal more than money and diamonds. All you've been thinking about for ages now is money because you haven't got it to make the film with. So maybe you've lost sight of what it is you're actually trying to do. Which is to tell everybody about what happened to people like Libby and her David and your Cyril and – and Barbara and her father and me. And yourself. It musn't all turn into dead history, the sort of stuff this house is filled with.' And she waved a comprehensive arm and he could almost see the shadowy dusty rooms with their clutter of tea chests and piles of papers.

'It's dead, all this. Papers and documents and – nothing to make your skin crawl on the back of your neck, nothing to make your belly as tight and as hard as a – as a pregnancy, full of pity and understanding and sheer *knowing*. All that you can only do with real people telling how it was, real people showing everyone the marks on them. That's what your film is for. Telling everyone the true story of what happened and how it happened and why it happened – if there is any "why", which I'm not sure about, but you have to try. That's more important than any sort of – oh, I don't know – retribution for Mayer. What you have to do is use him to make the film, and then when you've done it, you do what you like about him. But use his money and make your film! Don't be a bloody fool. You've no right to indulge yourself with childish views of what's right and wrong about stealing. That doesn't matter. Mayer only stole things – money, nothing important. He didn't hurt people – at least, this time he didn't. As for what he did all those years ago – put it in your film, you bloody fool! What better way do you have of getting back at him? *Telling* everyone!'

He was staring at her, almost hypnotised by the glitter she seemed to throw off and now, as she stopped speaking, he tried to think; and the thoughts came out aloud.

'It's what I want to do, more than anything. Just use his money, make my film, and tell everyone what he did and how he did it, and what a bastard he was. If he was a bastard, of course –

that's part of the hell of it. Whenever I think of him as a bad person, I just can't see it. I keep seeing the man who talked to me about the Dufy painting and the music he played and – he isn't a bad person, he can't be. And yet he is, and it's all so . . . How do I lie to him enough to get the money from him? Will Monty help there? He might. He's as miserable in his own way about all this as I am, I think. I just don't know. Oh, Miriam, what the hell am I to do? I'm in such a goddamn state I can't even think. Oh, Miriam.'

And he put his head down and let the feelings wash over him, a great tide of pain and memory and guilt and shame and loneliness; he didn't care what happened or what he looked like. He wanted only to rid himself of a flood of sensation that was so very painful that he could have burst, and he sat there with his chin on his chest and waited; and it came like a storm of rain, tears that filled his eyes and his nose and made him choke; and he had to lift his head to breathe at all and felt his eyes tighten into hot slits and his nose run as the weeping increased and the misery ballooned inside him till his ears rang and he knew his head would burst soon, very, soon now.

He didn't know quite how it happened, but she was holding him and crooning into his ear, and rocking him like a baby, and he heard the words murmuring at the back of his mind – Momma? Frieda? But he knew it wasn't, knew it never had been, that it was Miriam who was holding him and knew too that her dress was wet beneath his cheek, pressed as it was against her.

For the first time, a wriggle of adult embarrassment lifted in him and he raised one hand to wipe away the wet from his face, to protect her from it, for he was ashamed to do such a thing to her, and his hand touched her body and through the wet fabric he felt her become taut and knew at once what had happened to both of them.

His tears went on but they were different now, not so painful, more a release than an ugly bursting sort of pain, and he lifted his face and put his cheek against hers and held on tightly, and felt her skin move beneath his. Or was it? Was it his own body that was moving against hers? Of course it was; and though someone at the very back of his mind was shouting at him to wait, to treat her better than this, not to let it happen, he couldn't stop himself. And he didn't need to. Her hands were as eager as his as she pulled at his clothes, and her mouth as hot and hungry, and they clung to each other and rolled and turned on the creaking old sofa as the cat in the corner of the room watched them with angry eyes and the fire collapsed and died in the grate. But they noticed none of it.

She stirred against him and then started to shiver, for the fire had gone out and the room was cold; he woke suddenly and felt her tremors against him, wrapped her warmly in his arms and put his face against hers. But still she shivered and after a moment he rolled her gently on to her back and then followed so that his own body covered hers, and after a while she stopped shivering and murmured in his ear, 'You're better than a blanket,' and giggled softly so that her breath whispered across his cheek and made him in his turn shiver a little. But not with cold.

Kissing was enough for a while but then he knew the hunger was rising again and very deliberately he stopped himself, and settled his head down in the space between her shoulder and chin and rested there and she took a deep slow breath and relaxed; and he knew he had been right. She needed time and peace before she could cope with such a flood of experience again and he thought then with sudden anxiety, *Oh God, I so want her to be happy*.

And he lifted his head so that he could see her in the dimness and said urgently, 'Are you happy? It's important you're happy,' and she laughed again and said, 'Oh, yes, I'm happy. I never thought I could be, ever, but I know now that I am, and – oh, Abner, it doesn't matter what happens after this. I'm *happy*.'

'That's OK then,' he said and tucked his chin down again, and lay there, half dozing and half listening to her even breathing as the thin light in the dark window lifted and flattened and brought a chill morning creeping into them.

She had fallen asleep again and he moved very gingerly, not wanting to disturb her, but, of course, he did, and she whimpered a little in her sleep; he bent over and kissed her mouth again, and felt her lips curl into a smile beneath his and was content.

'I'll find you a blanket,' he said and pulled himself to his feet and stood there, awkwardly trying to untangle his clothes from around his feet. They had hurled themselves into their explosion with such vigour that neither of them had thought of clothes and now one leg of his pants was tangled round the other and his socks were twisted on his feet, and he knew he looked a complete idiot and was rewarded with yet another giggle from the sofa.

'I used to think about sex sometimes, and it was always so polite and tidy – not a bit like this.' And she pulled at her own clothes, getting out of them, and a bra came snaking out from beneath her and landed at his feet and they both laughed.

She rolled off the sofa and stood there in the half light, pimpled with the cold but clearly unashamed of nakedness, and that pleased him almost more than her passionate responses had a few hours ago; that she, who had been so remote and so difficult to know, could be so comfortable with him now filled him with a confidence that startled him and he stood and looked at her, knowing he had a silly grin on his face and not caring at all.

'Breakfast,' she said. 'Hot breakfasty things. You had nothing to eat last night and neither did I, and I actually have food here. Go and wash and shave – the things are still there from the last time – and I'll do the same upstairs and then there'll be breakfast.' And she went across the room, and it was light enough now to see that her back was deeply dimpled just above the cleft of her buttocks and her hips were every bit as sensual to look at as they had been to touch and be embraced by. Abner felt need lift in him again and wanted to laugh at his own importunity; he followed her out of the door and turned away to the kitchen for the cold wash he so definitely needed.

The breakfast things were very breakfasty; coffee and orange juice, oatmeal – she laughed when he refused to call it porridge – and quantites of hot French toast, a delicacy she hadn't tried till he showed her how to make it. Together they beat eggs and dipped bread into it and fried it in spitting butter, laughing a good deal like children playing at house; and ate it covered in gritty sugar in a somewhat shamefaced way, because, as Miriam said, 'Eating sugar is the greatest modern sin there is.'

The kitchen wrapped them about in warmth from the fire and the red shaded lamp and the smell of the food, and he never wanted to leave it; but eventually he had to move and stood up to collect dishes to carry them to the sink.

'You're house-trained,' she said lightly and got up to help him.

He wondered if he should tell her of the girls there had been before her, the liberated tough American girls who wouldn't be caught dead picking up a dirty dish for a man. It had been they who had trained him and who, it could perhaps be said, had trained him to be a lover, too. But he bit all that back; there would be time, plenty of it, to share with her these other aspects of his past life. They had talked of the painful childhood years, and soon he would have to talk of the better college years, the working years, and bring her up to date on them. Because he knew, even if she didn't yet, that the rest of the years that he had to live belonged to her, whether she wanted them or not.

They washed up in silence as though both were grieving a little at the parting that had to come and then she said suddenly, as she spread the damp tea towel on the fireguard to dry, 'Well? Have you decided?'

'Yes,' he said after a moment. 'I've decided.'

'What?'

'I – must I say?'

'Yes.'

'I'll do it your way,' he said at last. 'I shan't find it easy, God knows. I'm a bad liar, always have been. When it matters. But I'll lie and tell him that the boy with the apples is Monty.'

'What?' She stared at him, her hands, which had been rubbing her freshly washed hair up into an aureole, quite still at each side of her face. 'You'll tell him *what*?'

'I thought about it, while I was shaving. And it just came to me. Monty will let me. He'll be glad to, I think, in a way it will help his guilt. I'll give Mayer a script that ends with Monty as the unmasked boy with the apples. But the film I'll make once I get going – that'll be the real truth.'

'Can you get away with that?'

'I'm damned well going to try. I'll do more digging round. I'll get Brazel on the mat, somehow. I'll twist him into a fall and a submission – you watch. He'll tell me the truth eventually. And I'll put it into the film I'll make with Mayer's money and to hell with the consequences. Just you bloody well watch me.' And he brought out the British adjective with great pride and a laugh, and she laughed back and stood there, rubbing her hair again in the warm lamp light and wrapping him in her happiness.

He stopped at the front door as he reached it, and turned to look at her. She had followed him from the living room, ready to see him on his way, and said not a word.

'I think perhaps I should say thank you,' he said.

'It's better than apologising. But I don't want that either. Just be happy.'

'I am.'

'Then that's the way it should be.' She pushed the door open and they stepped out into the sudden sunshine of the spring morning. There was a bite in the air of departing frost but beneath that a warm promise of sun to come, and she shook her head as she looked at the blush of green on the bedraggled privet hedge at the end of the scrap of front garden.

'This is too much,' she said. 'Even the damned weather's getting sentimental on me.'

'I know,' he said. 'I was thinking something similar. Only not sentimental. More loving.'

'Don't talk about that! I can't cope with that. Not yet. It's enough to be happy. Love is something else.' And for a moment the old Miriam was back, watchful, edgy, unapproachable. But he wasn't worried. He'd known the other Miriam too well to be concerned.

'I don't have to talk,' he said. 'It's enough to feel it.' And walked down the path. 'I'll call you this afternoon, Miriam. And for God's sake, get this house sold will you? It's time you came to live in London. I can't keep on trailing down here, can I?'

'Why not?'

'Because I've got a movie to make,' he said and went along the street towards the main road, whistling between his teeth.

Thirty-Six

He stood for a long time after hanging up the phone, staring out of the window at the clutter of buildings, which looked in the light of the murky Californian sun as though they had been made out of pasteboard and balsa wood, and waited for the wave of feeling to subside. It had caught him with such surprise that he actually felt sick.

But it's real, a corner of his mind insisted. It's fantastic! It's what every bastard in this stinking business wants, and you've got it! You're the right side of forty, and you've done it. You've cracked it. Great, fantastic, magic, the whole bit.

So why, the rest of his mind retorted, do I feel so low? What the hell's the matter with me? Why feel so sick and so . . . ?

The door behind him swung open and she came in, balancing a tray with glasses in one hand and pulling the food wagon behind her. 'I sent the man away – I thought you might still be getting dressed. Here, give me a hand with this.' And then she looked at him and, at once, set the tray down on the bed with a rattle of the glasses, and almost ran across the room to him.

'What's happened? What's the matter? You look awful.'

'I – nothing. It's great – I'm fine. Here let me fix those things.' Abner crossed the room almost blindly, stumbling a little, meaning to bring the wagon further in and to set chairs beside it. But she wouldn't let him and put an arm round him; she took him over to the other bed and sat him down, her arm across his back.

'Now, tell me what's happened. I heard the phone and I thought – ' She went a little white around the mouth suddenly. 'Is it Frieda?'

'Frieda?' Abner looked puzzled and then shook his head. 'No, it's nothing to do with Frieda. I spoke to her this morning. She still won't come, no way will she come, but she says she'll watch on the TV. Which is quite something for her. No, it's nothing to do with Frieda.'

'Then, what is it?' Miriam was getting angry now as anxiety got the better of her, because he still looked drawn and very distressed and she peered more closely into his face and hugged him closer, suddenly desperate with fear. 'Don't be ill, my darling. Oh God, don't be ill. I couldn't stand it.'

He managed a laugh. 'Why the hell should I be ill? I'm in great shape! No, it's nothing like that. It's nothing at all, really.'

'You've been working like an idiot for two years,' she flared, allowing her anger to comfort her. 'You're exhausted. I told you it was crazy.'

'Listen, Miriam, I'm sick of this. I told you right at the start, and I tell you again, making a film is not one of your nine-to-five affairs. You work all the hours God gives while the film's on the floor and on location and – '

'And you drive yourself nearly into the ground all through the pre- and post-production as well, what with using people who aren't actors and all the misery of that; and then there's the editing, and you did all that too, and the dubbing and – '

'I know, I know,' he said wearily and got off the bed and went to the window to stare out of it again. 'But take it or leave it, that's what making films is about for me. They're my films, not a team's efforts. Mine.'

She was still sitting on the bed, watching him, and he turned round to look at her. She looked marvellous, in a long white dress which was very simple but made her dark eyes seem even darker and her neck extra long beneath the tight crown of dark curly hair. She'd picked up a little tan here in Los Angeles, and it suited her. Abner said impulsively, 'You look better than any one I've seen here. And the place is lousy with actresses.'

'Don't change the subject,' she said. 'What happened to make you look like that?'

'Dave phoned.'

'Shandwick?'

'Who else? That one. If I turn my back on him for a minute he's got another deal set up, another incredible idea and – he's done it again.'

'What is it now?'

'He's got an offer of fifteen million to make – well, pretty much what I like. I can go right ahead and do the East European breakdown film. Distribution, marketing, the whole thing. It's just the sort of deal Speilberg got after ET.'

She sat and stared at him and caught her breath. 'Oh, Abner!'

'Yeah. Oh, Abner,' and he turned back to the window again.

She watched him carefully and then said, 'So what's the matter? Does Monty not want you to – '

'Monty!' Abner said and his voice was solid with scorn. 'I can't get any help from Monty! He's just happy to be getting what he's getting from *Postscripts* so he can sit on his damned Majorcan terrace and rot. And he's getting enough to rot from now till kingdom come. He's got no opinion either way. And if he did have, I can tell you he'd be jumping up and down and screaming excitement, just like Dave. Grab it, take it, make more, more, more!' He turned back to her, and held out both hands, in a childlike gesture. 'Miriam, what the hell's gone wrong? It's all gone so wrong!'

'You're too successful,' she said flatly. 'Is that it?' And he took a deep breath of gratitude for the speed of her awareness.

'Yes,' he said and let out the long breath and came back to sit beside her. 'Yes. That's it exactly. It wasn't supposed to be like this. I wanted to make *Postscripts* for Hyman, for your Barbara, for David Lippner and his mother, for all of you. For Cyril and all the other Cyrils – '

'Cyril,' she said and let out a little bark of laughter. 'He's the happiest man I ever saw. He's sitting up on the roof by the pool, talking his head off to some journalist and gobbling pizza. You're the best thing that ever happened to him, Abner. How often is it that a man of his age ends up playing himself in a film and then gets this much attention for it?'

His lips quirked. 'That, I admit, is one of the more satisfying things that came out of it all – he was wonderful. Wasn't he wonderful?'

'The whole film was wonderful,' she said gently. 'Everything about it was, and still is. It'll be around for as long as people need to know what happened and what it all meant to the people like us who came after. It's an important document, Abner. Don't grieve over that.'

'I know all that! I'm not the sort of self-effacing fool who

doesn't know when he's done good work. I know it's good.
What I didn't expect is that it would turn out to be so – so bloody
commercial.'

She leaned against him, settling her head into the curve of his
neck above his open shirt collar and he smelled the familiar soap
and clean hair smell of her and relaxed a little. 'You're getting
awfully English, my love, living with me. It's no sin to be
commercial, is it? So the film's a success – what's wrong with
that?'

She sat up then and looked at him. 'It's amazing, though. It is,
isn't it? Over a hundred million at the box office.'

'A hundred and ten million at the last count,' he said gloomily.
'Dave gave me the latest figures.' And now she did laugh.

'Oh, Abner, you are funny! Isn't it great to know that so many
people care about the film, want to see it enough to hand over
their money like that? You're not being paid for nothing. You're
not stealing it – '

'It feels like it,' he said then, and put his hands over his face.
'Oh, God, it feels like it. I remember – I keep remembering –
Isaac saying that he felt like he'd have walked over dead bodies
to get what he wanted and I did just that.'

'He said nothing of the sort. He said he'd do it to survive. And
you did too. I don't mean you walked over bodies, but that you
had to survive as well. The way you were about what happened
to your parents and what that did to you – if you hadn't made
Postscripts, Abner, I don't think you could have gone on. You
don't know how close you were to breaking up.' She set her head
into the curve of his neck again, 'I know because I was, too. You
pulled me out of the morass when you pulled yourself. Working
on *Postscripts* was – well, if I never do another thing in my life,
that made it worth living for.'

He held her close, resting his chin on her curly hair, feeling the
resilience of it and relishing it; but still the sick feeling lurked,
deep in his belly.

'It's not that easy,' he said after a long pause. 'Not that easy,
whatever my intentions, whatever the value of the work. Don't I
diminish it in some way if I get so rich out of it? I never meant
that to happen, I truly never did. But it's happened. Well, it
won't last for always. What with Monty's share – and God
knows he's got a big one, what with his agent's cut and the extra

cut for the use of his name in the early scripts – and the share
David Lippner has, and the chunk that goes to the Holocaust
charities, I could get through the rest in a matter of a couple of
years.' He tipped her chin up then so that she had to look at him.
'Well, we both could.'

'You're damned right,' she said sturdily. 'I've got no hangups
about spending money. Why should I have? I had enough bad
years, enough when there wasn't enough of anything. I earned
my share of the loot on my job. I'm a bloody good researcher – '

'Bloody good,' he said gravely.

' – so I'll take what's coming and be glad of it. You should do
the same. This is childish quixotry.'

He pushed her away gently and got to his feet again, needing
to move around, and began to pace the room. 'I know,' he said.
'You think I don't know that? That's part of the whole bloody
confusion. I made *Postscripts* to get over the sickness of the guilt
I felt because I wasn't in the camps and my parents were, to get
over the loss of my parents' involvement in my childhood, to deal
with the sheer pain of being alive when so many were dead, and
all that happens is that I get more guilty than ever. Oh, Christ,'
he said then and turned to look at her. 'Do you know that I keep
feeling I wish I could be Matthew Mayer?'

'Sitting in his hiding place somewhere, listening to his music,
staring at his paintings, all on his own?' she said and shook her
head. 'You can't mean that.'

'No, I don't mean that. I'm glad we brought him down in
England at any rate, glad that it all came out, glad he had to run
like that. No, what I mean is, I wish I could be as he seemed to be.
Quite free of any guilt. For anything at all – for what he did as a
boy, for the way he stole all that property from the dead – I can't
see how he could be that way. And I wish, just sometimes, I wish
I could be the same.'

He went back to the window and stared out again, remembering. He recalled the day that had been meant to be so glorious,
when he had taken Mayer to the viewing room to show him the
uncut print, the one on which Mayer had expected to see Monty
Nagel pilloried as the adult version of the boy who had sold his
own people for a bag of apples, but had seen himself instead. The
actor Abner had found had been a miracle, had managed to
convey the mixture of ruggedness and fragility that was the

contradiction of Mayer, had looked like him, even sounded like him; and, of course, Abner had used Mayer's name, even shots of the outside of his office in as loving a reconstruction of his own inner sanctum as Abner had been able to devise for a set. And Mayer had sat there in the viewing room in Wardour Street and watched the film and said nothing. And at the end had stood up and looked at Abner and made a little bow, an oddly courtly little gesture.

'Well, there it is,' he'd said in his normal relaxed voice. 'There it is. You think you've hurt me? Think that if it will help you. But I did what I did because it had to be done and I have no regrets. If I hadn't, would they have survived any better? They caught me and I would have died too if I hadn't played the game their way. And dead men are of no use to anyone. So I played it their way and I've had no guilt about it, ever. I still haven't. As for the property of the dead – pfui! The dead are dead. I put their money to good use, for lovely paintings and ceramics, beautiful objects that will always live when people corrupt into slime, for music and books. Such things mean more than dead men. If this film you've made helps you with your juvenile guilt, Mr Wiseman, then you are fortunate to find comfort so easily. But it won't, you know. The sort of guilt you have will never go away.'

'Perhaps not,' Abner had said. 'But it's been eased by making this film. And using the money you stole to do it. And bringing you down with it. Oh God, but that's eased it.'

'Bringing me down?' Mayer had got to his delicate little feet and walked down to the screen end of the viewing theatre, to stand leaning against the low wooden bar that separated the screen from the seating area. His face couldn't be seen then; just the silhouette of his massive head with its thick springing hair. 'Bringing me down? You foolish creature. Do you think I'm so easily toppled? I have millions put away – millions.'

'You won't keep them long once the film is released and people see it. And it will be. For all the great power you're supposed to exert you can't stop it. I've told Jo Rossily all about you. She's seen this rough cut – and she's an honest woman, Mayer. She'll get the film out whatever you try to do to stop her. And I'm ready and willing to help finance her in the future when you no longer will – or can. This film will make money – I know that – so you're not the power you were.'

Mayer waved one hand, an elegant little movement that left jerky traces of itself against the silvered screen behind him. 'Such childish retribution you've planned. You think you can hurt me? Of course you can't. I will walk out of here when I'm ready, and I will go about my business again in my own way. Not here, perhaps. Not as Matthew Mayer perhaps. I have a splendid collection of other personae I can use. In Germany, possibly. Or America – though I find it rather brash for my taste – or possibly France or Switzerland, or even South America. I'm well cushioned in all these places, you see. You can't hurt me and you can't stop me doing what I choose.'

'I shall stop you. I'll get the police to – '

He laughed with genuine amusement. 'My good creature, you have no proof! They will never arrest me, just on your say! No, by the time you can convince them of how evil I am, I'll be long gone. Don't you realise I was aware of all you were doing? Don't you understand that I was watching you all the way? Venables made a stupid mistake in the way he gave you that first cheque, of course – if he'd done it properly I could have blocked you then. But I credit you where I must. You saw the danger of losing your project to him and so to me, and sidestepped it. But Heller and Garten watched you too. I've had plenty of time to organise myself. I shall go away, Mr Wiseman, not because I'm afraid of you, or ashamed of your revelations, but because I'm bored. I need the stimulus of a move. You've done me a service, believe me.'

He stopped then, and came back up the slight slope of the viewing theatre to the door that led out. 'And you won't try to stop me physically, because you're too aware of your own guilt in just being alive when so many died for you to be able to set a finger on me. But before I go, Mr Wiseman – ah, such a wise man! – let me tell you, *you were not there*. You did not experience what I experienced. Your life was a gift to you that you take for granted, and expect to be given love and approval to go with it. Me, I worked for my life, fought for my survival, and learned very early how little real value love and approval have. I prefer music and books and paintings. This is love turned into something worth having, not your mawkish sentimentality. Goodbye Mr Wiseman. You have your film. Many fools will be moved by it, I have no doubt. They'll make you rich because of that and then how will you live with your conscience? Poor fool of a Wiseman! You hadn't thought of that, had you? Well, you will. And you'll remember what I told you. Good night, Mr Wiseman.'

And he had bent his head in the sketch of another bow, and walked out into Wardour Street, taking Abner's glorious afternoon with him, and disappeared. The next day he was gone from his office in Mayfair, leaving a silent but clearly distressed Rowena behind, but taking his books, his records and his paintings, and no one had seen or heard from him since. Not even, it seemed, Rowena, who vanished too. However much Mayer's partners scurried about in despair trying to find him, people like Alex Venables and Simmy Gentle, all of them had found no trace. And that had been that.

Perhaps, Abner thought, staring out at Los Angeles in the late-afternoon sunshine, perhaps Mayer would come back in his own way, as he had said he would to do his own thing somewhere else. That man was born to survive. Not like me.

'Sooner or later you've got to forget it, Abner,' Miriam said, and came to the window to join him. 'I'm beginning to do it. I'm even beginning to be able to forgive her. How's that for a change?'

He looked at her sharply. 'What?'

'Barbara, Basia. The teller of stories of hell and damnation to little girls at bedtime.' She turned a slightly twisted smile on him, and he saw her eyes were brighter than usual and thought, she wants to cry. I've hurt her – and he reached to take her hand.

'It's all right,' she said. 'It only happens sometimes. I'm getting over her. And Geoff. It's quite agreeable in a way to be able just to say to myself – I'm sad because my parents are dead. It's normal to do that, to mourn them properly. You haven't done that for Hyman yet, have you?'

'Of course I have – long ago. He's been dead two years.'

'So what? Time has damn all to do with it. You're still trying to get over his loss.'

'How can I grieve his loss, when I never really had him?' he said then, almost savagely, and then bit his lip.

'You see what I mean?' she said as his eyes, too, brightened dangerously. 'You've a long way to go yet. There's still Frieda to deal with, isn't there? As long as you think about the right things and don't blame the wrong ones.'

'Blame the wrong ones?'

'If you get into a great lather over having a huge success with *Postscripts* and don't use the benefits sensibly then you'll be blaming the wrong things. What you have to do now is look at yourself and decide the best thing for yourself. Here and now. Not the little boy who was so shut out of love. Not the man who uncovered the diamond scam – though it was a good thing to have done, and you certainly stopped it happening – none of those. The here and now, Abner. Where do you go from here? That's what matters. If you choose wrong, fair enough. But don't, if you *do* make the wrong choice, try to blame what went before. It'll be because of you, now, that you make the choices. No one else. Oh hell, I'm ranting on. Do I make sense?'

'I think so,' he said. 'I just wish it was so easy. Forgetting what leads up to the here and now – I'm not sure I can.'

'It's not forgetting so much as looking at it differently. I did that after – you made me do that.'

He smiled down at her, for again she was standing very close. 'I did?'

'Well, there was a sort of line drawn, wasn't there? It isn't every day you get to have sex for the first time. Before there was the old me and afterwards – well, it was all different. I could start from there, that here and now, instead of always looking backwards.'

'You want to be careful. You'll have all the sisters after you, suggesting it just takes a man and his trusty weapon to change a girl's life.'

'It wasn't just that!' she said, suddenly angry. 'It was all of you – I mean it was both of us. It was – oh, damn you to hell and back, you know perfectly well what I mean!'

He managed to laugh, and was grateful for that. It made the sickness, already receding slowly, move away even more. 'Yes, I know, I shouldn't tease. I'm sorry.'

'Listen, Abner, tonight – is it going to be all right? Can you deal with it? It looks like you'll easily snatch the award you're up for, you know. I've been listening to the TV. They're all making odds – Speilberg's *Sleepstate* and Chetwynd's new one are the only Best Picture contenders, but you could have your own golden doorstop by the time the evening's out. Are you ready to deal with that?'

'Such a nightmare for a movie-maker,' he said mockingly and then put both arms round her and held on tightly. 'Oh hell, Miriam, I'm scared shitless.'

'That's all right then,' she said and her voice was muffled because he was holding her so close. 'That's the way it ought to be. But don't blame it all on guilt. You can't expiate it for the whole world, and you can't expiate it for yourself. Just tell the stories and get on with living, OK?'

'OK,' he said and kissed her hard.

'And I must now go and re-do my face, and you must go and get dressed properly,' she said calmly and extracted herself. 'The sandwiches'll be curly and the champagne warm by now, but will you have some? I can't see you eating any dinner tonight and you need something inside you to keep you going – that's why I ordered it.'

He laughed. 'You get more like a Jewish mother every day.'

'Well, I'm not, nor likely to be. Don't start that again.'

'Who's starting anything?' He was feeling better by the moment. She was, as always, the most exhilarating person to be with that he knew, the only one who could bring him back to common sense. He loved her more with every day that passed and that was a problem in itself, the way she was.

'As long as you don't. We'll think about all that later. Not now.'

'And who's fighting the past now?' he said and then held up both hands in mock surrender as she turned to flare at him. 'Pax! Not another word, I promise. Only, while you're dishing out the common sense, remember to lick your spoon occasionally, hmm? Now, forget the sandwiches, I'll eat dinner. Go and get yourself fixed up and get someone to haul Cyril down from the roof. We've got to be moving soon. It's gone six.'

'Right,' she said. And flashed him the broadest of grins. 'Oscars, here we come.'